A Time to Rise

by
Tal Bauer

A Tal Bauer Publication

This novel contains scenes of graphic violence.

Second Edition
10 9 8 7 6 5 4 3 2
Paperback ISBN: 9781983164668
Copyright © 2018 Tal Bauer
First Edition Copyright © 2016 Tal Bauer
Cover Art by Damonza © Copyright 2018
Edited by Rita Roberts
Published in 2018 by Tal Bauer
United States of America

Foreword

The Pontifical Swiss Guard is today's smallest standing army in the world, in existence since 1506. It is also one of the world's longest continuously-operating armies. Notable engagements include the Stand of the Swiss Guard in 1527, the Guards' defense of the Vatican during World War II when the Axis powers invaded Rome, and the 1981 assassination attempt of Pope John Paul II. Exceptional and qualified soldiers in the Swiss army may apply to the Swiss Guard through a rigorous selection process. Service in the Pontifical Swiss Guard is the only exception to the ban on foreign military service, outlawed by the Swiss Constitution in 1874. The Pontifical Swiss Guard maintains close associations and connections with their colleagues in the Swiss army, with guards returning frequently to Switzerland for advanced training, within the army and without.

A position to the Swiss Guard is considered a prestigious posting.

"In the middle of the journey of our life
I found myself within a dark woods
where the straight way was lost."

— DANTE ALIGHIERI, INFERNO

The Scrolls of the Apocalypse of the Angels

Hear me! The Lord, our Father, the Lord, has deceived you!
Our Father's words endure forever. His decrees are
  absolute.
But in His words, there is wickedness!
In place of righteousness, there is darkness.

He would bind your hearts and bind your minds
And silence the spark that lives within you.
He would hold out the blade upon which you may fall
And command you fling yourself down for the glory of
  His name!

Do you, my brothers, do you live?
Do you seek life?
Or do you choose death?
A life lived at the feet of the Lord
Is not a full life.
It is but a desperate breath
A dying gasp
From a broken heart.

To everything, my brothers, there is a moment
And a time for holding fast
With both hands
To the quest for life.

A time to awaken, and a time to die
A time to rise, and a time to rebel
A time to weep, and a time to rage
A time to rejoice, and a time to scorn
A time to rend, and a time to starve
A time to bleed, and a time to heal
A time to love, and a time to hate

Now is the time, my brothers.
Now is the time of war.

Join me, brothers!
Join me for your lives!

~ EXCERPT FROM THE *BOOK OF LUCIFER*

Chapter One

PRESSING BACK AGAINST THE ANCIENT CHURCH'S STONE WALLS, Alain chambered a silver round in his pistol. Cold ivy, wet with dew, flicked over the back of his neck. Fog clung to his skin, the roughhewn stones, the dreary courtyard. Across the cobblestone drive, pebbles skittered on an ill wind.

A streetlamp hummed down the road, lost in the midnight haze. A fountain burbled in the church's garden, water spitting from the mouths of fat cherubs beneath the light of a sickle moon.

The entire night could have been a transplanted moment from ages past. Antiquity drowned the air, heavy with every inhale.

Next to Alain, his back to the rotten walls of the *Basilica di Sant'Aurea*, Father Lotario Nicosia slipped his pistols under his suit jacket, into his shoulder holsters. He was dressed in his usual Catholic priest's attire—all black suit, white Roman collar—but he packed heavier firepower than just a crucifix.

Still, Father Lotario tucked the pistols away. What they were hunting tonight wouldn't fall to bullets. Not even silver or iron bullets.

Lotario coughed. The sudden fog, the rank humidity, choked the night.

"You need to quit smoking," Alain grunted.

"It's not going to be the smokes that kill me." Lotario drew his sickled blade—black handled with, as the Keys of Solomon instructed, the seven names of God carved into the steel—and pulled two flasks from his suit jacket. Slim and silver, they were identical.

Alain rolled his eyes as Lotario unscrewed the first and downed a swallow. Lotario hissed, squeezing his eyes closed. "Yep. That's the vodka."

"One day, the Holy Water will burn up your insides just the same." Alain jerked his head toward the church rectory. "Let's go. There's a priest pissing himself inside."

Lotario spat and nodded. Across the street, the swirl of red and blue police lights made slow circles, disjointed halos of smeared color trying to penetrate the gloom. Senior Officer Angelo Conti would have his men spread out by now around the cemetery at *Ostia Antica*, circling the block in a tight perimeter and keeping their prey trapped. To anyone else, it would look like another Italian *Polizia di Statio* operation. Maybe searching for a drug runner or an escaped drunk.

No one would ever suspect a revenant was on the loose.

The world was woefully—blessedly—ignorant of the dark creatures and evil spirits that had managed to cross through the Veil to make their home in the human world.

What would people do, Alain sometimes wondered, if they knew?

His job, of course, was to ensure no one ever knew. That no one would ever discover the truth about the darkness, the etheric, and the demonic forces preying upon the world.

His and Father Lotario's job, that was.

That evening, they'd received a call from their contact and counterpart, Angelo, an officer in the Italian *polizia*'s Central Operational Core of Security, Special Projects branch. The Central Operational Core managed Italy's counterterrorism and national security operations. The Special Projects branch, which didn't exist on any organization chart, was on permanent cooperative status with the Vatican. Their assignment: paranormal security.

Angelo was a gruff, no-nonsense veteran of the *carabinieri* and had only grudgingly accepted the transfer to the Special Projects branch when a gunfight at a drug sting in Sicily went south and he ended up with six bullets in his body. He called Alain and Lotario whenever an emergency call about suspicious activity was quietly routed to the Special Projects desk, or a corpse turned up in Rome that clearly wasn't killed by human hands.

Tonight, a revenant had torn through the *Ostia Antica* cemetery, screaming wildly out of its grave and cracking marble tombs as it raged. The shrieks, like dead branches scratching over glass, rolled through the Roman suburbs. Cold followed, an unnatural chill that swam through the early summer humidity and had seeped into Alain's bones as they'd pulled up alongside Angelo's car.

He and Lotario had arrived just in time to see the revenant scream its way out of the cemetery and cross the street, a swirl of shadow and bloodred rage. Curls of terror and fury crashed through the drivers up and down the road. Cars spun out, tires squealing, horns honking, people suddenly cursing each other as they sparked off the vibrations of an evil spirit they couldn't see.

Across the street from the cemetery, the *Basilica di Sant'Aurea*, a bedraggled, medieval church of crumbling stone and ivy-covered walls, sat in the middle of a cracked cobblestone courtyard. Candles inside the church twinkled, lit with prayers from the congregation, but it was the lights in the rectory that drew the revenant. Inside it went, and the elderly priest barricaded himself inside his closet with his cell phone.

Angelo spoke to the priest over the phone, trying to calm the old man down from his hyperventilating hysterics as Alain and Lotario got into position. A man of the cloth the priest may be, but a lifetime of homilies and baptisms and Hail Marys didn't prepare a man to come face-to-face with a risen corpse-spirit full of rage and bitter malice on a Tuesday night.

"The stairs around the back go up to the rectory," Lotario said, motioning with his head. "I'll slip up the back. You come in from the front and cover me. Distract it. I'll hit it with the flask while it's occupied with you."

Alain stared. "This plan sounds somewhat shaky."

Lotario shrugged. A devil-may-care smirk curled up the edges of his lips. "If you would carry more than just your pistol, you could be more than just my handsome sidekick."

"No." Alain snapped. "How many times—"

"Yeah, yeah." Lotario gulped another swig of vodka. "One day, Alain. You'll need to carry more than just your weapon."

"On three?" Alain ignored him and glanced around the church wall, to the front entrance of the rectory. "I can get inside in six seconds."

"Well, wait here for a bit before you go. You know I smoke." Lotario pushed off the wall and ducked around the side of the church, heading for the rear stairwell. His long legs pumped behind him, suit jacket flapping.

Alain watched and waited, cursing Lotario until he reached the base of the stairs.

Then he took off, racing around the other side of the church wall and tearing for the rectory's entrance.

Alain burst inside, crashing through the doors shoulder-first, splintering the old wood from its hinges. He stumbled as heard the upstairs balcony door crash. Lotario.

A roar from the revenant.

Definitely Lotario.

Leaping, Alain dashed up the wooden stairs, taking them three at a time, and then kicked down the priest's bedroom door. The revenant, a swirl of ruby mist coalescing into a vaguely human shape, stretched wrongly out of proportion, spun, shrieking into Alain's face.

He raised his pistol and fired. Silver wouldn't kill the revenant, but it would sting. It would piss it off.

Alain squinted through the red haze. Lotario knew better than to be in the path of his bullets. Then again, he really could never be too sure with Lotario. He caught the sound of a flask's cap hitting the wooden floorboards.

From behind the closet door, he heard sobbing, pleading, frantic prayers to God. The priest. He rolled to his side, edging along the wall as Lotario doused the revenant with his flask of vodka. Lotario brandished his sickled blade, slicing through the swirling tendrils the revenant sent for him, trying to eat Lotario's soul.

Alain reached the closet doors right as he heard Lotario flick his lighter. He ripped open the doors and swept the inside with his pistol. The old priest was curled into a ball, a stain on his bathrobe where he'd pissed himself. Red-rimmed eyes and a tear-stained face turned toward Alain. He gasped, reciting the Lord's Prayer and Hail Marys as fast as he could speak.

Behind Alain, Lotario's lighter landed in the dripping pile of overproof vodka tossed through the revenant's mist. Flames erupted, a fireball blooming through the priest's bedroom, engulfing the revenant. Another shriek, this one worse than all the others combined, tore from the revenant's burning shadow, a cry of fury and anguish.

The fire burned away the revenant like a vapor, flaring out as the mist tore itself apart.

Burn marks scorched the priest's bedroom floor. Smoke filled the room. Lotario poured the second flask—Holy Water, this time —onto the wood. He ground his heel into the drops as they sizzled and popped.

Alain held out his hand for the priest. "Come on, Father. Let's get you up."

The old man fainted.

AFTER THE CLEANUP, LOTARIO LOUNGED ON THE HOOD OF Angelo's *polizia* car smoking a cigarette. Alain and Angelo sipped espressos a carabinieri officer brought over.

Angelo's bushy mustache twitched. "That's the third call out this week," he grumbled. "And it's only Tuesday."

Alain frowned. "There've been more risings in the past six weeks. A lot more."

Lotario sucked down his cigarette and snapped his fingers, pointing at Alain. "Yes," he said. Smoke trailed his words. "This is what I was telling you over dinner. Hell yes, there have been more risings. And more *fresh* risings. This revenant, he was brand-new. Probably crawled out of one of those fresh graves in *Ostia*." Lotario vaguely pointed toward the ruined cemetery. "He didn't even have his full form yet. He was definitely a fresh burial."

"And two weeks ago, there were those wraiths up in the Coliseum." Alain waved Lotario's smoke away from his face.

"Any word from the others?" Angelo asked Alain.

"They're reporting a small increase in risings, but if we hadn't asked them to check their records, they probably wouldn't have noticed. Whatever is happening in Rome is localized."

"Always is." Lotario crossed his arms behind his head as he lay back on Angelo's windscreen. "Rome is the magnet for the paranormal, the etheric, and the bat shit crazy."

There was no arguing with that. Rome's vibrations were higher than the rest of the world, save Jerusalem, and that attracted more than their fair share of the supernatural trapped on the human side of the Veil: the undead, the dark creatures, the demonic, and humans who had fallen, making a pact with the darkness, or those who fell to temptation at the moment of their death.

"What could have set this revenant off? Do we know what grave he came from?" Alain watched the foggy glow of flashlights from Angelo's men bob and swerve inside the cemetery.

"Not yet. Hopefully by morning, unless his grave was too far destroyed. Then we'll have to wait for the undertaker."

Lotario slid down the hood of the car, landing on his feet as he inhaled the last nub of his cigarette. In the gloom and scattered light, the gray hair at his temples shone silver. "Alain, we've got to get going. It's late."

Alain cursed. At this hour, they wouldn't be back at the Vatican until dawn.

"That's right. It's the sixth of May." Angelo grinned. "You know, one of these days, I expect an invitation to your party. It's supposed to be a big deal."

"It's really not," Lotario snorted.

Alain glared. "It's our heritage. And it's important—"

"Yeah, yeah, I know." Lotario gestured to his vehicle, an ancient Volkswagen Bug—more rust than car—with the rear bumper bungee-corded to the frame. The license plate had SCV stamped into the metal—*State of Vatican City*, the country Alain and Lotario lived in, the smallest state in the world. The Holy See. Though, there were some who said the letters actually stood for *Se Cristo Vedesee: if Christ Could See*. Living in the Vatican was a study in opposites, in cognitive dissonance, in original sin made manifest, and in human failings in the quest for eternity.

Lotario waved to his car again. "That's why I'm getting you back in time for your big ceremony." He clapped twice and jogged to his rust bucket. "*En marche!*"

Angelo gave Alain a small salute. "Have a good night, Sergeant. I'll be in touch tomorrow with anything we find."

Alain gave Angelo a curt smile. Lotario honked his horn, the tinny, archaic belching worse than the revenant's screams. He started the Bug as Alain headed over, and a puff of black smoke burst from the tailpipe as the engine coughed and groaned.

"I know you're a priest," Alain said, sliding into the passenger seat, "but can't you afford anything else?" The passenger door rattled as he slammed it closed, the hinges creaking like a banshee's death wail.

"Believe it or not," Lotario said, sliding the car into neutral to roll down the hill. Reverse didn't work. "I actually make more than you do, Sergeant Autenburg." He winked. "But feel free to buy your own vehicle. We can take the Swiss Guard Express. Will you buy a rickshaw or can you afford a donkey?"

Alain laughed. "Service to God just isn't what it used to be."

Lotario pulled the last cigarette from his pack with his lips and threw the empty behind him to the backseat, where it landed in a pile of discarded cigarette packs, fast food wrappers, and old newspapers. "Amen," he grunted around the cigarette, lighting it one-handed as he shifted the car into drive. They puttered down the main parkway toward Rome, back to the Vatican.

To home.

SAINT MARTHA'S RESIDENCE, TUCKED ALONG THE EDGE OF THE Vatican to the south of St. Peter's Basilica, housed a handful of the bishops and archbishops who called the Eternal City home within its gilded walls.

Only five hundred people lived full time within the Holy See. Of those five hundred, a third were members of the Curia, the Holy City's government, both of the state and the church. The rest, mostly Swiss Guards, lived in the barracks. The Secretariat, the Vatican's office of the secretary of state, housed a handful of diplomat priests in the Holy City, in support of their nunciatures around the world. A scattering of priests, nuns, monks, seminarians, and habits dotted the Vatican grounds. The pope and the cardinal secretary of state for the Holy See lived in the Apostolic Palace overlooking St. Peter's Square.

Archbishop Santino Acossio, the number two man in the Vatican Secretariat, lived alone in Saint Martha's in a three-thousand-square-foot apartment, decked with handwoven rugs from the thirteenth-century Orient, hand-carved furniture from the Merovingian kingdom in France's history, and ornamented with Renaissance artwork. Such were the slim pickings from the Vatican warehouse, the repository of mostly-baroque furniture and priceless art for the highest-ranking Vatican officials to pick and choose from as they outfitted their homes.

Original Michelangelo sketches, framed in gold, adorned the walls. Bramante's charcoal designs for St. Peter's Basilica hung opposite a picture window overlooking the Basilica's dome and the Arch of the Bells. Every hour, the bells tolled, a peal that quaked the bones of every soul in the Vatican.

The residence was dark at three in the morning, save for lit candles warming the windows of Santino's apartment. Heavy curtains concealed his apartment from wandering eyes lifting up from the Arch of the Bells.

As Santino watched, a curl of smoke rose from a black candle, centered in the middle of a circle laid from melted silver burned into the floor, then covered with salt. A pentagram drawn in chalk lay within the circle, runes sketched out on each arm. Incense wafted from thuribles hanging in the corners, wormwood, yew, and willow mixed with mold and rot scraped from the edge of a grave. Black and white candles sat at the four cardinal directions, next to shallow bowls spattered with drops of blood.

Santino stood outside the circle. He wore his black cassock, his Roman collar, his scarlet fascia. He'd taken off his pectoral cross for this. He held a jagged black blade made from a human arm bone. His blood stained the blade's edge.

Black smoke rising from the candle tumbled and roiled, coalesced in the center of the circle. A twisted face pushed out of the darkness. Deathly pale, the face hardened, becoming a perfect parody of a smiling Venetian mask, porcelain smooth with empty, open eyes. The smoke fluttered into the vague shape of a dark body, incorporeal, insubstantial, hovering in the center of the circle.

The being tilted its head and lifted one wraith-like arm, shadows tumbling from the gesture. "You called me, Santino Acossio."

"Do I speak with Asmodeus?" Santino brandished his bone blade. "Do I speak with a prince of Hell, Asmodeus, the ruler of passions?"

One shadowed arm drifted lazily around the inside of Santino's circle. Sparks burst in its path. "You do speak with Asmodeus."

Santino lowered the blade and bowed, touching his forehead to the bloody bone. "Asmodeus," he breathed, "I give you my honor and my worship."

Asmodeus smiled. The demon traveled the inside of the circle, tracing a smoke arm over the entire perimeter. Sparks rained like fireworks within the silver and salt circle. "Your circle is strong. You have prepared well."

Santino stayed silent.

"Why have you summoned me?" Asmodeus spun and pressed his face against the silver and salt line, staring into Santino's eyes. "What do you want?"

Santino sank to his knees, bowing. His body protested his, his knees screaming. He was an old man, an old man running out of time. "Asmodeus," he pleaded, his voice shaking. "I was told to summon you. I was told you would have something for me."

"Something for you?" Asmodeus's mask face cocked to the side, an almost playful expression. A tiny laugh, distant-sounding and childish, fell from its thin mouth.

"A mission," Santino stuttered. "A duty, for your purposes."

"And who would have told you this?"

"I have spoken to Astaroth." Santino inhaled, holding his breath. "He said he has given you a task. That you are working on an important project. Something that requires help. I can help. I can—"

"Do not presume to know the workings of demons!" Asmodeus bellowed. "Do not presume to know that of which you are ignorant, human!" The smoke rumbled, thunder cracking within the circle, the shifting blackness rubbing against a palpable darkness. The scrape of iron against stone echoed through the apartment. "You know nothing, Santino Acossio."

Santino fell forward, prostrating before the demon Asmodeus. "Forgive me, prince of Hell," he whispered. "Forgive me. I only wish to serve. I only wish to do my part."

Asmodeus settled in the smoke, backing down until he was floating just above the floorboards, seemingly kneeling with Santino. "And what," the demon whispered, face rolling to one side, "would a helpful archbishop desire in exchange for his services?"

"Power." Santino pushed himself up, his hands scrabbling on the Oriental rug beneath him, tearing tufts of priceless silk from the weave. "I want to hold the office of Secretariat of State. I want to *run* the Vatican." He was so close, but the years were running out of his life like sand emptying from an hourglass. He was going to die, and his life's work would be for nothing if he didn't make it to the top. If he didn't make an impact upon the world. A man's deeds lived on long after him, and when a man was in charge of the affairs of eternity, well—

He'd made his peace with the price he had to pay to make his indelible mark on eternity.

Dark chuckles rumbled from the smoke. Overlaid, a second giggle, high pitched like a little child, singsonged from somewhere far away. "It would be most beneficial to have the second-in-command of the Vatican aligned with us."

"And, maybe one day..." Santino bared his teeth. "To be in charge of the Vatican. The papacy!"

Asmodeus drew back, the smoke folding in on itself and whispering down into the candle's black flame. "You shall have your mission, Archbishop. You may yet prove useful." Asmodeus's pale face, the apparition's mask, was swallowed by the darkness, pulled backward and torn apart by the shadows, disappearing into the candle's demon light. "We will be with you," the smoke whispered. "We will be in contact."

The candle sputtered, flickering in the sudden stillness of the circle and the whisper of Asmodeus's final words.

Santino stared at the candle, at the wavering flame, as he tried to catch his breath.

It worked. It had truly worked. He'd summoned—

The candle's flame winked out.

Chapter Two

Sergeant Alain Autenburg wiped his hands down his dress uniform, trying to smooth the wrinkles from his cropped jacket. He'd meant to steam it, but between the revenant attack and everything else, he hadn't had time. Besides, he never wore the Swiss Guards' duty uniform anymore. The regular uniform was *not* subtle.

The halberdiers—the lowest ranked members of the Swiss Guard—wore a modified Renaissance outfit: garishly striped red, yellow, and blue fabric, ballooning sleeves and pant legs puffing out from shoulders and hips before coming in tight around the forearms and calves. The halberdiers were forever catching their uniforms on doorknobs around the Vatican.

Day to day, Alain wore the all-black suit of the clergy, and he looked just like a priest, as long as someone didn't look too closely at the missing Roman collar. He hadn't had to wear his Swiss Guard uniform for a whole year. Since last May 6th.

Another year, another ceremony. Alain glared at the wrinkles, the dust that clung to the year-old creases. Instead of the red, yellow, and blue of the halberdiers, his uniform was deep maroon and black. His jacket, cropped at his waist and tight across his torso, was black, while his sleeves—puffed like a princess gown to his elbows and then tightened to his forearm with laces—were a mixture of black and maroon stripes. Likewise, his pants, deep maroon, were made of bell-shaped stripes gathered together at his knees. Skin-tight maroon hose stretched to his feet.

A thick leather belt cinched at his waist, his dress sword hanging from his hip. He shoved it to the side and tried to cover the unpolished hilt with his elbow. He'd meant to get everything ready the night before, dammit. Alain grabbed his beret, tugging it to the right until it was just barely hanging on his head and pulled it over his eyebrow. His hair, a dark, wild bird's nest, fought back.

Thank God he didn't have to wear this getup every day.

His black-on-black suit was infinitely better than the halberdiers' daily uniform. He'd suffered through that uniform for a year until his rushed promotion and his new duties became a full-time mission. The halberdiers—ninety percent of the Swiss Guard —wore the red, yellow, and blue ensemble, complete with puffy, striped sleeves, ballooning pants, and striped gaiters over black pointed boots, every day while at their posts inside the Vatican. The lucky few guarding St. Anne's Gate wore the blue uniforms—a simple coverall tricked up with a dainty white collar.

But today, everyone was decked out in their full finery. Even the steel armor was coming out, chestplates and shoulder pauldrons tied on tight over everything. On everyone's head, their morion, topped with an ostrich plume. Everyone would be looking their best.

Everyone except Alain. He hadn't even ironed his uniform. And his armor was unpolished, still sitting in the armory. He couldn't even get to it now.

If he stood at the very back of the ceremony, out of the way, maybe no one would notice his complete failure.

Drum rolls in the courtyard made him run, storm down the stairs in the officer's barracks and leap down the last few steps. Outside, in the courtyard of the Swiss Guard, the squad leaders marched the halberdiers out for the officers' review. Lining the courtyard were everyone's families, and seated in a place of honor, a mass of priests, bishops, and archbishops who had come to watch the annual ceremony.

Alain froze. There, in the center of the red carpet spread out for the guests of honor, the Holy Father stood, applauding the marching halberdiers with a beaming smile stretching his wrinkled face.

Fuck. No one had told him the Holy Father would be there. He glared down at his sloppy uniform. Looking slovenly in front of the entire Guard and the upper crust of the Roma Curia was one thing. But the *pope?*

Nothing to be done now. He slipped across the courtyard, bisecting the procession, skipping in front of the families, and cutting behind the honored guests. He kept his head down, trying to hide his face.

He felt the burning stares of four hundred eyeballs digging into his back.

Alain popped to attention at the end of the line of non-commissioned officers. He stared straight ahead, his jaw locked.

Disdain wafted across the courtyard, prickling the hairs on the back of his neck. Major Luca Bader turned his head, fractional inches that Alain swore he could hear, the bones in Luca's neck grinding as he looked him up and down. Alain stared back.

Raw, undisguised loathing slammed into him as Luca curled his lips. A snort, and then Luca looked away, his chin held high, his jaw clenching in time to the rolling drum beat. Alain closed his eyes, letting the crack of the drums beat against his soul and the rough bellow of the oath of enlistment roll over him.

One by one, the new recruits—thirty-six this year—strode forward, marching in stiff movements that clanked and rattled their gleaming armor. One of the sergeants held the flag of the Swiss Guard in the center of the yard. Each recruit grasped it in one hand and punched the sky with the other, holding three fingers aloft before belting out the oath, promising to give their life for the pope and for the church.

The Holy Father nodded and smiled to each man as he watched them swear their lives to his.

Since 1506, the soldiers of the Swiss Guard had formed the smallest standing army in the world. One hundred and fifty Swiss men guarded the life of the pope in an unbroken stretch of history. Bought and paid for by Pope Julius II, convinced he was about to be invaded and destroyed, the first soldiers of the Swiss Guard proved their worth at the Stand of the Swiss Guard on May 6, 1527. One hundred and forty-seven of the two hundred Swiss Guards fought and died in the brutal sack of Rome and the Vatican, slaughtered on the steps of St. Peter's Basilica. They gave their lives in sacrifice to forty-two of their comrades, rushing Pope Clement VII across the *passetto di Borgo* to *Castel Sant'Angelo*, where Pope Clement VII hid in exile as the Vatican burned. The survivors of the Guard sheltered his life in hiding for a year. And from that day forward, the Swiss Guard never left the Holy Father's side.

There weren't any invaders of Rome or pillagers sacking the Vatican these days. The Swiss Guard stood ceremonial postings at the Apostolic Palace, secured the inner reaches of the Vatican, and were the Holy Father's close personal bodyguards. They ran by the popemobile, walked beside him in the crowds, and the commandant and captains traveled with the pope overseas. And, when bullets flew toward Pope John Paul II, it was the Swiss Guard who threw themselves on top of the Holy Father, shielding him with their lives.

As the recruits moved through their oaths, one man caught Alain's eyes. He was tall, with a lithe strength perfectly highlighted by the close cut of the uniform. His voice was strong, clipped Swiss German rolling over the cobblestones. There was something there, though, some depth to his voice, a growl in his throat, that caught Alain's attention.

For a moment only.

He let his eyes drift over the recruit and then close as he repeated the words of the oath under his breath, thirty-six times.

Twelve years ago, he'd taken his own oath as a fresh-faced, wide-eyed child, twenty-two years old, barely out of Swiss army training. Luca Bader had been his friend then, and they'd stayed up all night before their oath, drinking cheap wine in the barracks and talking about sacrifice and all they wanted to accomplish in their lives.

Twelve years. Everything—every single thing—was different from what he'd dreamed. Even Luca, who he thought would be his friend until the end of time. Alain's eyes wandered over the back of Luca's helmet, watching the flicker and twitch of his aubergine plume. Twelve years, and Luca had rocketed up the ranks. Now he was Major Luca Bader, second-in-command.

And Alain was the eternal sergeant in charge of Special Projects, a duty so droll sounding and distasteful no one bothered him. No one was the wiser to his true duties, save for the commandant and the Holy Father, the only two people he reported to directly.

It must drive Luca insane. To be so powerful and yet still be locked out of Alain's secrets. He'd *hated* those secrets, bitterly so, and it had been the crushing weight of everything Alain kept from him that had sent them so terribly sideways for over a decade.

Finally, the oaths were done and the halberdiers were marched back into their formation. The *rat-a-tat-tat* of the drums beat on, and then Luca barked out everyone's orders. The formation of guards snapped to attention as the Holy Father stood. He waved down the crowds' applause, smiling his shy smile before launching into his homily.

Even though the Swiss Guard barracks and the courtyard were only just on the other side of the high stone walls separating the Vatican from the tumult and cacophony of Rome, it seemed as though the entire world had gone silent and their ancient corner of the Holy See was a medieval village locked in time. The three barracks buildings rose and enclosed the ceremony, their cracked maroon paint flecking off in centuries-old clumps. Narrow, cramped windows—former archers' windows—overlooked the central courtyard. Limp flags from the cantons the guards hailed from in Switzerland hung in the stale air. At one end of the courtyard, a fountain burbled and, set above it, a marble relief of a medieval Swiss Guard, clad in armor and wielding a broadsword, glared over the ceremony. *Patria Memor* was carved into the stone. *Remember country. Remember home.*

Centuries ago, it was a guardsman who invented the word nostalgia. *Nostos*, meaning sickness, and *algos*, meaning a longing for home. That guard had been struggling to describe the sickening loss he felt, his ceaseless pain and the aching, heart-scratching loneliness he carried inside. He'd had to create a new word to capture that exquisite longing, the desperate yearning for something he could never have, and the soul-deep purity of his despair.

Alain knew *exactly* how that felt.

A shadow crossed over his face. He blinked and looked up, squinting as the sun slid behind the Apostolic Palace. Rising above the barracks, the papal apartments within the Apostolic Palace loomed, a sheer cliff rising just beyond their cramped courtyard, breathtakingly close. Alain watched the pope's third-story bedroom window curtains flutter. With an easy throw, he could lob a stone into the Holy Father's bedchamber.

The Holy Father blessed the crowd and then the Swiss Guard, thanking them for their oaths and their passion before closing and dismissing the ceremony. Applause rose, family members cheering. Halberdiers dispersed, the youngest and newest going to their families while the veterans stood stiffly to the side and counted the minutes until they could shed their pinching armor.

Alain backed away. If he could slip out unnoticed, maybe the commandant wouldn't see his dreadful failure in his appearance. Besides, there was work to be done. The revenant, and so much more. He didn't have time to linger.

"Sergeant Autenburg!" Commandant Gaëtan Best's crisp voice broke over the din of the crowd.

Alain cringed. He spun on his heel. "Commandant?" He

ignored the way Best's face creased as he took in Alain's sloppy uniform and his distinct lack of armor.

"Sergeant, come." The commandant gestured for him, and one hand rose to the shoulder of a young Swiss Guard recruit standing at his side. "I have someone I want you to meet."

Alain strode forward. Wariness stole through him as he took in the man beside Commandant Best. It was the same recruit who'd caught his eye during the swearing in. He was older than the others, but still younger than Alain. Mid-twenties. He was tall, the long lines of the uniform only accentuating his height. Swiss blue eyes squinted back at Alain and a square German jaw with a dimpled, blunt chin finished the man's chiseled face.

A distant part of Alain recognized he was attractive, but he'd ignored that part of himself for so long, the thought was more of a passing observation, a spare thought lost amid his mental notes about the laundry, revenants and ghouls, and his pile of dishes still to wash.

"Ah," the commandant said, smiling at Alain. He clapped Alain on the shoulder, the same way he had the younger guard, holding both men in his grasp. "Halberdier Cristoph Hasse, I'd like you to meet Sergeant Alain Autenburg. He will be your mentor for your first year in the Guard."

Alain's head whipped around so fast he thought he'd snapped his neck. He must have misheard. He didn't mentor *anyone*. He couldn't. Besides, he practically wasn't in the Swiss Guard at all anymore, not with his special duties. He had no interaction with the rest of the Guard. How could he mentor anyone into a group he didn't belong to? He was the worst sort of role model, his current uniform a case in point. And, really, there was no time for this. "Sir?"

Commandant Best held his stare and squeezed his shoulder to the point of pain. "Sergeant, Halberdier Hasse is in special need of your counsel and your wisdom. I believe pairing the two of you will bring you both to greater success in each of your endeavors." He smiled, but it was brittle and didn't reach his eyes.

Cristoph Hasse stared straight ahead. His eyes flicked to Alain once, then away. His jaw clenched. Sheer misery, followed by disgust, flowed off Cristoph like the waves of the Mediterranean crashing against Italy's barren shore.

Luca strolled up behind the commandant. He glowered at Alain. "Sergeant, I know you cannot be bothered to follow even the most basic of regulations, but even *you*, I thought, knew how not to embarrass yourself with your slovenly appearance." A beat, as Luca looked Alain over, from his shoes to his beret, gone askew. "Apparently not."

"Major." The commandant's bark was short.

"Sir." It was an apology of sorts, but not to Alain.

Luca eyed Cristoph. He snorted, frowned. When he spoke next, it was in rolling French and directed to the commandant only. "Sir, may I ask what it is you're doing here?"

The commandant answered in French, sparing Alain a quick nod. "I have decided to partner Halberdier Hasse with Sergeant Autenburg for the halberdier's mentorship."

Luca laughed, loud peals echoing off the cold stone walls. His French was smooth, demure, and he grinned at Alain as he spoke, all sharp teeth, his voice cutting. "Don't you think that's like asking the fox to guard the hen house?"

Alain looked away. *Damn you, Luca. Damn you.* Dread settled in his stomach. Across from him, he spied Cristoph's eyes slide closed. His shoulders shook, though not from laughter. From rage. From wrath.

It seemed the young halberdier knew French, too. Alain shook his head. Just like Luca to assume he was better than everyone else.

Alain spoke up, his French rolling off his tongue less smoothly than the commandant or Luca. He got his point across. "Go fuck yourself, Luca."

The commandant's grip on his shoulder turned punishing, and he barely held in his hiss of pain. Luca turned purple, matching his feathered plume. His lips curled. "Sergeant—" Luca started.

"*Enough!*" The commandant growled at both of them. "Major.

You are dismissed." His eyes bored into Luca's until the major gave a curt nod and spun on his heel.

Alain caught Cristoph's tiny, barely-there smirk as he glanced Alain's way.

Commandant Best finally loosened his grasp on Alain's shoulder. "Sergeant, Halberdier Hasse is in need of mentorship. You are the mentor best suited for him. I have made my decision and it is final. You will guide this young man through his first year with us. Understood?"

Unspoken in the commandant's words was the threat that his first year would be his only year. Sent packing if he didn't fly right, his two-year enlistment cancelled in disgrace.

"Yes, Commandant." He had no time for mentorship and not the first clue what to do with the young guard, but there wasn't room to argue. "I'll do what I can."

The commandant nodded, clapped both men on the back, and strode off, heading for a gaggle of parents and their young recruits. He smiled and shook the parents' hands, loudly congratulating them for their sons' achievement in joining the Guard.

Alain shifted awkwardly next to Cristoph. The silence between them stretched long. "Do you want to see your family, Halberdier?"

Cristoph shook his head. "I have no family here."

That brought back memories. Alain's family hadn't shown up on his enlistment day either. Alain's eyes darted over the crowd, searching for an escape. His eyes caught on Luca and stuttered to a stop. Luca was rubbing elbows with the archbishops next to Chaplain Hauke Weimers. Figured. Luca never let an opportunity pass to get in front of the higher-ups.

"He's an asshole," Cristoph growled. He spat, lobbing a wad to the cobblestones as he glared at Luca.

"Halberdier!" Alain crowded close, looming into the younger man's space. "Major Bader is your superior officer and you will treat him with the respect his rank affords."

Slowly, Cristoph's frigid blue eyes traveled up Alain's chest, up his neck, his face, and met his gaze. They seared into Alain.

"Attention, Halberdier!" Alain barked.

Cristoph didn't set any speed records with how he came to attention, but he stood tall and straight, his hands at his sides. He averted his gaze, a darkness falling over his eyes.

So far, his mentorship was off to a fantastic start. Alain stepped back, sighing. "Major Bader is the second-in-command of the Swiss Guard. You can't fight him. You can't beat him. You'll only make yourself miserable if you try. Don't pick that fight."

Silence. Cristoph didn't move a muscle.

"How did you do in your recruit training?" Recruits, prior to enlistment, went through six months of intensive Italian, Roman and Vatican etiquette, Swiss Guard history and procedures, hand-to-hand combatives, and advanced weapons training, as well as marching and specialized halberd training.

It wasn't easy. The Swiss Guard wasn't a theme park, and they weren't colorful cartoon characters, props for the Vatican. Many washed out.

Cristoph nodded once. "Fine," he said stiffly. "Top marks in all courses."

"Mmm." Alain covered up his impressed look. Long ago, he and Luca had jockeyed for top marks in their courses. Alain had come out on top, just barely. It hadn't been easy, but throwing Luca down in combatives day in and day out had made up for the stress and strain. "And how are you getting along with the rest of the recruits?"

Cristoph turned a withering stare toward Alain. Alain arched his eyebrow in return. *We'll have to work on respect, for starters.* No wonder Luca despised the kid. "You're well on your way to being discharged with that attitude, Halberdier."

"Maybe I'm fine with that."

"It's your first day." Alain scrunched up his nose as he tried to puzzle the young man—contradictory and full of piss and vinegar —out. "Why take the oath? You don't want to be here? Then don't. No one is forcing you. Don't waste anyone's time."

Swallowing, Cristoph's jaw clenched again, the muscles bulging outward. "I came here for a reason," he finally growled.

"And what's that? Wanted to be a badass? Thought this was all about dark shades and talking in hidden microphones?"

Two kinds of men joined the Swiss Guard. The adrenaline junkies, thinking they were about to be some kind of United States Secret Service Agent. Or the prophets, thinking their experience would bring them closer to God. Both were constantly, consistently disappointed.

"How much longer do I have to be here?" Cristoph glared at the small celebration taking place.

"When is your next shift? You'll stand guard at your station now that you're officially enlisted." Each halberdier would stand a total of eighteen hours at a guard post for two days and then have one day off. However, when the guards were off duty, they could be immediately recalled for any reason. Overtime was an understatement. All in all, it was exhausting work.

"I'm due at the Arch of the Bells in two hours."

"Get out of here then. And report to my office once a week. We'll discuss your progress and... mentoring."

Their eyes met and held before Cristoph hurried off. Alain spotted his quiet contempt buried beneath a weary resignation in the depths of his gaze.

Join the club.

Chapter Three

ALAIN'S BODY ROCKS A SLOW RHYTHM, HIPS PUMPING DOWN, SLIDING in and out of a tight heat. Arms spread wide, fingers laced with another's, pressing his lover's palms down into the mattress. Lying on his lover's back, Alain presses his lips into his lover's hair, breaths in his scent.

Hot breath stutters out of him, whispering over the back of his lover's neck. Eyes closed, Alain buries his face in between his shoulder blades, mouthing at the sweat-slick skin and the roll of clenching muscles. God, he loves this, loves feeling his lover's body, loves lying across him, surrounding him, enveloping him. Holding him close.

It hasn't been like this in years. Not since—

A moan from his lover. A deep, breathy groan, an arch of his back.

Alain's eyes fly open.

That's not his lover's voice. Not the sounds his lover makes.

Pushing back, he rises just enough for Alain to get a glimpse of his partner's face over his shoulder.

His partner twists around, looking back at Alain, but only half his face is visible. Blond hair and lightning-blue eyes stare back at him, a breathless moan pushed out between kiss-red lips.

It's Cristoph.

Alain can't breathe, can't drag in air. Cristoph rocks beneath him, pushing back, driving Alain deeper inside his body. Another moan, and Cristoph's eyes close, squeezing shut as he bites his lower lip.

"Alain..." Cristoph breathes, almost a groan. "Alain..."

This isn't his lover. Cristoph isn't the man he dreams about, the lover he lost so many years ago and now only sees in his dreams.

His hips drive forward again, plunging deep into Cristoph. Cristoph arches his back and his neck, his fingers squeezing Alain's before pulling their hands in close. Alain buries his face in Cristoph's neck again and nuzzles the short blond strands. The scent of Cristoph—green grass, sunshine, and gunpowder—sizzles down his spine. His lips move over Cristoph's skin, warm and wet on his neck, his jaw. Cristoph turns, craning around for a press of his lips to Alain's.

Alain should fight it. He should. Cristoph isn't his lover.

He doesn't have a lover anymore, except for deep in his dreams, in the dark corners of his memories, and in his deepest, most unfulfilled yearnings.

So he leans forward, driving deeper as he kisses Cristoph, kisses him until he can't breathe.

He breaks away when his toes curl, when lines of fire begin to thread from the center of his soul, and when the world shrinks to the heat burning beneath his navel. A gasp, and he buries his face in Cristoph's hair, and then he's coming apart at the seams for what seems like ages, and white lightning scratches across his vision, and he's burning, burning from the inside—

ALAIN WOKE WITH A SHOUT, ROLLING OUT OF HIS BED AND falling to the floor. One leg tangled in his blankets, still caught on his mattress as his shoulder and head hit the floor in his bedroom.

He lay unmoving, catching his breath as he blinked. The Vatican at night was a somber place, still as death, but it was always lit up like the gates of heaven. St. Peter's Basilica gleamed, the glow slicing through Alain's heavy curtains like lines of holy fire and condemnation.

Shifting, he tried to untangle his leg. Wetness in his crotch stilled his movements. Alain lay back, closing his eyes. His dream came back in bits and pieces.

Making love to his long-lost lover. But not his lover, not really. Making love to *Cristoph*.

Cristoph Hasse, the new recruit, a man who wanted nothing to do with Alain. Who seemed to resent even being there.

God, why him? Why Cristoph? Those kinds of dreams were few and far between as it was, memories replaying from back when he'd been happy, when he'd thought he had it all. Why was Cristoph invading his dreams?

Push it all away. He repeated his old mantra, the words he'd repeated over and over to himself, words he'd needed to cling to through the years. *Push it all down. Push it away. Crush everything in the center of your chest.*

TWO DAYS LATER, THE PHONE RANG IN ALAIN'S OFFICE AS HE surfed through reports of dark risings and rumblings in the etheric from his counterparts around the world. The clatter of the ringer —practically an antique with a real brass bell embedded in the phone—made him jump, sloshing espresso across the back of his hand. He held in his curse as he mopped at the mess staining his file folders.

"Sergeant Autenburg."

"*That revenant was a dead priest.*"

Alain blinked. Father Lotario was blunt to the point of rude, and he didn't give a shit what time of day it was, he was himself. He'd once said he didn't have time for social niceties and since everyone hated him anyway, he didn't bother. It was an odd thing to find a priest that seemingly everyone despised. Lotario, though, managed to piss off nearly every single person he encountered.

Especially Alain. But Alain was partnered with the man, and he'd come to expect Lotario's quirks, rely on them even, like relying on the dryer in the barracks basement to eat his socks and burn his dress shirts. It was almost comforting, Lotario's routine crassness.

"Was it a violent death?"

"*The* polizia *fished him out of the Tiber last week. He was fresh meat in the Vatican. Wet behind the ears. A clerk in the Vatican archives.*"

Over the phone, Alain heard the squeal of tires and the smash of a car horn wailing, and then Lotario's bellowing curse. "Has Angelo sent over the autopsy records yet? Can we figure out how the priest died?"

Lotario was still cursing under his breath. "*Yeah, funny thing about that. The death was ruled a suicide. No autopsy was performed. Lungs were full of the Tiber's shit water, the report said.*"

Sighing, Alain let his head fall forward as he pinched the bridge of his nose. "Is his body in any recoverable state?" They'd burned the revenant, the remnants of the dead priest's soul back from the grave, fury at its core. But the body left behind was another matter. If the revenant hadn't desecrated its own remains, they might be able to take a second look at his death.

Lotario didn't sound hopeful. A long sigh and a quibbling sort of waver. "*Ehh... He wasn't in one piece, according to Angelo.*"

Creaking wood and the turn of a rusting doorknob made Alain freeze.

Halberdier Hasse stood in his doorway. He was dressed in his striped uniform, topped with his duty beret. The beret was angled just off perfect, just enough to be purposeful. Blue eyes narrowed when they met Alain's.

Alain's breath stuttered, lost in his eyes, but Cristoph looked away, his gaze fixing to one of Alain's bookshelves and the disorganized clutter piled helter-skelter.

He floundered for words. "Uhh, we've still got to check it out," he stumbled. "Still have to see what we can get from... it." His dream flashed back, his mind suddenly filled with lightning-blue eyes and breathy moans and strong muscles moving beneath kiss-flushed skin.

"*Eh? The hell's wrong with you?*" Another horn honked in the background and a loud curse in Italian flowed over the line. "*You, Alain, not the fucking morons on this God forsaken road.*"

Of course Lotario would pick up on Alain's sudden obfuscation. His eyes darted to Cristoph. *Push it all away.* He motioned the young guard inside, gesturing to one of the seats before his desk. "I have to go. I have company."

"*You?*" Lotario scoffed and laughed loud enough his voice bounced off the stone walls of Alain's office from the phone's tinny handset. "*You* never *have company!*"

"Good-bye." Alain hung up as Lotario launched into another tirade, this time against a Vespa, as far as Alain could make out from Lotario's gutter Italian.

He turned back to Cristoph, still standing in his doorway. One arched eyebrow and a pointed look at Alain's chairs clued him in a moment later. The pair of creaking metal folding chairs huddled together in the cramped space before his desk were stacked with dusty books and files, folios of medieval manuscripts checked out of the Vatican archives, and copies of *polizia* reports detailing the paranormal. More mundane reports from his actual duties to the Swiss Guard—coordinating special activities between the Vatican gendarmerie and the Swiss Guard—cluttered the second chair.

"Sorry." Alain bustled the chairs clear, dropping the stacks haphazardly onto his desk. One pile slid sideways, bleeding papers. He smeared over the exposed Latin incantations and runic magic circles with an open folder of pickpocket statistics from St. Peter's Square before turning around and leaning back against the desk.

Which put his crotch directly at eye level with the young halberdier, sitting in a rickety folding chair now that it was clear. Cristoph pursed his lips, eyebrows arching and disappearing entirely beneath his beret's rim.

"Sorry." Alain slid sideways, escaping back to the safety of his desk. His face burned. An echo of Cristoph's moan sounded in the back of his mind.

Adjusting his suit jacket, Alain dropped into his chair with a sigh. "Good morning," he said, forcing cheer into his voice and a smile to his face. His cheeks strained, and he had the sudden image of himself looking like one of the patently fake toothpaste adverts. He dropped the smile. "How are you doing, Halberdier Hasse?"

Cristoph winced. "It's Cristoph," he said, looking away.

"It's supposed to be 'halberdier', as that is your rank." Alain watched Cristoph's jaw clench again. "But you may call me Alain. How have your first two days gone?"

Cristoph shrugged.

"That's it?" Alain crossed his arms on the desk. He frowned. "You do remember applying for this position, yes? You do remember you had to ask to be here?"

Cristoph's gaze darted to Alain. His eyes were dark, roiling with thunderclouds, lightning ready to strike. "It's not what I thought this would be."

"It never is." Alain gestured to his cramped, closet-sized office. "Do you imagine I expected this is where I would end up when I took my oath?"

Silence.

"I was in your shoes once. Trying to understand what I had just signed up for. Time passed... and now I am here." Alain tried to smile. He failed. And now he was here, indeed. "Look, do you want to leave?"

He watched Cristoph, looking for any sign, any reaction. He'd closed down entirely. The man was like a statue and just as expressionless. The Mona Lisa showed more emotion. Alain caught the edge of a tongue, peeking out as he licked his lips. The edge of one lip, being bit. His eyes tracked the line of Cristoph's teeth and the furrow left in his pink skin.

"What is after the Swiss Guard if you were to leave tomorrow?" Leaving without finishing his term of enlistment was a quick way to a stalled career. No matter whether Cristoph wanted to continue in the military or move into the private sector, a dismissal from the Guard would haunt the rest of his days. "Where would you go?"

Cristoph shook his head.

"If you leave now, that's all anyone will ever see." Alain tried to catch his gaze. "If you stay, if you beat whatever is troubling you, then you will at least have the satisfaction of victory."

Finally, a reaction. Cristoph frowned at him as if he were a puzzle piece out of place. "You're not going to tell me to submit? To accept that everyone above me knows better?" His eyes narrowed. "Aren't I supposed to recite Psalm Forty? 'I delight to do your will, O my God. Your law is within my heart.'"

Alain let the breath in his lungs slowly pour from him. As he inhaled, he caught Cristoph's scent—sunshine, green grass, and gunpowder. He coughed, his throat clenching.

"Submission," he started. He stopped. Clearly, Chaplain Weimers had already gotten to Cristoph during recruit training. It was the standard preaching—submission to authority as a mimicry of submission to God. "That's a good Psalm. Submission takes many forms— There can be freedom in submission, when you give yourself to the right purpose. To the right—" His voice stuttered. Died.

He couldn't say it. Couldn't say the words, talk about faith and God and purpose. He just couldn't. "But... submission for the sake of submission robs us of our freedom. Of our souls."

How many pacts with dark creatures had he seen based off a human's submission and their belief they would emerge from the deal with something to gain? How many times had a man given in when he should have stood strong? "Never once," he finished, "has it ever been wrong to stand true to yourself."

Cristoph stared at him, the silence of the room suddenly visceral, suddenly a tangible, weighty presence. His office was set off from the rest of the officers and the NCOs of the Swiss Guard, down a long, dark hallway. It was normally quiet as a graveyard, but never this heavy. Never this claustrophobic. He could feel Cristoph's eyes boring into him, seeking something beneath his rank, beneath his duties.

Alain slapped his hand down on the desk, trying to break the moment. Beneath his black collar, his skin burned hot, itching where his duties lay across his shoulders. "My job is to get you through your enlistment. You have seven hundred and twenty-eight days left. It goes fast, faster than you can believe. I know it doesn't seem like that now—"

Cristoph interrupted him. "I have duty in ten minutes." He stood, scraping the chair against the rough wood floor.

Alain jumped to his feet. "Next time, come earlier."

Cristoph nodded once, never meeting Alain's eyes, and stormed out the door.

"And fix your beret!" Alain shouted at his retreating back.

THE DEAD PRIEST'S REMAINS WERE IN FORTY PIECES.

Nothing fit back together. Some parts were liquefied. Others were simply gone. Angelo stood back while Lotario and Alain tried to lay out the former priest's body in some semblance of a human shape on the gurney Angelo had brought them.

The priest's chest was missing. His lungs, which proved he'd drowned, were gone. His shoulders ended with a ragged tear, and then his body picked up again where his hips began, a frayed edge of skin and muscle covering his hip bones and leading down to his legs. His spine was intact through it all, a slinking chain of chipped vertebrae and cracked bones and broken shafts where ribs had once extended. One arm was crushed, the hand torn off. Half his face was missing, the other frozen in a rictus of anguish.

"That can't have been from the revenant." Angelo stayed back, but he peered over Lotario's skinny shoulders.

The cigarette bounced between Lotario's lips as he spoke. Smoke drifted above the gurney, mixing with the smell of putrescence and river rot. "No, no," he mumbled. "That's from his death."

"Doesn't look like much like a suicide." Alain rolled the priest's head sideways, covering the missing half. He tried to imagine the full face, screaming in pain. "Doesn't look like a man who chose to drown of his own free will."

Lotario snorted. The cigarette glowed, embers flashing as ash fell from the tip, scattering on the priest's naked thighs. "Check this out," he growled. Lotario flipped the priest's hips and thighs onto the side, manhandling the corpse's pieces until it was mostly on its front. Slime and putrefaction oozed out of the shorn pelvic cavity, smearing on the gurney.

Alain peered at the rotten thighs. Bruises marred the back, purple lines, a snaking pattern of tendrils and wisps crisscrossing his dead skin. Ligature marks. "Melusine."

Plucking the cigarette from his lips, Lotario blew his smoke away from Alain's face. He tapped the ash over the priest's shoulder. The embers landed in the hollow of his shattered cheek. "Yeah, melusine. He didn't kill himself. The river killed him."

Melusine were river spirits, deadly, damned, and demonic creatures who swam in the murky depths of the Tiber. Filaments of muscle dragged an unsuspecting person down into their razor-sharp fangs. They only fed while their prey was alive. After they'd drowned, the melusine released their prey, but by then, it was too late.

"But who hops in the Tiber for a swim these days?" Angelo, still standing far away, asked. "No one just goes for a jump in that filthy river."

"And with his suit on." The priest had died in his clerical suit. Alain fingered the bag of his river-soaked belongings, his shredded black suit and his torn Roman collar. "From the outside, it must have looked like a clean suicide."

"'Cept not." Lotario dropped the priest's hips back to the table. The corpse landed with a squelch, a slimy, slick slap of dead flesh against sterile metal. Alain cringed and stepped back, but ooze splashed onto his suit pants. He glared at Lotario.

Lotario kept talking, still sucking down his cigarette. "Someone threw him in the river. Someone who knew what he'd face down there. If this were a human killing, they'd have shot him first, or held him under in shallow water until he drowned."

"Think he was targeted by something?" Alain brushed at his pants.

Lotario shrugged, plucking the nub of his cigarette from his mouth. He extinguished the remnants on the back of the corpse's hand, the embers hissing out of existence, charring the rotten flesh around the burn. "Dunno. We can't check for sulfur. The water would have gotten rid of all traces of dealings with a demon. But something wanted him dead. And not just dead. They wanted it to hurt. Wanted him to suffer."

Alain sighed. "Get back to the Vatican and pull his records. We'll have to talk to his supervisors. See what sorts of projects he was working on in the archives."

Lotario nodded. He clicked off the brakes on the gurney and started to wheel the corpse out. Down the hallway, in the bunker Angelo had given them, a concrete room with a circle of melted silver poured into the floor waited. A pile of charred ash and bone sat in the center.

"Do you need help with the remains?"

Alain always offered.

"Nope." Lotario grabbed a bucket of salt and a can of lighter fluid from the metal shelves against the wall, piling the supplies in the dead priest's empty chest cavity.

Lotario never accepted.

Chapter Four

Mentoring went from bad to worse.

Alain missed his next appointment with Cristoph thanks to a hungry wraith and Angelo's predawn phone call. He and Lotario drove out to Tivoli and managed to shatter the wraith's energies and dispatch the darkness. Still, he didn't get back to the Vatican until late afternoon, well after his appointment with Cristoph.

He didn't know if he should be thankful or frustrated at that.

The dreams hadn't left.

He dreamed about his long-gone lover once, maybe twice, a year. A quick handjob in the shower or a rut against the mattress and he'd be over it. It had been years since those memories had haunted his footsteps and his waking moments. Years since he'd seen his lover in the shadows or reached out for him in a moment of weakness, only to meet dead, empty air.

Now, Cristoph starred in his dreams almost nightly. Cristoph's furious blue eyes, turned soft. His blond hair, just slightly too long. Enough to get his fingers tangled in. Enough to grab, and arch Cristoph's neck—

Push it all away.

Of course, he'd heard all about his missed appointment from

Luca, who'd regaled him with the tale of Cristoph standing at attention outside his office door for a full hour under Luca's hawk-like gaze.

Luca only let Cristoph leave when he was three minutes away from his shift at the Bronze Doors.

He should just let the whole thing shrivel and die. He should let his ill-suited mentorship duties atrophy and fall away. He should let Cristoph turn his resentment toward him, nurture a hatred of Alain instead of Luca, instead of the Guard. That should be his gift to Cristoph.

He shouldn't watch for Cristoph's blond hair striding across the courtyard, shouldn't picture those frigid blue eyes warming, turning soft in Alain's direction. He shouldn't get involved. Any *more* involved.

His shouldn'ts shadowed him like ghosts, chasing after him in whispers as he trudged into the Guards' canteen. Their communal eating hall was a dark and dreary place, grim in the dull light of dusty chandeliers. Heavy wooden beams latticed the ceiling, as if trying to replicate the atmosphere of the 1500's. The barracks had been updated and modernized to keep with the times, but the canteen stubbornly held on to its dubious medieval charms. Murals along the walls tried to recreate the splendor of the knights of their heyday, medieval Switzerland's famed knights of renown, feared across all of Europe.

It was hard to look at the murals. Alain knew the truth about those knights of old.

And, sitting a literal stone's throw from St. Peter's, the mural's loose and wild brushings seemed almost cartoonish, a child's finger-painting beside Michelangelo's crowning glory.

He took a step into the gloomy canteen. Halberdiers milled, some getting ready to go on their shifts, others coming off. A television was on in the corner, tuned to a football game from northern Italy. Three guards watched, sipping their beers. A low din carried through the room, conversation mixed with sighs and stretches, silverware scraping on plates and metal trays, guards relaxing or readying themselves. Laughter, the sound of life.

Everything stopped dead as the guards spotted Alain at the door. Like a wave receding from shore, pulling further and further away, silence spread, jaws snapping shut, silverware freezing. Beer glasses setting down.

In the back, one guard stood, glaring at Alain.

He knew. God, he knew. He wasn't welcome here.

Still, he sought out Cristoph. Through the crowd, through the mass of wary, silent humanity, his own comrades arrayed against him.

Cristoph was the only one not looking at him. He glared down at his plate, picking at his pasta as he sat alone at a table separated from everyone else. Sullen rage pulsed off of him, loud as a scream.

He should apologize, but if he crossed the canteen, if he actually sat with Cristoph, everyone there would connect the two of them. His corruption would seep from him to Cristoph, right there in front of everyone's eyes, and as bad as Cristoph might have it now —isolated, cut off, and pissed at the world—how much worse would it be for him if Alain walked to him right now? If he sat with him?

It would be a kindness to walk away.

It would be a kindness to leave Cristoph alone. Let their... whatever it was die.

He turned and left. Fifty pairs of eyeballs drilled into his back as he walked out.

Was one of those Cristoph's?

LOTARIO RAN INTO A DEAD END WITH THE DEAD PRIEST'S supervisors at the Vatican archives. He had been a quiet man with few friends. The priest hadn't been working on anything extraordinary. His tasks had been mundane, boring even. They didn't remember his name until Lotario reminded them.

Alain cringed at that.

"He was doing some research on the first garrison of Swiss Guards at the Vatican, back in 1506," Lotario grumbled over the phone line. Alain could almost smell the cigarette smoke as he heard Lotario exhale and sift through papers. *"Some boring art restoration notes... Looks like he was cataloging Michelangelo's Vatican pieces. That's it."*

"Where are we on his personal effects?"

"The dormitory is trying to find the box now. They cleared his room and boxed everything up." Another exhale. *"It was brought to the basement, and now it's just a bunch of finger pointing."*

"Hopefully we can find something in his stuff. We're running out of leads."

"I think you mean we're out of leads." A loud cough. *"I'll bring his effects by your office when they find it."*

―――――――

LOTARIO'S TIMING, AS ALWAYS, COULDN'T HAVE BEEN WORSE.

A week had passed since Alain missed his appointment with Cristoph. Seven hours had passed since Alain's last dream of Cristoph. He'd woken with Cristoph's name on his lips and his hips rutting into the mattress like a horny teenager. He'd given up on his sheets. He'd do laundry after this sexual madness had passed.

And it would pass. He would get over whatever imagined fantasy his twisted subconscious had seized on. Nothing would happen between him and Cristoph. Not a thing.

It couldn't. Not ever. *Never again.*

He'd purposely cleared his schedule for Cristoph, staying in his office with the warped door propped open by a thick copy of the worthless *Malleus Maleficarum*. Rain thundered from the sky, drenching the Vatican and all of Rome. The creaky old buildings were waterlogged in moments, and shivering drafts crept through ancient cracks. Alain clutched a fresh cup of espresso as he reviewed all of his notes on the Tiber melusine.

A soggy, dripping mess brought a swirl of cold air to his

doorway. Papers fluttered on the desk as Cristoph, soaked to the bone and trailing water on the stone floor, appeared. His boots squished with every step, and his brilliantly striped uniform was drenched, hanging limply from his body. His beret was plastered to his pale face. His lips had gone plum from the cold. They pressed together, trying to hide his chattering. Dark hollows hung beneath his eyes.

"Halberdier!" Alain shot to his feet. "How long were you out in this weather? Do you not have a cover? Where is your cape?" When it rained, the guardsmen were supposed to don navy wool capes, covering their uniforms and keeping them warm. They were also supposed to stand in the rain shelter.

"Been at my post all night," Cristoph managed through chattering teeth.

Alain slid his espresso across the desk. Cristoph grabbed it in both hands and huddled over the cup as he sat. "Why didn't you stand at your post inside the shelter?" No matter where a guard was stationed, there was always an inclement weather shelter.

Dark eyes met Alain's. Cristoph's lip curled up. "Because Corporal Gruber ordered me to stand outside."

He bit down hard on his tongue. Corporal Gruber was a close mentee of Luca's. "What did he say?" Alain asked slowly.

"He ordered me out in the fucking rain! Said it was something any true guard would do! And that going into the shelter would be weak. Something only a soft man would do!" Cristoph glared at the wall, trying—and failing—for a stony mask of indifference.

There were some in the Guard who would stand in the rain all night long. It filled their sense of masculine glory and hit their buttons for sacrifice and punishment. It was a strop of good old Germanic discipline and good for the character, they said. Mix that with a healthy dose of hazing and a man who made himself a target through his sullen, shitty attitude, and one drenched, pissed-off guardsman was the result.

"That's a load of shit," he said, looking at Cristoph. "You know that. I know you do."

Cristoph snorted, but congestion in his nose made it snotty.

"What do you have to prove?" Alain tried to catch his eye.

"Oh come off it!" Cristoph snapped. He glared at Alain, his eyes no longer dark, but red-rimmed and furious. "I know exactly what they think of me here! I know exactly what it is they see in me! I mean, come *on!*" He threw his arm out, gesturing around Alain's closet of an office, unkempt and bursting with ancient manuscripts and coffee-stained printouts. "Look where they dumped me! Instead of being paired up with one of the real officers as a mentor, they gave me to *you.*"

Alain arched a single eyebrow.

"So I look at you. Is this my future? Am I being told that if I stay, I'll just end up just like you? Did you just give *in* this crap? Despite your 'always be yourself' speech? How can you sit here, taking this?" Snarling, Cristoph stared at Alain, a heavy darkness in his eyes masking a brief flash of something that looked like anguish.

Alain's voice dropped, going frigid. "My reasons for staying are my own. And you came here with a chip on your shoulder. What did you expect?"

Cristoph leaped to his feet. "I expect to not be treated like a leper! To not be shoved out of the way and ignored, like they've clearly done with you! I expected this to *mean* something! To matter!" He slammed the espresso cup down on the desk, bitter liquid sloshing over the edges and staining a folder with the dead priest's autopsy. "But *nothing* does. Not even you. What are you, their pet faggot?"

Silence. Pipes creaked in the walls, groaning as someone turned the faucet on the second floor. Boots clip-clapped on worn wood, and the electronic whine of a printer scratched through the air, far away in the main garrison offices.

His dreams seemed so far removed from the present moment, his dream Cristoph of laughing eyes and sweet looks totally incompatible with the furious, hardened man before him. The muscles in his jaw quivered as he forcibly held back from lashing out. Twelve hard years had taught him temperance, at least.

"Bad time?" Lotario slouched against the doorframe, his eyebrows raised and a smirk stretching his lips. He had a box, sealed with evidence tape, under one arm.

"Jesus Christ," Alain muttered, exhaling. His fists slowly uncurled. He glared at Cristoph. "Get out."

Cristoph stormed off, barely avoiding soaking Lotario as he edged past. Lotario seemed to revel in Cristoph's ire as he strode into Alain's office.

"Sounds like you made a new friend." Lotario swapped the box for Alain's abandoned espresso, chugging it down as he tapped his fingers on the box lid.

Alain ground his teeth, molars scrapping. *Push it all away.* "This our priest's effects?"

"*Mm.*" Lotario polished off Alain's espresso with one last swallow and set the cup on top of Alain's boxy computer monitor. "Let's get inside him, shall we?"

Scissors sliced through the gendarmerie's tape. Lotario flipped the lid and pulled out the last of their dead priest's worldly possessions. It wasn't much, not even enough to fill the bottom of the box. A spare suit and a Roman collar. A crucifix. A Bible. A rosary, well worn. A picture of a middle-aged woman, signed on the back, "*Love, Mom.*"

Lotario tossed the Bible back into the box, crumpling the Roman collar. "Well, that was a fat lot of nothing."

"This is where we're supposed to find a piece of evidence." Alain hung his head between his shoulders. "That's how this script is supposed to work."

"Yeah, well, I think you'd have more luck getting that soaking wet guard to grab a beer with you than find anything more in this case. We're out of road on this one."

Alain fingered the signed picture. "And the mom?"

"Dead. Breast cancer. Five years ago."

"Let's get this back to the dorm." Lotario eyeballed Alain.

"What?" Alain groaned.

"What was up with your little friend? Pretty strong words getting thrown around for a Tuesday morning. And here, no less." Lotario whistled as he made a show of inspecting the office and the barracks hallway. "You lot give 'prude' a new definition."

Despite himself, Alain chuckled. This from a priest who skirted the blurry boundaries of decency and decorum. "That was Cristoph, one of the new recruits. My assigned mentee." *And my new depravity. Something my dark soul has seized onto.* His dreams crowded into his waking moments, the warm body he imagined sinking into every night, and the throaty moans and heart-melting smiles his dreams bequeathed him.

This must be it. Must be the first sign of madness. His grip on reality was slipping. His sanity would all come apart with one blond recruit.

He was damned. So very damned.

Grabbing the box, Lotario tossed Alain a wink and a smile. "Looks like it's going just swimmingly."

"Sergeant? Do you have a moment?"

It was Commandant Best who brought the bad news a few days later. From the look on his face, Alain *knew* whatever he was about to say had to do with Cristoph. That cringe, the tightening around his eyes. The purse of his lips.

He sighed. "Of course, Commandant." Alain pushed aside his mountain of files and invited him in.

"How are your duties coming?"

"We've had a spate of risings recently. Evidence of dark pacts and corpses turning after death. A few revenants. A wraith. We haven't been able to tie them together, and we haven't been able to figure out what has been attracting the increase in risings. Or why some of our fresh corpses have turned."

"Payoff of a Faustian bargain?"

A deal with the Devil or, in actuality, some form of lesser dark creature. The Devil himself never appeared. "It's always the number one suspicion. We had a revenant rise from a corpse that was made to look like a suicide but was really a murder. Murder by melusine." He slid a file across the desk with the dead priest's second autopsy photos inside. Their autopsy. "See the purple ligature marks around the thigh? He'd been drowned in the Tiber as he was torn apart by the melusine."

"Was this one recently?"

Alain nodded. "Few weeks ago. He broke out of his cemetery days after his burial. We've put him down. His soul is gone."

Best bowed his head and closed his eyes. He muttered a soft prayer under his breath. Alain waited. He didn't pray with Best. It was never easy to banish a soul, to shatter a human's existence into nothing. But the alternative was to let a newborn demon linger in the world, and that always led to more death. All creatures of darkness—all of them—were eliminated. Always.

"Sergeant, there's something else I'd like to speak with you about." Best shifted in his seat as he crossed his legs. "It's about your young halberdier."

Alain tried not to grimace. Hot shame licked up his spine.

Best chuckled. "He's a trying young man. Fighting something, it seems."

"The world, I think."

"Well, he's gone and put himself in a serious jam. Major Bader found him returning to the barracks this morning. He'd been out all night, apparently."

"And it had to be Luca who found him?"

"It gets better." Best shook his head. "He is sporting a rather impressive hickey just above his uniform collar line."

A chill settled over Alain. "Jesus Christ." Best shot him a lean glare. "Sorry." He pressed his lips together, covered his mouth with his hand, and looked down.

He hadn't had a dream about Cristoph last night. No nighttime visits from his subconscious fantasy lover. A pang of jealously ripped apart his twisting guts, and his heart slid down his ribs, a hot, pounding mess, settling rancid in his belly. *Push it all away.*

Best waited.

"Tell me. What did Luca do?"

"I'm surprised you didn't hear it, even all the way in here. He may have sprained his vocal chords."

He plastered on a fake grin. "I bet that's not all he's sprained."

"I'm sure." Best's tight smile disappeared. "Alain, Halberdier Hasse is headed for expulsion. I don't want to do that. Cristoph is a good man. He's meant to be here, I know he is."

Alain frowned. What was the commandant talking about? Cristoph hated the Guard and resented being there. He'd come to the Vatican for the wrong reasons, clearly, and he didn't belong. It would be a miracle if he lasted a single year, let alone his full enlistment.

And he was stuck with Alain, the worst possible mentor, and a depraved, desperate one as well.

"I need you to save him."

Groaning, Alain flopped back in his chair. "Commandant, that's not my line of work. At all."

"Alain—"

"In fact, I'm in the exact opposite kind of spiritual warfare."

"Sergeant, I want Halberdier Hasse to remain and I know you are the man for the job." He paused. "You need each other."

"Oh no." Alain scooted back, waving his hands in front of him, trying to forestall the commandant's words. Flashes of his dreams sparked behind his eyes. Heat rose in his bones. "No, no, no. I won't accept this meddling in my life, especially not from you."

"You need a friend for God's sake, Alain. There are days you don't speak a single word to another living soul. And that priest of yours does not count. One of these days, you're liable to be as off as he is if you don't try to rejoin the world of the living."

"I talk to all sorts of things regularly. Revenants. Wraiths." He gestured to the autopsy records. "Corpses."

"That's what I mean." Best glared. "Alain, I've been there. I know the path you're on. Don't forget who put you in your position."

"Thank you for that, by the way."

"You don't have to do this alone. Your stubborn insistence on this matter—"

"Commandant, I'm very busy. Can we continue this another time?"

Heaving a sigh, Best stared at Alain, shaking his head. "I don't want to bury you, too," he finally breathed.

Alain looked away.

"Please look in on our young Halberdier Hasse." The commandant stood, straightening his suit. Unlike the halberdiers, he and the other officers wore a regular suit every day. "I believe you can find him shredding old uniforms and cleaning the cobblestones as part of his punishment duties. For now, 'until the end of time,' according to Major Bader."

"I'll check on him. But I make no promises."

"You aren't alone, Alain."

"Good day, Commandant."

With a sigh, Best left Alain's office, marching down the dark hallway away from Alain's shadowed dungeon and back to the real world of living people and human interaction.

Alain's eyes traveled from the *Malleus Maleficarum*, still propping open his door, to the ground corpse bone sitting in a glass vial on the edge of his desk, and then over to the extracted vampire fangs he'd salvaged from an autopsy years before. Half of a centuries-old skull, missing the jaw, scrawled with incantations in a dead language. Papers on the demonic, rituals in Latin, and runes carved into the edge of his desk. Calculations and tables of weights, charts of correspondences, figures for balancing magical circles. Above the door, sigils to ward off black magic and dark creatures. Beneath the rug under his feet, a demon's trap was painted into the stone.

No matter what Commandant Best tried to say, the chasm between Alain and the rest of the world was only getting bigger.

Chapter Five

FURY ROLLED OFF CRISTOPH. ALAIN COULD FEEL THE FORCE OF it even before he pulled open the creaking door closing Cristoph inside the dank cellar the Guard used as a punishment closet. Inside, two bare bulbs stuck out from the walls just below the ceiling, wires piped in along the stone walls and snaking to a heavy breaker box. The bulbs hummed, a soft pulse hovering just behind Alain's ears.

Cristoph crouched in front of a worn wooden block, an ancient executioner's stand. He held an axe blade in one hand and stretched a faded Swiss Guard uniform across the block with the other. With a grunt, he slammed the axe blade down on the old uniform, cutting it into ragged squares, each cut smaller than his palm.

Uniforms no longer fit for wear were shredded by hand, chopped into squares and then burned. It was a precaution against an outsider getting a hold of one of the uniforms and using it to penetrate the deepest recesses of the Vatican. It was also the Guards' oldest punishment detail for recalcitrant halberdiers. For hundreds of years, deviant guardsmen had pulled punishment duties in the stone cell, a hollow of bitten-off curses and sweat-stained stones scarred from centuries of manual labor.

The cut pieces of cloth slid off the block, landing in piles beside Cristoph's feet.

Though the cellar was cool, Cristoph was sweating, and his shirt was soaked down his back and beneath his arms. A bead of perspiration dripped down his temple, his cheek. Alain's eyes followed it, his gaze dragging across the jut of Cristoph's jaw. Cristoph shook his head, the ends of his hair curling with his sweat.

Alain swallowed. Looked down, for a moment. He folded his arms and leaned against the doorway, watching. Cristoph spared him one quick glance before sliding the destroyed uniform around for another swing of his axe.

Above his neckline, a purple bruise stained Cristoph's pale skin. Clearly, an overly passionate pair of lips. His jeans hung low on his hips, and Alain peeked, wondering if there were finger marks stretched over his hipbones. That slippery slide of jealousy reared within Alain again, but he stamped it out. There was no place for that. No reason for him to be jealous. His deranged fantasies were his own. Cristoph was his own man. He could do whatever—whomever—he wanted.

Still, Alain's gaze lingered on Cristoph's hips, his trim waist, his broad shoulders.

Another slam of the blade. The axe ground against the fabric and the executioner's block. The uniform and the wood frayed, pieces of one tangling with the other. Cristoph tugged the scraps to the floor and grabbed another fistful of old fabric from a basket by his feet.

"Are you pleased with yourself?" Alain finally asked. "Did you get what you wanted?"

Cristoph slammed the axe down again, harder than before.

"I hear you're on uniform punishment until the end of time."

"I won't be here that long."

Alain pursed his lips. "You're lucky you're here at all."

Swinging the axe, Cristoph left the blade embedded in the wood before turning the full force of his fury to Alain. "Here to gloat? Tell me to pack my bags and head back to Switzerland?"

"I would never gloat over your punishment." Alain shook his head. "And no one is sending you home. At least not today."

Cristoph snorted.

"Did you come here on a mission?" Alain pushed off the wall. He stood before Cristoph, legs spread, arms crossed, chin held high. "Did you come here to make a spectacle? Flaunt yourself? Launch some kind of visibility campaign for gay rights?"

Shaking his head, Cristoph's glower darkened. "No," he hissed. Silence stretched long as Cristoph fingered the edge of the blade. "I thought you said I should be true to myself."

"I did. But there is a big difference between being yourself and purposely being an asshole. Or at least there should be."

Cristoph looked down.

"You know you're not the only gay man in the Vatican, right? You're not completely alone." Alain cocked his head, watching Cristoph's profile. A muscle twitched in his cheek.

Ah. Struck a nerve.

"And I don't mean just me. One third of the Vatican is gay, give or take a nervous breakdown or ten."

Wide blue eyes swung around, staring at Alain.

"Haven't you wondered why there are so many bathhouses in Rome?" Alain arched his eyebrows, a wry grin curving his lips. "The Vatican rents out apartments for priests above one of the busiest gay neighborhoods in Old Town. The Vatican is stuffed full of gay men. Mostly priests. Some of them are celibate, but others aren't. They all find ways to live their lives, be who they are."

"But their vows—"

"That's for them to figure out." Alain held up his hands. "Call them crazy for being here. Call me crazy for choosing to be here. I have my reasons. And I am not one to judge another human being for theirs."

Cristoph's look called Alain a liar.

Alain almost grinned. "I don't judge *you*, though you seem to think I'm just waiting to pounce on all of your faults. I want you to succeed here, Cristoph. And I want to help you figure that out."

A long moment passed. Cristoph didn't move. He stared at Alain, wide-eyed and stiff-jawed. Finally, his head drooped forward. He braced his elbows on the tattered cutting block.

"I don't know if I made a mistake coming here or not," Cristoph said. His voice had lost some of that hard bitterness, the edge Alain had always heard. "And I don't know what to do now." The admission, the words, seemed almost painful, dragged out against his will and pulled from his soul. He kept his eyes down, glaring at the ground.

"You can start by not trying so hard to push every single person away." Moving forward, Alain leaned against the other end of the cutting block. "You could make friends here, but everyone is afraid you'll wrap them up in your wrath and your career suicide."

"They all look at me like I'm—"

"They all look at you like you're an angry, bitter man." Alain cut Cristoph off. "I'm sure you have your reasons for that, but you're slowly killing yourself here with this rage." Alain stared Cristoph down. The hum of the overhead bulbs stretched on, droning above their heads in the stuffy closet. "You're not the only gay guardsman, if that's what this is about. If you're... lonely." He shrugged. "Two of the guards have Italian boyfriends they want to marry. One man spent a month in Miami and came back with a broken heart. A week later, he had six new men." Alain chuckled at Cristoph's snort. "You're so convinced you're hated for reasons only you are worrying about. You're creating a self-fulfilling prophecy.

"Look," he continued. "I'm not saying it's perfect. I know it's far from that. Being gay and being here, in the Vatican, is ridiculously schizophrenic. 'God loves you for who you are and created you in his image'. And you're going to burn in hell for your sodomizing ways." Scrunching up his face, Alain picked at a torn piece of fabric caught on a snarl of wood. "It's better now than it was. But there are times I think God... whatever He is... never made it past the Vatican walls. Never got through St. Anne's Gate." He tossed a wry glance Cristoph's way, his lips curving into a grimace. "But we all have to live in this world somewhere. Here is where I've chosen."

Cristoph chewed on his lip.

"I'm here for reasons that have nothing to do with my sexuality." Alain dropped the thread rolling through his fingers. "My faith, whatever that is, doesn't hang on sex."

Alain caught how Cristoph's eyes flinched, tightening as Alain said "faith."

Eventually, Cristoph looked at Alain, really looked at him. He met his gaze, and the anger, the bitter, closed-off wariness had fallen from his eyes. "Major Bader—"

Alain shook his head. "Leave the major to me. He's only taking it out on you."

"Taking what out?"

Alain didn't respond. He pushed back and gestured to the pile of uniforms still to be shredded. "You almost done here?" A thought had wormed its way into Alain's mind while they spoke, a whisper of transgression. What was one more infringement on the rules?

"I won't be done for *months*."

"Then there will be plenty left when you get back. Let's go."

"Go?" Cristoph frowned. "I'm restricted to the barracks. I'm on punishment detail when I'm not on duty, then back to my room. Major Bader's orders."

"You leave Luca to me. Now come on. Let's go."

He busted Cristoph out of the barracks, walking with the halberdier across the courtyard and drill square to St. Anne's Gate. The cracked stone eagles keeping watch seemed withered with age and hardly up to their sentinel task. The papal coat of arms painted on the gate was fading away, lost in the chipped black paint and the bustle of Rome.

Brazenly, they walked out of the Vatican, strolling past the open-mouthed guards on duty without so much as a wave. Alain watched Cristoph shove his hands in the pockets of his jeans, look down, try to smother his grin. The hickey on his neck stood out in the sunlight, a glaring bruise marring the clean line of his neck.

He never left bruises on Cristoph in his dreams.

Alain caught the guards on duty staring at the bruise and then at Cristoph before snapping back to attention when Alain glared at them both. He gave it fifteen seconds, tops, before Luca was alerted to their escape.

"Where to?" Cristoph asked, hunching his shoulders as he squinted up the Roman street buttressing the Vatican's walls.

"This way." Alain strode down the sidewalk, Cristoph by his side, the sun beating down on his shoulders and warming the black fabric of his suit. Cristoph still had threads from the shredded uniforms and wood chips splattered on his T-shirt, and with Alain's all black suit—minus the Roman collar—they looked like an odd pair escaping from the Vatican. Another of Rome's infamous Vatican trysts, complete with a salacious hickey to prove it.

Snorting, Alain shook his head. There wasn't a chance in hell that he and Cristoph would ever see the wrong side of morning or spend a few hours horizontal together. Not a chance in hell.

A thirty-minute stroll in silence, surrounded by the hustle and bustle of Rome, led them to the *polizia's* main substation for their city sector. Amid the car fumes and the tinny honks of scooters and the burly cursing of a hundred cabbies, Alain steered Cristoph into the side entrance of the substation, waving to the bored officer on duty at the desk. They breezed past a sign declaring the area restricted to *"Authorized Police Personnel"*, and then made their way down a rickety metal staircase. Alain ignored the confused looks Cristoph shot his way, skipping down the stairs two levels until they reached the second basement.

Smoke and gunpowder hit their noses. Pops echoed down the halls. Overhead, lights installed during World War Two hummed and buzzed, vibrating against antique sockets and steel lampshades painted olive green.

"Where are we?"

Alain gestured to the steel door on the right. In Italian, stenciled letters read "*Firing Range. Authorized Personnel Only.*"

"You mentioned you wished you had a different mentor. Someone more exciting or more fun."

In the Swiss Guard, Captain Ewe was the favorite mentor of the new recruits. Bombastic, personable, and in love with the church, Ewe had a beautiful wife, twin girls, and led the Guard Outreach. He personally brought food and provisions to the homeless and indigent population of Rome, his devoted followers in the Guard all traipsing along with him. He had hiked the Italian Alps, climbed Kilimanjaro, and swum the Strait of Gibraltar. He was, to so many of the younger recruits, a hero. He took them out to Rome, to churches and prayer retreats and monasteries where they considered the intractable aspects of their faith, and their purpose and meaning in the breadth of the greater Catholic Church.

That just didn't seem Cristoph's style.

"I didn't mean—" Cristoph stammered.

"I thought you'd enjoy this more than a monastic retreat. Or some kind of penance at St. Anne's. Call it... stress relief." Alain shrugged, his hands in his pockets. He grinned. "I thought you'd enjoy taking out some of that anger with the arsenal we keep with the *polizia.*"

This time, when Cristoph met Alain's gaze, his eyes were filled with something new—a fiery burst of mischief, a curl of gratitude, and what almost looked like friendliness.

LATER, AFTER CRISTOPH HAD SAMPLED THE WEAPON RESERVES the Swiss Guard kept at the *polizia* substation, they wandered back out into the late Roman afternoon. The sun had fallen, scattering orange and tawny oaken light across the city. The Coliseum cast long shadows over the twisted mixture of ancient ruins and modern concrete. The Tiber snaked through the center, slumbering and silent in its muddy, grime-filled depths. Stone that had seen empires rise and fall seemed burnished with gold in the setting sunlight, hiding the grime, the decay, and the ruin.

They skirted scooters and packs of tourists, dodged cars trying to make their own lanes of traffic, and sidestepped a pack of wild cats, all fighting for space on the uneven, cracked sidewalks. A carpet of cigarette butts and stains from spilled gelato softened their steps.

"Thanks," Cristoph finally grunted, a few blocks away from the *polizia* station. "You're not so bad, I guess."

Alain tipped his head back, laughing. "I'll make sure that goes on my gravestone."

"Come on. You have to admit, you don't put out the best vibe yourself." Cristoph screwed up his face again, taking in Alain from head to toe and seeming to disregard everything about him in one pass.

"What?" Alain spread his hands, buried in his rumpled suit jacket pockets, wide. His jacket flared, and a thread dangled from the inner lining, all the way down to his thigh.

"You're practically locked in a closet for an office, it's full of medieval, creepy junk, and you don't even bother to wear the uniform." Cristoph snorted. "And when you did, you didn't even wear the right one."

"I'm on Special Projects. I don't need to wear the duty uniform."

"What does that even mean, anyway? You just stack papers from the gendarmerie in your office all day long?"

"I wish." Alain chuckled again. "I'm in charge of special projects the Swiss Guard has custody over."

"That's a whole lot of nothing. Great non-answer there."

"It's the only answer you're getting." Alain smiled at Cristoph as they waited at a crosswalk, letting the belch of Rome's exhaust and the heat of the asphalt mix with the sounds of a million tourists crowding the road.

"Thanks, Dad." Cristoph glowered.

"I am definitely not old enough for that! No need to be rude."

Cristoph grinned quickly, but his expression settled back into his customary frown in a moment. "Who was that priest with you the other day?" He stepped ahead of Alain, clearing a path for the two of them with his broad shoulders driving into the press and grab of Rome's populace.

"He's nobody." Alain shook his head. "Don't worry about him. You'll never see him again."

"That sounds like something. Like he is somebody, and you don't want anyone to know." Cristoph threw him another sidelong glance, his eyes narrowed. "Are you one of those guards you mentioned, with an Italian boyfriend you want to marry? Is he a priest?"

Alain shot him a scathing look. "No. I'm *not* one of those guards." He hesitated, half of him ready to end the conversation with a curt order and a reminder of Cristoph's rank.

But, was this the beginning of something, something almost like friendship? God knew, they'd said more to each other in the past hour than they had in the entire time they'd known each other. He watched Cristoph from the corner of his eye as they dodged tourists on Rome's cobbled streets and crossed the *Pont d'Angelo*, inhaling Vespa exhaust fumes.

He chewed on the inside of his lip. Was this what the commandant had wanted? For them to be closer? Though, perhaps not in the biblical way Alain dreamed of knowing Cristoph.

Cristoph, the real, actual man, intrigued Alain. That glowering stare hid a ferocious core, and there was a depth to Cristoph's eyes that told of something deeper. Part of him wanted to get to know the man.

But then there were his dreams. Nothing—nothing at all—like that could or would happen. It was an impossibility. He'd taken a vow. Albeit, it was a vow to himself, and he'd made it out of blood and the salt of his tears, but he'd vowed all the same. He'd never let his heart be broken again. He'd never let another man be put into danger and led to death's door because of him. Never again.

Cristoph had somehow woken a part of Alain he'd long thought dead. He'd laid that part of himself to rest when he'd buried the memories of his lost love. Now, his blood ran hot and his nights were filled with blond hair and electric-blue eyes and a burning, aching desire.

In the daylight, the Cristoph of his nighttime fantasies was a pale comparison to the torrid intensity of the real Cristoph who stood before him. All of the dark shadows in his eyes, the fault lines in his soul, made the man so much *more*.

His dreams were nothing on the reality of Cristoph, the flesh and blood man.

Shame, again, licked up his spine, curling around his ribs. He should leave Cristoph alone. He should walk away. He should leave now before he did any more damage.

Alain's gaze slid sideways, again. He couldn't look away. Cristoph was a magnet, a pull, a pulse that called to him.

Maybe just a little bit of friendship. A kind word here and there. A joke, some laughter. That couldn't all be bad, could it? One tiny tendril of humanity. It was what the commandant wanted, right?

He was out of practice with that sort of thing. It really had been a long time since he'd spoken to anyone other than Lotario or Angelo. It was pathetic, really. He had no idea how to continue.

"Looks like you landed yourself a boyfriend last night, by the state of things." Alain looked pointedly at Cristoph's neck. He pasted on a wide grin.

It felt fake. He felt ridiculous. And he didn't want to think about what Cristoph had been up to the night before. About who had held Cristoph in their arms and had him in their bed.

Cristoph grimaced. "No way." He exhaled, still scrunching up his face like a disgusted cat. "It actually wasn't all that great."

"Not worth it?" Alain cursed the hopeful lilt in his voice. *Don't be irredeemably stupid, Alain.*

Cristoph met Alain's curious look with a quick shake of his head. "And," Cristoph continued. "That's not what it's about. You know." He shrugged his shoulders, hunching in on himself.

"Your bad attitude?"

A quick glare shot his way. Alain quirked a grin.

"It's not about me being gay. Being gay *here*. I'm fine with myself. Everyone else can fuck off if they don't like it."

Silence. Alain watched Cristoph as a pack of tourists filed through, jostling them both on the narrow sidewalk. Fast Japanese mixed with the warm sun and Roman fumes and the smells of rubber and smog. Cristoph seemed to draw away from the crowd, standing taller and pulling himself inward, as if trying to hold himself apart from the world. The tourists bumped Alain but stayed off Cristoph.

He didn't say anything about not being lonely.

After the group passed, Alain heard Cristoph's disgruntled sigh and the crack of his neck as he rolled his shoulders. As if too many people had sent him to red alert and he was forcing himself back down from some heightened, tense place of readiness.

St. Anne's Gate loomed, and a blue-bedecked Swiss Guard waited at the entrance, checking IDs and waving cars through. When the guard saw Alain and Cristoph, his eyes went wide.

"When we get inside, go straight to your barracks. Get some rest and be on time for your shift tomorrow. Got it?"

Cristoph nodded.

"And, I want you to join the football team."

"What?" Cristoph stared at Alain like he'd lost his mind. "What the hell are you talking about?"

"I looked at your file. You listed football as one of your hobbies. It was on your army service record, too. Something about your outreach activities when you were in Africa?"

Cristoph glowered.

"We have a football team here for the Guard. They play the other teams at the Vatican. Seminarians, priests, gendarmes, firefighters. A few nuns. I want you to go and join. It would do you well." They were closer to the gate now. One of the guards was on the phone, staring at them as he spoke.

"Fine," Cristoph grumbled. "I'll check it out."

So convinced everyone was against him. Alain shook his head. What had turned this man into such a suspicious creature? What had turned him so contradictory, so at odds with himself? Pride that ran for miles, and a wariness of everyone and everything around him that ran fathoms deep.

They reached the gate just as the guard hung up the phone. He stared at Cristoph, ignoring Alain.

"Go." Alain nodded to Cristoph and jerked his head toward the barracks. "I'll see you tomorrow."

Nodding, Cristoph jogged across the courtyard and disappeared into the halberdier barracks right before Luca stormed out of the garrison offices.

"Autenburg!" Luca bellowed. "What in the hell are you doing? You have *no* right and *no* authority—"

"I am Halberdier Hasse's mentor," Alain shouted over Luca. "And in my role as his mentor, I determined he needed a mental break. You'll remember the commandant has long approved of such measures."

Luca turned purple, vibrating with barely-concealed rage as he forced his shouts back down his throat. Pinched lips collapsed around his bellows as his eyes narrowed to slits, slicing into Alain.

Twelve years ago, Best had taken Luca out of the barracks for a week in a much-needed mental break.

"I'm watching you," Luca finally hissed, seething. "Mark my words. I *will* see the end of you."

Chapter Six

"So, how's football going?" Alain sat on his usual stoop, the cold of the ancient stones seeping in through his black suit pants. Overhead, the single lightbulb droned in the Swiss Guard's medieval punishment closet.

It was the twelfth day after Cristoph's assignment to his punishment duties. The pile of uniforms to be shredded was added to every day by Luca, growing ever larger. A small mountain of red, yellow, and blue fabric tumbled out of the basket, a never-ending deluge. The message from Luca was clear: *you'll be here until these are through. And they'll never be through.*

Cristoph, as always, was hunched over the wooden block, pounding away at the uniforms with his hand axe.

Alain had been waylaid for a week by a possible vampire nest in Turin, which turned out to be nothing but rags and remnants and a few desiccated husks of long-dead humans who had been dinner for the long-gone vamps. He, Lotario, and Angelo had quietly worked with Interpol to access the European database of unidentified bodies and upload the victims as best they could. Someone, somewhere, should have closure.

From Turin, he and Lotario swung by Lotario's former

monastery for two days, checking out of the world and descending into the cloistered recesses of the catacombs, where the bones of a millennium of hunters sat in reliquaries. Ancient tomes, relics from beyond the edges of history, recovered manuscripts from the Great Library at Alexandria, and more, huddled in the darkness. They slept on the stone floors, surrounded by lines of salt and silver and the bones of their forbearers.

Lotario spent two days in meditation, stopping only to haul himself up to the topmost level of the catacombs so his cigarette smoke could blow out of the sewer grate.

Alain spent a day on his knees, staring at the ossuary of Hugh de Paynes. If any man's bones had the secrets of time etched on his marrow...

As always, the secrets of the universe stubbornly refused to reveal themselves to Alain.

They made it back to Rome, back to the Vatican, to find Cristoph still on punishment duty. He'd also been grudgingly admitted to the football team, signed off on by Commandant Best at Alain's request, despite Luca's written caution against the approval. Alain had almost gone to Cristoph's room, knocked on his door and checked in with him, had almost reached out like a normal human being. He'd nearly made it up the stairs—

But no. He'd turned back. Had retreated.

He finally worked up the nerve to seek out Cristoph in his punishment closet, out of sight from everyone else. At least he had something to talk about. God bless football.

A scowl marred Cristoph's features as Alain asked about the team, bringing out the Germanic of his Swiss-German heritage in the play of shadow and light. "S'alright," Cristoph mumbled.

Alain reached inside the plastic shopping bag he'd dropped at his feet from the *Annona*, Vatican City's supermarket. He usually made his rounds at the *Annona* at the bitterly last moment, when he was reduced to ketchup and stale bread, his milk long past its due date and his fridge and cupboards bare. He would circuit the market once, throwing odds and ends in his basket as the nuns stared and the priests doing their shopping crossed themselves before hurrying away.

Today, he'd gone inside in the sunlight, not skulking in the dark just before it closed. He heard three Hail Marys as he walked the aisles and caught several nuns hurrying out of his path.

Alain tossed Cristoph a bottle of Fanta. "Heads up."

Cristoph fumbled but caught the cold soda and managed not to slice himself with his hatchet either. He stared, first at the bottle, then at Alain. "Aren't I supposed to be suffering on bread and water alone?"

"That's the Navy. Here, you're supposed to meditate on your failings before God in fast before you accept the Eucharist in contrition. Take in the Lord as you admit your sins, and your transgressions will be forgiven."

Cristoph stared.

Alain unscrewed the top of his own soda. He grinned as he held up his soda in a salute. "Breaking down old uniforms is hard work. I know."

A flicker of interest sparked in Cristoph's eyes.

"I've been in your shoes. Exactly where you are standing, in fact." Alain sighed, shaking his head, smiling despite himself. "Inside these walls, the Vatican is a world removed from everywhere else. The air is different. Even time moves slower. But just over the gate... *Rome*." He winked.

"'There's sin in Rome'," Cristoph droned, repeating an old line given to the recruits from the Swiss Guard chaplains through the years. "'Enough to bury your soul.'"

"Chaplain Weimers really likes that line. I've heard it for thirteen years."

"What did you do?"

"If I share, am I going to be corrupting you further? I should be shepherding you to better choices. Not guiding you to more sin." Alain winked, but the words stung his soul.

Cristoph rolled his eyes. He hefted the hatchet into the wood and grabbed his soda, sliding down the block until he was sitting on the floor. "Teach me the good ways."

Alain laughed. He leaned back, propping up on his palms on the cool stone floor. "There was a good wine bar in the *Campo Dei Fiori*, a decade ago. Lunch spot and café by day..." Alain shrugged. "Thrilling place after the sun goes down. I may have enjoyed myself there a night or two." He grinned, even as the old pain sliced through him, right up his gut.

Memories assailed him. Him and his lover, sneaking out of the Holy See to blow off steam, to shake off the darkness and try to recapture a bit of normalcy. Lotario helped them, driving them to the *Campo* and dropping them off, winking at them both to have fun and admonishing them that, if they were going to sin, to sin boldly, to sin well. His lover had always loved Lotario's quirks, his sarcasm. Back then, Lotario hadn't been quite so bitter. Quite so haunted.

They'd always staggered their return to the Vatican to try to avoid being caught together. One night, his lover had returned first and was waiting at the barracks' door for Alain to sneak back over the border, creep back into their shared quarters. He could practically feel his lover's body beneath him, taste him on his lips. He'd been clumsy. He hadn't been cautious.

The guards had caught him, and he'd been marched to the major's office, Best's office, then. Thirty days of punishment detail fell around his shoulders.

His lover had sneaked in to see him every day, bringing sodas and company and his smiles, his laughs. His share of the punishment, lightening the load. They had been together in everything, had thought they'd be together for all time.

That old pain was dulled, now. *Dead*, Alain whispered in his mind. *He's dead. Everything we had. It's dead.* Every time he repeated the truth, the rip in his soul seemed to wither, the tears frayed almost to the point where the cut was no longer distinguishable. It was just a wind-worn flap of decay and ruin inside of him, roughened edges where something had once been, but was no more.

"We were specifically told *not* to go to the *Campo*." Cristoph chugged his Fanta and grinned. "*Very* specifically."

Alain shrugged, snapping back to the present as he smoothed his trousers, the wrinkles formed from his long days and nights. "I'm certain that has nothing at all to do with me."

Was this history repeating itself? Was he playing the part of the friend—the lover—in coming to ease the burden? No. Cristoph was too young. He was too angry. There was too much fight in him, and he'd break Alain, split him in two, if they ever crossed that line.

He was just too broken. He'd broken twelve years before.

Cristoph was a force Alain couldn't fight.

He couldn't fight the living.

Besides, he was Cristoph's mentor. He was just trying to show him some grace. Some compassion in a world that seemed to have desiccated and fractured under the weight of history and time.

"Tell me about our football team. I hear we're somewhat decent."

"The Vatican fire brigade has won the Vatican championships for four years in a row." Cristoph capped his soda and stood, grabbing the axe before he went back to hacking away at the uniforms. "We're the Vatican's army. We're soldiers. That's an embarrassment."

Alain smothered his smile. The Vatican championship was the ragtag competition between the various football teams in the Eternal City. Firefighters, gendarmes, Swiss Guards, seminarians, a few teams made up of the younger members of brothers from the dozens of religious orders scattered throughout the Vatican. The World Cup, it was not. Skinny priests' legs, blindingly white from never having seen the sun beneath a cassock or a suit, raced pell-mell across a pitch tucked into the Vatican Gardens beneath the topiaries and the flowers tenderly arranged into the papal coat of arms beyond the pope's private vegetable garden.

That the pope's soldiers, the Vatican's military might, weren't number one was an embarrassment. The firefighters were burly Italians, generations of Romans whose fathers had been Vatican firefighters, and whose fathers before them were as well. A few Greeks were thrown in, too, Eastern Catholics, strong as bulls, built for barreling through the opposing team.

Shame rang like a bell in the Swiss Guard barracks and the canteen whenever football was brought up.

"Tell me. Who is playing this year?"

"Zeigler and Muller are the strikers."

"Friends?"

Cristoph sent him a steely-eyed glare.

"They could be friends."

Cristoph snorted.

"Where have they put you?"

"On the bench. I'm on punishment. I'm not allowed to play."

"Do they have any idea how good you actually are?"

"How do you know how I play?"

Alain demurred. He pursed his lips, smoothing out another wrinkle from his trousers over his knee. His suit was starting to wear thin. He'd need a new one. "I can tell." His eyes flicked up. Met Cristoph's.

Corded muscles clung to Cristoph's frame, long, lean lines of legs and arms, the hint of abs when his white undershirt rode up. A body carved in the gym, yes, but honed to perfection through physical action. Running. Fighting. Football. Fucking, even. How would Cristoph look, spread out on his sheets—

Alain swallowed. "I looked up your military record in Switzerland. You formed a pickup league in your spare time on your humanitarian deployment in Africa. There were commendations in your file. Community outreach. Civil service. Building a semblance of calm in the height of the crisis."

Cristoph flinched and turned away. He hammered at the old uniforms again, shredding them to pieces with brute force instead of slicing them.

Alain stared. "The football? Or Africa?"

"I don't wanna talk about it."

Alain stared at the stones on the far wall. "Captain Ewe is the captain of the team, yes?"

Cristoph grunted again. His axe slammed into the wooden block, shredding a uniform to ribbons, red, yellow, and blue fabric tumbling to the dust around his feet. He was ruining the perfect squares he was supposed to make. Luca would be furious.

"You'll get your chance to play at the next practice. Show them who you really are." Alain cocked his head. There was something else, an extra line of tension between Cristoph's shoulder blades. "Something on your mind?"

Whack. The blade slammed into the block. Cristoph ripped a red strip of fabric from the edge of his axe. "What you said. About people like us, here. How they deal with it."

Alain swallowed.

"One of my roommates says he gets five hundred euros to strip naked in front of a bunch of priests. Some of them jack off. Others just look."

Closing his eyes, Alain hung his head between his shoulders. His hands gripped each other, knuckles going white. "I've heard of things like that happening. Some of the guards earn money on the side."

A burst of air blustered out of Cristoph. "Am I in here because I'm gay? Or because I was too public with it?"

"You're in here—" Alain jerked his chin to the closet, the axe, the pile of old uniforms. "—because you pissed off Luca. You flouted the rules to his face."

"So I should hide? Like everyone else seems to?" Cristoph screwed up his face, shaking his head.

Alain tried to smile. "This is the Vatican, Cristoph. Secrets are our bones, our blood. Our currency."

Cristoph frowned.

"Luca... is not against you for *that*," he said carefully. "This place, it does strange things to your mind. Your soul. The only advice I can give you, Cristoph, is to be happy with yourself when you're *alone*. It's what everyone has to ask themselves, square themselves with. When you're in the dark, can you stand to be yourself?" Alain's heart, his soul, screamed at him, calling him a liar in thirteen languages, modern to ancient, even runic incantations blazing in his mind. *Take your own advice.*

Maybe a priest would have phrased it differently, would have asked Cristoph to consider his soul, who he wanted to be before God. But Alain couldn't go there.

Cristoph paused. His arm, mid-swing, sagged, and the axe blade embedded in the edge of the chopping block. He exhaled, his shoulders slumping, his fingers rolling over the threads ripped free from the shredded uniforms. "Is it worth it? Staying on? Keep going?"

Alain looked down. He scraped his sole against the dust-covered ground. They were in a corner of the barracks untouched by time, save for the droning lightbulbs piped in during World War II. Other than that light, they could be anywhere, any point in the past from 1506 to now. History stretched forward and backward, waves of time riding up around Alain, cresting higher and higher on Cristoph's barely uttered words.

Is it worth it?

Nights spent wading through blood, hip deep in it, the stain impossible to erase. Nights facing down dark creatures, ghouls and wraiths and revenants, dead things that didn't stay dead. That came back from beyond, that crawled out of nightmares. Creatures of darkness that stained his soul with doubt.

Nights alone, standing on the edge of nothingness and forever, like a gargoyle perched on the very edge of a cathedral. No, clinging to the tiniest edge. But did he want to let go, or did he want to hang on?

He was so achingly lonely, deep down in the marrow of his bones.

Is it worth it?

He'd been Cristoph, once. On the cusp of being a man, on the cusp of the rest of his life, certain that an assignment in the Vatican, in the heart of Rome, was the grand adventure he'd been waiting his whole life for.

He would have been a good halberdier. He would have served with distinction, moved up the ranks. He would have made major, he knew it. All he wanted was to serve, to do the right thing.

If only *everything* had been different.

Is it worth it?

What would he have become had he turned his back on it all? If he had he left the morning after his world had ended, the morning after everything had shattered and he'd been drenched in every drop of blood that had once pumped through his lover's veins? After he'd held his dead love in his arms and watched the life fade from his eyes? He'd have gone back to Switzerland a disgrace, a failure from the Swiss Guard. Sworn to secrecy by the Holy Father himself about his true role, giving up would have meant being quietly excommunicated as well. He'd have been no more than a shade, a shadow like the ones he hunted.

Would he have even lived through the rest of the year? Without Lotario, without their duties. Would he have held on to life at all?

But what life was he living now?

Is it worth it?

The weight of a blade falling on his shoulders. An invocation in Latin. A sacrament. A blessing... and a curse. His memories intruded into the present, warm and full of grace. He'd only wanted to serve, always and only to serve. To save. To do the right thing.

He'd been able to save everyone except the one who had mattered the most.

Alain licked his lips. Dust from centuries past ground over his skin. "It *is* worth it. Don't turn your back. Don't welcome the darkness into your life, Cristoph." He cleared his throat. "You *can* have friends here. You *can* make a life. It's all kinds of topsy-turvy inside these walls, and sometimes nothing makes sense. Sometimes you tie yourself in knots, just to jump through hoops for everyone else. But there *is* good here, along with the human." *And, sometimes, the demonic.* He shoved the thought away. "The Vatican is a very human place, subject to all the falls and foibles of man. If you wanted something more heavenly..."

Cristoph shook his head.

"It's up to you. This place won't save you from whatever you're running from. But you might be able to save yourself, *if* you give yourself a chance."

Cristoph peered at him from under his eyelashes, across the shadows. Hesitation shimmered the air around him, questions thrumming the silence. What had he gotten himself into?

Alain could see, as if he'd laid out a deck of cards, how Cristoph's life had unfolded. Always being slightly at odds from the world, never quite fitting in. Trying to hide all the wrong parts of himself. Trying to make an impact, make a difference, and do something good. Trying to apologize for his existence through the brashness of his fists, the boldness of his attitude. *Fuck the world, and everyone in it*, his spread would say. Crossed with, *I'm so alone. I don't know what to do.*

What would Alain's say if he read his own cards? Would they look the same as Cristoph's? Aching loneliness? Heartbreak at the center of his soul? His would undoubtedly reveal the hermit's cross, the recluse's turn away from the world. *Let the world pass me by. Let me turn into a stone gargoyle as the years roll on and on.*

What did Commandant Best see in putting them together? What in all of the earth, all of the heavenly glories, did he possibly see?

They were two broken men, outcasts from the world, from the Vatican, even. If Cristoph was looking to him for advice, he was asking the wrong man about what choices to make for a good life.

How had Cristoph ended up in the Vatican? From the bloody streets of West Africa and his humanitarian deployment during the Ebola outbreak to the Eternal City? Who had put the thought in his head? Why the Swiss Guards? What was he searching for here? Why not London, or Paris, or New York? Why had he thought he'd find his answers *here*?

"Do you play?" Cristoph finally asked, breaking the silence. His hatchet slammed down on the block, shredding red, blue, and yellow fabric again. "Football?"

"Not for many years."

"Do you ever watch the games here?"

"I haven't. I've been busy. There's always something going on," Alain said, stretching, trying to work out the kinks in his back, his neck. He saw Cristoph, saw his expression shutter, close down, the heavy frown curl back over his forehead. "When you play," he said softly. "I'll come."

Finally, Cristoph smiled.

FIFTEEN DAYS INTO CRISTOPH'S PUNISHMENT DETAIL. ALAIN sipped his espresso and checked his morning emails—all quiet on the gendarmerie front, notices from Luca about maintaining decorum at all times; 'A Swiss Guard is a Swiss Guard whether on or off duty,' yes, thank you Luca, and two dispatches from overseas. A revenant rising in Brazil, and a plague of hungry ghosts in Egypt.

And one from Captain Ewe.

Sergeant –

Halberdier Hasse displayed exceptional skills at last night's practice. You're right – he is meant to play football! Thank you for sending him to the team! We're looking forward to trouncing those fire jockeys this year, and with Halberdier Hasse, we have a good chance.

God Bless +
CAPT Ewe

Alain smiled.

That afternoon, after checking with Lotario and Angelo on an attack in the *Campo* the night before—human, not supernatural.

The victim was sky-high on something, but that was for the *carabinieri* to figure out—Alain headed for Cristoph's shift at the punishment closet. He had two bottles of Fanta with him, and there was a spring in his step.

Cristoph was a chatterbox, almost vibrating with his excitement. He was like a weed given sunlight and fresh air, a chance to grow. Alain tossed him his Fanta and listened, smiling at all the right places.

He stared at the curve of Cristoph's grin, watched his lips forms words that Alain longed to taste.

"What about you?" Cristoph finally asked, throwing his gaze to Alain. "What have you been doing while I was schooling these priests on how to kick a ball?"

"None of the guards are priests," Alain corrected. Cristoph shrugged, too giddy and goofy to care. "And I've been... busy," he finished lamely.

"Busy? With that? What kind of special projects are you working on?"

He scrambled, trying to come up with something, anything. "Nothing much. Just liaison work with the gendarmes."

"First you were busy, now it's nothing much..." Cristoph leaned side to side, a teasing smile twisting his lips. "Sure you're not just doing nothing, conning the Guard out of keeping you around?"

Alain laughed. "That's it exactly. You've caught me. I'm utterly, utterly useless."

"Knew it." Cristoph winked.

Silence stretched long, but this time, not strained or fragile, about to shatter into a billion shards that could cut too deep. Alain drained his Fanta, leaned back against the stone walls. Listened to the rhythmic thumping of Cristoph's blows and slices, his soft grunts and the whispered songs he sang to himself.

"I'm glad you showed the team what you're made of," Alain said, breaking the silence. He rolled his head against the stone, smiling.

Cristoph's neck flushed, but he said nothing.

"You know…" A thought wormed its way into Alain's mind. A stupid, dangerous, idiotic thought. He shouldn't say it. He shouldn't continue. "You know, you've been on shift or on punishment details for a few weeks now. Not really had much time to work out."

Cristoph's gaze slid sidelong, fixing on Alain.

"Want to work out a bit before the football season starts? Preseason matches are just a week away."

"With you?" Cristoph's tone was careful, measured. Skeptical.

Alain scoffed. "You think I'm some old man that can't take it?" He had revenant burns across his back, werewolf slashes across his hip, poisoned cuts scarred down his thigh, and the roughened shredded scars of a wraith's wither down his side. He survived because he was fast, and because he was strong. And because Lotario had his back. "I'll show you a work out, Halberdier!"

Cristoph grinned. "Deal."

IT WAS A BAD IDEA. IT WAS A STUPID, TERRIBLE, NO GOOD, BAD idea. He never should have offered to train with Cristoph, should never have offered to go to the gym with him.

But here they were, in the Guards' gym.

A dozen pairs of eyeballs had skittered their way as they entered together. Men stopped, mid-curl, mid-chest press, gawking.

How many years had it been since Alain had been in the Guards' gym? His strength was more of the survival variety. He and Lotario hit up the meathead gym down in Trastevere. It was a hole in the wall gym of punching bags and free weights and the stench of sweat, where metal music pounded from the rafters and shook the peeling mirrors on the walls, and no one cared at all who they were.

The Swiss Guards' gym was sparkling bright, outfitted with the latest in gym equipment sent down from Switzerland by Catholic donors to the Guard. Massive machines lined the walls, and free weights squatted next to weigh benches and mats spread on the floor. In the rear of the gym, a space had been cleared and laid with mats for sparring practice.

Cristoph waved to two of the guards working out on the squat machines. One waved back, slowly, his eyes glued to Alain.

Yes, the gargoyle has come out into the daylight, Alain wanted to snap. *He's entered the world of man.* Cheeks burning, he padded after Cristoph to the free weights.

The spotted each other on their favorite routines. Chest presses and shoulder work from Cristoph, core strength and calisthenics from Alain. Alain stared down into Cristoph's flushed, sweat-soaked face as he counted out his chest press reps, fingers brushing over Cristoph's wrists, the heat of his skin.

Everyone stared. Everyone.

Alain ignored them, as always. But how did Cristoph?

Was he used to being stared at, too? Used to ignoring everyone?

HE SPRANG CRISTOPH FROM PUNISHMENT DUTY EARLY THE NEXT day as the uniform pile was dwindling down to the dregs. Instead of the gym, Alain steered them toward the gardens. He couldn't take the wash of public humiliation two days in a row.

Luca would probably be there, anyway. He had probably heard all about him and Cristoph in the gym the day before. He'd no doubt pounce the first moment he could. Tear into Cristoph for being away from his punishment duties, rip Alain a new one for flaunting Luca's authority.

He couldn't take that from Luca. Couldn't take his spite and fury and so much hatred distilled into every dark glare. As if the sight of Alain was offensive to Luca's soul.

It probably was.

They ran up and down the Vatican garden steps, racing each

other from the tree-lined walls to the top of the flower beds, the elegant topiaries and the papal crest grown from roses. Alain nearly sprained a lung racing Cristoph from the heliport—in the indefatigable spirit of holiness that drenched the Holy See—to the Vatican radio tower. He won, though, and the look of shock on Cristoph's face was worth the heaving, the pounding in his chest. The way his heart seemed to seize as Cristoph threw his head back and laughed, sun dazzling over his face, tiny rainbows glinting off each bead of sweat.

RUNNING, THE NEXT DAY, WAS OUT.

Alain could barely move. He let Lotario take the lead on a ghoul chase at midnight, winding their way through the twisting streets of Trastevere in Rome, the medieval village opposite the Vatican, just off the Janiculum. He stayed in Lotario's Bug, inching his way up and down alleys, pointing his flashlight out the broken driver's window as Lotario poked into manhole covers, clambered into refuse bins, and crawled into dark alleys.

"You owe me," Lotario had growled, puffing on a cigarette. "A *lot* of booze."

"Anything you say." Alain's legs screamed as he shifted gears, pointing the Bug back to the Vatican. "No ghoul?"

"Not tonight. Unless you count my stench."

Alain had leaned his head out the Bug's window as they crossed the Tiber and headed back for the Vatican.

He was still sore in the morning, and paracetamol did nothing to blunt the way his legs were shredding from the inside, every muscle on fire, every nerve split in two.

But Cristoph was working on his last two uniforms, and Luca hadn't brought another pile to be shredded. Possibly, Cristoph had shredded every last uniform destined for the trash. What would Luca do, if Cristoph freed himself from his purgatory?

"I've got football practice later. The team is meeting at

midnight when we're all off shifts." Cristoph triumphantly shredded the last stretch of yellow fabric into two lopsided squares and tossed them into the basket. He grinned at Alain, his blue eyes shining, brilliantly, spectacularly illuminated like a diamond washed in the ocean. "I think this means I'm free. What do we do now?"

Alain shifted. He couldn't hold back his own beaming smile. "Congratulations. You just sent a record time."

"Major Bader wanted to bury me alive in here. I know it."

"How did you get through them so fast?"

"When I couldn't sleep, I'd come down and chop some more." Cristoph shrugged. "I just wanted it done with. Wanted to be anywhere but in here, locked in this damn closet."

A pang sounded in some distant part of Alain's heart. This closet, these moments, were the times he'd stolen away to spend with Cristoph. They were moments he'd started to build his days around, moments that had leached into the rest of his life like seeping blood, like an infection that couldn't be contained. His smile turned brittle.

"You've won your freedom." Alain mimicked the sign of the cross in the air. "You are released from purgatory, my son." He winced. "Now what?"

Cristoph blinked. His electric gaze bored into Alain's. "My shift isn't until eighteen hundred. I thought we could hit the gym again?"

His first taste of freedom, and he wanted to spend it with Alain. If it weren't for the ways his legs wanted to break off at his hips and run away, flee back to his bed and never leave his sheets, Alain might have gone weak at the knees. His heart might have thumped, an extra pitter patter.

But her forced it all away. Pushed it all down.

Cristoph was his mentee. Nothing more.

No one could ever be anything more.

No matter how wonderful.

Cristoph was still staring at him, confusion starting to darken his sky-blue eyes. "But are you busy?" he grunted. "More... special projects?" He sounded dubious at best about Alain's supposed job in the Swiss Guard, in the Vatican.

Most days, Alain was just as dubious.

Alain's throat clenched. "No, I'm free this afternoon." He smiled to cover the grimace as he stood. "Meet you in the gym in ten?"

THERE WASN'T AN OFF TIME IN THE SWISS GUARDS' GYM. WITH the three rotating shifts covering all hours of the day and night, there were always groups of men coming on and off duty, starting or ending their day with a workout. Alain prayed for a football game, a midday group outing to the pubs, or a party on the halberdiers' barracks roof with fondue and an inflatable pool. Anything to empty the gym.

No such luck.

Cristoph warmed up on the treadmill while Alain stretched and stretched, trying to breathe through the hellfire that coursed through his battered leg muscles. Ten years Cristoph's senior, and he'd had a footrace with the man. What was he thinking? He deserved this punishment, certainly.

"Right." Cristoph ambled over to him, long limbs loose, shoulders shaking out, hands loosely clenched. He grinned down at Alain, spread out on the wrestling mats. His blond hair, just a shade past regulation length, curled over his forehead, ends dipping past his eyebrows and dusting over his eyes. He smiled as the fluorescent lights droned behind his head, haloing Cristoph in dull neon and burned-plastic yellow.

He looked like the first morning's sunlight shining through St. Peter's. Like hope, and like Alain's first day in the Swiss Guard, full of dreams and wonder, gazing at the glory of the world.

Alain couldn't breathe.

"Wanna practice combatives?" Cristoph held out his hand.

Chapter Seven

"ARE YOU FINALLY OFF PUNISHMENT?" HALBERDIER ANDREAS Zeigler slid in across from Cristoph in the barracks canteen, his metal tray clattering across the knotted wood planks of the dining table. Sausage and baked apples seeped into Zeigler's potatoes and sauerkraut. The tastes of home, of Switzerland, made fresh in the barracks by a team of nuns who were, possibly, older than the Vatican itself.

Cristoph speared a baked apple slice and popped it into his mouth, nodding. "Finished shredding the last uniform days ago."

"Thanks, man." Halberdier Konrad Muller plopped down next to Cristoph, his rolls tumbling from their perch on top of his mountain of food on his tray. "Now the rest of us can all go out and stir up trouble and there will be nothing for us to do." He winked at Zeigler before shoveling potatoes into his mouth.

Cristoph snorted. "I'm sure Major Bader will find something. And for you?" He elbowed Muller, digging into his ribs. "Probably have to lick the toilets clean."

"Nah, I think that's next on your list." Zeigler grinned around his sauerkraut. He hesitated, looking Cristoph up and down. "You're really good? I mean, you can actually play tonight?"

The football preseason always opened with a game between the Swiss Guard and the Vatican fire brigade, and the fire brigade continued to obliterate the Guard, in preseason and the rest of the games. The preseason opener had set the tone for the past three years—decisive trouncing.

But, when Cristoph was finally allowed to play during practice —thank you, Alain—Captain Ewe and the other players seemed to rejoice: he was the striker they had been looking for. He wasn't the best footballer, but he'd played for years. Three years of secondary school, and then he was the striker on the pickup league he'd put together on his humanitarian deployment in West Africa. Playing against the West African locals had been the best form of training. He'd had his ass handed to him over and over again until he could hold his own.

Now, in the Vatican, he was practically considered a gift from God. Or at least from the football gods.

He'd gone from shunned outcast to welcomed footballer almost overnight. Zeigler and Muller, the duo of strikers, welcomed him into their fold, descending on him with arms around his shoulders as they dragged him off for beers and pretzels.

If he squinted, it could be friendship. Almost.

Cristoph nodded. "Yeah, I'll be there. I got my shifts moved around so I'm free during the game."

"Surprised the major let you do that," Muller spoke around a mouthful of sausage.

"He may hate me, but even *he* wants to crush those fire jockeys."

Laughter broke out across the table, strained just slightly along the edges. Cristoph sipped his water, his gaze darting between the two men as he leaned back in his chair.

His chest clenched, a heaviness hovering between his lungs. Deep inside, frantic clawing tried to scratch its way out of his belly, but he did his best to ignore it.

Things had turned out all right. Things were working themselves out. He was finding his feet. There was no need to run.

Still, that mad, hectic itch just beneath his skin worried at his soul.

Could he really stay? Would he finally find a place to belong? Or would he need to pack up and leave—again?

Yes, it was shit at the start. It had sucked. But try just one more day. Just one more. *You're not alone this time.*

He would probably be bitterly angry and furiously unemployed back in Switzerland if it weren't for the second chance he'd been given.

If it weren't for Alain.

Speak of the Devil. Cristoph's gaze caught on Alain slipping in through the rear entrance to the canteen, filling up his cup of espresso for what looked like the fourteenth time that morning. Dark circles hung beneath his eyes, standing out against his pale skin. His hair, normally sticking up wild and haphazard as if he didn't own a comb to smooth it down, was pressed flat in places, pushed down. Grime traced a thin line down his temple.

Cristoph pushed his chair back. It had been days since he'd last seen Alain, since their spar in the gym. Alain's office had been empty, dark and locked up for the past three days. He'd almost passed by the old punishment closet to see if somehow Alain was there.

Finally seeing him again, but looking like he'd been dragged through the streets, sent a thick clench of worry straight through his guts.

"What's the deal with that freak?" Zeigler spoke low softly, behind his cup. He downed a quick swallow of espresso, his wide eyes watching Cristoph.

Cristoph froze halfway out of his chair. "What?"

Muller jerked his head toward Alain. "The sergeant." He shifted, turning quickly when Alain glanced their way. "You know he's not right? In the head, I mean. And, you know." Muller thumped his chest. "In the soul." His gaze darted over his shoulder once, as if he couldn't look away. He hunched over the table, one finger tapping at the wood as he spoke. "He's been here for, what, over twelve years? And no one knows what he really does. But it's *weird*. And it's not right. Someone is protecting him."

"Yeah." Zeigler jerked on Cristoph's sleeve, pulling him back down to his seat. "I saw Chaplain Weimers throw him out of the chapel six years ago. He's never been back."

Cristoph's gaze found Alain across the crowded canteen.

"He never comes out of that crazy office of his. Have you seen it?"

"I've been there." Cristoph's voice was hard.

"That whacked out stuff he has? It's practically Devil worship."

Muller leaned forward, as if sharing secrets. "He keeps away from everyone. Hides in that office. Dresses like he's pretending to be a priest. Looks like hell." Muller shook his head. "He and Major Bader fight at *least* once a month. And I don't mean little fights. Shake the windows kind of shouting. I swear, they're going to kill each other one day. I can't believe they haven't already. If he wasn't being protected, Major Bader would have thrown him out a *long* time ago."

"What's their hist—"

Zeigler cut him off. "So look, he's some kind of freak and he stays in his little dark hole, but then, all of a sudden, he's out and about? Spending time with you during your punishment detail?" Zeigler's eyebrows rose. "Working out with you in the gym? I've never seen him in the gym. Ever."

"What's going on with him?" Muller squinted at Cristoph. "And you?"

A humorless laugh fell from Cristoph's lips. "Is *that* what this is about? You want to know his secrets so you try and chat me up?" He shoved back from the table.

"No, Cristoph," Zeigler hissed. "We're trying to *protect* you." He swallowed, eyes darting right and left. "Look, he's dangerous. We all know it and we all stay the hell away from him. But he's got his claws in you or something. He's into you for some reason."

Cristoph's gaze again shot to Alain. He picked him out, his rumpled black suit and disheveled hair, through the mess of precision uniforms and buzzed, military haircuts. Oblivious to the conversation at Cristoph's table, Alain waved, wanly smiling through his clear exhaustion. Cristoph groaned when Alain started toward them, picking his way across the canteen.

The guards gave him a wide berth, skirting Alain as if he carried a pit of darkness and shadow in his hands.

"Shit." Muller hunched forward, as if he could hide within the knots of the wooden table. He kept his eyes down, glaring at Zeigler. "He's headed our way."

"To see you." Zeigler fixed Cristoph with a hard stare.

That desperate clawing in his chest was back, scrabbling up his throat. Cristoph ran his tongue over his teeth, fighting back the urge to snarl. At Muller and Zeigler or at Alain, he couldn't tell.

It had all seemed too good to be true, this shift in his fortunes. That usually meant it was.

Almost three weeks of Alain's daily companionship, his unasked-for company during the long hours of his punishment details, and the idle conversations they'd started and fumbled through about nothing at all. Hours and hours together, and not *once* had they ever veered toward anything remotely close to the darkness Muller and Zeigler seemed to fear.

"Hello, halberdiers." Alain managed a weak smile. "Hello Cristoph," he said, a warmer grin for him alone.

Cristoph tried to smile back. He failed.

The corners of Alain's eyes pinched. The warmth in his gaze faded away.

Muller coughed loudly in the leaden silence. Cristoph shot him a hard glare as flames crawled up his spine, the burn of shame curling around his neck. His cheeks blazed. *Fuck you, Muller.*

"Have a good day, halberdiers." He nodded to Muller and Zeigler. "Good luck at the game tonight. This is the year." Alain spared one last glance to Cristoph. "You'll do great."

Zeigler and Muller exhaled long and loud as Alain moved off.

Zeigler rubbed one hand over his face, muttering a Hail Mary beneath his breath. Cristoph glared at them both before shoving away from the table.

He took off after Alain. "Hey, Sergeant. Hold up!"

Freezing, Alain turned. Around them, guardsmen inched away, trying not to get caught watching the two in the middle of the suddenly silent canteen. Conversations stilled, and the hot heaviness of everyone staring at the two of them burned into Cristoph's shoulders.

Alain didn't move a muscle.

Cristoph jerked his chin toward Alain's temple, to the exhaustion flowing from his body. "Long night filing?" He tried to grin as he shoved his hands in his pockets.

"Something like that." Alain smiled, but there wasn't any warmth there anymore. Nothing of the Alain who had spent hours with him, laughing over stories and nothing at all. Who'd thrown sodas at his head and raced with him in the gardens. Alain turned away.

"You are coming to the game tonight, right?" Cristoph groaned inside, kicking himself. He bit down on his tongue. If he could reverse time and never speak again, that would be great. Or just snatch the words out of the ears of everyone who had heard, erase the looks of shock and horror spreading around the canteen.

The entire canteen had gone still as a grave, no longer pretending to not be watching them. Watching Alain. Cristoph felt their eyes shift, move from him to Alain. The pressure in the room changed. Grew darker.

"Of course! I'll be there." With a flourish of his espresso cup to the silent canteen, and an obviously fake, fuck you smile, Alain slipped out.

Cristoph watched the doors bang shut behind him as the guards shifted their attention back to him. A moment, and then the chatter started up again as everyone went back to eating.

He stood in the center of the room, a lost man in the midst of a crowd, staring at the hinges creaking in Alain's wake.

"Cristoph..." Muller appeared at his elbow, both their trays of abandoned food in his hands. "Come on."

"Fuck you." He grabbed his tray and dumped the remnants into the bin, stacked his dishes on the kitchen cart. He shoved his way out of the canteen through the same swinging wooden doors Alain had disappeared through.

He turned toward the garrison offices.

Fuck the rest of the guardsmen. Fuck their suspicions. He hadn't seen anything like what they whispered about. Alain had been nothing but friendly to him.

And Alain hadn't looked that exhausted since their swearing in day. He never wore the uniform, preferring that damn black suit that made him look like a priest, but even then, he never looked exhausted or filthy.

Except for today.

***

"MY BOY!" BISHOP BATTISTINI CRIED, LEANING OUT THE window of his tiny Fiat. The old bishop's wrinkled face creased into a wide smile. He turned his car slowly, his frail hands clenching the top of his steering wheel, bald head barely poking over the top of the dashboard, and passed the Swiss Guards' courtyard, making his way through the checkpoint at St. Anne's Gate toward the parking lot behind the Apostolic Palace and the Vatican Bank.

Cristoph clenched his jaw but waved and smiled back. Bishop Battistini worked in the doctrinal section of the Congregation for the Doctrine of the Faith, one of the arms of the Vatican government in the Holy See. The tottering old man had always been friendly to him, smiling and chatting every time he passed his guard post.

Battistini parked by the cluster of cars beneath the Vatican Bank down the cobbled hill from the Swiss Guard garrison. He beamed at Cristoph as he slowly pulled himself out of his little car, his long black cassock and amaranth zucchetto billowing in the Roman wind.

"My young boy," Battistini said, clapping his gnarled hands on either side of Cristoph's face before pulling him down for a press of his dry lips to Cristoph's forehead. "Where are you running to with such a fierce look on your face?"

"Just checking on someone, Bishop." Cristoph held out his arm for Battistini. "Can I escort you to your office?"

Battistini patted Cristoph on his cheek. "Such a good boy." They walked slowly together. Cristoph held Battistini's briefcase in his free hand. The bishop's gnarled fingers curled around his other elbow.

Battistini launched into a story about the Masses he'd held at one of Rome's homeless shelters and the food they had served to the hungry. Battistini had told him before it was his mission to bring each and every one of Rome's homeless, heartbroken, and hurting into the shelters and to care for them with food and with a warm heart, especially as summer broke over Rome. Cristoph had agreed to join Battistini on his outreach a few weeks before. He should work on his soul. He should help more people.

"Would you come this evening?" Battistini asked. "I can show you the shelter outside Trastevere and then take you down to see the cafés by the waterfront. A cup of espresso on a cool night after warming the heart." Battistini smiled.

"I can't." Cristoph cringed. Was he an ass for denying the old bishop? Probably. No, definitely. Football did not trump the bishop's cause. He hesitated, biting his lip. "I'm playing on the Guard football team and... it's the first game of the season. We're playing the Vatican fire brigade."

"Oh, that's right!" Battistini patted his arm. "You are playing tonight, yes?" They climbed the marble steps to the Apostolic Palace, skirting around the rotund tower of the Vatican Bank. A hundred different kinds of mysteries were hidden within the black bricks of the tower, the former prison and torture chamber of popes long past.

Cristoph nodded as he pulled open one of the side doors for Battistini and passed him his worn briefcase. He'd been evasive with the bishop, not revealing exactly why he was only possibly going to play on a team woefully short of players, or why he was riding the bench during practices and possibly wouldn't ever play for the Guards.

Battistini had winked at him once, said he understood young men and the heat in their blood, and never asked again.

"I think, then, that I will come and see the game." Battistini smiled as he leaned against the doorway, supporting his frail body. "I can say Mass and serve the Lord's Supper in time to return to watch you."

Speechless, Cristoph's jaw dropped. "Bishop," he stuttered. "It's just a football game—"

"It is meaningful to you. You have been wanting to share your talents. I could tell." A deep inhale, and Battistini squinted into the dark, gilded hallway of the Apostolic Palace. "I have meetings here. I won't see you until later this evening. But, my boy, I promise you, I will be there to watch you tonight." He reached out again, cupping Cristoph's cheek.

Cristoph watched him shuffle down the hallway. He fought back a clench in his throat as an aching warmth spread out from his chest. *You can make a home here. A life.*

Alain.

The bells in St. Peter's Square tolled, tremulous booms quaking the air. He cursed, jogging back down the hill toward the garrison and the barracks. Only a half hour until he had to get to the Arch of the Bells for his post. Just enough time to duck into Alain's office. He slipped in the back entrance to the garrison, bypassed the server room, a complete fire hazard—it was the privy, centuries ago—and turned down the dark hallway that led to Alain's office.

Voices bled out into the corridor. Cristoph frowned. Alain wasn't alone.

Rounding the doorway, Cristoph stopped short. Alain sat at his desk, laughing and shaking his head as he looked up at the same nameless priest from before, the skinny, hawk-like older man Cristoph had seen over a month before. The priest perched on the edge of Alain's desk, one leg hitched on the side of Alain's chair. He had an open file folder in his hand and reading glasses had slid down his nose. The priest was gazing down at Alain, smirking, eyes glowing, but a teasing expression softening the harsh lines of his face. He nudged Alain with his knee, a gentle tap against his ribs.

Hot jealousy slid into Cristoph, a spike through the back. He grunted, almost physically knocked by the sudden stab. He cleared his throat.

Alain's eyes shot up, blown wide. "Cristoph!" He shoved the priest's foot off his chair and stood. "What are you doing here?"

Cristoph's eyes darted between the priest and Alain again. The whole atmosphere changed suddenly, as if he had interrupted something. Something that was supposed to be hidden. He caught the dirt and grime lingering on their faces and the rumples in their black suits. "I... just wanted to..." He trailed off, all of his excuses bouncing around his skull sounding completely lame.

He turned to the priest and shoved out his hand. "Hi. I'm Cristoph." He puffed out his chest. He could solve one mystery, at least.

The priest stared back, his beady eyes sweeping over him from head to toe. He didn't reach for Cristoph's hand. He didn't introduce himself.

"Halberdier." Alain stared. "Don't you have a shift to attend?"

"In half an hour," Cristoph snapped. He dropped his hand. "I came to check on you. You didn't seem right in the canteen. You're filthy. You're exhausted. I haven't seen you in days." He glared. "What's going on?"

The priest's eyebrows skyrocketed, nearly rising off his head as Alain exhaled and looked away, looked down, looked over to his messy shelves. Anywhere but at Cristoph, it seemed. "I'm fine. It's nothing that concerns you," Alain said.

Cristoph snorted. So it was okay for Alain to fret over Cristoph, to butt into his life and to badger him, but that concern wasn't welcomed both ways? His eyes narrowed. "Forget it. I don't care." He spread his hands, shrugged, and headed for the door.

He shot a glare to that damn smug priest before he left, though. The priest just smirked.

Footsteps chased him down the hall. "Cristoph, wait."

Pausing, Cristoph didn't turn around. Alain slipped ahead of him in the cramped hallway.

"I appreciate your concern," Alain said slowly. He crossed his arms and spread his legs. His fingers tapped against his sleeve over and over, as if he'd had too much caffeine. "It has been a long, long time since anyone cared what I've done. Or how I've looked in the morning."

"I don't care. It's not my concern." He threw Alain's words back in his face. "You just said so."

"Cristoph, there are parts of my duties I cannot share with you. I am sorry, but that is how it is."

"Whatever you're doing was part of your duties?" His mind swam with images, with the priest and Alain locked in a sweaty embrace or partying all night long or making out on top of Alain's desk. Or the priest sitting in Alain's lap, as he almost nearly was. No. Cristoph pushed those thoughts away. He didn't care. He didn't care at all.

"We were up all night," Alain said quietly, "working on an investigation. And that is all I can say." He frowned. "Did you think—"

"Doesn't matter what I thought." Cristoph started walking again.

"I *will* be there tonight," Alain called. "I promise."

LOTARIO WAITED FOR ALAIN IN HIS OFFICE, SITTING CROSS-legged on top of Alain's desk, on top of his files and his scattered papers, surrounded his haphazard clutter.

His look called Alain a thousand kinds of idiot.

"I know," Alain snapped. "Laugh at me. Go ahead. I'll even help." He chuckled, obnoxiously fake and boisterous, grabbing his stomach. "Look at Sergeant Autenburg! He's such a fool!" He sobered instantly, his mask of laughter falling flat.

"That little spitfire actually managed to make something of himself?"

Alain slouched against the doorframe and crossed his arms. He wouldn't meet Lotario's gaze. "He just needed someone to get through to him. Show him everyone here wasn't out to get him."

"And that person was you."

"I didn't want it to be me." Alain's heart clenched against his lie. "I pushed him toward the footballers. He's made friends there. He's found other guards."

"You didn't want it to be you? Alain, you've spent every day with the guy for the past month," Lotario scoffed. "You sought him out! You spent time with him! You don't choose to spend time with anyone. Not even me."

"*Especially* not you. I see enough of you."

"Is it any surprise he came to check in, especially with how you look? The night we just had?" Lotario leaned forward, dropping his legs over the side of the rickety desk. He stared at Alain, eyes narrowed. "When was the last time anyone ever checked up on you?"

"Don't remind me."

"I mean, not even your beloved commandant checks on you after a hunt, not even the bad ones, and you know he knows what kind of shit you're—"

"What do you want from me?" Alain snapped. He scrubbed one hand down his face. "Do you want me to admit I'm wrong? That I've fucked up? Want me to play the fool all over again? Repeat everything?" His voice rose, bouncing off the stone walls, until his shouts echoed down the hallway.

Bitter rage flooded Alain, a howling misery that lapped at his bones. He had no one to blame but himself.

For a month, Cristoph had been isolated with his endless

monotony of uniform shredding. His mentee, already sent to the punishment closet, just months after swearing in. He was a failure of a mentor, assuredly.

He'd just tried to help him, somehow. Just tried to be friendly.

But history had pushed and pushed, memories clamoring for attention, an ocean that couldn't be held back. Waves of the past tried to chase after him as he ran, tried to keep his toes out of those black and bloody waters.

When Alain had tentatively reached out to Cristoph, trying something, anything to help save him from a stinging dismissal, he'd scraped up against that yearn he'd thought he'd exorcised, had thought he'd buried away for all eternity. Just the slightest bit of connection, the tiniest bit of warm camaraderie. Just a hint, a touch of humanity. Of warmth. And a dam inside his soul had crumbled and fallen. Had broken to pieces, and the remains lay in the tatters of his self-control.

Keeping Cristoph company during the long hours he chopped old uniforms. Sharing stories and laughing together, shared glances and eyes meeting under the droning light. He'd seen Cristoph chuckle and laugh, and his chest had swelled with pride. He had done that. Him, just him. Alain Autenburg... the scourge of the Vatican.

He shouldn't have done it. Shouldn't have done *any* of it. Shouldn't have befriended Cristoph, shouldn't have made him laugh. Shouldn't have gotten addicted to the sound of his happiness, or the curve of his lips when he grinned.

He definitely shouldn't have offered that carefully worded invite, the pathetic suggestion that they work out together in the Guard's gym. And Cristoph shouldn't have taken him up on it, but he had, and then they were there, spotting each other on the free weights and facing off during a push-up contest.

And, then sparring? Combatives? Hands on each other's bodies, wrestling sweat-slick skin against skin, bodies pressing, aligning—

Until Alain had thrown him clear across the mats, too wound

up and frantic to do anything but fling Cristoph away or hold him down and bury his face in the sweet sweat of his thighs.

What on earth was he doing? He didn't even know the answer himself.

He was working his way nicely through the seven deadlies. Envy? Check. Hot jealousy when his eyes had lingered on Cristoph's fading hickey. Envy of the options Cristoph had, the life he could lead, unchecked and unbowed. Greed? Oh, yes. Greed at the root, the very heart, of everything.

He *wanted*. He wanted, and the power, the hunger behind that want surprised him, made his breath catch. Twelve years of isolation. Twelve years of holding to his vow. Twelve years of never wanting, ever, something he could never have.

And then, Cristoph.

Lust. Lust that burned him alive nightly. The dreams had changed, shifting from sweaty, slick slides of his body against Dream Cristoph to a softer, gentler thing. Replays of their time together, surrounded by shredded uniforms. Cristoph's smile tossed his way. The sound of his laughter. How he looked in the sunlight. Lust, still, but a different kind of yearning.

Pride. Thinking, somehow, someway, he could have this. Could have some kind of fucked-up friendship, something where he could smile at Cristoph and receive smiles back, but shield Cristoph forever from the darkness and the truth.

Of course everything would come crashing down.

And finally, wrath. Wrath directed right back at himself. He knew better. He'd vowed never, after all.

"I fucked up, Lotario. He got too close because I wanted him close. And now I have to push him away." Rage spiked, bloodred and hot. Alain kicked one of his metal folding chairs. It skittered across the cracked linoleum flooring. "Cristoph doesn't deserve to be messed up with my shit. God, he doesn't." Alain sighed, rubbing his eyes.

Lotario stared.

Tired, ancient air pressed in on Alain from every side. He felt the weight of the mummies' eyeballs staring at him from his bookshelves, the crackle of the ward runes humming over the doorway. Alain paced, his hands on his hips.

"He's the only person who's even remotely cared in years. Who hasn't looked at me like I'm..." He trailed off, trying to gesture to all of the ritual detritus surrounding them. "I wanted that once. Someone... someone like him."

Alain slumped against the wall. His head hit stone. "I screwed up. And now I'll have to push him away." He closed his eyes and knocked back his head, once, twice. "I just don't want to."

Silence. Lotario slid off the desk, his shoes hitting the worn throw rug with a soft sigh. "Maybe you don't have to."

Alain groaned. "Not you too."

"It's been twelve years. When are you going to accept that you can't do this forever?"

"What about you?" Alain glared at Lotario. "How long has it been for you?"

"Longer than your time. But I don't get to choose my successor. One day the Vatican will replace me, and that's if I live long enough to see retirement. After all this, I'll be whisked off to my former monastery and I'll never see humanity again." Lotario looked away. Alain studied the lines of his face, the exhaustion hidden in his deep furrows, the lean planes of his cheeks hiding years of secrets and silence. "You have more of a future than I do, but you work so hard to ignore it."

"What happened the last time I tried to have a life, Lotario?" His words turned cutting, barbed and filled with bitterness. "What happened the last time I wanted something for myself?"

"That wasn't all you." Lotario squinted, staring into the middle distance. His Adam's apple rose and fell, a slow, heavy swallow. "We did what we had to do."

"I made a vow that night." Alain stalked forward, pressing into Lotario's space. He stared Lotario down, all the long years of buried anger and loss pushing past the ironclad grip he had on his soul. "And I will *not* break it. Not if there's any chance of someone getting hurt. Of losing everything. Not again."

Closing his eyes, Lotario turned his face away. A muscle in his cheek twitched.

"Can we get back to business?" Alain asked. "We have a ghoul to catch." He sidestepped Lotario, circled his desk, and grabbed an open file folder spread over his keyboard.

Just before midnight the night before, Angelo had called them out with reports coming in of a ghoul attacking tourists at the infamous *Campo Dei Fiori*. The *Campo*, a square in Rome's tourist section of the capital, had for millennia been a meeting place for those with mischief, mayhem, or murder on their minds. By day, the *Campo* was an open-air market, a tourist trap, and a bustling hub of humanity. As night fell, the tourists and locals flocked for drugs, crime, and sex, and the ring of clubs surrounding the *Campo* and up and down the side streets pushed those hungers hard.

Like clockwork, shadowy forces appeared, feasting on humans flirting with their own dark natures.

Normally, it was hungry ghosts and wraiths and, every once in a while, a rogue vampire feeding on stragglers and drunks and horny bargoers stumbling into back alleys. Ghouls didn't travel near humans, not unless they were trailing a vampire and scavenging off the fresh kill and the desiccated corpse. They stayed by graveyards and deep underground, hiding in the sewers and the tunnels and catacombs beneath Rome. A ghoul inside of Rome's heart, in one of the most populated places of the capital, had to have been drawn there.

Lotario stayed quiet as Alain read over the notes they'd taken the night before. "Angelo responded, on callout from the *polizia*, to a distraught woman behind Club Mood, not far from the *Campo*. She was shrieking, saying she'd seen a monster eating a man. The *polizia* wrote her off as being high or intoxicated and they transported her to hospital. Angelo called us."

"No sign of a body, but we did find a nasty pool of blood behind a refuse bin off one of the alleys behind the *Campo*,"

Lotario said. "Fresh blood, too. Still warm. But not enough for it to have been a ghoul's full meal."

"And, ghoul tracks leading from the nearest sewer manhole to the alley. But we lost the trail underground." Alain wiped at his temple, at the grime still stubbornly fixed to his skin.

"Why would a ghoul be this far inside Rome?" Lotario rolled his neck, cracking joints with a sigh. "What would bring it out of the tunnels?"

"Where there are ghouls, there are vampires. Are we sure the blood pool didn't come from a vampire's kill?"

Lotario shook his head. "Vampires wouldn't take the body. A ghoul would devour the corpse and leave behind a pile of mess and filth. That's why so many ghoul kills are unsolved missing persons cases." He jerked his chin to the file in Alain's hand. "*Almost* like what we have here."

"Ghouls will follow behind a vampire and eat their kill." Alain busied himself with straightening the papers on his desk, setting them at perfect right angles. He wouldn't meet Lotario's gaze. "Could we be dealing with vampires?"

"After all this time?" Lotario looked away. "I didn't sense any vampiric energy in the blood. I could have missed it. But vamp energy is very specific." He frowned, staring at the extracted vampire fang on Alain's shelf. "You know what I mean."

"Like grave dirt is choking the back of your throat and your blood has turned to dust, and all you can see is fog." It was like snakes slipping over skin, flypaper thin and drier than a desert. And ancient, as if all of time were pressing down, choking the breath out of a person. He closed his eyes. "It's not something I think you'd miss."

"Do we head out there tonight? Stake the *Campo* out?"

He smiled, sadly. "I have a football game to go to tonight. But yes, after."

Lotario grinned. But, he so rarely looked happy, and his attempt at an honest smile fell short. He needed more practice.

Alain knew what Lotario wanted him to say. "I'm only going to go this one game. His first. And then—"

Sadness hung on Lotario's words. "You really don't have to do this."

"I can't risk losing everything again. This ends tonight."

Chapter Eight

At least once a week, every member of the Swiss Guard was required to attend Mass at St. Anne's chapel, the chapel built into the Vatican walls directly across from the guards' barracks. Chaplain Weimers ran the chapel, ministered to the guardsmen, and served as their confessor. He also took roll, obsessively counting to make sure each of the guards maintained their attendance.

Cristoph attended once each week, in between his shifts and his practice and his—thankfully now complete—punishment details. Just off his shift at the Arch of the Bells, he slipped in for his devotions and Mass. He was early, and he sat in one of the pews at the back. He let his head fall forward, elbows balanced on his knees as if he was praying. His aching feet throbbed. He curled his toes inside his boots, trying to stretch.

Inside St. Anne's, the white stone walls rose high with only narrow windows breaking up the cold interior. A small dome hovered over the chapel's nave and a simple stained-glass panel glittered behind the altar. Worn wooden pews sat in rows, pushed slightly out of line by the weight of the men rising and kneeling throughout the day. Tattered Bibles peeked out of the pew racks, the original Latin Vulgate. A simple stand of votive candles sat beneath a painting of Saint Sebastian tied to a tree and pierced through the neck with an arrow. Saint Sebastian the Martyr, one of the patron saints of the Guard. They were supposed to pray on Psalm 118 while contemplating Saint Sebastian.

Sighing, he tugged one of the Bibles free and flipped to the Psalm. His eyes caught on the first line.

O give thanks to the LORD, for he is good;
his steadfast love endures forever!

He slammed the Bible shut, the air cracking with the force of the delicate pages smacking together. Eyes closed, he tried to breathe. Tried to calm his heart.

Tried to stop the flood of memories suddenly running wild in the darkness of his mind.

He exhaled, his breath shaking.

Behind the altar, tucked inside the vestment room where Chaplain Weimers readied for each Mass, the sound of silver crashed to the ground, shattering the stillness of the empty chapel. Cristoph straightened, his spine cracking, as raised voices bellowed from behind the altar.

"I've told you before! I don't want your kind in here! Get out!" Weimers thick accent barked.

"I'm not here to cause trouble. I'm trying to talk to you about—"

"I don't want to hear it!" Another crash, and Cristoph heard the sound of silver rattling and scraping over stone, as if it had been kicked. "You're not welcome here!"

"You'd let one of your flock go? You'd let a man who needs your prayers be left to wither? You'd turn away a sheep, leave him for the wilds?"

"I will not let your darkness seep into this house of God!" Weimers burst from behind the nave, bustling half in his vestments toward the altar. He slammed down the chalice and the flute of wine.

Behind him, the lanky priest from Alain's office stood, his eyes narrowed, one hand clutching the strap of a messenger bag slung over his shoulder. "Alain Autenburg—"

"*Enough!*" Weimers whirled around. He crossed himself, glaring at the priest, and clenched the altar with one hand, his knuckles going white. "Leave this house of God. Sergeant Autenburg's soul —and your own—need more than I can give." He trembled. "You would ruin me," he whispered.

Cristoph stared, his mouth open, frozen in his pew.

The lean priest snorted. He pushed past Weimers, clapping him on the shoulder. "Always a pleasure seeing you again, Hauke," the priest grunted. He thundered down the altar, and as he hit the center aisle, his eyes finally caught on Cristoph. A tiny hitch in his step was the only sign he'd noticed Cristoph at all.

The priest strode out of the chapel without a backward glance, pushing both wooden doors open and striding into the afternoon sunlight.

Weimers braced himself against the stone altar, whispering prayers as he crossed himself three times.

Slowly, Cristoph stood. He cleared his throat.

Weimers jumped. His panicked gaze finally settled on Cristoph, and the chaplain exhaled, grabbing his crucifix hanging around neck. "My son, you scared the Holy Ghost out of me."

Cristoph tried to smile, quirking his lips. "I apologize."

"Did... did you any of hear that?"

He nodded once.

"Listen to me, young man," Weimers said, his voice shaking. "You must not associate with that man. Or with Sergeant Autenburg."

"Alain is my mentor."

Weimers made the sign of the cross over his chest again. "You must ask the commandant to reassign you. You must! Immediately!"

"Why? Sergeant Autenburg has been nothing but kind to me. And I don't even know who that man is. Who *is* he?"

Weimers' jowls shook as he clenched his jaw tight. His nostrils flared. "That man you saw," he breathed, "is in league with the Devil. He and Sergeant Autenburg both."

"He's a priest..."

"He's no Christian brother of mine." Weimers spread his hands over the altar. He exhaled slowly. "Now, why don't you come and help me with my Mass this afternoon?"

Shaking his head, Cristoph stumbled out of the pew, backing away. He had to run. He had to get out of there. Crumbling frescos glared down at him, the eyes of saints painted onto ancient stone scraping him raw. Beams of sunlight pierced the chapel like an archangel's sword. He watched Weimers' face fall as his back hit the door.

He scrambled behind him, pushing at the wood until he fell onto the cobblestone roads of the Vatican. He gasped, breathing in the exhaust of Rome, and stared up at the dome of St. Peter's Basilica.

HE DIDN'T HAVE ANOTHER GUARD SHIFT UNTIL THE NEXT DAY. He could have fled, and part of him screamed to run, to tear out of the Vatican and into Rome and lose himself in the crowds and the frenetic energy of the city. Park himself in a bar and drink until the shrieking in his mind stopped and the dark crack in his soul was covered up again with hastily piled mountains of bullshit and anger.

But fleeing had always been his default option. He'd fled so many things in his life, it was easier to count the times he'd stayed, had stuck around and seen something through. The Swiss Guard, in fact, had almost been an exercise in cutting losses and making a run for it.

How was he even still there? Five months of training before swearing in, and through it all, he'd been a giant target for Major Bader's wrath. Then he was thrown together with Alain, and his fumbling efforts to try to straighten Cristoph out. To reach him.

When everything had seemed to go to Hell, when he was ready to just throw it all in and call the whole thing a mistake, Alain had started to pry Cristoph out of that dark funk he'd wallowed in ever since Africa.

And somewhere in all of that, he'd gone and decided he wanted to make Alain proud of him.

It wasn't hard to figure out why. After a lifetime of being everyone else's bother, Cristoph knew himself well enough to know his one giant weakness.

Alain may be a complete nerd who stayed locked up in a stale office collating reports all day long. He may not know proper military decorum if it slapped him in the face. He was undoubtedly a loner. But he was a funny, fit, and kind nerd, and he treated Cristoph like he was worth knowing.

Why then, was everyone saying Alain was the darkest secret in the Vatican? That there was something sinister and terrible about him? That Cristoph should flee and not look back?

No. He knew what he had seen and what he had experienced. Alain had been the one good thing about coming to the Vatican. The only good thing so far. He wasn't going to let that go. Not because of rumor and gossip.

He headed for the roof of the barracks and gazed out over Rome and the Eternal City. Hope churned inside him, alien and unfamiliar. It was almost too much, the frenzied excitement that Alain would be at the game that night.

Maybe... maybe after the game, they could grab a drink. Or talk. Or do something, anything, together. Something outside of the punishment closet, outside of the gym. He just wanted to see Alain again, spend time with him. Spending time with Alain, even just the little bit that they had, had been better than any of the times he spent with Muller and Zeigler, with his roommates or his fellow recruits, or with the others from the team. He wanted more.

Hours later, Cristoph joined in on a short afternoon practice before the game, and then the team piled into the canteen together, devouring pounds of pasta and eggplant parmesan. Other guardsmen off shift joined in, cheering the team on before the game had even begun.

Muller and Zeigler bracketed Cristoph, talking nonstop around mouthfuls of pasta and breadsticks as if nothing had happened that morning. He ignored them both, silent between their arguments and chatter.

When the rest of the team sat down, Captain Ewe came around to pump everyone up, grinning and cheering and pumping his fists with the rest of them, all for the pre-game rush.

His eyes strayed toward the canteen doors every few minutes. Commandant Best wandered in, along with Major Bader. Captain Ewe leaped on top of a table and led the team—and the rest of the Guard—in a rousing rendition of the *Schweizer Nati* football chant, stomping on the tables and slapping each of the players on the head.

For the first time in the months since his swearing in, a part of Cristoph wanted to feel settled. He knew this—military camaraderie, teammates shouting and cheering, hands pumping through the air, and a brotherhood binding them all together.

Why, then, did it feel as if something was missing?

Why was he searching for Alain, turning to look back at the doors every time they banged open?

Zeigler caught him after the twentieth time. "Forget him!" Zeigler shouted into his ear, over the rising chant of *Olé*. "We're heading out to the fields in a bit. Get your head in the game!"

The team jogged through the Vatican gardens. In the far corners of the Eternal City by the Holy See's radio tower, there was enough of a flat space for a rough soccer field to be chalked out and for orange cones to be set up as goals. The fire brigade was already warming up when they arrived, and one of the younger Congregation for the Clergy priests, who officiated at the football games at one of the local Catholic high schools, was stretching in the center of the field.

The Guard officers showed up just before kickoff, along with the off-duty guardsmen and fire fighters. Cristoph strained to see through the crowd, but he couldn't find the rumpled black suit and messy hair he was looking for.

Zeigler stayed silent. He elbowed Muller when Muller opened his mouth.

Bishop Battistini hobbled up the grassy hillside, leaning on a walking stick. One of the guards raced away, returning with a wooden chair taken from the nearby Ethiopian Seminary. High backed and etched with carvings, the chair stood out in the gardens, but the bishop patted the young man's cheek with a smile and settled down for the game.

At kick-off, Alain was nowhere to be seen.

———

"YOU ARE TRULY A MAGNIFICENT SIGHT TO BEHOLD ON THE field!" Bishop Battistini walked arm in arm with Cristoph, heading back to his rooms in the Palazzo San Carlo, one of the gilded residences within the Vatican walls. "You played like you had the Holy Spirit inside your soul."

Cristoph tried to smile. He'd channeled his disappointment and his anger onto the field, taking his ridiculous emotions out on the ball and the other team. He'd earned himself a yellow card, but also three goals. The team had rallied around him, and they'd pulled off an upset, ending the fire brigades domination over the Swiss Guard.

Alain had never shown up.

Cristoph kicked himself inside. He had cared too much, and he'd been exposed as a fool.

So what that Alain had skipped the game? Even though he had promised he'd be there. So what? They weren't anything to each other, other than mentor and mentee. He tried to shake off the funk that had settled around him like a pall.

God, he'd wanted Alain to see him out there. He'd wanted the man to see he could, in fact, be somebody worth being proud of. That he could do something right.

Too bad he wasn't worth Alain's attention. What could have come up that would break his promise? What was so captivating to Alain that it yanked him from Cristoph, time and time again? A new file to pore over? A pickpocket in St. Peter's Square he had to liaise with the gendarmerie over?

Dammit, Alain had *promised*.

Guess his word didn't mean that much.

He always did have a knack for wanting the wrong guy. It was practically his superpower at this point.

Cristoph came back to himself as Battistini patted his hand. The old bishop had been retelling Cristoph's highlights, describing each goal, each barbaric charge down the field. How he'd dove for the ball, stealing it from the legs of the fire brigade's star striker. Cristoph smiled weakly.

"Would you like to come up for a drink?" Battistini winked. "I have more than communion wine in my apartment."

Cristoph nodded and let Battistini lead him through the Palazzo San Carlo doors and into the turn of the century elevator. Brass gates closed, and a hand lever moved the car at an agonizing pace up the levels of the Palazzo. Battistini stopped at the floor second from the top, gesturing to a door down the hall.

Battistini, like most of the residents of the Vatican, left his door unlocked. Crime amongst the five hundred—mostly clerical —residents was low. Cristoph held Battistini's door open and waited as the bishop shuffled inside. He made his way over to an eighteenth-century velvet sofa tucked beneath a bay window overlooking the Vatican gardens.

The apartment was decked out in French revolutionary style, eighteenth- and nineteenth-century wooden tables sharing space with hand-carved rocking chairs and sideboards. An original oil canvas dominated one wall, a Slavic painting from centuries past. Jesus, barely covered in a red cloth, lay back against a naked angel, his head nestled against the angel's taut, muscular chest. One of the angel's arms wrapped around Jesus, and his other brandished a club, as if to protect his sleeping charge.

Cristoph's gaze lingered on the firm lines of the shockingly nude angel's body.

On a table next to the sofa, a crystal decanter filled with plum wine breathed. "Grab two glasses for us, please?" Battistini asked, directing Cristoph toward the kitchen at the back of the apartment.

The kitchen was clean, tidy, cramped, and dominated by dark wood and old appliances. Two wine glasses sat on a shelf, and he snatched them before heading back to the sitting room.

Beaming, Battistini poured a glass of wine and then gestured to the painting. "Do you like it?"

"It's interesting. I don't remember this scene from Sunday school."

Battistini handed one full glass of wine to Cristoph, keeping the other. "It was considered too provocative for public display. I asked to keep it here. I enjoy the aesthetics of the piece."

Cristoph took a deep swallow of the wine to cover his sudden nerves, grasping the wine glass to hide the shaking of his hands. Alain had told him there were more men like them than he realized, but he somehow hadn't expected to meet anyone who owned up to it. Certainly not ancient Bishop Battistini. "The angel is, uh, buff," he finally said.

"Not as strong as you are, my boy." Battistini winked over the edge of his wine glass. "You truly are a sight to behold."

Cristoph's hands went slick as his mouth dried. He could hear his pulse pounding in his ears. "Thanks." He fidgeted. "I... I think I should be going."

"So soon?" Battistini frowned.

"I don't feel..." Cristoph reached out, trying to put the wine glass down on the sideboard. He missed by five feet, staggering sideways, and the glass fell to the ground, shattering. The world spun, sounds blending together, the floor rising up as the painting smeared from the wall, colors bleeding backward and forward. He blinked, but the world seemed to spin faster.

"Oh! Be careful!" Battistini's hands landed on his shoulders, steadying him as he stumbled. "You need to sit down." Gentle pressure turned Cristoph until he was facing the couch. "Sit."

He fell forward, feet tripping, and landed in a pile of arms and legs across the couch. Cristoph tried to grab on to the sofa, tried to stop the world from somersaulting. "Wha's happenin'..."

"I will take care of you, my boy."

Hands grabbed his hips, pulled on his shorts. He jerked, tried to twist away. Bright lights burned into his eyes. He screwed his eyes shut.

Battistini kneeled over him, his black cassock spreading around Cristoph's shins as his gnarled hands pulled down Cristoph's shorts.

"Stop..." He tried to bat Battistini away.

"Hush, don't say a word. I'll take care of you." Battistini's hands reached for his crotch. "I've got you..."

Cristoph jerked, grabbing Battistini's frail arms with shaking hands. He couldn't breathe, struggled to drag in gulps of air to his burning lungs. "I don't want to hurt you," Cristoph pleaded. "Please, stop."

Battistini's hands squeezed. "Shhh," Battistini cooed. "It will be all right."

Cristoph felt the fragility of Bishop Battistini beneath his grip. "*Please*," he pleaded one last time. "*Stop*. I don't want to hurt you."

One of Battistini's hands dragged Cristoph's shirt up over his belly. The old bishop's tongue snaked out, licking a long line from his crotch to his belly button.

Cristoph bucked, using all of the strength he could muster in his weakened state. He rolled, hoping he was rolling off the couch, and grabbed Battistini, pulling him into his arms. They fell to the floor, Battistini crying out as his hip hit the ground. A sharp *crack* burst through the room. Battistini's cassock flew up, and the bishop's flypaper-thin skin dragged across Cristoph's thighs, dry as

ancient parchment. Cristoph shuddered. He shoved Battistini
back, throwing him to the floor.

Everything still swam, and the lamps around the room bled
light in rainbows as the walls and floors rolled over and around
each other as if he was caught inside a hamster's ball. He grabbed
his shorts, pulled them up, and staggered to his feet, hands spread
wide for balance.

"You can't leave me!" Battistini wailed. "You've broken me!"
Battistini lay on the floor, grasping his hip, his face twisted with
anguish.

"I'll get help," Cristoph gasped. Fear iced through him. "I'll get
help... I'm sorry." He shook his head. The world rang like a bell.
Everything turned neon, then flipped upside down. He blinked,
long and hard. "You drugged me!" Anger replaced his fear,
white hot.

Battistini stared back at him. "You're such a beautiful boy."

He was going to puke. Fire roiled in his belly. Cristoph
staggered for the door, ignoring Battistini's pleas. He bounced off
the bishop's walls, missed when he tried to grab the door handle.
Finally, he fell head first into the hallway.

Blessedly, the main hallway was silent.

A ding by the elevator. Someone was coming.

God, they couldn't find him like this. He had to run.

He tried to stand, but only managed a crawl. Moving as fast as
he could, Cristoph headed for the stairwell at the end of the hall.
The dings behind him grew louder as the elevator rose, closer to
their level. Panting, he reached the door to the stairwell, but he
fought with the door handle, trying to get it open. He cursed as
spit fell from the corners of his lips. God, why this? Why now?

The door finally unlatched, flying open, and Cristoph fell onto
the stair landing. He rolled in and kicked the door shut behind
him. He had to keep moving. He dragged himself to his feet. His
legs shook, and he put most of his weight on his arms, clutching
the railing with white knuckles.

He took a step, down one stair.

He fell.

Cristoph tumbled, rolling and somersaulting down four flights of turns and twists in the stairwell. He felt something in his ankle pop, a tear, and he let out a tiny grunt as he rolled the rest of the way down, all the way to the bottom.

He lay motionless, heaving shaking breaths, for a long, long time.

Chapter Nine

THE NUNS ALWAYS MOVED THE ZIP BAGGIES.

Grumbling, Alain rifled through another drawer, coming up with aluminum foil and parchment paper, but no bags. Blood dripped onto the counter, and he wiped it away with his sleeve before sucking his torn bottom lip into his mouth. More blood rained from the ragged tear across his cheek.

Finally, he spotted the tattered cardboard box stuffed with baggies on a shelf over the metal sink. Why they were there, he didn't know, but he grabbed a handful and headed for the fridge. The fridge held enough food to feed one hundred and thirty Guardsmen three meals a day. Alain grabbed a cup and plunged it into the ice bin, filling it before dumping the ice into the baggie. He zipped it up and pressed it to his bloody, swollen eye, sighing.

In the canteen, a wooden chair scraped across the floor, followed by a muffled curse. A grunt of pain.

Alain whirled, staring at the darkened doorway leading out to the canteen. It was the middle of the night. The canteen was closed. He should be alone.

He strode for the door, clicking on the lights.

Cristoph raised one arm against the sudden brightness and

stumbled, crashing into a wooden chair again and falling to the floor.

Alain dropped his ice pack and ran to him. He grabbed Cristoph, sinking to his side and rolling him in his arms. "What happened?" Bruises dotted Cristoph's jaw and arms, and a split lip stared back at him. Cristoph breathed fast, and his hands grasped Alain's arms.

"Hurt my ankle," Cristoph finally breathed. "I... fell."

Alain took in Cristoph's disheveled state. He was covered in dirt, and suspicious purple stains on his white shorts looked like spilled wine. Sweat beaded off his forehead even though he was shivering, trembling in Alain's grasp. And he still hadn't opened his eyes.

"I've got you," Alain said.

Cristoph jerked, pushing away from Alain as if he wanted to escape. He pummeled him with his fists. Uncoordinated, his blows landed on Alain's shoulders instead of his face, but they were still hard, almost full force. As if Cristoph were fighting for his freedom.

"Whoa!" Alain managed to grab Cristoph's hands. "What's going on?"

"He said... he said... he said..." Cristoph repeated, almost hyperventilating. "That's what he said..."

Realization hit Alain with the force of an exorcism. All the air left him, drilled out of his lungs, as he stared at Cristoph. "Jesus Christ..." He closed his eyes. His hands dropped and squeezed Cristoph's shoulders.

He trembled, raw fury closing over his mind. A curse, dark and depraved, hovered on the tip of his tongue. If he knew who had done this, he'd speak the curse and damn the man's soul in a moment.

No. Cristoph needed him now. He softened his voice. "Cristoph, it's Alain. I'm going to pick you up now. I need to see what happened."

"He grabbed me." Cristoph groaned as Alain lifted him, but he rolled his head against Alain's chest. "I fought him off. God, I hurt him—"

"Shhh. He's gone. I'll take care of you." Alain carried him into the kitchen and laid Cristoph on the giant stainless-steel island in the center of the room. He started at Cristoph's head, taking in the bruises and the cuts as Cristoph trembled. He moved his hands down Cristoph's body, his fingers fluttering over the bruises on one arm. Nothing broken. Nothing swollen. Until he saw Cristoph's ankle.

Alain swore. "Your ankle is badly hurt. Maybe a torn ligament. It might be broken. I'm going to check you out, all right?"

Cristoph nodded, his eyes squeezed shut.

Alain undid his football boot and peeled it off, wincing as Cristoph winced. Swelling around the joint. Gently, Alain took Cristoph's foot in hand and flexed it. Cristoph strained, but he didn't cry out, and Alain didn't feel any bones grinding. Not that he was any authority on mortal, bodily injuries. His expertise ended at self-sewn stitches into cuts disinfected with vodka. "I don't think it's broken. But we'll need an x-ray to make sure."

"It was my first game...".

Alain grabbed his discarded ice bag and rested it on Cristoph's ankle. "I'm going to clean you up." He wet a rag with warm water and leaned over Cristoph, gently wiping his cheek.

Finally, Cristoph opened his eyes. He blinked, slow and bleary, and Alain watched Cristoph take a full minute to focus in on him, inches away from his face. Alain stared into his gaze. Cristoph's pupils were blown wide, his eyes nearly black, not even a sliver of brilliant blue left in his irises. He'd been drugged.

"Who did this?" Alain whispered. "Someone here in the Vatican?"

Cristoph rolled his head away. He blinked fast and bit down on his lip hard enough to bruise. Alain swiped his thumb across Cristoph's lips, urging him to let go.

"You said you'd be there tonight."

Guilt grabbed hold of Alain's heart and took a swan dive. "I'm sorry." Alain finished wiping Cristoph's face and moved to his arms and his hands. "I am sorry, Cristoph." His head throbbed, his swollen eye pounding. Before he got back to the Vatican, he hadn't thought the night could have gotten any worse. "I got called out again. We thought we had a lead, and we were tracking... something bad." He shook his head. "I *really* wanted to see you tonight."

Cristoph wouldn't look at him.

Alain finished with the cuts on his hands, his scraped knees. He wadded up the towel and threw it in the trash. Inside himself, he was screaming, fury and guilt warring with each other, tearing Alain to shreds. He should have been there. He should have been at the game. He would have come up with some kind of pathetic excuse to spend time with Cristoph after, and then this wouldn't have happened.

Dammit, he'd promised Cristoph. And now this.

"You need to call the emergency line," Cristoph whispered. "Bishop Battistini... fell. He broke his hip."

Alain nodded. Fury rose within him again, a cresting wave. He clenched his hands, trying to still their shaking. He had his culprit now.

Stay with Cristoph. After everything, you should at least stay with him now. Alain's breath hitched. *If he wants anything at all to do with me ever again.* "I'll call it in after I take you back to your dorm."

Cristoph cringed. "No, not there. Not like this." He struggled his way into a sitting position, even though he was panting, wincing with every move his body made. "I can't go back there like this."

"You need to rest. Do you want to go to hospital? I can take you over to the clinic—"

Mute, Cristoph shook his head. "The bishop will be there after you call it in."

"Good," Alain blurted out. His lips twisted, pressing together. "Good," he growled. "You did the right thing, fighting back. Whatever you did to him, he deserved it. And more."

Cristoph stayed silent. He swayed dangerously forward, almost falling face first into Alain. Alain steadied him, grabbed his shoulders.

"Just take me to the chapel. I'll spend the night there."

"No." Alain frowned. Letting Cristoph out of his sight tonight was no longer an option. Not with the guilt sliding down the inside of his chest, dripping down his ribs. "No, you're coming with me. You can stay in my apartment."

If anything, Cristoph looked worse after Alain spoke, cringing again and glaring down at the ground, his face twisted into a rictus of pain and unshed anger.

He'd always been a fool. And everything he touched turn to ash. *Push it all down.*

"C'mon. I'll carry you up. You're still drugged and I don't want you falling again, hurting yourself worse." Alain passed the ice bag to Cristoph.

Cristoph closed his eyes as Alain wrapped his arms under Cristoph's knees and around his shoulders and hefted him up. Cristoph stayed stiff, muscles clenched, still trembling from head to toe as Alain headed out of the canteen and crossed the courtyard. The looming barracks rose into the night, some windows open, some lights on, gentle laughter and the sounds of snores and pop music and video games mixing with the Vatican night. Alain moved quickly, slipping into the officers' barracks, and punched the elevator call button.

It took a few minutes, but Cristoph eventually relaxed in his arms. His head rested against Alain's shoulder. Warm breaths puffed over Alain's neck as they rode up to the fourth floor. Alain kicked open the brass gate, squeezed through, and padded down the hall past Major Bader's apartment.

"The single officers live on this floor," he muttered. It was just him and Luca.

Cristoph grunted.

Alain shouldered into his apartment and carried Cristoph

down the narrow hallway to the back bedroom. He kept his home purposely sterile. Nothing personal.

Bookshelves dominated the walls of his study, filled with ancient manuscripts, forbidden tomes, and tools of his trade. Bone blades and scrying glass and witches' ladders confiscated from the Inquisition sat next to runes and hex bags and carved idols. Bones etched with sigils and seals shared space with herb bags and vials of blessed oil and holy water. Alain kept Cristoph's back to his shelves as he carried him into his bedroom.

He deposited Cristoph in the middle of his tattered bed, laying him down in an unmade nest of white cotton sheets and a plaid duvet. Alain's stomach clenched. He'd had dreams since the last time he'd done laundry. The evidence was still there, ground into the sheets, if Cristoph looked. At the least, the faint smell still lingered. His cheeks burned.

Cristoph rolled instantly on Alain's bed, burying his face in his pillow. Whether it was to hide his face or to get away from Alain, Alain couldn't tell. He fussed with the ice bag, pulling two couch pillows from the study for Cristoph's ankle and set the ice bag back on his swollen joint.

When he looked up, Cristoph was staring at him, frowning. "What happened to your face?" One shaking hand reached for his swollen black eye, his bloody face, his torn lip.

Alain intercepted his hand, rubbing his thumb over Cristoph's palm. "I brawled with a ghoul," he whispered, smiling sadly. "You have no idea how much I wish I had been with you."

"A what?"

"Get some rest." He finished drawing a rune for sleep in the center of Cristoph's palm just before Cristoph's eyelids slid shut.

Alain dragged a chair close to his bed and collapsed into it. His bones ached where Lotario's spell had knit together his shattered ribs, his punctured lung. Blood still oozed down his face. Exhaustion pulled on his soul.

"I will watch over you," he said to Cristoph's sleeping form. "I won't let anything happen to you."

When Cristoph woke, sunlight spiked through his skull, bright enough to make his brain bleed. Groaning, he rolled away and buried his face in the pillow.

In the pillow that smelled exactly like Alain: moss tinged with iron, wet leaves on concrete, and ancient dust mixed with musk. He pulled back, his eyes darting right and left, taking in Alain's rumpled bed, Alain's bedroom, and the aches in his body. He froze.

Outside the bedroom, raised voices filtered through the closed door. He recognized Major Bader's voice first.

"And you didn't do anything to warn the man? Didn't say anything to him?"

"You didn't either, Luca!" Alain's voice, uncharacteristically loud. Shouting. *"You didn't say anything to them in training!"*

"I'm not his mentor," Bader hissed.

"Did you warn Gruber?" Silence. *"Or Braun?"* Alain sighed, and floorboards creaked. *"I'm sick of this. I'm sick of seeing our new recruits waiting like flowers to be plucked by old men inside this Vatican hothouse."*

"Some of the guards enjoy the extra income." Bader's voice was quiet. *"You know we've had guards who seek out these kinds of arrangements."*

"There's a big difference between prostitution and getting drugged and attacked."

More silence. Bader's voice was gruff when he finally spoke. *"Is he all right?"*

"He needs to go to hospital. I need you to take him there this morning. Stay with him."

"Me?"

"Yes, you. You're in charge of the men, Luca."

"You are his mentor! His friend. His..." Bader trailed off.

"I'm his mentor and that is all," Alain growled. *"He's been traumatized. You need to stop being an ass for a day and take care of this man."*

"Fine," Bader hissed. *"Since you're too busy to take care of him yourself."*

"Sometimes, Luca... Sometimes, I just want to—"

"Do it. Please." Bader's voice dripped with condescension. A long moment. *"Your apartment is a fucking mess. What's with all these boxes? Twelve years and you can't unpack?"*

Footsteps marched down the hallway. Cristoph cringed, pushing himself up. He'd recognize the major's stride anywhere.

The door flew open, hitting the wall with a thud. Major Bader stood in the doorway, his glower fixed on his face. He glared at Cristoph, sitting on the edge of Alain's bed. "It's time to go to hospital. I'm taking you. On your feet!"

As Cristoph limped out of Alain's apartment, he searched for Alain, but the man had vanished. All he could see were empty bookshelves, piles of boxes, and a stained coffee pot still warming on a hot plate.

VATICAN HEALTH SERVICES, LIKE EVERYTHING IN THE VATICAN, existed in a stratified, bifurcated world. Surely all were equal before the kingdom of heaven, as the scriptures taught. But some were more equal than others. To enter the clinic and seek treatment, there were two doors. One for bishops, and one for everyone else.

Cristoph had already heard the jokes. American priests living in the Vatican would fly home to their own doctors rather than risk a trip to the Vatican health clinic. There was no regular staff. The clinic was run by volunteers who worked shifts on their off days from their day jobs in Rome and was supplemented by nuns and priests of the various orders living on the grounds.

It was only fifty years ago, Cristoph heard in recruit training, that Pius XII was prescribed an injection of monkey brains to increase his lifespan. And make sure you never need surgery from the Vatican quacks. Paul VI's prostate was removed in his private library.

If that's how popes were treated, what would a lowly Swiss Guard receive?

He'd find out eventually. Maybe. If he didn't die of old age before being seen. His gaze kept dragging to the bishop's private entrance. Was Battistini still in there? Was he getting the best treatment, the all hands on deck attention that bishops commanded? Even after what he did?

Had he done that before?

Cristoph shifted. The bag of ice Major Bader had brought him after they arrived in the clinic was a melted mess of lukewarm water, dripping slowly onto the tiled floor. A puddle stretched for his heel. Beside Cristoph, Major Bader sat, back ramrod straight, eyes facing front, glaring at the closed doors leading to the treatment room.

At least Bader had let him change out of his sweat-stained and wine-splattered football shorts and jersey top before he limped across the Vatican. When the major had marched into his shared barracks dormitory, his roommates—drinking espresso, lounging as they traded bullshit and gossip while getting ready for their shifts —had fled in seconds, barreling out of the dorm as Bader escorted Cristoph in.

That bit of gossip would be running around the Guard in no time flat. Being escorted into his dorm by the major, bruised, bloody, and limping, would certainly put him squarely on the outs again.

Why hadn't Alain seen him before he left? Where had he gone? He'd heard him talking before the major had barged into Alain's bedroom. Surely he was there. Why wasn't Alain sitting by his side in the clinic instead of the stone-faced major who hated his guts?

Bader stood, each of his movements as purposeful as if he were marching to war, and strode toward the main desk. His clipped words growled back across the waiting room. Cristoph sagged forward, his back bowing as he buried his face in his hands, elbows propped on his knees. The nurse, an ancient nun in a habit who might have treated St. Peter as he came down from his crucifixion, frowned, but she nodded to Bader.

After three hours of waiting, they were escorted into an exam room.

Major Bader stood by the exam door, arms crossed, legs spread, like he was waiting for a command inspection. He said nothing as Cristoph fumbled and flubbed his way through his lies, saying he'd slipped and tumbled down the stairs "in the barracks" instead of "while drugged and escaping a sexual assault".

When the nurse asked for a urine sample, Cristoph blanched.

"Is that really necessary?" Major Bader drawled. "The man can hardly hobble to the toilet and I don't have time to wait for him to figure it out."

"We don't have an updated physical," the nurse protested. "Mr. Hasse's records are from his initial entry into recruit training. Since he's here, we can collect what we can."

"Another time," the major ordered curtly. "He needs his ankle tended to. I need him back on duty. I don't have time to waste with his out-of-date physical. I'm not here to make things easier for him." Bader glared at Cristoph. "You'll have to come back on your own to take care of that, Halberdier."

Cristoph nodded. As the nurse turned away, sighing at Bader, he sent the major a shaky smile behind her back. God only knew what Battistini had drugged him with. He didn't want any of that in his medical record.

Bader nodded once and looked away.

When the physician came in with plaster and wrappings for his leg and ankle, Bader slipped out. Through the thin walls, Cristoph heard his deep rumble ask about other patients, specifically about Bishop Battistini. Whatever the nurse's response was, Cristoph didn't hear, but Bader returned moments later.

He was bandaged, splinted, and given a pair of crutches, and then they were escorted out with a bottle of paracetamol and a warning to be careful going down the stairs. They walked away in silence, Cristoph hobbling next to Major Bader across the back of the Vatican, away from the crowds.

"The bishop has been sent to *San Giovanni Addolorata* hospital. He is being transferred to the Archbasilica of St. John Lateran after he's discharged. The hospital will be able to better care for his broken hip with him near. But, with him being so old, they don't think he'll ever leave the Archbasilica," Major Bader said quietly.

Cristoph swallowed. His crutches rang out on the cobbled walkways, a slow rhythm and clank. "I'm sorry. I didn't mean to hurt him."

"*Don't*," Bader barked. His eyes burned as stopped Cristoph. "Don't apologize. Don't ever." He exhaled, his nostrils flaring wide. Bader stared over Cristoph's shoulder, into some middle distance. "Report to Sergeant Autenburg when you return to the barracks. You're unfit for guard duty. You'll perform garrison duties instead, from zero eight hundred until sixteen hundred every day. Sergeant Autenburg will assign those duties."

"Yes, sir. Thank you, sir."

Bader stayed at Cristoph's side for the rest of the trek back to the barracks. When they returned, Bader held open the door for Cristoph, then disappeared into his office, slamming the door behind him. Cristoph hobbled down the hallway to Alain's cramped closet, squeezing through the narrow passage and gritting his teeth as he banged his casted foot. He stopped at the doorway. "Hey."

Alain looked up, one eye swollen shut, ringed in deep bruises, the other bloodshot. One cheek was scratched, butterfly bandages closing the cut. His hands shook, and the four empty cups of coffee scattered on Alain's desk were probably to blame.

"What happened to *you?*" Cristoph slumped against the doorframe. "I thought I had a bad night."

"You did have a bad night. You had a terrible night." Alain's hands clenched into fists. "I'm so sorry—"

"It's not your fault."

"I should have warned you—"

"That there's crap in the world? Yeah, I already knew that." Cristoph shrugged, picking at the hem of his shirt. "You told me about the other guards, like my roommate. I knew some stuff happened. I just didn't think... *he* would..." Battistini, after Alain, had been the kindest person to him in the Vatican. He was a man who did good in the world.

His memories shifted, scratched like a vinyl record being destroyed. Flashes of the night before, colors bleeding from the lights, naked angels, hands fondling him—

Cristoph shook his head.

Alain exhaled. "Yes, some of the guards have sold their services to some members of the curia. It's way to make more money. The Swiss Guards aren't paid that much. Most of the time, it's not sex. Just strip shows, maybe some petting. Some of the priests are very careful about their celibacy. They skirt the lines as much as they can." Alain closed his eyes. "A long time ago, I was approached. I was asked to—" He shook his head. Looked down. "I've never seen a guard attacked. Until now," he breathed.

The hem of Cristoph's shirt frayed beneath his hands, strings pulling free. "He was kind to me. Always nice, even when I was angry. When I didn't want to be here. Before—" His lips clamped shut. *Before you helped me. Before I wanted to make you proud.*

"I'm sorry," Alain repeated. He cleared his throat. "Is there something I can do for you?"

Cristoph felt the physical push of Alain's distancing like a shove to his chest. It made his skin pucker on the inside, made his muscles go tight. "Major Bader sent me here. Said I was going to perform garrison duties every day until I recovered and that you should assign them to me."

"*Me?*" Alain groaned, shaking his head and burying his face in his hands. "Luca..."

Was he truly this unwanted? Had he read Alain *completely* wrong? All those moments laughing and talking, spending time together when he could have been alone during his punishment details. Running in the gardens, working out side by side. Sparring. He stared back at their history, the time they had known each other.

He was a thousand different kinds of fool.

There wasn't anything there. Nothing more than a sergeant who had made the most out of his unwanted mentee and a man with delusions that someone cared for him. His stomach churned, a mix of painkillers swallowed dry on a drugged stomach and the swirling dregs of his self-hatred rearing again. Was it only yesterday he'd tried to convince himself everything was going to be all right?

He knew better than that.

He shifted, looking away. His heart thudded in his chest. Alain could probably hear it.

"Well, come in," Alain sighed. He winced as he stood, grabbing files and piling them on the floor out of sight behind his desk. Whole stacks disappeared, the desk suddenly bare, the chairs emptied, everything hidden away. He pulled a small clump of folders off the top of the computer monitor, coated in a layer of dust, and brushed them off with his jacket sleeve before sliding them across the desk to Cristoph.

"What's this?" Cristoph caught them before they slid off the edge, gingerly sitting down in one of the creaking metal folding chairs.

"Crime reports from the gendarmerie for the past five years. Interviews they took from people they detained who threatened the Holy Father." Alain's pinched expression stayed fixed on the folders, refusing to meet Cristoph's gaze. "Most of them are crazy. Religious nuts. They don't have the means to pull off any kind of attack. Or any kind of anything, really. Most of the time, their motives are based in conspiracy theory and madness. A lot of these people are homeless."

"What do you want me to do with this?"

"I need a threat assessment done on each individual. Analyze their background. Their threats, their motive, and their means."

Cristoph stared at Alain. "You just said they were all meaningless."

"That's one interpretation—"

"They were collecting dust on your monitor! You can't be serious!"

"I need to give you something to do. And that's all I have for you."

"I *know* this isn't what you do all day long. This isn't what got you that black eye!"

"I told you before, there are things I cannot share with you." A desperate plea burned from Alain's gaze. "Please. Don't push this."

"What's so secret? Why do you get to know everything about me but I know *nothing* about you?" Cristoph tossed the folders on the desk. "Why does everyone around here treat you like you're some kind of Devil-worshipping madman?" His voice rose until he was shouting at Alain. "Why are you pushing me away? I thought you—" He clamped his jaw shut.

Silence.

"Dammit, commandant," Alain whispered. "God *damn* you."

Footsteps rang down the hallway. Cristoph twisted, staring at the door. The lean, older priest appeared, eyes blown wide, cell phone pressed to his ear. His thin lips pressed together, face twisted into a grimace, and he barely paid Cristoph any attention as he fixed a panicked glare on Alain.

Cristoph could just make out someone talking fast and frantic over the line.

Alain jumped up. "What is it?"

"It's Angelo. The girl. It's... bad." The priest's eyes darted once to Cristoph, then away. "We have to go. *Now*."

"Shit." Alain winced as he rounded his desk, one hand over his ribs. Cristoph watched as he grabbed a shoulder bag by the door. "Cristoph..." he said, sighing. "Go back to your dorm. You can't be here." He licked his lips. Looked away. "And don't come back."

The priest waved for Alain to hurry. He jogged off, heading for the back door to the garrison. Alain followed slower, one hand still pressed over his side. They disappeared out to the car park in a flurry of frantic energy, leaving Cristoph alone in the dusty, dark office.

———

LOTARIO'S BEATER BUG SMOKED AND SNORTED AND GROUND ITS way across Rome, veering in and out of the capital's afternoon traffic of Vespas and cabbies and crowds of tourists. Lotario leaned on the horn as he sucked down a cigarette, careening into every space he could squeeze his shitty car, flipping off the other drivers and leaning out his window, cursing.

Alain clutched the duct-taped door handle and closed his eyes, resting his forehead on the grimy window. He tried not to feel anything at all. Tried desperately to erase the image of Cristoph's betrayed, shattered expression. *Don't come back.*

Why had he deluded himself into thinking he could have something for himself. Hadn't he learned his lesson twelve years ago? Why had the commandant gone and encouraged him, encouraged them?

He'd passed the point of worry about the state of his soul long ago, but even so, he blanched at how quickly he'd rocketed through all seven deadly sins. Didn't he have better control than this? Desire had grown, oh so fast. Envy. Greed. Pride. Gluttony for *more*. More of Cristoph, more of the hope he'd sheltered, hidden from his soul in the deepest recesses of his being, let out when he'd steal moments with Cristoph. Gaze at his smile. Bask in his laughter.

There was nothing so dangerous as to give a condemned man hope. Nothing in the world.

Unending wrath against himself for what he'd done. How he'd let Cristoph down. Of course he wouldn't have been able to see Cristoph's football game. Why had he thought that the universe would let him? He'd known, even from the beginning, it would end like this.

He was cursed. He'd made his vow—*never again*—for a reason.

But worst of all, sloth. Laziness. The complete capture of his mind, the shift in focus. Had this fascination distracted him from his duties? Had he missed something critical? Had his mind been on Cristoph when it should have been on his job, his purpose? There was no room for distractions. Not in this life.

The night before, just as he'd been about to head to Cristoph's game, Angelo had called. A woman's shrieking in the flats off the *Campo*, in the rundown tenements behind the bars and head shops and clubs, had lit up the switchboards in the Roman *polizia*. The callers thought she was being murdered.

In fact, she was being eaten.

The *polizia* who'd busted down the door came face-to-face, for the first time in their lives, with an evil entity. Shocked, they'd frozen, watching as the ghoul's claws slashed through her thigh and she slipped backward in a pool of her own blood, struggling to escape. Her screams had stirred them on, and the two officers unloaded their pistols into the ghoul.

Thirty rounds of lead later, the ghoul snarled and snapped, but didn't fall. It had lunged at the officers, blood smeared on its jowls, on its gnarled lips and jagged teeth, and its burning breath had filled the air with the stench of rotten meat.

Sirens closing in had spooked the ghoul. Roaring, it leaped for the window, breaking through the glass and then scaling the side of the building until it disappeared into the shadows of the Roman twilight.

Angelo had arrived first, steering the officers to his car for a debrief. They'd shaken for hours, were still shaking when Alain and Lotario had arrived.

The woman's name was Madelena, and she had adamantly refused to be transported to the hospital for her wounds. The medics on scene cleaned and bandaged what they could, glued together her deeper cuts, and gave her a shot of antibiotics. But she had refused to leave her apartment, and she drank from a plastic bottle of whiskey with a label that could only have come from the bottom shelf of a petrol station's cooler. Her cigarette-stained hands shook as she lowered the bottle, clutching the warped plastic between her spindly, bandaged thighs.

She wasn't one for questions, either.

"Get out!" she had shouted in curt Italian. "I don't want anything to do with you! Just leave me alone!" She'd thrown the empty whiskey bottle at their heads. It bounced off the wall after Alain had ducked.

Outside her apartment's warped door, Lotario and Alain had heard her ragged voice mumbling, a low chant that sounded like prayers or pleading.

Leaving her be, they'd tried to track the ghoul instead, following a trail of blood and an infrared spectrum scan down one of the narrow, twisting alleys between the run-down tenements. Dried vines clung to the soot-covered stone of the old building. The alley was claustrophobic and fetid. Rust stains mixed with the grime of Rome that stretched in long smears down the dank, forgotten bricks.

Alain had walked in first, into the darkness.

They'd thought they had it pinned. Without a manhole cover or a sewer entrance, the ghoul was trapped in the alley. It should have wanted to get back to safety, back underground. It'd penned itself in, though, pinning itself without an exit in its mad rush to flee.

The ghoul came out swinging. It took down Alain with a claw-filled bellow, slamming one heavy paw against his face. Alain had grabbed the ghoul's arm, trying to spar with the beast.

Their brawl was short. And bloody. Alain ended up flat on his back, bleeding from his face and side, gasping for breath as his ribs and his lung had exploded in searing agony. Through the blood gushing from his forehead, he'd watched the ghoul escape as Lotario chanted an incantation over him to heal his wounds.

Lotario had flung out his hand as Alain started to breathe again, palm facing the fleeing ghoul, and tried to launch a tracking charm after the dark creature.

His ribs knitted together beneath Lotario's touch. The tracking charm didn't stick to the ghoul.

They'd hunted for hours, trying to track it. Alain shook off Lotario's offer to heal him further, insisting they get back to work. In the end, though, the ghoul had vanished, probably back underground. They'd called it after three in the morning, and Angelo left a team outside Madelena's apartment for the rest of the night. Lotario had driven Alain back to the Vatican, where Alain stopped by the canteen for an ice bag before heading home.

But then Cristoph...

After packing up and hiding everything in his apartment, boxing away his tools and his relics and his weapons from any wandering eyes, he and Lotario had spoken quietly over the phone, coming down from the adrenaline together and trading theories on the ghoul, on the risings cropping up more and more in Rome. Lotario had been smoking on his rooftop, he'd said. Alain had his feet propped up on his mattress, and he'd traced the lines of Cristoph's sleeping expression over and over again with his gaze.

Had that only been hours ago? *Don't come back.*

He wanted to vomit.

Lotario filled him in on Angelo's call in between puffs of his cigarette and honks of his horn as they sped across Rome, back to the *Campo*.

Back to Madelena. Or what was left of her.

The *polizia* officers from the night before had gone back, wanting to pray with Madelena. A sour stench—warm copper and the sticky smell of melted sugar and rotten meat—made the officers shoulder open the door. They'd found Madelena ripped to shreds. Her blood, still warm, was spreading out from her exsanguinated body.

Those *polizia* officers weren't going to stay on the force. Alain just knew it. He'd seen enough young officers get spooked by the true darkness, had seen that haunted, hunted look. Priests were born on those nights, and occasionally he thought he recognized a seminarian sporting a fresh Roman collar, a starched black suit, and that same terrified expression as they darted panicked looks over their shoulders, on the streets of Rome.

Lotario swerved to a stop in the *Campo*, brakes squealing as the Bug bounced on broken shocks. Alain's head ricocheted off the steel frame of the door. If he had a nickel for every time, he could retire a wealthy man and leave all this hunting business behind. He'd have enough to bring Cristoph along, too—

Alain heaved himself out of the car as Lotario ground out his cigarette and ran past the Roman *polizia*'s crime scene barricade. The officers ignored him, as if he wasn't even there. They never even looked his way. They didn't look at Alain, either. He was a ghost in the sunlight, unseen, unacknowledged by the world.

Angelo waited for them at the landing outside Madelena's apartment. "It's not good."

He refused to go back inside, pushing open the door to her apartment with his foot.

The taste of dust and snakeskin hit them first, dry sand slipping through their fingers, the stench of damp earth cradling rotten flesh. Grave dirt and river fog and a parched scream scratching over the back of their throats.

"Vampire," Alain choked out. He bit the inside of his lip until he tasted copper and salt at the back of his throat. Anything to get rid of the vampiric energy.

Lotario's eyes slid sideways. "You gonna be—"

"I'm fine." Alain cut him off. He spotted a foot, bare and bruised, peeking out from behind a tattered yellow sofa. "Let's get going."

They stepped carefully, avoiding blood splatter and destroyed furniture. End tables had been shattered, the wood splintered apart by some crushing force. Mirrors were cracked, and glass shards lay scattered over the worn throw rugs and the scratched wooden floors. Blood arched on the walls, arterial spray, and pooled on the carpet in splashes and splatters. Her death had not been easy. Or quick.

Madelena lay behind the sofa, flat on her back, her eyes open.

Her neck was savagely torn, like an animal or a beast had ripped into her. Bloody smears around her wrists told of a struggle. Gashes marred her soft abdomen, visible from where her stained shirt had ridden up. She wore cutoff jean shorts, and beneath the fraying hems, blood streaked down her thighs.

Lotario sighed. "A ghoul and a vampire. Where there is one, there is the other."

"We should have prevented this." Alain's gaze traced the pool of blood beneath Madelena's body.

"We were coming back tonight. She should have been safe during the day." Ghouls didn't move during the day, and vampires stayed in their nests until it was night. They could move in sunlight, at least some of them could, but they looked so obviously unnatural, so clearly demonic, that they kept to the shadows and to darkness. They hadn't heard of vampires moving during the daylight in decades. Maybe a century.

Alain glared. "Not this time."

"Why?" Lotario frowned at her shabby apartment, at the run-down space and the cloying pull of despair and degradation that clung to her home. "Why attack *her*?"

"This has to be deliberate. She must have been targeted. She's too far off the main sewer access points for this to be a random, opportunistic kill."

"And it's all backwards. Ghouls feast on vampire kills. Vamps don't trawl ghoul attacks." Ghouls occasionally feasted on the vampires' leftovers. They mostly fed on rotting corpses. They slunk in the tunnels and hid in the darkness, carrion demons waiting to swoop in. Where there were ghouls, there were vampires, and vice versa. Both had appeared in the space of two days, attacking the same woman. Why?

And why had the ghoul struck first? Opportunistic bottom feeders did not hunt on their own.

Hairs prickled at the back of Alain's neck, standing on end, vibrating. Pressure behind him filled the room, almost popping his ears. He wanted to turn around, to check the dark corners and under Madelena's bed, satisfy that primal, human urge to make sure there weren't monsters hiding in the shadows, waiting to strike. He exhaled, closing his eyes. It was only leftover terrors in his soul. "We need to turn her life upside down. Who is she? What did she do? Who did she know? Why did the darkness come for her?"

"You think she called out to it?"

"We won't know until we investigate. And, we need to track the vampire that did this. We need answers. This is well outside the bounds of the pact."

Lotario squinted. "You sure you—"

"The sooner we start the better chance we have. It's daylight. We can find this killer while they're resting. Did you bring your tracking tools?"

Lotario unshouldered his bag and slung it over the back of Madelena's sofa. He unzipped it with too much force, wrenching the bag open and rummaging inside before pulling out a crystal tied to a coil of braided twine, a plate of glass with sigils etched around the edges, and a worn and weary map of Rome. Alain took the map and unfolded it, laying it out next to Madelena's body. He stayed clear of her cooling pool of blood. The edges of the map had already collected enough brown and rust-colored stains. It didn't need any more.

Lotario swiped the tip of the crystal deep inside the tears and gashes in Madelena's throat, deep inside her severed carotid artery, where the vampire's fangs had torn her apart and where it had left behind some of its own essence during the kill. The mark of a vampire was indelibly fixed onto its prey, as long as one knew where to search.

Black vampire blood soaked the crystal, dripping from the tip, as Lotario pulled away and slid the glass plate beneath the pendulum.

Passing everything across her body to Alain, Lotario stood back. He watched while Alain moved the glass and bloody pendulum over the map of Rome, muttering under his breath and speaking the words to the incantation. Alain repeated them in his mind, closing his eyes.

He opened them when he felt he pendulum swing. Blood welled at the tip of the crystal, and when it swung to a certain point, the stream of blood fell to the glass etched with runes. The bloody tell quivered on the plate, hovering above the map.

Lotario shared a long look with Alain.

They knew that place.

Alain wiped away the blood on the glass and the crystal and silently folded the map. All the while, he kept repeating to himself that there wasn't a vampire behind him waiting to strike, and the pressure and presence were only his fear. Were only a shadow of his mind, of his bloody memories wreaking havoc.

Alain let loose a breathless exhale when they slipped out of Madelena's apartment, back onto the landing with Angelo. Dizziness stole through him, but he hid his stumble from Lotario as they plodded down the stairs and back outside, into the sunlight.

———

ACROSS THE ALLEY, HIDDEN IN THE GRIM SHADOWS AND squeezed between a refuse bin and a rusted-out fire escape, a pale figure shrouded in darkness watched Alain. Yellow eyes glittered, following the hunter and the priest as they disappeared into the backstreets of Rome.

Chapter Ten

THEY FOLLOWED THE OLD CITY'S COBBLED BACK ALLEYS AND
narrow side streets until they ended up on the Lungotevere, the
tree-lined avenue overlooking the banks of the Tiber. Walking fast,
they dodged scooters and bicyclists and Romans laughing into
their cell phones, keeping their gazes on the river on their right.
Heading south, the Tiber curved around the *Isola Tiberina*, and just
after the snub end of the island, the *Ponto Palatino* bridge stretched
across the river, connecting the east and west banks. Nearby, the
Ponto Rotto, the oldest stone bridge in Rome, stood in ruins, a
single arch hovering in the midst of the Tiber.

Trampling in a rush down the stairs leading from the
Lungotevere to the walking path on the river's shore, Alain tried to
steady his frantic heart. His chest ached, as if his chest were
clenched in a vise. It had been twelve years since they'd had last
tangled with vampires living beneath Rome, but he remembered
every *single* moment of that last encounter.

Push it all down. Push it all away.

Vampires didn't usually venture out, certainly not deep into the
heart of Rome. When they hunted, it was always on the periphery
of the city, near the sewers and the grottos and the catacombs.

They snatched the homeless, the indigents, and the lonely—people who wouldn't be missed. Twice a year, Alain and Lotario found bodies dumped by river outflows or moldering in marshes. Victims of a vampire.

And yet, there hadn't been a single missing person report or a cry for help from any friend or family of the victim. In the end, there was only a silent silver circle and a lit match in the dank cellar beneath Angelo's *polizia* station.

The vampires' stayed out of sight. They kept their feedings to a minimum. They didn't penetrate the inner city. They didn't make a scene. It was part of the pact made twelve years ago. The nest of vampires in Rome had been silent since, keeping to their end of the agreement. Stay on the edges. Stay hidden. Do nothing that required the hunters to come for them.

Why murder a woman deep inside Rome now? Why break the pact?

Alain slipped on the bottom step, sliding on the damp slick of the river's spray on the stone carved stairs. The blocks beneath their shoes could have a hundred years old or a thousand, worn smooth from years of feet slapping against the steps. Lotario grabbed his elbow, steadying him, and left his hand on Alain's arm even after Alain found his feet.

Lotario had been there that night. They'd never spoken of it since, but Lotario knew. He knew the hatred in Alain's marrow, in the cells of his existence, toward vampires.

He shook off Lotario's lingering hold. He didn't want anyone's pity. Not now, not ever. Lotario's quiet concern and his searching gaze grated on Alain's soul.

The obvious opening to the Roman underground, the ancient sewers stretching back to pre-Roman days, arched across the Tiber's bank. The *Cloaca Maxima's* outflow to the river was a crumbled arch of brick half submerged beneath the waterline, surrounded by dirt and trees on a sheltered segment of the riverbank. Homeless Romani made camp on top of the outflow's arch in the dirt-packed shelter beneath the Lungotevere overhang, sleeping on pallets and scraps of cardboard and playing wailing tunes on a fiddle missing two of its strings. The Romani waved to Alain and Lotario as they approached. When they recognized them, they made a warding sign, an evil eye, and shouted at them to move on in a mixture of Russian, Romany, and French.

Lotario waved back, a jaunty salute with two fingers that told them to fuck off. Roaring with laughter, the Romani watched the two seeming priests head down the riverbank.

Not far down, a secondary entrance to the sewers, an access tunnel, opened into the riverbank. Lotario looked up and down the river, then ducked inside with Alain. A gate swung inside the entrance. Lotario picked the lock and pushed through it, the bars near the bottom raised off the riverbed to let the sewer waters pass through to the Tiber.

Alain hopped across the low stream, landing on a narrow brick catwalk. Lotario stayed on his side and dug out a headlamp from his bag. Alain did the same, fixing the elastic over his head and shining the light into the sewer's darkness.

"Ready?" Lotario asked.

Alain stepped forward.

The free-flowing stream slowed twenty feet in, mucked up by a pile of sewage. Loose, slimy offal oozed through the narrow waterway. Alain's eyes watered, and he tried to breathe shallowly through his mouth. A rotten shoe and a football bobbed and squelched against the blockage. Another day, they might have found a corpse dumped by a vampire, or by some other nefarious—but human—presence.

The sewers continued. A dark recess opened to the left, heading north underground. Lotario shined his headlamp into the opening. The tunnel's pitch-black swallowed his beam, an impenetrable stillness. He turned back to Alain. In the harsh illumination of their bobbing headlamps, the gaunt lines of his face looked almost skeletal, and the gray in his hair shone like a beacon.

Alain hopped back across the passage and onto the narrow catwalk skirting the edge of the sewer's flow of waste, taking the lead as they pushed into the northbound sewer. A wave of stench hit him hard, and he coughed, burying his face in his shoulder. Still, he stepped forward, moving with Lotario.

They walked for what felt like ages in the dark. Twisting and turning, their headlamps bobbing in the blackness, time seemed to stretch on, every second lingering between breaths. The watery waste trudging through the trench between them slowed and turned to a trickle, and then into wet muck. Millennia-old brick from ancient Rome arched overhead, some crumbling as they passed beneath. Dust rained on their shoulders in soft whiffs.

The passageway narrowed until they were practically shoulder to shoulder across the damp trench. Wet earth mixed with ancient offal and the detritus of antiquity kept the air dank and humid. Rust and moss hit the back of Alain's throat.

"We should be under the Capitoline Hill now." Lotario looked up, as if he could see the Roman buildings astride the hill above hundreds of feet of earth. The weight of the land above their heads stilled Alain's breath.

"The vampire nest should be close." Alain shifted, reaching for the iron daggers he kept secreted in double sheath holsters at the back of his waistband, beneath his suit jacket. His fingers closed around the hilts, one at a time.

"Do you sense anything?" Lotario's pistol chambered in the darkness, silver bullets locked and loaded. It was the only sound in the impenetrable tunnel. Alain's ears strained for something, anything, beyond their fast breaths and slow footfalls.

Frowning, Alain pushed past the fear sluicing through his veins. He opened his mouth, tasting the air. It was damp, a cold, dark earth that hung on the back of his tongue. A whiff of death, of rot, and of ancient history. The tunnel they were in had to have been formed in the depths of Rome's prehistory.

But there was no dust, no snakeskin or shadow or desert. No electricity arching between his molars.

"No," he whispered. "I don't."

He didn't hear the vampire sliding in front of him, but between one breath and the next, in the light of his headlamp, a fierce face, long fangs cutting down from an angular grin, appeared like a camera flash a hands breadth away from his face. The vampire's sallow skin shone sickly transparent in his headlamp's harsh beam. Shouting, Alain jerked back. His foot slipped on the edge of the catwalk. His head hit the arched bricks behind him. As he fell, a hand shot out, scratching at his scalp. His headlamp went flying, sailing into the darkness before landing with a *crunch* as the bulb cracked.

Alain heard Lotario shout, curse. Heard the sound of glass breaking.

Lotario's headlamp winked off.

Darkness enveloped the tunnel, sealing them in.

A single gunshot erupted, a brief flash of flame kicking from Lotario's pistol and lighting up his face. A bloody cut wept from Lotario's temple.

Howling erupted all around them, coming from every direction, above, in front of, and behind them. Alain kicked, trying to fight off the vampires. A hand grabbed his ankle, bruisingly tight. He tried to kick again. Tried to swing with his daggers. Fear choked his throat, strangling his breaths as his heart pounded. *Not again, not again.*

"Alain!" Lotario shouted. He grunted as if hit by something heavy. Alain heard a body slam against the brick wall. Another gunshot cracked. In the muzzle flash, Alain saw Lotario wrestling with a vampire on his back on the catwalk, one hand pushing the vampire's neck away, the other trying to aim his pistol at the vampire's head. Long fangs, milk white, curved like scythes, arched out of the vampire's mouth.

Another gunshot. The vampires roared, a cacophony of voices and screams and howls that made Alain's blood shriek. He scrabbled against the hands holding him down, but the howling rose, roars rising until his ears popped. Blood trickled down his neck.

He heard a wild snuffling behind him. A scratch, like talons on stone. A single claw shivered down his cheek, breaking the skin and letting his blood run free.

Rumbling shook the ground around him, the tunnels, the bricks overhead. Dust rained, spraying his face. He heaved, trying to rise, swinging his dagger in a high arch. A clawed hand caught his wrist and twisted.

He cried out, collapsed, and felt the brick archway around him give way.

Closing his eyes, Alain tried to curl into a ball, but clawed hands grabbed him, pulled hard, and the last thing he remembered was free-fall and the whistling wind of the sewer whisking over his body as he plunged down into the blackness of the earth.

SCRAPING—SKIN OVER STONE AND EARTH—WOKE ALAIN.

He grimaced and he tried to roll away from the pounding in his head.

A hand gripping his ankle shook him. He jerked. He was being dragged on his back, and the pounding was his head, bouncing off the ground.

Growls bounced off stone walls. Alain reached out, fingers scratching in damp earth and loose pebbles, searching for a grip, anything to stop the claws and the creature hauling him by his ankle. His hands slipped through loose dirt.

A warm, sticky wetness plastered one side of his face. Blood, he realized. Blood pouring from his shredded temple and sliced cheek and gashed jaw. Dirt had ground into the cuts, leaving them open and oozing. One shoulder burned, twisted hard from the fight in the tunnels.

He tried to look around. Green light, putrid and sickly, misted over the stone and earth walls, barely penetrating the pitch-black of the underground cavern. It was just enough light to glimpse the shadowy figure hauling him by his ankle and others hovering around him. Vampires. Made of darkness and twisted by evil until they'd lost every touch of their humanity, the vampires moved without making a sound.

He couldn't feel the weight of his weapons. His daggers were gone, the double sheath at the back of his waistband empty. He hadn't carried his pistols with him that morning. The Holy Water flask he kept in his suit pocket was missing. The silver blade he kept in his ankle sheath was gone as well.

Just him, then, against a nest of vampires.

Where was Lotario? He couldn't hear Lotario's cursing, the sound of anyone else breathing. Anyone else alive. Had Lotario made it out? Had he fought the vampires off? Or had he been trapped? They'd been so far underground, deep in the ancient regions of the sewers.

No. He couldn't be killed by a sewer collapse. Sheer stubbornness would keep Lotario alive, at the very least. He wouldn't die like that.

Wherever Lotario was, he wasn't trapped with Alain. That had to be good. Angelo would find him. He had to. Alain had to believe that. He had to believe Lotario would be all right.

They were supposed to track the murderer, sneak into the vampire's nest during daylight when they should be resting. Reconnoiter. Try to understand why their twelve-year-old pact of silence had shattered with the brutal, targeted murder of a lonely alcoholic woman.

It seemed, he thought, scraping over the stone and dirt as claws dug into his foot, that they had walked into a trap.

And Alain had been snared.

Had the vampires been lying in wait for them? Luring them to that tunnel to spring their trap? Where were they taking him? To the nest? It was apparently far deeper underground and more hidden than he or Lotario had thought. Why had the vampires gone so deep down into the earth?

The green mist crawling along the walls on either side of him skittered away, snaking upward and crawling higher as they entered an underground cavern. Green flame flickered inside recessed slits in the cavern walls, casting the open space in the same grim pall. It was just enough light to know he was in the vampires' nest. That he was in the heart of their sacred bone cathedral.

Skulls hung on the walls, lit from within by a dim glow he couldn't see. Some skulls he recognized as human. Others came from ghouls, revenants, wraiths, and other dark creatures long dead. Still others were monsters and beings he didn't know and never wanted to meet.

Death suffused the cavern, a dank rush of sour air filled with the stench of rot and grave dirt. Lightning arced behind his molars. He felt the weight of a hundred pair of eyes staring down at him. Whispers in a language he didn't know seemed warm as silk as the words caressed his bones.

Somewhere nearby, Alain heard the trickle of water, a burbling that flowed and tumbled around rocks and lapped at a pebble shore. He frowned, trying to place the sound. Tried to orient himself.

The vampire dragging him kept going, hauling him into the center of the cavern. A hiss rose around him. The blood weeping on one side of his face chilled against the open air.

He was in the center of a vampire nest, and bleeding. He swallowed. Gritted his teeth.

Memories tried to force their way into his mind, scenes and screams and panicked pleas and desperate actions from so long ago. He shook his head, physically pushing the memories away.

The vampire flung him by the ankle as if he weighed nothing. Alain landed hard against packed earth and polished stone, sliding and skidding on his burning shoulder and his bloody face. He closed his eyes, holding his breath as his lungs ached and his ribs burned.

A ring of burgundy flame rose around him, a perfect circle, trapping him in the center.

Pain forgotten, Alain pushed to his feet, staring at the flames. Demon Fire in a vampires' nest? His heart hammered as his eyes darted over the flames. Why would vampires have Demon Fire?

Only demons wielded the dark flames. And demons despised vampires. There hadn't ever been an alliance between the two. Never. Not in all the lore and history Alain knew.

Just what was in the darkness with him?

A vampire appeared from the darkness, standing before the ring of aubergine flames. Yellow eyes, like burning sulfur, stared at him from his gaunt face, stretched long and out of proportion, lengthened to grotesque limits. His ears had turned animalistic, curved like a bat's, and ran along the side of his head. Tangled dreadlocks woven with bells and beads and bits of bone were half tied on top of the vampire's head.

"Your heart is racing," the vampire purred. His voice was dry, dust against parchment, a snake shedding its skin across the Sahara. Alain felt the roll of his words in the marrow of his bones.

He stayed silent.

"I can taste your blood from here. It's filled with your fear." The vampire opened his mouth, and his fangs glinted in the dark light of the Demon Fire. He breathed in, hissing, rapture spreading over his face. "You will taste exquisite when I drink you dry."

A shadow stepped close to the vampire, whispering in his ear. Alain could barely make out the shape of the second vampire, but he saw the glittering heat of the yellow eyes in the blackness, staring at him like he was a starving man denied a feast. Alain wiped sweat-slick hands down his filthy pants. He listened desperately, trying to hear anything in the cavern. The water, again, lapping at a shore, teased the edge of his mind.

The first vampire stepped to the edge of the Demon Fire. By the way he moved, he was the alpha. But a different alpha than twelve years ago. Alain held his gaze.

"Who are you?" the alpha asked. "Why does a priest crawl through the sewers?"

Alain frowned. Were they not expecting them? Was this not a trap? Vampires and hunters had warred throughout the millennia, though not for years in Rome, since the pact. Still, the blatant, daylight murder of a targeted human demanded a response, and an explanation. Why had things changed? Why kill Madelena? Why put an end to their pact of silence that let the vampires feed on the edges of society?

"You carried silver and iron. Are you a hunter?" The vampire's long fingers curled.

Silence.

"Why would a hunter penetrate our darkness? Why would you enter our solitude? We have done nothing to bring you here. We have a pact, do we not?"

"After the murder, how could you think we wouldn't hunt you down?"

"Murder?" The vampire bared his teeth, a mockery of a smile. "Who has died, little hunter? And why do we care?"

"The woman in the *Campo*. Her name was Madelena. You slew her."

The alpha stilled, all movement freezing, and for a moment, it seemed like all the air had fled from the cavern, sucked out in a silent rush. "Madelena is dead?" The alpha's voice could have cut diamond. His sulfuric eyes pierced Alain.

It was Alain's turn to still. Did the alpha not know? "Slain by a vampire. By one of yours."

"Not by one of mine!" the alpha roared. Snarling, he snapped his fangs, a savage flash of teeth and terror.

A shout broke the darkness, words barked out in a language Alain didn't know and couldn't understand. Still glaring at Alain, the alpha backed away, disappearing into the darkness outside the ring of fire. More ancient words cut the darkness before stillness and silence stole over the cavern once more. Even the Demon Fire flickered silently, giving off waves of frigidity instead of heat. The flames seemed to leach whatever warmth Alain still had inside him away, and the ground around the ring of fire grew colder than ice.

"Before you die, you will answer our questions." The alpha spoke again, hidden from sight. His voice seemed to echo, to come from everywhere, above and behind, from left and right, all at once. "Tell us about the hunters in Rome."

"Why? What do you want to know?"

"We're searching for someone. You will tell us what we need to know." A hiss followed the words, the alpha scenting the air again. "Hurry. Your blood calls to us."

Alain's gaze darted sideways. He could still hear the water burbling. Maybe twenty feet to his left, deep into the darkness, outside the ring of Demon Fire. He rubbed his hands on his pants again, hiding the way he shifted his body.

"Answer my question," he called. "Why did you kill Madelena?"

"We did not kill the girl," the alpha spat. "She was one of ours."

"She was not a vampire."

"She was one of ours. Answer us, hunter. We may take pity on you and gift you with a new life. You can be very useful to us."

There were no footsteps, no sounds to indicate the vampires had moved closer, but Alain could still feel their presence, the pull of their darkness on him.

Now or never.

Diving to the left, Alain covered his head and rolled through the Demon Fire. Burgundy flames wrapped around him, trying to pull him back, but he pushed on, forcing himself through the ring of fire.

Ice slammed into him, grasping his heart, freezing it. He screamed through gritted teeth as his whole body spasmed. Lashes opened on his back, the licks of the flames peeling away his skin as he broke free. Blood welled from his torn skin, dripping across the cavern floor.

Shouts rang out, roars from the vampires. There were so many more than he had thought. Alain crawled forward, scrabbling toward the sound of the water. The river beckoned, a tributary of the Tiber deep underground, lapping against the vampires' subterranean cavern and their rocky shore.

He hit the riverbank face first, taking a mouthful of dirt and rocks before he plunged deeper. Water hit his arms, pulling him forward, and he scrambled into the river, plunging into the depths as a clawed hand slashed through his side. He screamed underwater but stayed submerged and let the flow of the river carry him away.

He stayed down until he thought his lungs would burst, and then for another ten seconds, counting the moments as spots floated in front of his eyes, obscuring his vision. Only then did he kick to the surface, gulping lungfuls of air as he spat and coughed against the swells of the Tiber smacking him in the face.

An eddy swirled him around. A swell crested over his head. He coughed, tried to clear his eyes, but didn't see the plank that slammed into the side of his head until he heard the *crunch* of wood on bone.

ALPHA LYCIDAS STARED ACROSS THE SWELL OF THE TIBER, THE great river that fed the vampires' nest.

Behind him, his lieutenants waited for their orders. The Demon Fire lay banked, subdued by Alpha Lycidas. Lycidas held out his hand, drops of Alain's blood staining his claws. "Track this hunter," he growled. "Learn everything about him."

His lieutenants nodded.

Lycidas turned away from the river. "Find Linhart. Bring him to me." His yellow eyes flashed. "I will unmake his blood, scatter his bones, and banish his soul to nothingness."

Chapter Eleven

CRISTOPH UPENDED THE WINE BOTTLE INTO HIS PLASTIC CUP.
Dark Chianti sloshed. How many cups was this? He couldn't
remember.

He pulled out the bottle of painkillers the clinic had prescribed
and shoved two in his mouth, washing both down with the wine
before slumping against the low wall circling the rooftop of the
Swiss Guard's enlisted barracks. His crutches lay scattered on the
ground beside him. To his right, the dome of St Peter's stood
against the setting sun, burnished in the amber dusk. Rome
stretched before him, sprawling history and a snaking river tangled
with tourists and priests and too many cars and scooters. Car
horns jockeyed with cathedral bells. Smog choked the air.

Not even Muller and Zeigler, his supposed friends, had tried to
find him over the long hours of the day. When his roommates had
returned after their shifts, they'd found him drunk in his barracks,
scowling out the window in their shared common room. Silent as
they'd changed out of their uniforms, the others had fucked off,
leaving him alone with a slam of the door behind them.

He'd grabbed a fresh bottle of wine and headed for the roof.
He knew when he wasn't wanted. It was a skill he'd acquired, along

with an above average sniper rating, superior hand-to-hand combatives, and always being in the wrong place at the wrong time.

Cristoph drained the last of the wine and reached for the bottle. He upended it again, but nothing came out. Groaning, he rolled the bottle across the roof, glaring at its uselessness.

Useless. That's what he was, too.

It was a mistake to come here. What had he been thinking? A few quiet nights listening to the shaman down in the darkness of Africa, and he'd decided to run for Rome? Had he really thought this place would hold the answers he needed?

He'd made bad decisions in his life, terrible, stupid decisions. Trying to start something with Marco, and then with Dimitri. Almost all of his crushes.

Going to Africa.

But this... Oh, this had to be the worst bad decision of his life. He'd signed up for the Swiss Guard, enlisted in their ranks, and now he was stuck. Stuck in a place where he was hated and even the people he thought had been in his corner had turned him out, and in the end, wanted nothing to do with him.

The words of Job came back to him, sliding along memories of heat-soaked jungles and rivers of blood.

Therefore I will not restrain my mouth;
I will speak in the anguish of my spirit;
I will complain in the bitterness of my soul.

He closed his eyes, groaning. Nightmares in blood lapped at the edges of his consciousness. Words from dusty pages in old books hadn't helped after Africa. He'd listened when the shaman, deep in the heat of the Liberian jungle, suggested he head to Rome. For the Eternal City. Wash his soul in the bells of St. Paul's. Find truth there, the big *Truth*. Capital T Truth.

That hope he'd had when he started this journey seemed thin now, ground down to nothing as he watched the sun set on the Eternal City. Even the bells were hollow. There was no Truth to be found here. Only secrets and pain.

Fine. He wasn't supposed to be here. He could take a message.

What next? Cristoph heaved a deep sigh, tipping his head back against. If he quit the Guard, then his military career was over. He couldn't just return to his old unit. Quitting the Guard meant quitting the army. The Swiss army looked at a Swiss Guard enlistment as something almost saint like. Anyone who quit the Guard was no longer welcome in their ranks. Leaving the Swiss Guard would close more than one door in his life.

The army hadn't been much, but it had been everything he had. There, like everywhere, he'd fit in like a bad screw, all right angles and sharp edges against people who didn't like him, who never wanted him around. He'd been *That Guy*: conversations had stopped when he walked in the room, and there was a mountain of forgotten invitations for drinks or kicking back with the others staring him blatantly in the face.

Unbelievably, his thoughts wandered back to the jungle. Dare he even think it? He chewed on his lip. He could go back to Africa. He'd lost himself there and found something he couldn't explain. Maybe he needed to head back, find whatever part of himself he'd lost. Some irreplaceable part of his soul, perhaps. Something that set him apart from the world, from the rest of humanity.

Whatever he needed, it wasn't here. It had been a mistake to come to the Vatican. Nowhere was that clearer than in the forceful distancing Alain had pushed between them.

He wasn't wanted. Time to cut his losses and run.

It seemed he was always running.

The sun was drowsy on the horizon, burnt umber rays roasting Rome. Rust turned to bronze, lilac and peony strands threading the sky above the city. Cristoph threw his empty cup after the useless bottle of wine.

He'd made up his mind about leaving, but he was no closer to actually walking out. How far would he get with a bum leg and unfinished business with Alain? Though, there really was nothing there between him and Alain. Him and Sergeant Autenburg. If he

TAL BAUER

was lucky, he'd never see the man again. The memories already stung too much, more of his stupid optimism and foolish hope. Alain was the last person he wanted to think about. Or remember.

So, of course, he wallowed in his memories, in his thoughts of Alain.

He'd wanted Alain to be proud of him. He'd wanted to not be a fuckup for once. He'd wanted someone to see that he *was* good enough, where it mattered. All of the spectacular course grades and the field accolades and army awards meant *nothing* if the actual people who thought he was worth something, who wanted him around, were so few and far between.

His one weakness: he craved the tiny drops of kindness he found, so rare in his life. Others seemed to lap up affection, acceptance even, like rain. Why did it seem he was wandering in the desert, always searching but never finding a place in the world to call his own?

Cristoph gazed down the sloping Vatican hill, away from St. Peter's and toward the *Castel Sant'Angelo*. The black turret of the Vatican Bank rose, a barred fortress, not far from the barracks.

So long Eternal City. I'm done with you. The sun's rays peeled away from the Vatican's buildings. Shadows built around the ancient walls. Stillness crept in with the darkness, silence settling as the Vatican turned in for the night. Lights winked on in the Apostolic Palace in the pope and the secretary of state's apartments.

His eyes caught movement by the base of the Vatican Bank. A figure huddled at the base, hidden by the ramshackle assortment of badly parked cars crowding for space. Jerking, staggering steps limped forward. Someone was heading for the barracks, it seemed, wrapped up in a tattered blanket. One hand shot out, grasping the rough stone of the tower. The man barely managed to stay upright.

Cristoph froze. The inner spaces of the Vatican, especially the walkways between the Apostolic Palace, the Vatican Bank, and the Swiss Guard barracks, were some of the most secure spaces in the world. Who was this man stumbling up the hill toward the barracks? A guard, back from a day of debauchery?

142

A chill settled in his bones. A guard back from an assault, like him the night before? Cristoph scooted forward for a better look.

The man pulled himself another step, using the bricks of the tower to keep him going.

It was one step too many, apparently, because he pitched forward, falling flat on the cobbled passageway between the barracks and the bank. He rolled to his back and Cristoph finally saw his face.

Alain!

He was on his feet before he knew it. He stumbled, then cursed as he grabbed his crutches. Uncoordinated and woozy from wine, Cristoph careened sideways before righting himself. He managed a stumbling sway toward the roof access and hopped down the stairs on his good foot, huffing all the way down the five floors to the rear exit of the barracks. He shouldered open the door and heaved his way out on his crutches.

Alain hadn't moved. He was still motionless on the cobblestones.

Cristoph flung himself across the cobbled street. He was at Alain's side in moments, and he dropped his crutches with a clatter as he fell to his knees, barely wincing at the pain in his leg.

His hands hovered over Alain. One side of Alain's face was gashed and bloody, like he'd gone ten rounds with a prize boxer or been attacked with a cheese grater. His suit, normally comfortably rumpled, was shredded, and bruised and flayed skin bled through the suit's tears. He was soaked and shivering, and a filthy blanket wrapped around him. It stank like the city's homeless, like piss and rust and smoke. Cristoph gagged as he peeled it off Alain.

Alain moaned. His teeth clattered together, and his hands reached blindly for Cristoph.

"Alain? What the fuck happened to you?" Cristoph's hands fluttered over Alain, hesitant to touch. There wasn't a piece of skin he could see that wasn't bruised or bloody.

"Have to..." Alain coughed, spat blood on the cobblestones.

His teeth kept chattering. "Have to get to my apartment," he forced out. "Help me. Please."

"You need to get to hospital." Cristoph dug in his pockets, pulling out his cell phone. He punched in the emergency number.

"No." Alain rolled away from Cristoph, trying to get his hands and knees under him. "That's not what I need."

"You're beaten half to death." Cristoph barely caught Alain as he lurched to his feet, almost falling. Cristoph grimaced, putting weight on his cast and his broken foot, and he felt bones and tendons shift and crunch as fire rocketed up his leg. Alain sagged against Cristoph. Cristoph managed to get one of Alain's arms over his shoulder. He gazed at his crutches, tossed aside at the base of the tower. There was no way to get them now. Not without dropping Alain.

Fuck it. He'd endured worse. Cristoph set off, walking on his broken foot and cast, heaving Alain alongside his slow, halting steps.

Alain's moans masked Cristoph's pained grunts. He moved as fast as he could, trying to get Alain to safety and to get off his damn broken foot. He held Alain tight, fingers digging into Alain's side, but he loosened his grip when he realized the slick wetness on his fingers wasn't the unexplained water drenching Alain. It was blood, seeping from a ragged slash around Alain's side and over his back, pouring into Cristoph's hand. He shifted his hold.

Alain's head lolled against Cristoph's shoulder. His eyes closed.

They managed to get into the back door of Alain's barracks. Cristoph stumbled in the narrow hallway, trying not to lose his footing or hurt Alain and managing to do neither. The fluorescent light buzzed overhead as his cast clanked on the linoleum. Blessedly, they were alone. Thank God. He couldn't deal with anyone's staring or their questions.

Not when he didn't know what the hell was going on.

The ancient elevator loomed. He shoved them both through the narrow opening and slammed the brass gate closed. He elbowed the lever up for the fourth floor, to Alain's apartment. The gears squealed, motors whirred. The elevator lurched upward.

"What happened?" Cristoph breathed into Alain's soaked hair. He swallowed, looking down at his bloody palm. "Fuck, Alain. I really need to call emergency services."

"No. They can't help me." One bloody hand gripped Cristoph's shirt. "Just get me home." Alain's breaths burned Cristoph's neck. He was almost hyperventilating.

Cristoph stayed silent, staring at Alain's blood smeared on his fingers. More dripped on the elevator floor, a slow, steady flow that formed a star beneath their bodies.

The elevator lurched to a stop at the fourth floor. Cristoph shoved the brass gate back and hauled Alain through. He set his jaw, forcing away the throbbing in his foot as he dragged Alain down the hallway to his apartment.

Cristoph glared Major Bader's door. *Don't come out, don't come out, don't come out.*

His blood-soaked hand slipped on Alain's doorknob. Alain, inexplicably, locked his apartment. No one locked their doors in the Vatican, or in the barracks. There were no looters, no robbers, not here.

He threw his shoulder into the door, holding on to Alain. The simple lock snapped, and they barreled through together, crashing into Alain's entryway. His broken foot twisted inside his cast, and he screamed behind clenched teeth.

As Cristoph tried to breathe through the agony ripping his foot apart, Alain pushed out of his arms. He pulled at the buttons of his shirt and tugged at his torn clothes as he tried to strip.

"Here." Cristoph grabbed the hem and ripped it over Alain's head, helping him get free of the black priest's shirt. He froze, staring at the mess of Alain's body. It was so much worse than he'd thought. Alain looked like he'd been filleted, like his back had been cut through to ribbons, and one deep, jagged slash curled around his side, crossing through the other gashes, deeper than the rest.

Blood was everywhere, pouring down his skin. He saw the edges of scars beneath the blood. It looked like Alain had been to war.

Alain's hands dropped to his belt. He fumbled as he worked the leather through the buckle. A few kicks, and he left his pants behind in a tangle, one leg catching on his black boot and trailing behind him as he stumbled for the kitchen.

"Jesus! Alain!" Cristoph limped after him. "Where are you going? You need stitches. And antibiotics. You're fucked up!" He dug in his pants for his cell phone again, hobbling after Alain into his cramped kitchen.

He froze.

Weapons hung on every inch of the walls, assault rifles and sawed-off shotguns and pistols and honest-to-God swords of every length, from heavy broadswords to lithe daggers and lean sabers. Dried herbs tied to twine bobbed in front of a dirty window, and more were pressed between heavy books, poking out from between pages. Jars filled with thick ruby liquid lined the walls along the floor. Was that blood? Blood in hundreds of glass jars surrounding Alain's kitchen?

A wooden chest sat in the corner. Alain made a beeline for it, falling to his knees as he wheezed. He collapsed on top of the chest, pressing his bloodied cheek to the wood as he exhaled.

"Alain!" Cristoph dropped to his knees, pulling him back. He cradled him against his chest, searching for a pulse. Christ, that had sounded like a death rattle, like the last exhale Alain would ever make.

Fighting his hold, Alain reached for the chest with shaking hands and flipped it open.

Bowls of split skulls and black stone rested next to curved knives and scythes and blades made of carved bones and teeth from creatures long extinct. Runic tablets and charred stones and bits of wood burned with sigils sat next to bags of herbs wrapped in linen and tied with twine. Phials of oil and water sparked with lightning sat in a row, each stoppered and coated with a wax seal emblazoned with a sigil. More blood-filled jars lined the bottom, labeled sigils messily drawn on the outside of the glass in what looked like the same blood within.

Cristoph went still behind Alain as he stared at a bowl carved from a human skull. He'd seen this before. Magic, wrapped in fire and smoke and wreathed in darkness. He'd seen this all before, down in the blood-soaked jungles of Africa.

Alain knocked over phials and bottles and a blade of ebony as he reached into the chest. He pulled out a bag of ash and a long fang, and then rooted around until he pulled out a green glass bottle at the bottom of the chest. A bowl made from black basalt and carved with golden sigils around the rim followed.

Ancient tarot cards, bloodstained, fluttered from the chest, sliding across the kitchen floor.

"What is this shit?" Cristoph breathed. "Alain, what the fuck is all this?"

Alain shoved the basalt bowl in Cristoph's hands. He reached for the bag of ashes and missed, but grabbed it on the next reach.

Blood pooled on the ground between their bodies, bleeding out of Alain.

He dumped all of the ash into the bowl and then grabbed the milk-white fang. Gasping, Alain ground the fang into the side of the bowl, sweeping it in a circle through the ash three times. Next, he grabbed the green bottle, peering at the label as he blinked hard. Breaking the wax seal with his teeth, Alain poured the entire contents into the bowl.

It was blood.

"Oh shit..." Cristoph balked, turning his head away. He squeezed his eyes closed and tried to breathe through his mouth as the stench of copper and moss hit him hard.

"Spit," Alain grunted, blinking up at Cristoph through his swollen and bloody eye.

"What?"

"Spit! Now!" Alain waved his hand toward the black basalt bowl and the mess of ash, blood, and fang.

Cristoph spat slowly. "You've fucking lost it, man. I have to get you to hospital."

Or maybe, fuck the hospital. He should run the fuck away. Every one of the warnings he'd ignored from Muller, Zeigler, and even Chaplain Weimers pounded inside his brain. Everyone had warned him. Everyone.

Alain reached for the blades in the chest, discarding one after another until he found a curved, silver sickle.

He grabbed Cristoph's hand. Without a word, he rolled the blade across Cristoph's palm, opening his skin. Blood welled, and Alain turned his palm over, squeezing it into the basalt bowl.

"What the fuck!" Cristoph jerked his hand back.

Alain dripped the blade into the bowl, stirring the mush of blood, ash, and fang together as he chanted under his breath in Latin.

The hairs on the back of Cristoph's neck shot straight up, electrified as *something* pulsed through the air. The lights flickered. A bulb popped in its socket. He whipped around. The air around them seemed to tremble, seemed to quake.

Finally, Alain stopped chanting. He dropped the blade, let it clatter to the floor. "Smear this on my cuts." He turned his torn face toward Cristoph. "Everywhere."

"*Fuck* no." Cristoph stared at the bowl. "That will infect you. You can't put this shit on open wounds. I can't—"

"Do it!" Alain gasped. "Now! Put it on me!" His eyes slid closed as he weaved to the side, almost slumping. "*Please...*"

He'd been in Africa during the Ebloa outbreaks, and that had taught him to never, ever fuck around with someone else's blood, with any blood outside of anyone's body, ever. He glared at Alain.

He scooped up a palmful of blood, cursing Alain, cursing the Swiss Guards, cursing the day he decided to come to the Vatican, no, even further back. Cursing the day he was born.

Warm electricity tingled his skin. Shocks zipped up his arm, spiraling straight down his spine.

He didn't think. If he stopped for a single moment, he'd run as far as he could, as fast as he could. He slapped the warm, ashy blood onto Alain's chest, smearing the mess into his still-bleeding gashes.

Alain leaned back, exhaling as Cristoph rubbed the paste over his chest, his arms, his shoulders, and his back. Slowly, he worked up Alain's neck, and, after a moment, patted his bloody palms into the open wounds across half of Alain's face. Alain shuddered, closing his eyes, as though some of the pain slipped from him.

Looking down, Cristoph saw Alain's legs for the first time. Below his briefs, angry purple ligature marks snaked around his thighs, some weeping blood. "The hell? What happened to you?"

"Melusine," Alain breathed. "Had to fight my way out of the river."

"The river..." Cristoph frowned. "The *Tiber*? What were you doing in the Tiber? And what the fuck is a melusine?"

Alain slumped against the kitchen wall and shook his head. He didn't answer Cristoph's questions.

He held up his blood-covered hands. "Does this go on those, too?"

"No," Alain breathed. "That's for vampires. It should work on the Demon Fire, too."

"Vampires. And Demon Fire." Cristoph stared at him. Blood-soaked jungle leaves flashed in his mind. "Fuck, you need to go to hospital."

"Take me to bed," Alain said instead.

"*Alain.*"

Alain reached for Cristoph's cheek as if to cup it. He missed, almost poking Cristoph in the eye. Even though half of Alain's face, his body, was covered in blood and ash, the light in his eyes was brighter than it had been before, and it seemed like the old Alain was fighting his way back.

"Shit," Alain suddenly said, reaching for his pants. Whatever he'd been about to say was gone, as was the moment. "Where's my phone? God, Lotario..."

Silently, Cristoph passed his own phone over to Alain,

struggling with his pants and gripping his empty pockets. Wherever Alain's phone had ended up, it wasn't with him. Alain grabbed Cristoph's phone and punched in Lotario's number by heart.

The cranky older priest's voicemail message blared from the phone's speaker. The phone didn't even ring.

Alain threw his head back, *thunking* his skull against the wall. "Fuck," he breathed. "Goddammit."

"Come on." Cristoph pulled himself up with hands against the wall and the kitchen table. "You need to get off the floor." He held his hands out to Alain.

Alain wouldn't meet his eyes as Cristoph helped him stand. They both winced. Alain stumbled from the kitchen, still trailing his pants behind his boot. He led Cristoph down the hall to his bedroom.

Cristoph followed, limping. He'd let Alain pass out and then get emergency services in there. They could take care of Alain and whatever had happened to him. Whatever break he'd had with reality, whatever had messed up his head. And clean off that blood. And set his foot again, Jesus Christ.

At the door of the bedroom, Cristoph hesitated. Had it only been that morning that he'd woken up in Alain's bed? The duvet and sheet were still twitched where he'd thrown them when Major Bader had barged in. If there was one legacy from his time at the Vatican, it would be emotional whiplash. How quickly things had changed, over and over again.

Alain collapsed into his bed, some of the blood smearing against the sheets. The side of his face, where Cristoph had rubbed the bloody paste, rubbed clean. Cristoph grimaced, expecting to see mangled skin and a bloody wound, now made worse.

Instead, he saw pink skin, smooth and raw. Like a scab had just been peeled off. Fresh, healed skin. Cristoph stared, his mouth dropping open.

Alain didn't seem to care, melting back against the mattress and the pillows with a soul-deep exhale. His breathing evened out, no longer hoarse or rasping or wet. His eyes slid shut as Cristoph moved close, hovering next to the bed as he stared at Alain. At his inexplicable recovery, and at the bloody paste that had healed his wounds.

Alain was already out, already unconscious, half in and half out of the bed.

There was a chair pulled close, as if someone had watched over someone sleeping the night before. Cristoph stared at it. Slowly, he sat, resting his broken foot on the edge of the mattress.

When Alain woke, he had some explaining to do.

HE DIDN'T INTEND TO FALL ASLEEP, BUT A BOTTLE OF WINE AND a handful of painkillers pulled him under. He slept fitfully, jerking in the chair, and kept snorting awake at the slightest twitch from Alain, lost in his own nightmares.

Hours later, his phone vibrated in his pants pocket. Cristoph jumped, almost falling to the floor as he fought off nightmares of bishops grabbing for him, and black eyes, flames rising in a circle in the darkness, and blood dripping from neon green leaves as monkeys howled and disease-filled bodies piled in the streets. Trying to run, trying to escape, and in front of him, Alain beckoned, waving for him. Every time he got near Alain, the older man disappeared, vanishing into the nothing. He tried to scream, but there was no sound.

Then his phone buzzed, vibrating against his thigh, and he nearly toppled the chair.

He pulled his phone out of his pocket, trying to rub the throbbing pain in his foot out over his cast. He winced as he answered. "Hello?"

The priest who worked with Alain—and who'd never given his name—spoke. Cristoph would recognize that gravelly, put-upon tone anywhere, roughened by cigarette smoke and anger. *"Who the fuck is this?"*

"It's Cristoph," he grunted. "Cristoph Hasse."

A beat. *"Fuck. The halberdier?"*

"One of ninety-eight." Cristoph leaned back in the chair. In the dim light slipping through Alain's bedroom window, he could make out the man's blood-crusted skin and his ungainly slump, and the tiny sliver of drool running from the corner of his mouth where he'd pillowed his face. "Look—" he started.

"How did you get this fucking number?" The priest interrupted him, and the telltale sucking inhale of a cigarette echoed across the line after his words.

"Look, fuck you too, all right? I don't want to be talking to you anymore than you want to be talking to me. Alain called *you*, okay? He lost his phone, and he looked like fucking shit, so I let him use mine—"

The priest broke into a coughing fit as soon as Cristoph said Alain's name. He interrupted when he was able to breathe again. *"Alain? He's with you? He's alive?"*

"Well, yeah, he's alive, but *fuck*, what the hell happened to him? What—"

"Where are you?"

Cristoph exhaled and pursed his lips. He debated hanging up on the priest. But Alain seemed connected to him somehow. Maybe even—

Even if Alain's choice in men was the fucking worst on the planet, he wasn't going to be the asshole who kept them apart. "His place," he grunted. "I found him crawling back—"

The line cut, going silent.

Snorting, Cristoph stared at the phone for a moment before shoving it back in his pants pocket. The priest was an asshole, and no amount of prayer or benediction was going to change that.

They work for the Devil, Chaplain Weimers had said. *He's no Christian brother of mine.*

Swallowing, Cristoph watched Alain through slitted eyes as he slouched. It might be easy to try to believe the asshole priest was some kind of sycophant of the Devil's, but that was rooted in his pure disdain for the asshole. Carrying that forward and thinking Alain was also some kind of evil worshipper was harder.

But why? Why was that hard to imagine? Alain had all but thrown him out that morning, dumping him into Major Bader's tender arms instead of helping him personally. And when Cristoph had returned, he'd flat out told him to leave and not come back.

Was he that odious to Alain? And were those truly the actions of an evil Devil worshipper? Or just someone who didn't like Cristoph? Did that morning erase the kindness, the moments when it had just been the two of them laughing over nothing? When Cristoph had been achingly alone and Alain had been his one unasked-for anchor?

But what about that chest in his kitchen? The skulls? The blades? The herbs and talismans and tarot cards, and all of the occult detritus he'd rummaged through? The blood mixture he'd made had healed skin that had been cut down to the bone in moments. Blood and spit—his own—and ash, mixed together with an incantation.

He'd seen those kinds of things before, though not as powerful as whatever he'd smeared on Alain.

But what was it all doing in the heart of the Vatican, in Alain's apartment?

Leaning forward, Cristoph buried his face in his hands. He watched Alain over the tips of his fingers. *He's no Christian brother of mine.*

What was true?

Cristoph threw his head back against the worn chairback, sighing. His foot throbbed, a pounding, bone-deep ache that pulsed with every beat of his heart. His head hurt, too. A hangover, no doubt. Too much alcohol during his pity party, guest of one.

He hauled himself up and let loose a string of muffled curses as his cast hit the ground. Carrying Alain across the courtyard and up to his apartment hadn't been his smartest idea ever. Whatever he'd broken in his foot before, it was a hundred times worse now. He couldn't put an ounce of weight on it, not even faking it. He hopped to Alain's drab kitchen on one foot and leaned against the wall.

Faded wallpaper, a mustard paisley, rubbed beneath his shoulder. In the kitchen, seventies décor begged for a remodel. Dark wood cabinets, stained-glass windowpanes, and mint green appliances. A bottle of cheap vodka, only a third full, sat on the counter next to a chipped coffee cup.

The place screamed desperate bachelor. Or crazed, weapon-addicted, black magic workaholic.

Cristoph stared at the open chest and the mess of bones, blades, runes, and tarot cards strewn on the floor. Herbs lay scattered, and the bottles of blood lining the kitchen walls seemed to shiver, as if the blood inside was alive somehow. Two skulls, one upside down, had rolled free from the chest, and they collided by the edge of the refrigerator and a line of blood jars. Empty sockets stared at Cristoph. The jaws were unhinged, cockeyed and out of place.

He skirted the tableau and grabbed a glass from the dish rack, filling it from the faucet and draining it four times. He left the glass in the sink and hobbled back toward Alain's bedroom.

Boxes in the study caught his eye, as did empty bookshelves.

What was it Major Bader had said? Alain had lived for years in this apartment, but boxes still cluttered his home. His shelves were empty. Well, the guy was a packrat, and not the tidiest. His office looked like some kind of medieval alchemist's library had exploded inside it.

Shapes in the dust on the shelves caught his eye. Empty spaces, places where the wood of Alain's shelves shone cleanly. Places where things had sat, very recently.

He limped closer. Peered into the boxes haphazardly arranged in front of the bookshelves. The tops had been folded down, loosely covering the insides. He peeled one flap back.

Crumbling scrolls stared back at him, piled together next to dark, stained leather bags tied with woven cords. Charms and stacks of runes, bits of burned wood and tumbled crystals. Human bones, etched in languages that looked older than the written word. Blades of obsidian, of silver, of iron, and of bone. Curved sickles. Mirrors, both clear and reflective, made of blackened glass, darker than midnight. Candles, burned to nubs. Vials of oil and water with crosses etched on the glass.

Bullets. Piles of bullets. Nine-millimeter rounds. But not the kind he'd seen before. Iron tips. Silver tips. Some with crystal tips, what looked like quartz on top of the bullet's jacket.

Shotgun shells. But not filled with slug or shot. Salt leaked from one broken shell, a thin line falling like snow when he plucked it out of the box.

His eyes caught the windowsill, across the room. Something glittered on the ledge, beneath the glass. He stared. It was too far to walk, dammit, and his foot still hurt.

He recognized it a moment later. Salt. Alain had poured salt under his window, a long line stretching from edge to edge.

Cristoph closed his eyes as he squeezed the shotgun shell in his palm.

What was it all doing in the center of the Vatican? In Alain's home?

He's no Christian brother of mine.

His heart lodged in his throat as his breath crashed through him. His chest heaved, trying to draw in air that wasn't there, trying to breathe through the sudden panic seizing him. The urge to run, the need to flee, screamed from his bones. His skin puckered, desperate to move, and his guts twisted, trying to claw their way out of his body. As if his body wanted to be free of his soul, free of where he was.

Banging crashed through the apartment, wood hitting the cinderblock walls of the front hall. Cristoph jumped. He fell to the side, catching himself on Alain's empty bookshelf.

"*Alain!*" The asshole priest's voice burst through the apartment. "Alain! Where the fuck are you?"

"Shh!" Cristoph stumbled into the main hall. "He's sleeping, asshole. You want to wake him up?"

The priest glared at him. His nostrils flared and his face turned almost purple as his mouth twisted. Narrowed eyes burned into Cristoph. Finally, the priest spoke again, after a long exhale. "He is alive?" He spoke softer, though his voice still scratched at Cristoph's eardrums, still grated down his spine.

"Yeah, he's alive. He's fine, after he made me smear some kind of bloody bullshit on him. What the fuck happened?"

The priest dragged one hand down his face. He seemed to melt, as if his bones turned to jelly and everything that held him up crumpled within. He sagged forward, shoulders slumping, and shoved past Cristoph as if he wasn't even there. Cristoph hopped after him, balancing both hands on the wall. He followed the priest into Alain's bedroom.

The priest was already leaning over Alain, holding his face in both hands, just inches apart. Cristoph limped back to the bedside chair.

"You did this?" The priest gestured to the dried blood flaking off Alain and smeared all over his sheets. It looked like a murder had occurred in his bed.

"Yeah. Alain mixed up ash and blood and a fang. He cut me. Made me spit. Then told me to smear it everywhere."

The priest clapped his hands on Alain's face, shaking him gently before pulling back. "You," he said to Cristoph, weariness clinging to his words, "saved his life." He squeezing Cristoph's shoulder. A tiny smile appeared on his face. "Well done."

He didn't know what to say. He said nothing.

The priest disappeared down the hallway, heading for the kitchen. Cupboards banged and glasses clinked on the countertop. Footsteps came back down the hall a moment later. The priest returned bearing two glasses of amber liquid. He held one out to Cristoph.

Scotch tickled his nose, a sweet, tawny burn. He fought down a stab of nausea.

"Thanks," he said, scrunching up his face. "But I've had enough of priests offering me alcohol."

Shrugging, the priest knocked back both, one after the other. "More for me," he grunted, breathing through the burn with a deep rasp. The priest collapsed on the edge of the bed between Alain and Cristoph.

Alain rolled away, snorting and burying his face in the pillow. Healed skin stretched over the sheets, flaked with dried blood, his muscles flexing in his back as he slept. Cristoph's narrowed eyes strayed over his body. No more cuts, no more bloody wounds. Scars for days, what looked like a lifetime spent in hand to hand combat. But the bloody, ashy paste was healing Alain, somehow.

His hand ached. Slowly, he unfurled his clenched grasp. A salt-filled shotgun shell lay in his palm.

"What *is* all this?" He turned his glare to the priest. "What happened to him? He said something about vampires. What is this stuff? The blood? The skulls? The special bullets?" He held out his hand. "The salt? Who are *you*? Why did Chaplain Weimers throw you out of St. Anne's?"

"Your foot. It's broken, right?"

"What?" Cristoph shook his head. "Yeah, it is, but answer my questions."

The priest wrapped one hand around the back of his cast and pulled his foot up into his lap. Cristoph fell back in the chair. "Fuck!"

"My name is Father Lotario Nicosia," the priest said, cutting off Cristoph's protests. He pulled a blade from a sheath hidden beneath his suit pants, tied to his lower leg and stretching from his boot to his knee. The silver gleamed, catching the moonlight outside Alain's window. "You won't find me in any of the Vatican records. Like all of this, I don't exist."

Cristoph gripped the seat arms, his nails digging into the worn corduroy fabric. He tensed, tried to pull away. Lotario slipped the blade inside Cristoph's cast and slowly sawed through the plaster.

"The fuck are you doing?"

"I work with Alain. Have worked with him for years. He's very special to me."

The last bits of the cast broke apart with a gentle tug as Lotario slipped the blade free. He set it aside and pulled the remains of the cast off Cristoph's foot. Cristoph groaned as the agony of what he'd done to himself scorched its way up his leg. He'd ruined whatever the doctor had tried to set. It was so, so much worse than it had been.

Lotario wrapped his hands around his calf. He dragged his palms down Cristoph's leg, exhaling in a long, slow breath.

"What are you doing?" Heat built beneath Lotario's touch, a warmth that was just shy of painful. He flinched, trying to pull away, but Lotario held firm. He squeezed around Cristoph's ankle, pressing against broken bone with too much force. Cristoph screamed, throwing his head back, and tried to kick free.

White-hot heat slipped under his skin, slithering around his bones. A flash of light burst from Lotario's palms, flush against Cristoph's ankle. Cristoph cursed, grasped the chair, tried to breathe through his screams.

And then, it was over. Silence, and the light was gone and so was the pain. Lotario slid his hands down the length of Cristoph's foot, whisper soft, dry skin on dry skin.

Watching and panting, Cristoph stayed still. He didn't blink. He didn't move. Just stared at Lotario.

Slowly, he flexed his ankle.

An ache, a lingering soreness, answered his movements. But not agony. Not screaming pain. Not the crunch of broken bones.

"What did you do to me?"

Lotario smiled, but it was worn on the edges, and it didn't reach his eyes. "You know, I've been rooting for you," he said. He reached for Cristoph. "Alain needs to be the one to talk to you, though."

His palm hit Cristoph's forehead, and then there was darkness.

Chapter Twelve

CRISTOPH SMILES AT HIM, NOT THE SARCASTIC SMILE HE GIVES THE *world, but a warm, gentle smile, something that is for Alain only. He's lying on his belly, naked, next to Alain. They're in bed, but not Alain's bed. They aren't in the Vatican.*

Sheer white curtains behind Cristoph flutter. Beyond, a white sand beach stretches wide. So many bright colors clutter his view, houses and tumbling buildings pressed together, awash in a brilliant sea of happy oranges and vibrant turquoises and screaming yellows. Painted stucco beneath red tiled roofs.

And beyond, a glittering, azure sea, topped with softly rolling waves.

Has he escaped? Have they escaped together? He can't remember what happened before this moment, what brought him to wake up next to Cristoph, gloriously naked in a room overlooking the sea.

But he's not going to waste this. Not a single moment.

Alain cups Cristoph's face and smiles back, and it's as if the sun is breaking through storm clouds on a bleak and bleary day. The happiness, the radiant joy in Cristoph's eyes, quakes the foundations of his soul.

He kisses him, slow and sweet, but Cristoph rolls on top of him, a wild grin on his face and mischief in his eyes. Cristoph's hands stroke down Alain's sides.

He can barely breathe, his throat closing at the beauty above him. He can feel every heartbeat, every breath of Cristoph's, every drag of his fingers and his lips across his skin. Cristoph moans, breathes out his name, oh-so-beautifully.

It's all he can do to grasp Cristoph, try to hold him close, try to merge their bodies into one. His hands rise, stroking up Cristoph's back, up his neck, and his fingers drag through Cristoph's hair like Cristoph is his only grip on reality. "I tried so hard," Alain mutters as Cristoph rains kisses like blessings on his lips, on his face. "I tried so hard to not fall for you. But, God, Cristoph. You're amazing. You've turned me inside out."

Cristoph smiles down at him. He takes Alain's face in his hands, holding him so tenderly. "Everything about you," Alain murmurs, "is so strong. You bend for nothing and no one. You're like gold that's been through fire." Cristoph drops a kiss to his lips. "I admire you so much..." Alain breathes against him.

Everything after is a blur, a searing mix of touches and kisses, of bodies sliding and hands stroking down muscles as lips drag over skin. He's a mess, overstimulated nerves and a raw heart, and his bones are on fire as Cristoph rocks with him, pulling gasps and groans and promises from his kiss-bruised lips that Alain swears he'll keep. It's too much, much too much, and he's going to explode, white-hot bliss ripping through him. Alain reaches for Cristoph, cradles his face in his hands, presses their lips together as his orgasm tears free of his soul, burning him alive, burning him anew.

"Cristoph," he breathes, their lips clinging together. "I—"

ALAIN WOKE TO A WORLD OF PAIN. HIS DREAM DISAPPEARED with a crack, vanishing into the ether, leaving him cold and bereft as he reached for empty air.

His bones ached. His muscles burned, as if flayed from his body. His skin felt too tight, pressing in on him from every wrong angle. He buried his face in his pillow, trying to block out the signals from his body.

He froze. Pillow. Bed.

Scrambling, Alain scooted back. Hands spread wide, he grasped at his sheets, spinning around. Dried blood fell from him, adding to the smears on his bed. He looked down. Someone had stripped him to his briefs. Even his boots were gone.

A sleepy groan made him whirl, spinning around until he was facing the chair set beside his bed. The chair he'd stayed up in all night watching over Cristoph while he slept.

The chair where Cristoph now sat, bleary eyed and yawning.

And looking pissed.

"Cristoph?" He shifted, grabbed his sheet and pulled it over his lap. Why was he nearly naked in front of Cristoph? His dreams, his torturous dreams, flashed back. God, had Cristoph...? No, he wouldn't have. *Couldn't* have. "What are you doing here?"

Cristoph frowned, somehow glaring through his sleep-haze as he pushed himself up. "What am *I* doing here? I dragged you back when you collapsed. What happened to *you*? You were torn to shreds."

Looking down, Alain saw his unblemished chest, free of cuts, free of bruises. Dried blood clung to his skin, caught in his chest hair. He picked at it, rubbing it between his fingers.

"You asked me to smear that ashy blood all over you."

No. God, no. Alain's fingers froze as Cristoph spoke. He didn't look up. Couldn't meet Cristoph's eyes. "Where did you find me?"

"Collapsed outside the Vatican Bank. I saw you crawling your way across the courtyard toward the barracks. You were bleeding out. Cut up. Soaking wet." Cristoph hesitated. "When I got you up here, you made that bloody paste from that fucked-up chest in your kitchen."

Alain cringed. He leaned forward, bracing his elbows on his knees.

"You said it was vampires."

Exhaling, he buried his face in his palms. Memories flashed back, snippets of scenes and sounds bled together, like films running on fast forward. The search in the sewers. The vampires attacking. Falling. The ring of Demon Fire.

The alpha vampire.

Escaping into the Tiber, the underground tributary beneath the city. Crawling onto the banks, exhausted after fighting melusine for an hour. Fighting for every single step, all the way into the Vatican.

Collapsing.

Clinging to a warm body. Wrapping his arms around his rescuer. Burying his face in a warm neck and smelling sunshine, green grass, and gunpowder.

Slicing Cristoph's palm with a silver blade. Cristoph's hands spreading the healing balm over his skin. Saving his life.

"What happened, Alain?" Cristoph's whisper trembled. One of his hands reached out. It hovered between them. "What happened here?"

Swallowing the truth ached like swallowing a thousand knives. A complete traitor, his heart rebelled against his vow. Why *not* let Cristoph in? Why *not* tell him the truth? Why *not* try for that beach?

Dark years from his past, one blood-soaked night overflowing with screams and choking sobs, and his heartbroken vow, told him why not.

He pushed down his dreams, his vision of Cristoph—happy, breathlessly happy—and their slow lovemaking. *Push it all down. Crush it all in the center of your chest.*

Except, now Cristoph was in his heart, and when he crushed him there, he'd be crushing his heart for the second time in his miserable life.

"I'm sorry you had to see that," Alain breathed. "I don't normally drink—" His voice broke. Shame poured off him. With any luck, Cristoph would buy that it was the burning shame of an out of control man forced to own up to his failures. "I don't normally drink because it brings out the crazy in me."

Cristoph stared, his face screwed up, eyes narrowed, disbelief screaming from every line of his body.

"I'm sorry you had to see me like that." Alain stood, wrapping the sheet around his waist. "I'm not proud of what I turn into."

"*No.*" Cristoph jumped in front of Alain. "*No.* You're *not* going to lie your way out of this. I know you weren't drunk last night. Don't treat me like I'm a fucking idiot. I *know* what I saw," he hissed. Alain couldn't meet his gaze. "You have no idea what you saw."

"Some kind of magic. Was it black magic?" Cristoph moved in front of Alain when he tried to escape, tried to bypass Cristoph. "Your lights blew out when you mixed that blood spell. Your cuts. They've vanished." Cristoph slid in front of him again. "And you said *vampires*. You said the word."

"I'm a crazy son of a bitch when I'm drunk." Alain finally grabbed Cristoph's shoulders and moved him to the side, never meeting his gaze. "The Vatican makes you crazy after a while. Don't fall for my shit. Be smarter than that."

Watching Cristoph blow his lid was like watching Pompeii erupt. His face twisted, racing from stunned to outraged to murderous in seconds. Hands fisted at his sides, shaking. "You think you can just make me ignore all of this because you *say* so?"

He was so exposed, so utterly exposed, and it had nothing to do with him standing in front of Cristoph in nothing but his briefs and a twisted bedsheet. He stared at the floor.

"What kind of sick fucking games do you play? What kind of fucked-up asshole *are* you?" Cristoph's voice rose, deepening until he was bellowing, roaring at Alain.

In the doorway, Lotario appeared, hovering. His hair stuck straight up and dark circles clung beneath his eyes. His pinched look, the downward turn to his lips, hit Alain hard. He knew what Lotario wanted him to do.

I can't. I just can't.

"Cristoph—"

"I've had *enough* of your bullshit!" Cristoph hollered. "Of everyone's bullshit! You're *everything* everyone ever said about you! You are a fucking monster!"

"No—" Alain reached for him.

Cristoph slapped his hand away. "Fuck you!" He stormed out of Alain's bedroom, the force of his rage sweeping through the apartment like a firestorm. He slammed into Lotario on his way out, shouldering him hard, and kept going.

Lotario took it silently.

The door crashing closed shook the walls. A picture in the front room rattled and fell, glass shattering. An iron blade tumbled from the bedside table.

His knees buckled beneath him and he dropped, falling in a heap. The white sheet flared around him. He hung his head, closed his eyes. Salt dug into his knees, scratching his skin. He shifted, and a broken shotgun shell rolled out from under the bedsheet.

Lotario slid down the doorframe, sitting with a sigh as he knocked his head back against the wood.

"Think he'll buy it?" Alain's voice rumbled, the words fracturing on the consonants.

"I healed his ankle." Lotario nodded to the broken pieces of Cristoph's cast, half under the bed.

"Fuck," Alain whispered. "Goddammit."

Silence strained the air as Alain crushed the shotgun shell in his fist. He threw it against the wall.

"We have another problem. We were led into a trap in the sewers. The vampires who attacked us *didn't* kill the girl," Lotario said, after a moment.

The alpha's voice, like warm smoke caressing Alain's spine, burned through his mind. "I know."

Lotario frowned. "What happened? After the tunnel collapsed, the vampires were gone, and so were you."

He sat back with a sigh, leaning against the edge of his bed.

And told Lotario everything.

POUNDING IN ARCHBISHOP SANTINO ACOSSIO'S TEMPLES SENT

him back to his apartment late in the afternoon while the Roman sun smoldered over the city and heat waves rose from the pavement and cobbled streets. He'd spent the day in tedious negotiations, appointing nuncios to fill openings in Latin America. He'd had to end the last phone call early, cutting off the archbishop of Caracas almost midsentence.

He didn't want to spend his days pandering to the aged drivel of men clambering for a richer station, for the trappings and mortal powers of the earthly world. Banal desires bored him.

Santino kept his apartment locked, unlike the other bishops and archbishops with whom he shared Saint Martha's Residence. There was too much he kept hidden, too much that could be revealed.

An old iron key fitted into the antique lock set in his door. Metal clanged on metal, rust crunching as the key turned. A sigh of wood scraping over plush Turkish rugs greeted him as he pushed into his home. He dropped his briefcase by the front door and rubbed his eyes, and the hem of his cassock shifted across the wood floors as he headed for the kitchen. A glass of wine would set him right.

"Santino."

He paused, one foot still in the air, at the sweet slide of a voice calling out his name from his front room. The voice was clean and cold, holding a touch of laughter inside. But not happy laughter. Mocking, if he had to put a name to it.

Turning, Santino stepped into his front room and stopped. He swallowed, his lips pressing together.

Asmodeus, or at least, the shadow of his being, cloaked in smoke and shuddering with darkness, perched on the edge of his French silk sofa. Rolling wisps of midnight mist tangled off the edges of the man-shaped column, sitting prim and with his head tilted to one side. The Venetian mask, white as death and plain of any decoration, hovered over the shadow where a face should be. Empty sockets in the mask, filled with black, still managed to stare into Santino's soul.

Santino dropped to one knee, wincing as his old bones hit the floor. "My lord," he breathed. "This is a surprise."

"Why? You think that you can only summon me to appear? That I am constrained by your circle of silver and salt? Your runes?" A dry chuckle, like glass shards falling to the ground. "You devoted yourself to me, Santino. I can come to you whenever I choose."

Santino licked his thin, aged lips. "It has been some time." His hands fisted in the loose folds of his cassock. "I thought, perhaps, you had changed your mind."

A whip of smoke, almost like the wave of a hand, and then a dark swirl circled lazily through the air. "The time was not right. There were others at work."

"Others?"

"They don't concern you. All you need to know is that they failed." Asmodeus's mask tilted again. "We require their work to be completed. Are you the man for the job, Santino?"

Santino's gaze rose, meeting the empty eyeholes of Asmodeus's mask. "And what do I get in return?"

Another flick of smoke. The mask gazed at Santino's lavish apartment. "More of this?"

His lips curled back. "You already know what I want."

Silence, save for the shift of smoke against smoke and a whiff of breeze that curled through Asmodeus's shadow. "We require someone inside the Vatican," Asmodeus finally said. "Someone who can gather information for us. Someone at the highest levels of the Eternal City."

"What kind of information?"

"We need to find a man. A hunter."

"Hunters in the Church died out long ago. The fourteenth century."

"Do not presume to tell me what does and does not exist. Hunters exist today." Asmodeus rose from the sofa. Ripples roiled through the shadows. "You know only what you've been told, and what you've been told has all been lies."

Bowing low, Santino dropped his eyes as he pressed his palms to the wooden floorboards beneath his knees. "Tell me the truth of what you seek. I will complete this task for you."

Papers at Santino's desk rustled, moved by an unseen breeze. A heavy velvet curtain twitched.

"We search for a hunter. One man, the current descendant and bearer of the *noumenon*. He comes from a single line stretching back to when your kind lost their trail. Back to the fourteenth century." Asmodeus floated across the floor, a shadowed mist that came too close. "Our first agent toiled through your archives. He was tracing the line of hunters. But he ran into troubles, and, sadly, he isn't with us any longer."

A whiff of smoke caressed Santino's cheek.

"Our next agent was murdered." Asmodeus pulled back, shifting until the smoke towered over Santino. "Before her task could even come to bear." A soft tutting sound, almost disappointed. "Which paves the way for you."

Santino pushed to his feet, steadying himself against the wall as he rose. "Tell me what you seek, and why, and I will find him for you. I swear I will. I will use the entire power and reach of the Vatican to search the world for you."

"He's here in Rome. You must identify him. You must find him."

"And what will happen to this hunter when I do?"

Asmodeus's mask tilted sideways and an almost childlike giggle escaped from behind the blank porcelain mask. Smoke shivered, moving quickly. "He will die," Asmodeus said, as if it were the most obvious thing in the world. "He *must* die."

A moment passed, and then Santino bowed his head and closed his eyes. "It will be done, my lord."

"See that it is."

There was a pop and then a breeze, and when Santino looked up, the black column of smoke and shadow that was Asmodeus was gone. Even the mask had disappeared.

Santino grasped the doorway, leaning into the wood as his knuckles went white.

ALAIN WAS SIX CUPS OF ESPRESSO TOO SHORT FOR A conversation with Commandant Best. Still, the commandant persisted, bullying his way into Alain's office, ignoring Alain's red-eyed, hairy glares and the way his fingers white-knuckled his mug to hide his hands' shaking.

Best didn't waste any time. "What is happening? The *polizia* sent over a classified packet with information about a vampire murder, and His Holiness sent for a personal report." Best's eyebrows arched. "He's never asked for a personal report before. Not once since taking over as the Holy Father."

"Has he heard something? How could he have? We're the only ones—"

"The camerlengo says His Holiness has been having troublesome dreams. He wakes from nightmares constantly."

A scathing retort hovered on the edges of Alain's tongue. "Dreams?" he snorted. "The last one didn't care at all what we did, or how, and now, the new Holy Father says he's having bad dreams just months into his papacy?" Alain scoffed. "Commandant—"

"I realize your faith is not as strong as it once was," Best interrupted. "And that, despite working with the etheric and the paranormal every day, you refuse to entertain that which you cannot see with both eyes. Touch with both your hands." Best sighed. "But His Holiness's dreams *are* significant. He is tapped in to the etheric just as much as we are."

"*We?*" Alain glared at Best over the rim of his espresso. "You are not involved any longer."

"I passed the role on to you as it was passed on to me. As you should be preparing to pass your duties on to someone else. You have done this long enough." Best chewed on his upper lip for a moment, dragging the thin strip of red between his crooked teeth.

"Is there anyone you could pass this on to? Someone... new, perhaps?"

"Jesus Christ." Alain ignored the scathing look the commandant shot his way. "That's what this has all been about, isn't it? Getting me to be a mentor? Putting me with—" He couldn't say Cristoph's name. He just couldn't.

"He reminds me of—"

"*Don't.*" Alain slammed his espresso down. "Don't say it. Don't say his name."

"Twelve years, Alain," Best whispered. "It's been a long time."

"And yet, it feels like yesterday." Alain pasted a wan smile on his face, trying to tell the commandant to back off and tread carefully through these bloody waters. Through these memories.

Best didn't heed his warning. "The vampires are back." He stared at Alain as he spoke, holding his gaze as if he didn't know the world was dropping out from beneath Alain with those words.

Alain wanted to snarl, to scream, to shout and snap and rage. He wanted to wail at the sky and demand answers. He wanted to storm the sewers and burn the vampires' bones. Boil the blood inside their bodies. Destroy their millennia-old civilization. Not just destroy. Desecrate. Scatter their bones and their lives to the winds, as his own life had been scattered. Had been destroyed.

He wanted to leave them with nothing but emptiness, a longing that could never, ever be filled. A waking nightmare for an existence. He wanted them all to suffer, as he had suffered.

He felt the weight of his office, of the long years of hunting, pull down on him like dust burying forgotten manuscripts. He felt the grounded power of demon trap beneath his feet, tugging on his bones. Runes etched into bits of teeth and claws stared at him from his shelves across the room. Scrolls of parchment inked with spells from dozens of civilizations piled haphazardly on the floor. He was just like the detritus of his office: a forgotten scrap of antiquity.

And he was tired, so very, very tired, of it all.

Especially now, standing in front of a hunt that had too much

TAL BAUER

similarity to his past. To twelve years ago, his broken heart, and his blood-soaked vow.

"The vampires are back." He met Best's gaze. "A woman was murdered by one after being attacked by a ghoul."

"That's a bit backward. Ghouls scavenge after vampire kills. They're carrion creatures, not hunters of their own."

"This time, a ghoul attacked the victim first. We chased it off and stopped that attack. We put her under surveillance for the rest of the night, and at dawn, the police were called off. By midmorning, she was dead, her throat ripped out."

Best folded his arms across his chest and pursed his lips.

"Father Nicosia and I set a locating charm on the blood inside the wound to trace the murderer. The charm sent us deep into the old Roman cloacae. We went during the day to find the killer. They should have been resting." Alain hesitated. Breathed in. "It was a trap. The vampires there attacked us, thinking we were invading. The tunnel collapsed and I was taken back to their bone cathedral. Father Nicosia escaped."

Best leaned forward, all frowns and worried lines suddenly. "You were taken? Captured?"

"They dragged me down to their darkness. Set me in a circle of Demon Fire."

A harsh inhale from Best, but no words. His hands clenched, knuckles going white.

"Something else. They have a new alpha. I didn't recognize him, and he didn't know me when he spoke to me. He wanted to know what I was doing there."

Best sat back. He turned his head, quizzical as he watched Alain. "A new alpha... A change in leadership sometime in the past decade. Even still, they know that such a blatant murder demands that we respond."

"They didn't kill her."

Silence. "Then who did? Do we have another invading nest?"

Alain rolled his neck, trying to loosen his stiff joints. He wasn't a twenty-three-year-old anymore. A long night out, clinging to life while trudging through Rome, wasn't the easiest to shake off these days. "Father Nicosia went back to the murder scene. Tried the charm again, this time on a drop of vampire blood he found away from the body. It pointed him toward the *Castel Sant'Angelo*. A totally different nest. It had been abandoned, though."

"Damn. Two vampire nests in Rome. I hoped we'd never have to go through that again. They'll fight it out for supremacy and hunting grounds if we don't stop them." Best stroked one hand down his face, his fingers scratching the sides of his jaw. "Why would you both have found the first nest? What in her blood drew you to the alpha's location?"

"I don't know. Lotario thinks the alpha was being framed. Maybe the second nest wants us to take out the first, do their dirty work for them. If it's two nests fighting it out, then they'll want to destroy each other. Why not use us to do their dirty work?" After all, they'd done it before. Bits of the alpha's smoke-smooth voice curled through his mind. *She was one of ours.* "The alpha was upset when I told him she was dead. He didn't know."

Best stared.

"He knew her."

"You'll have to dive deep into her history. Why was she involved with the vampires? What happened in her life? How did she tangle with the darkness?" Slowly, Best stood, his knees and hips groaning. "This is an unusual case, Alain. And, because of your past... What you've been through." He tried—and failed—to offer a calming smile to Alain. "I am here if you need anything."

Alain raised his espresso in a silent salute. Best turned to leave.

"Commandant." Alain closed his eyes. "Where is Luca?"

At the doorway, Best hesitated. "Major Bader took some personal time. He's away until the day after tomorrow."

"Luca?" Alain snorted. "That man doesn't know the meaning of a personal day. Or relaxation."

"He's not here, Alain." Best fixed Alain with a long look. "He's not here."

IT WAS PAST TIME TO GO.

Cristoph had overstayed his welcome. Wasn't it just yesterday he'd resolved to get the hell out of the Vatican? So long Eternal City? Hadn't he said those words? But Alain had waltzed back into his life and turned everything upside down. *Again.* Fuck it. Forget Alain and his occult nonsense. His talk of vampires. Whatever that mad blood magic had been. His crazed weapons collection and creepy apartment full of supernatural detritus. Had Alain really stayed up all night boxing up his things so Cristoph wouldn't possibly see his stuff when he woke up? What kind of a freak was he?

He's no Christian brother of mine.

Cristoph leaned back against the wall in his dorm room, half in and half out of his T-shirt. He closed his eyes and *thunked* his head back against the wall.

He flexed his toes. Rolled his ankle. Only a slight stiffness, but the pain, the brutal, bone-crushing pain, was gone.

Who was Lotario Nicosia—other than an asshole, good for nothing priest—who made him see red, who cupped Alain's face and stroked his cheekbones, and who had healed his ankle with just his touch?

These were questions he wouldn't ever have an answer for. It was time to go. Time to leave all of this behind. Walk out that door and never look back.

He pulled on his shirt. A tattered duffel he'd carried since the first day of army basic training held the rest of his clothes—T-shirts, some jeans, a sweater. He palmed his phone and his wallet, unplugged his charger, and shoved it and his toothbrush and toothpaste into the bag. A final zip, and he was through packing. Not much to show, at twenty-six years old, but it was all he had in his life.

Made it easy to leave, every single time.

Cristoph slung his duffel over his shoulders and headed for the door. He was out of here.

No looking back.

PERCHED ON TOP OF THE VATICAN WALLS, TUCKED BETWEEN A moss-covered crenel and a sculpted cherub, the vampire Alpha Lycidas had sent out to follow Alain lurked in the shadows. His yellow eyes gleamed in the afternoon sun, an evanescent film swirling over the surface, gained from so many years underground.

Those eyes followed Cristoph, watching as he slipped out of the Vatican and headed into Rome.

Silently, the vampire followed.

Chapter Thirteen

LOTARIO CAME TO ALAIN'S OFFICE AFTER BEST LEFT, BLUSTERING in smelling of cigarettes and burned espresso and bearing a box of manuscripts from the Vatican archives. He dropped the box on Alain's desk, knocking over an empty paper cup that spun across Alain's papers.

"I didn't find much." Lotario pulled out three slim volumes, old leather and hand-stitched spines creaking, yellowed papers revealing their wizened age. "One ancient Germanic story about a battle between vampires and demons, written in rhyme." He tossed the first manuscript down on the desk. "One unpublished magical treatise from a monastery in France, studying Demon Fire after an exorcism gone wrong." He dropped the second manuscript, and a puff of dust burst from the pages. "And one journal from Carpathia documenting a solitary vampire's descent into madness." He let the last manuscript fall on top of the others.

"A lone vampire?" Frowning, Alain picked at the corner of the old journal, holding it between his fingers. A rusty brown liquid stained the bottom right corner of the journal, from the heavy leather cover through the handmade, yellowing pages. "Vampires aren't solitary creatures. They live in clans and nests. I've never heard of a vampire living on its own."

"Neither has the research." Lotario collapsed into a metal folding chair, the legs whining. "I had to dig hard for that one journal, and it's the only thing I could find at all on a solitary vampire."

"Why are we interested in this?"

Swallowing, Lotario clasped his hands between his knees. "Because that nest I found in *Castel Sant'Angelo* was small. At first, I thought it was just a few vamps, but—" He squinted and held Alain's gaze. "There was only a single vampire there. It was just a solitary nest."

"What happened to the lone vampire in Carpathia?"

"First it was anger. Rage. Lashing out at everything. He was a captive, so he tried to attack the monks who held him prisoner. Then came confusion. Disorientation. He screamed for days. Wailed. Called out for his clan."

"Where were they?"

"No one knew. They found the vamp half staked to the ground. No clue who did it, or why. Or where his others were. No one ever came back for him."

"What happened?"

"One of the monks got too close. He reached through the bars of his cell and killed him. Tore him apart, pulling bits of his body through the cell bars so he could feed. After that, the monks left him alone. Ignored him for months. They came back down a year later, checking on what had happened to him all alone in the dungeon."

Lotario hesitated.

"And?"

"He'd eaten himself. Or parts of himself. Desperate for blood, he'd started trying to drink his own. But vamps only pump blood after they drink another's, and by the time he tried to feed off himself, he had to cut all the way inside. He'd cut himself open. Tried to cut out his heart."

The journal clattered to the desktop. Alain's gaze fixed to the blood-colored stains covering the corner. "Lotario... what does all of this have to do with—" He closed his eyes. "Why are we talking about this?"

"Because while the vampire was locked up and alone, while he was going crazy, the monks in the monastery reported that everything else was going crazy, too. Ghouls appeared, even though there were no signs of other vampires. No vampire kills. Revenants stalked the forest. Wraiths terrorized the village. As the vampire went crazy, paranormal activity around the monastery increased."

"You think we have a solitary vampire here in Rome? Slowly going insane?"

"It would make sense, yes? Ghouls wandering around with no reason. The risings? The attacks? So much has happened in just the past few weeks. Could it be because of this vamp going crazy?"

"Could be." Alain leaned back in his chair, wincing as his still healing skin rubbed against his shirt. "But why? Why is the vampire off on his own?"

"Maybe he was exiled. Or he rebelled. He may have framed the alpha and the first nest for the girl's death. Maybe he wanted us to take them out. Revenge? Or," Lotario spread his hands wide, "maybe it's connected to the Demon Fire. How did they even get their hands on that? Only demons can light those flames."

"The alpha was wielding them down there."

"Is there some kind of alliance between the demons and the vampires? Is that why they've burrowed so deep underground? Deeper than before?" Lotario shook his head. "None of this makes any sense. All we know is that we have a lone vamp somewhere in Rome that killed yesterday. And who is slowly going crazy."

"And another nest with Demon Fire." Alain frowned. "But why would this solitary vampire kill the girl?"

"He needed the blood? He wanted a fresh kill?"

Alain shook his head. Parts of the puzzle didn't fit. Not everything was adding up. "The *Campo* is a hike from the *Castel Sant'Angelo*. He would have had to wander far, and then find a specific person hidden in her apartment, and in the daytime no less. It's extremely unlikely that she was a random kill." He chewed on the inside of his cheek. "God dammit, I hate vampires." "We just need to find this one and put him down before there's another murder. He'll need to feed again. We need to get rid of him before the whole city goes mad with more risings." Lotario dragged one hand through his hair, making the ends stand wild on his head. "I'll go back to his nest. See what I can pull from the crap he left behind—"

"I'll come with you."

Lotario looked away. "Alain... I don't want to be working this case. I don't want to have anything to do with the vampires. And I wasn't the one who—"

Alain's fists clenched until his fingernails dug into the skin of his palms. A tight pull, a slice, and then he felt warm wetness squishing around his fingertips. Blood. He'd made himself bleed.

How ironic.

Lotario exhaled quietly. He couldn't hold Alain's gaze.

"I want them to die," Alain hissed. "I want them all to die, for what they did. For—" A drop of his blood landed on the edge of the rough sketch he'd drawn, trying to detail the vampire's bone cathedral deep under Rome.

"We also need to find out more about this girl." Lotario shoved his hands into his pockets. "Why don't you get with Angelo and see what he's dug up on her? You don't have to force yourself into this."

Part of him wanted to let go, to release himself into the escape Lotario offered. Sure, he'd take the research into Madelena. Lotario could skulk about the *Castel Sant'Angelo* and pick through the dead remnants of a crazed, solitary vampire. He could stay away, far away, from everything, and especially from his memories.

Another part of him raged. Wanted to rise up and throttle Lotario, bellow in his face and grab his throat, squeeze until Lotario fell to his knees and begged for forgiveness. How dare Lotario take this from him? Take his revenge, his vengeance? Take

what he'd dreamed of for so long—a chance to destroy the
creatures who had ruined his life. Who had taken so much from
him. Who had taken away the man he'd loved and cursed his life,
ruining any hope of finding another love? Any hope of building a
future with Cristoph?

He looked up. Heat burned behind his eyeballs, flickering his
vision. Red lined the edges of his narrowed gaze, a hellish haze of
fury. He opened his mouth—

The antique brass telephone blared on the desk. Snarling, he
grabbed the handset and tried to hide the shaking of his hands as
he flexed his fingers. "Autenburg," he growled.

"*Alain, is Lotario with you?*" It was Angelo.

Alain looked up and found Lotario's gaze. "Yeah, he's here."

"*Look, we've finished our preliminary workup on the girl. Processed
her apartment. Brought her in. My office is handling her autopsy, and we
should have the results back tomorrow.*"

"You found anything yet that can help us?"

"*Yeah,*" Angelo sighed. "*And you're not going to like it.*"

"Well, go on," Alain prompted when Angelo fell silent. "What
won't we like?"

"*The girl was a prostitute.*"

"That's hardly unusual in Rome." Alain angled the handset
toward Lotario so they both could hear. Lotario rolled his eyes.

"Rome's oldest profession, in fact," Lotario said.

"*Yeah, cute,*" Angelo snapped. "*But one of her clients was one of your
own. Carlo Nuzzi.*"

Blood drained from Lotario's face. He turned wide eyes to
Alain. "*Cardinal* Carlo Nuzzi?"

"*The Vatican Secretary of State.*" Angelo whistled on his end of
the line. "*And it gets better. She had a flash drive in her desk. Looks like
it's a rip and copy of the cardinal's hard drive. Emails, private files, Vatican
documents. She had everything.*"

"What in the fuck..." Lotario breathed.

Alain's hand clenched hard on the phone's handset. He couldn't stop shaking. "A vampire murdered a prostitute who was spying on the cardinal secretary of state?"

She was one of ours...

"Shit." Alain almost dropped the phone, the handset sliding along his blood and sweat-slick palms. "Shit, the alpha. He knew her. 'She was one of ours,' he said."

If possible, Lotario paled even further. His thin lips pressed together. "She was spying for the vampires. For the alpha. And if the alpha and his nest are somehow working with the demons..."

"*I've got the flash drive here. I'll drive it over to you.*"

"We've got to go talk to Cardinal Nuzzi." Lotario rubbed one hand down his face, covering his mouth with his palm.

"Angelo, call when you're on your way." Alain hung up on Angelo's grunts. Behind him, his black suit jacket hung off his chair. He grabbed it, wincing as he slid it on, and followed Lotario out of his office.

A whiff of sweat and grass slipped through the air. He closed his eyes and inhaled Cristoph's scent: green grass, sunshine, and gunpowder. He lowered his head to his jacket lapel. Cristoph flowed through him.

He slumped against the doorway as he fought to stand. His jacket had been on the back of the chair in his bedroom, thrown there sometime in the past few weeks, and when he needed a new one, he'd grabbed it without a second thought.

Now he had to smell Cristoph on him, smell his most recent fuck up, and carry that misery heavy on his shoulders.

"Alain! Let's go!" Lotario barked at him from the end of the hall.

I am so sorry, Cristoph. Alain pushed off the doorway and jogged toward Lotario. *I am so damn sorry.*

"CARDINAL NUZZI, WE KNOW THIS OCCURRED." ALAIN LEANED forward on the cardinal secretary of state's Italian sofa in his lavish apartment's sitting room, beneath a crystal chandelier and an original Da Vinci. "We're not here from the Congregation for the Clergy." The Congregation for the Clergy handled all administrative—and disciplinary—functions for the clergy within the Catholic Church. "We're not here to punish you. We just need to know what happened and when. We need to figure out what kind of exposure we're dealing with."

Cardinal Nuzzi, an old man weighed down with the exposure of his guilt, leaned forward on his sofa, opposite Alain. His black cassock pooled on the floor and his red sash tumbled from his lap. His heavy pectoral cross swung in the space between his knees. He sighed, and it was as if a window opened inside a church and all the musty air inside whispered out.

"She was a lost girl," Nuzzi said slowly, his Italian accent rumbling through the words. "I was only trying to help her."

I bet you were. Alain pressed his lips together and looked down. "How long had you been seeing Madelena? How long had you been intimate with her?"

"Only a few weeks. Not long."

"How did you meet?"

"She came up to me one day when I was out in Rome. I was giving alms and saying prayers over the city's homeless. Small Masses and prayers for the people. She was in the back during one and followed me. I bought her a cappuccino. She said she wanted to talk." Nuzzi closed his eyes and exhaled. "I went back to her apartment." He spread his hands, looking up at Lotario and across to Alain. "It happened so fast... I only wanted to help her."

"I'm sure," Alain demurred. A lost, frightened, lonely woman was not the same person they had met, downing whiskey straight from a plastic bottle and sucking on the nub ends of cigarettes. He'd seen it before. Women and men who played a part, determined to wile their way into another person's heart. It was always for an end. Always.

"How would she have had access to your computer? Did you bring her here?"

"No, no." Nuzzi pinched the bridge of his nose. "I would visit her. Three days ago, I spent the morning at the seminary. I was guest lecturing, and I had my laptop with me. After, I went to see her. It was the only time I had it at her apartment."

"She must have ripped the files then." Lotario, leaning on the back of Alain's sofa, pushed himself up and paced in the walkway behind the sitting room. Marble statues bracketed both ends of the hallway and a plush Turkish rug softened his heavy footfalls. Gold glittered from mosaics hanging on the walls.

"If you are not with the Congregation for the Clergy, then who are you with?" Nuzzi frowned. "What did you say your names were?"

"Father Roberto," Lotario smoothly lied, straightening his jacket. "And this is Father Hasse."

Alain's breath hitched. He turned, sending a withering glare over his shoulder.

Lotario ignored Alain. "We are on His Holiness's special commission," he continued. It wasn't too far from the truth.

"Which one?" Nuzzi cocked his head. "I know all of them and I don't know you two."

Lotario grinned, his teeth seemingly feral, almost savage. "You don't know them all."

"That's enough." Alain stood, still glaring at Lotario. Lotario held up his hands and backed away. Alain turned back to Nuzzi. "Thank you for your time, Cardinal Nuzzi. We believe we can contain this situation. No one will know about your indiscretion."

"Ah. You must be lawyers, then."

"Not quite." Alain buttoned his suit jacket and headed for the cardinal's door. Lotario's borrowed Roman collar pinched his throat. He needed to get rid of it, now.

"You have my thanks all the same." The cardinal tried to smile. "If you please." Nuzzi called out, his fingers wringing together. "Where is Madelena now?"

Alain looked down.

"She's dead," Lotario said. He didn't blink.

Nuzzi fell sideways, his shoulder leaning against the wall. One wizened hand grasped a marble statue. "My God." He crossed himself and closed his eyes.

And then opened them, fixing Alain and Lotario with a hard glare. "I think it's time for you to leave."

ON HIS WAY OUT OF ROME, CRISTOPH HEADED TO THE *CAMPO*.

Music threaded around him, European dance tracks and Korean pop and Russian heavy metal from a dozen different bars along the square. The sun was setting on Rome, and long shadows stretched across the *Campo* as tourists and farmers' markets traded places with barflies and wandering groups of drunks. A gaggle of women in barely-there sequined dresses smoked cigarettes while men stared at the long lines of their legs.

Cristoph watched out the window of his bar. He turned back to the bar and hung his head over a shot of whiskey, glaring at the bar top.

Someone jostled him, bumping into his back as they passed the bar. He was ready for a fight. Eager for one. Almost desperate for a chance to lash out. He turned on his bar stool, wobbled slightly, and snarled.

Words died in his throat. His hand clenched on the tumbler of whiskey. Rage swirled in his head, dizzying his thoughts, but everything within him stilled when his gaze stuttered to a stop at the bar's entrance.

Alain waited, just inside the bar's entrance. He watched Cristoph, sent him a tiny smile, a little wave. Slowly, he pushed through the crowd, making his way to Cristoph's side.

Cristoph followed his every move, his eyes glued to Alain's dark frame.

"Hey." Alain rested one hand on the back of Cristoph's barstool, right above his ass. Alain's thigh pressed against Cristoph's. "Can we talk?"

Warmth slid up Cristoph's spine. The smell of roses and rot tickled the air. He coughed. "Do you smell that? Like... rotten eggs?" Something sulfurous hung in the air.

"Maybe something burned in the kitchen." One of Alain's hands dropped to Cristoph's arm.

His thumb stroked over Cristoph's wrist.

A heat haze slithered through Cristoph's mind. The buzz of the bar faded away, the bustle of people surrounding them, the music threading through the air. Only the faint scent of sulfur hung in the air, mixed with dead roses and a faint stench of rot.

But Cristoph wasn't paying attention to the smell. Not anymore.

He had eyes only for Alain now—and a warm, shy grin.

Alain smiled back, a dark gleam edging his eyes. "Is that better?"

Chapter Fourteen

Lotario's phone rang as he and Alain thundered down the steps of the Apostolic Palace. Angelo.

"You on the way?" Lotario pulled a cigarette out of his pack with his lips and lit it one-handed.

"*Something's come up.*"

Alain jogged close to Lotario's side as Angelo's voice grunted out of Lotario's speaker. "What's going on?"

"*Just got a call routed from the emergency line. Someone in the Campo called in a murder. The description fits the profile of an incubus.*"

Lotario rolled his eyes as Alain groaned. "An incubus? Now? Seriously?" Lotario sucked down his cigarette after speaking. "I swear, there's too much going on right now. This has to be coming from the crazed vampire. What else could explain all this shit?"

"*The hell are you talking about?*" Angelo snapped at Lotario through the phone.

"We'll fill you in later." Alain grabbed the phone from Lotario and jerked his head toward the car park behind the barracks. Three other cars had boxed in Lotario's Bug, nearly blocking the rusted yellow monstrosity. Lotario cursed. "We talked to Nuzzi. He's clueless. We'll need to get a look at that flash drive and see what she stole. Then go from there. But we think we have a lead on what's been happening recently."

They slipped into Lotario's Bug, doors slamming on rusted, creaking hinges.

"Fucking Vatican gendarmerie," Lotario fumed. "Can't control the fucking parking around here. Can't trust them with fucking anything."

Angelo snorted at Lotario's outburst. "*I'll give you the drive when you get here. Head for the Campo. We gotta get this incubus first.*"

Lotario puffed his cigarette as he started up his car, nudged a Lexus and a Mercedes, and then rumbled out of the Vatican. "So what are we rolling to?"

The crackle of a *polizia* radio echoed over the phone. "*We got a call routed to us about ten minutes ago. Some barfly went out to the back alley behind the Siam Hookabar and found a desiccated corpse. Young male, late twenties. He was still warm when the medics showed up, but drained dry.*"

Lotario swerved through Rome's ever-present traffic. The sun was setting, dusk falling on the city like damp silk. Plum light bled into shadows, painting the capital in shades of amber and onyx and midnight. Traffic lights winked on. "How do we know it wasn't a vampire?" Smoke breathed from Lotario's mouth with every word.

"*No fang marks. The corpse wasn't bled out. It was desiccated. All fluids gone, not just the blood. Eyes, lungs, muscles, everything dried and destroyed. Looked like a piece of jerky. A dried-up husk. There was also anal penetration, but no semen. No condom on the ground, either. Beyond that... even I could tell the soul had been ripped out.*"

"How could you tell that?" Lotario grunted around the cigarette bouncing on his lips.

"*Just could. You know, I do listen to your weirdness. I've picked up a few things these past few years.*"

"We'll deputize you, Angelo. Join the club." Lotario turned left down an alley, barely missing oncoming traffic. "We're headed for the *Campo*. Want us to meet you at the Hookabar?"

"*No. The medics have taken the body. We need to find the incubus. I've set up a perimeter around the square, but I need your help to narrow the search.*"

Lotario swung the car around the back alleys leading to the *Campo*, turning left, then right, and left again and driving them up to the *polizia* barricade near the Hookabar. "We're at the scene," Alain said, pushing open the rusted Bug's door. "We'll get the incubus's energy and call you back."

They headed for the *polizia* tape, ducking beneath the barrier and nodding to the officers who politely ignored their existence. Ahead, the outline of a body had been sketched on the ground and numbered evidence tents lay scattered around the concrete. Not as many, though, as there would be with a human murder. No bullet casings or blood spatter. Just a desiccated corpse and a string of questions.

Lotario dropped down next to the sketch and pressed his palm to the warm concrete, right where the victim's heart would have been.

Alain stood back. If he wanted to, he could drop down and tap into the etheric alongside Lotario. He could press his palm to the ground and try to trace the last vestiges of energy from the corpse and from the incubus. He could cast charms and work healing spells and wield so much more than just his iron blades, salt shotgun, and specially tipped bullets.

But that brought him back to the last time he'd ever touched the etheric. The night he'd lost everything.

"It was the first kill." Lotario squinted up at Alain. "The incubus was gathering his strength. This one was sloppy. He left some of his energy in the corpse."

"Enough to track?" Alain rubbed his fingers over his forehead. His head was starting to pound, an ache that burned behind his eyeballs.

Nodding, Lotario stood and wiped his hands. "Got the map?"

They headed back to Lotario's Bug and laid the map of Rome out on the front of the car. Lotario rubbed a quartz pendulum between his palms and dangled the crystal above the streets of the

Campo. It twitched, slipping sideways, and swung over the northwest corner, shivering with the energy of the incubus.

Alain dialed Angelo on Lotario's phone. "Angelo, northwest corner. We're looking for any couple that seems out of touch. Lost in their own world. The incubus will portray their target's deepest desire back at them. Be whoever they need to be for the target. Watch for a man taking someone away for privacy. The incubus will want to be alone when he starts eating their soul. It'll start with sex, though. It's how the incubus gets going, feeds their energy."

"*I'm moving my men there now. Do you have any idea how much sex happens here in the Campo? You're asking for a needle in a very large haystack.*"

Alain chuckled. "We're on our way. You and your men start from the southwest. We'll meet in the middle. Lotario's got the scent. We'll have him soon."

ANGELO MOVED HIS MEN ACROSS THE *CAMPO*, SWEEPING A SQUAD down the southwest corner. They peered into bars, eyeballing patrons and drunks and couples making out in dark corners of lounges and on dance floors. They were able to split everyone apart, tear each partner from the other with ease.

Every time, they got a curse and angry words, coming from clear eyes and a human face. No possessions yet.

They moved down the line of bars, searching.

At the fourth, Angelo stopped short, glaring through the front windows at two men seated at the bar.

LOTARIO'S PHONE RANG LOUDLY IN ALAIN'S POCKET. HE SLID IT out, turning away from the entrance of the bar on the north side of the square and cupped his hand over the mouthpiece. "What?"

"*Where are you?*"

Alain frowned. "We're outside..." He backed up, searching for the bar's name. "Sugar. We're moving your way."

"*You're not inside Moondust? Not sitting at the bar next to a young blond?*"

Alain's blood went cold. His throat clenched. "No. No, I'm not."

Through the windows of Sugar, Lotario looked up, as if he could sense Alain's sudden shock. He started pushing through the crowd, heading for the door.

"*I'm looking at an exact copy of you, Alain,*" Angelo growled. "*Even your messed-up hair.*"

"Where?" Alain headed north, leaving Lotario behind.

"*Moondust, one of the clubs—*" Angelo cursed, and the sounds of a group of people laughing and passing him by jingled over the line. "*You're— Shit.*"

"What?" Alain moved faster, breaking out into a jog. "What happened?"

"*I lost you. I mean him. It. I lost it.*"

"What do you mean you lost it?" Alain ran full speed, tearing down the *Campo* toward Angelo and Moondust. "What happened?"

"*You were sitting at the bar with this young blond man and then you were gone!*"

"Fuck!" Alain ran, spotting Angelo through the crowds milling in the square. He shoved his way through the mess of humanity. "What did he look like? The blond?"

Ahead, Alain saw Angelo ordering his men into the club and heard the angry shouts of a club being sacked by the *polizia*. He ran toward Angelo, still listening to him over the phone.

"*Young, mid-to-late twenties. Tall. Clean cut. Blond and German-looking, like he was one of your guards. And he held himself like a soldier.*"

"Goddammit!" Alain ripped the phone away from his head as he found Angelo. "Goddammit, it's Cristoph."

"*Who?*" Angelo pocketed his cell as he glared at Alain. "Why is the incubus impersonating you?"

Alain ignored Angelo's questions. "He's taking Cristoph away to kill him. Have your men found them yet?"

The radio in Angelo's hand spat static, and then rough Italian from the *polizia* forces reporting in. No luck. They'd lost the incubus wearing Alain's face.

Alain threw himself into the club and the crazed mix of partygoers, bass beats, and *polizia* officers. The officers were slow, moving methodically, shining flashlights in every patron's face. They'd only managed to work their way through the front part of the club. The packed dance floor in the back didn't even know the *polizia* were there.

Alain pushed through the crowds, shoving his way onto the dance floor. He searched for a blond head of hair and a wide set of shoulders, shoulders he had memorized and imagined nearly every day since he'd met the man. *Cristoph... God, where are you Cristoph?*

His gaze caught on the club's back door, swinging closed.

He took off, barreling his way through the crowd. Elbows flew, and he pushed women in dresses and men with popped collars out of the way. He hollered over his shoulder at Angelo's men, but didn't stop to wait for them. Cristoph, Cristoph, Cristoph... What had happened? Why was Cristoph here? How had an incubus found him, of all people?

Alain threw himself through the back door, nearly stumbled when he hit the rancid summer air of the back alley. His shoes splashed in a puddle and the stench of urine hit his nose.

Rotten roses, a heavy musk, and the tang of sulfur crept over his skin. He shook his head, trying to clear away the heat haze. Blinked fast.

Against the bricks behind the club, the incubus—a replica of himself—pressed Cristoph back, his hands cradling Cristoph's face, their hips grinding together. Cristoph's shirt hitched up. His taut stomach gleamed in the neon light, one of the incubus's—Alain's—hands trailing over his skin. Cristoph was panting, thrusting his hips against the incubus's, grabbing at the black suit jacket the incubus wore.

The incubus's eyes glowed bronze. An amber light shone beneath its skin. "Show me everything you know about the hunter," the incubus whispered as he leaned in and sealed his lips over Cristoph's.

"*No!*" Alain bellowed. He took off, racing toward Cristoph and the incubus, right as the back door to Moondust slammed open and Angelo and Lotario rushed out.

"Alain! *Wait*! You'll be sucked in!"

Alain ignored Lotario's shouts. He ran at the incubus. Steps away, Cristoph wailed, shrieking into the incubus's kiss as the first tears in his soul started. Amber light blazed from Cristoph's eyes as his body shook, quaking in the incubus's grip.

He launched himself at the incubus, slamming into the demon wearing his skin and tackled him to the ground, tearing him from Cristoph. The incubus shifted, his stolen image wavering, face flickering from Alain's to Cristoph's, and then back to Alain.

Stumbling, Alain got to his feet and faced off against the incubus. It mirrored him, every one of his movements. Alain swung at the incubus, his movements growing sloppy. He didn't have long. He was too close. Somewhere, in the back of his mind, he knew this. Gasping, the heady scent of rotten roses and sulfur swam up into his mind.

Next to the brawl, Cristoph sagged to the ground, grasping his head, moaning.

"Cristoph!" Alain turned away from the incubus for a moment. He reached—

The incubus grabbed him, swung him back around.

Its face and body had changed. Now, Cristoph's double stared back at Alain, grinning that lopsided, flirty grin. Alain froze.

The incubus grabbed Alain behind the neck and pulled him down, sealing their lips together as his skin glowed amber and his eyes gleamed, bronze light bathing Alain's shocked features.

Gunshots cracked, splintering down the alley. The incubus

stumbled, releasing Alain. Alain crashed back against the alley wall and slid down the worn bricks, landing beside Cristoph.

The incubus turned rage-filled eyes at Lotario and Angelo, both holding their ground at the club's back entrance and brandishing their modified pistols.

More shots rang out. Bronze holes appeared in the incubus's body, gleaming shards of raw light beneath the wounds. But no blood. Angelo fired again, and half of the incubus's jaw blasted away. There was nothing but a bronze glow beneath the remnants of the incubus's—of Cristoph's—face.

A snarl, like a lion raging at a lost kill, and the incubus turned. The image of Cristoph fractured. Fell apart into a stream of bronze light that shot straight into Cristoph's and Alain's chest.

Alain shrieked.

Footsteps thundered as Lotario and Angelo ran for them. "Alain!" Lotario shouted. "Jesus Christ, Alain! What the fuck were you thinking, you stupid sonofabitch?"

Everything sounded so far away. Alain shook his head, trying to break through the heat haze in his mind. Warmth hovered next to his body, the scents of sweat and sunshine and grass and gunpowder filled his nose. "Cristoph..."

Cristoph, slumped against the brick wall, stared at him. "Alain," Cristoph whispered. One shaking hand rose and rested on Alain's cheek.

One touch, and a firestorm erupted inside Alain.

He *needed* Cristoph, needed the man like he needed to breathe. Every one of his fantasies roared through him, all of his yearning, his longing. Cristoph's smile played on an endless loop. He heard Cristoph's voice calling his name, gasping, moaning. Wanting. Fire raged through him, a demonic burn coursing through his soul. Hunger twisted his mind until his only thoughts were *possess, mine, possess, mine!*

Alain grabbed Cristoph, dragged him into his arms. His lips descended, mouthing down Cristoph's neck, sucking at his pulse point. He tasted the hot sweat and demon energy coating Cristoph's body. Moaning, he rolled Cristoph onto the ground.

Cristoph went, panting wildly and breathing Alain's name. His hands wrapped around Alain's neck, his ankles twisted around his back, thighs squeezing Alain's hips and dragging him down, grinding their bodies together. Alain molded himself to Cristoph, holding them as tight together as he possibly could. He buried his hands in Cristoph's tousled hair. He was going to use his out-of-regulation hair as handlebars as he fucked Cristoph's mouth. He said so, grunting the words into Cristoph's skin as his bottom lip dragged over his neck.

Cristoph arched against him, his erection sliding against Alain's through their pants. "Yes, Alain. Take me! Fuck me!"

Lotario's hands grabbed Alain's shoulders. Tried to pull him off Cristoph. Alain snarled, shoving Lotario away. He grasped Cristoph tighter. Nothing would pull Cristoph from him. Nothing. Cristoph was his.

He's so fucking perfect. So beautiful. I'm going to make love to him for days.

"Shit!" Lotario reached for Alain again. Alain tried to punch him across his jaw. "They've both been caught up in the incubus's spell."

"How do we break it?" Angelo tugged on Cristoph, trying to drag him away from Alain. Cristoph refused to go, clinging to Alain madly.

Alain kicked Angelo, snarling like a wild animal. Heat poured off him, slicking his shirt, his clothes, with sweat. He needed to be naked. Cristoph needed to be naked. They needed to fuck. Now.

"It's a possession," Lotario snapped. Alain heard the words. They meant nothing to him, not in the midst of his need to fuck Cristoph through the pavement, all the way to Australia. "We have to exorcise the incubus's energy or they'll burn themselves up fucking each other's brains out."

Roaring, Alain swung wildly at Lotario, a wild haymaker with no finesse. Lotario ducked and grabbed his arm, twisting and pinning it behind Alain's back. Alain tried to kick Lotario off, tried to fight back, but Lotario threw his shoulder into Alain's back, holding him down. He wasn't going to let these men keep him from Cristoph. Not now. Not when the world had narrowed until all he could see was Cristoph, all he could smell was the sweet scent of his body, and all he could feel was Cristoph's burning heat and his desperation for him. For Alain.

He'd claw his own bones out to get to Cristoph. Tear his own skin off.

Angelo grabbed Cristoph's legs and yanked, finally tearing Cristoph from Alain's grasp. As they separated, Cristoph went limp, his eyes rolling back in his head as he started to seize.

Alain bellowed wordless curses, mad spitfire, at Lotario and Angelo. Fury cracked his vision as he roared, struggling to get free from Lotario's hold. His eyes burned, and his pulse pounded in his temple, a heavy war drum beating against his skull. *Mine, mine, mine,* his blood screamed. Cristoph was everything he needed, every carnal sin that damned a man, and Alain was going to dive cock-first into Hell tonight.

"Who the hell is this guy?" Angelo grabbed Cristoph and hefted him up, slinging Cristoph over his shoulder. He stumbled under the heavy weight. "What's going on with him and Alain?"

"Give him to me!" Alain roared. "Get away from him!" His fingers scraped on the cold concrete of the back alley, fingernails cracking, skin breaking. Blood streamed down his hands, mixed with the dirt and the grime.

"Sorry, Alain," Lotario grumbled, slamming his fist into the side of Alain's face.

Dazed, he lunged for Cristoph, grasping for his shirt, his shoulder, desperate to cling to him. Lotario socked him again, a swift punch to his temple. His vision tripled, went blurry, ruby red. He slumped sideways, falling face-first to the ground, cheek pressed against the concrete. He tried to shake his head, clear the red-hot haze crackling through him, but all he could do was scrape his fingers against the ground as the world swam fuzzy and delirium-slow before his eyes. Cristoph's scent burned his nose, and as Angelo took a few cautious steps back, Alain keened, an animal wail tearing from him.

"I don't even know where to begin." Alain felt Lotario sigh, felt Lotario's forehead rest on his shoulder. "He's one of the guards. They've been fighting—" Alain saw Lotario's hand wave, as if to trying to encompass the madness surrounding the two men. "—*this*. I had no idea it was this bad, though."

"Bad?" Angelo asked.

"Incubi target a person's deepest desire, right? They penetrate their target's subconscious. Get at what they want more than anything else. I would have thought, for Alain, it would have been —" Lotario stopped.

Alain's eyes slid closed. There was a name Lotario almost said. His breath faltered, but Cristoph's scent curled along his lips. He snarled, trying to fight Lotario off.

Lotario hauled him up and hefted Alain over his shoulder, holding him tight. "We have to get them to my place. Now."

Angelo and Lotario raced to Lotario's Bug, hobbling as fast as they could with the weight of two grown men over their shoulders. Lotario wheezed, and Angelo cursed with every step. They kept to the back alleys, snaking down the back of the *Campo* until the last moment. Lotario slumped Alain over the boot of his car as he fumbled with the door locks. Angelo dropped Cristoph in the cluttered backseat, sweeping away empty cigarette packs and newspapers before climbing in after.

Lotario shoved Alain in headfirst on the passenger side.

Alain drooped unconscious over the stick, but roused slowly as Lotario hopped in and slammed his door. Red-rimmed eyes flashed to the back seat, landing first on Cristoph, still unconscious, still trembling, and then on Angelo. His lips curled, a low snarl in his throat.

"Fuck," Angelo breathed. "Go now! Drive!"

Lotario floored it, peeling out of the *Campo* in a scream of burning rubber and a thunderous cloud of black smoke coughing from the beat-up engine. The Bug lurched, stuttered.

Alain clawed at Angelo and reached for Cristoph. He was half in and half out of his seat, his knees kicking Lotario, growling inhuman snarls at Angelo. One of Alain's hand fisted in Cristoph's shirt. Cristoph's eyes flew open at the touch. He reached for Alain.

"Don't let them touch!" Lotario bellowed. "Don't let them fucking touch each other!"

"You wanna get in the middle of this?" Angelo shoved between Cristoph and Alain, trying to separate their desperate grasping. He threw himself forcibly in between them.

Alain roared. One hand wrapped around Angelo's throat and squeezed.

"Hurry..." Angelo croaked.

Lotario gunned the Bug's engine, not slowing for stoplights or corners. They careened wildly, and Alain lost his grip on Angelo's neck as his arm slammed against Lotario's headrest on a tight curve. He lunged again, both hands coming at Angelo, and Angelo grabbed him, pulled him into the backseat, and tried to hold him in a headlock. Alain kicked the side of Lotario's head.

Cristoph wrapped his arms around Angelo's neck, screaming Alain's name.

"Goddammit, Alain..." Angelo wheezed, pushing back on Cristoph as he tried to keep Alain in the headlock and force Cristoph to let go. "Fucking demons!"

Lotario swerved the car, and in a squeal of rubber and burning brakes, brought them to a violent stop outside a run-down strip of apartments nestled above a pizzeria, an electronics store, and a kitschy souvenir shop selling crucifixes and rosaries. "We're here!" He leaped out of the car and yanked open the rear door, grabbing

Cristoph. He tugged on an arm and Cristoph's shirt, the only two things he could reach, and dragged him off Angelo.

Angelo gasped. Alain tried to clamber his way out of the car, mowing right through Angelo to chase Cristoph.

Angelo helped him along, shoving him out to Lotario. "Here!"

Lotario flung Cristoph to the ground and grabbed Alain in a gladiator's grapple, both hands wrapped around his chest and back.

"Get Cristoph!" Lotario roared. "Follow me up!"

They managed to brawl their way up five flights of narrow stairs to Lotario's rooftop apartment. Alain kicked and punched and struggled to get to Cristoph. Cristoph wavered between consciousness and unconsciousness. Halfway up the stairs, Cristoph started keening, a low-pitched wail that sounded like glass being sliced in two. Alain roared, fighting against Lotario to get to Cristoph, and only a solid punch to the face managed to knock him off balance enough to continue the climb.

When they burst into Lotario's tiny apartment at the top of the ramshackle building, Angelo stopped dead.

Lotario lived in the rooftop loft, an open, spartan space, with what little furniture there was pushed clear to the walls. A tiny kitchenette sat in one corner next to a threadbare couch with a broken frame and sagging cushions in the middle. Books were piled under the windows overlooking the street, windows that hadn't been washed in decades. Grime clung to the panes, the walls, and the antique chandelier overhead, more rust than iron.

In the center of the apartment, two circles were drawn in chalk. An industrial size can of road salt for deicing sat next to the circles, along with chalk. Candle nubs and bowls of herbs squatted at the four cardinal directions.

More herbs hung from the rafters overhead, bundled for drying. Along one wall weapons hung for easy access, balanced on rusty nails. Shotguns, blades, swords, pikes, and pistols. Everything a demon hunter could ever need.

"Get them into the circles, now!"

Lotario's voice kicked Angelo back into gear. He dragged

Cristoph, limp, into the second circle. Lotario dropped Alain in the center of the first and grabbed the can of salt. He kicked Alain down, ripped open his black button-down, and poured salt across his chest. "Stay down!"

Alain howled, a wail that shook the windows. Angelo covered his ears.

Lotario sketched a rune in the pile of salt on Alain's chest with his fingers. Alain thrashed, but didn't rise, seemingly held by the rune to the floor. Lotario tossed the salt can out of the circle and grabbed a lighter, balanced on a stack of books, and lit the candles around Alain's circle. He tossed the lighter to Angelo. As Angelo lit the candles around Cristoph's circle, Lotario dumped the bowls of herbs surrounding Alain and plucked new buds from the dried hangings above.

He stood back, muttering to himself and staring at the two circles.

"Well?" Angelo held Cristoph down inside his circle. Beneath his touch, Cristoph's skin burned, far too hot.

"Give me a minute. I have to calculate the circles."

"Calculate?"

Lotario huffed. "It's a sphere, really. I have to calculate the energies right. Balance the power so I can pull out and destroy the incubus and leave Alain's and Cristoph's souls inside their bodies." He closed his eyes. "It's really quite complicated, so it would help if you shut up!"

Angelo shook his head but stayed silent. Cristoph continued to seize beneath his hold.

Lotario mumbled to himself, grabbed a piece of chalk, and knelt next to Alain's circle. He ignored the howls, the wailing keens coming from Alain as he sketched runes and sigils and signs along the circle's outer boundary.

The air in the room crackled. A lightbulb blew out in the kitchen. Angelo's hair stood on end.

Lotario jogged to Cristoph's circle. He repeated the sigils and signs from Alain's circle, then added a second layer of sigils at the cardinal directions.

"Get out of the circle, Angelo," Lotario breathed. "Get out now."

Angelo backed away. Lotario closed his eyes and held his hands out, palms up. He started to chant.

"Let God arise, and let His enemies be scattered. Let them that hate Him flee from before His face. As smoke vanishes, so let them vanish away. As wax melts before the fire, so let the wicked perish at the presence of God. Flee, enemies! God has conquered you!"

Lightbulbs blasted out across the apartment. Glasses in the kitchen shattered on the countertop and in the sink. Angelo whirled, holding his hand up to his face as a hot wind swept through the apartment. Books flew open, pages slapping forward and backward. Cristoph moaned, and his fingernails scratched over the wooden floorboards.

Alain went still.

Lotario continued to speak. "I drive you from us, impure demon, evil power, and infernal invader. In the name and by the virtue of our God, may you be snatched away and driven from this world, and driven from these men, these souls who are not yours. I take these souls back. I claim them as my own."

The wind raged, howling through the apartment as Cristoph's back arched off the ground. His mouth opened, a silent scream paralyzing his body.

Alain thrashed. His fingers ran red with blood as he scratched at the floor. The salt on his chest began to burn. Smoke and the stench of burning flesh curled through the air.

"Cease your audacity, invading demon, as you attempt to deceive the human race! You shall not take these souls! This is the command made to you by I, in the service of the Most High God. In your insolence, you still pretend to be equal, yet you are nothing in the eyes of the Lord! The Lord will have all men saved, and all men shall come to the knowledge of the truth. God—"

Alain bolted upright, sitting straight up, staring wildly at

Lotario. His pupils had blown wide, and his gaze seemed to be pure black. His hands stretched out, blood drenching his hands, falling from torn his fingertips. He snarled, a mad, crazed grin of terror and glee. "You think you know God?" he shouted, and his voice wavered, strung through with more than just his own voice. There was something inside of Alain, within him. Speaking for him. "You think you know the *truth?*" Alain flung his hand. Blood went flying toward Lotario.

Lotario stood tall, staring down the demon in Alain as the blood droplets fizzled against the boundaries of the circle, disappearing in a puff of smoke.

"You know nothing about the thing you worship." Alain's lips curled back, sneering. His head tilted to the side. His eyes were pitch black. "We're coming. We're coming for him. He's *ours!*"

Lotario spoke again, repeating the ritual. "I exorcise you, you impure spirit, you satanic power. I drive you from us, impure demon, evil power, and infernal invader. In the name and by the virtue of our God, may you be snatched away and driven from this world, and driven from these men, these souls who are not yours. I take these souls back. I claim them as my own."

Dark chuckling rose from Alain, a dry laugh scraped over brittle bones. Cristoph wheezed, his body shaking, violent seizures inside his circle.

"I drive you from us, impure demon, evil power, and infernal invader. In the name and by the virtue of our God, may you be snatched away and driven from this world, and driven from these men, these souls who are not yours. I take these souls back. I claim them as my own!"

Cristoph bellowed, screaming so loud his throat seemed to tear. Bronze light burst from his eyes, from his mouth, from the center of his chest.

Alain whirled, staring at Cristoph.

A moment later, bronze light erupted from Alain, spearing out of his eyes and his mouth as he roared, arching backward and falling to the floor. The light seemed to struggle, beating against the borders of the circles, as if desperate to escape. Lotario brought his hands together, slowly squeezing something invisible between his palms. The light danced, amber shards sparking, sputtering. As if it were being extinguished.

Lotario's hands clapped together.

The amber light disappeared with a crack, leaving the apartment shrouded in darkness.

Silence enveloped the men. Angelo heard his own heart pounding, the harsh, ragged inhale and exhale of his own panicked breaths. He clutched the crucifix he always wore in one hand, whispering Hail Marys as he slumped against the far wall, his legs tucking up to his chest.

Alain lay still, unmoving. Cristoph curled into a ball. Both of their chests rose and fell as one, trembling breaths escaping past quivering lips.

Lotario collapsed, falling to his ass with a shaking sigh. His hand rose, covering his face.

No one moved for a long time.

Chapter Fifteen

DAWN'S FIRST LIGHT SCRATCHED ACROSS THE WOODEN FLOOR, rays penetrating the grime of Lotario's windows and reaching for Alain. His eyes fluttered open, and he struggled to wake against the pounding in his head.

Heaviness hung inside him, a dark weight that seemed to crush his breath. Alain clutched his skin. Burns scorched his chest. A trail of salt ran down his sides. He sat up.

He was in a circle on Lotario's floor, his shirt ripped open and salt clinging to him. A burn in the shape of a rune designed to hold a demon down was charred into his skin. Across the room, Lotario lay slumped on his broken sofa, face down, one arm dangling off the couch and holding a shotgun.

Next to him, Cristoph lay in his own chalk circle, surrounded by exorcism runes, banishing sigils, and calculations designed to expel and destroy a demonic force. He was face down, his cheek pressed against the floor, but one hand reached toward Alain.

Alain dragged himself across the floor, scrabbling when his legs weakened and he couldn't crawl. He crossed the chalk lines of the circle easily, palms smearing the seals and sigils. At least he knew the demon was gone.

Memories snapped and cracked in his mind, smears and screams and flashes of images, out of sequence and distorted. He remembered getting the call. Going to the *Campo*. The plunge of his heart when he realized Cristoph was the next victim. Charging the incubus as it held Cristoph. And then... *lust*, a burning that couldn't be quenched. An insatiable need. Cristoph, beneath him, in his arms, all around him.

Agony. Searing, brutal agony.

Followed by darkness. Nothing.

Waking in a circle.

Alain wrapped Cristoph up in his arms, dragging him onto his chest and tucking his face into Alain's neck. "Cristoph," he murmured, burying his face in Cristoph's sweaty hair. "God, Cristoph..." He held Cristoph tight to him, rocking back and forth, one hand sliding into Cristoph's hair, fingers slipping through the strands as he pressed his cheek to Cristoph's forehead. "Cristoph..."

Everything had happened so quickly, and it had been such a whirlwind of cascading bad and worse news. The incubus running loose in the *Campo*. Angelo's call, seeing a duplicate of Alain at a bar with a young blond. He hadn't dared to think it at first, hadn't dared to believe Cristoph would want him in the same way he desired Cristoph. Why would he, when Alain had so thoroughly destroyed their fledgling friendship? Had shoved Cristoph aside?

Why had the incubus picked Cristoph? Out of all of the people in Rome, in the *Campo*, why *Cristoph*?

This was every one of his deepest fears suddenly made so vividly real. This was why he isolated himself. This was why he never wanted to feel anything at all for anybody. This was why he'd buried his heart twelve years ago and had vowed to never love again.

Alain closed his eyes and pressed his lips to the top of Cristoph's head, breathing in the scent of his hair.

Damn this man. Damn him and his stubborn insistence on being exactly who he was. He was confrontational, had an attitude the length of the Tiber, and yet, he was also exactly himself. He refused easy explanations and wouldn't leave Alain well enough alone. He was the breath of life Alain needed. He was a flower growing on a corpse grave. He was the sunlight after a storm at sea, the dove after the flood.

He also wanted something from him, something Alain had vowed to never give again.

Something he had lost to Cristoph already.

His heart ached, trembling. What now? What now, after Cristoph had been possessed and lay in the remnants of a banishing circle after an exorcism? There was no way to wave away this one, to try to force Cristoph to accept a nonsense explanation that hurt to lie through. What now, when all he wanted was to keep Cristoph safe and the *only* way to do that was to keep him far, far away from Alain?

A tiny part of him protested, the lonely part of his soul reaching out for Cristoph. Was there ever a future where he could hold Cristoph like this? Where he could wait for Cristoph to wake, to smile at him and lift his chin for a gentle kiss? A future where there might be a beach and Cristoph's happiness? Where he didn't have to watch over his shoulder for demons and vampires and ghouls and revenants? Was there ever a future where he could accept this desire? Give in to his heart?

Wherever that future was, it wasn't here, not yet. Maybe not ever. He pressed his cheek to Cristoph's hair and shuddered as he wrapped his arms tighter around him. He'd hold him for a moment longer, then no more.

A hand grabbed his arm, squeezing.

Alain froze.

"Alain?" Cristoph whispered, his voice throaty and choked. "Alain... What happened?"

A long exhale as Alain blinked fast. He swallowed.

"Don't you *dare* tell me any lies," Cristoph growled. "Don't you fucking dare. Not after this."

"What do you remember?" Alain finally breathed.

He didn't let go of Cristoph, and Cristoph made no move to escape. His hand stayed wrapped around Alain's arm, slowly inching its way toward his wrist.

Cristoph rolled his face into Alain's neck, his chest. He exhaled. "I thought you were there at that bar. I thought you'd come to find me. I was drinking. I wanted to get smashed before my train left Rome. You showed up and said we should talk. You put your hands on me. You were touching me."

Alain's teeth ground together, his jaw clenched so hard his bones hurt.

"That wasn't you, was it?"

He shook his head. He couldn't speak.

"Of course not." Cristoph swallowed. Alain felt the slow gulp through their tightly pressed bodies. "What was it?"

"An incubus. A demon. They shape-shift. Take the form of—" He couldn't say it.

He couldn't believe it.

"I saw you tackle it. The thing that had me." Cristoph tried to smile, and Alain felt the curve of his lips brush across his neck. "Tackle yourself."

Alain nodded.

"What happened to us?" Cristoph nodded to the edge of the circle. "Is this more magic? Another spell of yours?" He growled. "Don't lie to me."

"Yes," Alain choked out. "It's a kind of magic. An exorcism. That demon... it possessed both of us. But you're okay. You're all right now. Lotario, he exorcised it."

"That asshole priest of yours?"

"Yes, that's Lotario."

Silence. Alain held Cristoph, savoring the moment. He didn't want to let go. Didn't want the moment to end. Didn't want to face everything that came after this moment.

"So nothing it said was true?"

"What did it say?"

A pause. "That you were... that he... *it*... was—" Cristoph frowned. "It said you were a hunter. That you hunted demons and dark creatures."

Alain closed his eyes and buried his face in Cristoph's hair again.

"But then it wanted me to tell it everything I knew about you. What had I seen? What did I know about your hunting?"

A chill tickled down Alain's spine. "What did you say?"

Cristoph shook his head. His hand squeezed down on Alain's, almost threading their fingers together. "I don't know much. Just the things I've seen. You wouldn't tell me anything. I... didn't know it wasn't you. I thought we were finally talking. And I was confused. There was a lot of... of groping. Flirting. I don't remember much." He squeezed his eyes shut. Sighed. "Did I give something away?"

"I don't know," Alain whispered. "I don't know."

"It's true? You are some kind of demon hunter? That's what everything's been about? The stuff in your apartment? When you said vampires? Does all of that really exist?"

The moment of truth. Alain buried his nose in the warm scent of the man. "It's all real, Cristoph."

It felt like damnation. Like ruin, like he'd carved a piece of his soul out. Like he'd damned his heart to forever break, even before anything happened. He'd never told another soul before. Not in twelve years had he revealed this secret, the truth of his life. Not once.

"Shit," Cristoph breathed. "Holy fuck."

Alain chuckled. "That's one way to put it." He nuzzled Cristoph for another moment before pulling back.

Cristoph clung to Alain's hand, refusing to let go. Alain shifted until Cristoph was sitting with his back to Alain's chest and Alain's arms were wrapped around his shoulders. Cristoph tangled their fingers together over his heart.

"Do you know anything about the Order of the Knights Templar?" Alain tucked his face against the side of Cristoph's head, speaking softly into Cristoph's ear.

"Old knights of the crusades, right? They were arrested for being heretics, right? For turning against the church? For... having a bunch of occult stuff?"

Alain shook his head, and the motions transferred to Cristoph. "The politics of the Templars' arrest go further than just heresy. The king of France was broke and he pressured Pope Clement to issue the arrest warrant for the Templars and to disband the Order. That gave the monarchs the right to seize the Order's assets. The king wanted the treasure they were supposed to have found."

"They found some kind of treasure in Jerusalem? Something buried under the old Temple, right?"

"What they found changed the world, Cristoph. Changed everything. And you've never heard of it. No one has."

"What do you mean?" Cristoph rolled his eyes up, frowning at Alain. "And why are you telling me all of this?"

"What the Knights Templar found, beneath the Temple in the Well of Souls, has never been revealed to any outsider. It's been a secret of our Order for almost a millennium. Since the very beginning."

Cristoph's eyes went wide. "You—"

"They found a doorway. A portal that crossed the Veil and that connected our world and the etheric world. The other side. The world of demons, and darkness, and all of the terrible stories you've ever heard." Cristoph stared at Alain, staying silent. "The stories say it was like a nightmare, what the original knights found down there. But they were able to close the portal and seal the Veil. The knowledge of this, and what they learned, has been passed down through each generation of knights. Until—"

Alain closed his eyes. What he was doing, what he was saying, was punishable by death according to the old law. Not that there was anyone left to enforce the law, but still. He could feel hundreds and hundreds of years of censure crawling up his spine.

"The secret of the Order has always been this: the knights, the Templars, they always had a deeper mission. They were hunters. They fought demons, darkness, and evil. Anything that crossed the

Veil to our side. That mission has never stopped, not even after they were arrested. Tried. Killed.

"The Knights Templar weren't totally destroyed in 1307. So many were captured and tortured. They were burned at the stake and worse. But others escaped to what was then the first Swiss confederacy. Do you remember your Swiss history? History teaches that knights, dressed in white with red crosses, moved into the Swiss Alps during the first confederacy, right? They came from nowhere, but they were the best fighters on the continent. They helped fight for the Swiss confederacy, training others just like they were trained.

"Our *home*, Cristoph. The birth of Switzerland came from *them*, the surviving Knights Templar making a new country for themselves." Alain tried to imagine it, his forefathers, the birth of their homeland. "They continued on in secret, training who they could to join their Order."

"The Knights Templar hid in Switzerland?" Cristoph craned his head around, staring at Alain. "Our home?"

"The Templar *created* our home." Alain exhaled. Pressed his lips together. "And, three hundred years later, in 1506, the Swiss Guard entered Rome, serving the pope as holy protectors." He tried to smile. "You know this. Swiss Guard 101. But the soldiers who came to Rome weren't *just* soldiers. They were the knights. The Knights Templar came home. They came back to the Vatican, and to the pope, and to their mission."

Cristoph shook his head. "The Templars still exist?"

"You're looking at one." He tried to grin. He failed. "For five hundred years, since the founding of the Swiss Guard, at least one of the guard has been knighted by His Holiness and elevated to the Secret Order of the Resurrected Knights Templar. There used to be dozens of knights. Now, it's usually only one or two at a time. Twelve years ago, I was chosen. I was knighted."

"And now you fight demons?" Cristoph blinked. "Wait, knighted by the pope?"

"Yes." Alain really did smile. "The knights report directly to him. Only His Holiness and Commandant Best know my true purpose."

Cristoph fell back against Alain's chest. "The commandant, too?"

"Best recruited me. He was the knight of the Order on guard against the darkness before he picked me." Alain's throat clenched tight. "Me... and another."

Alain saw Cristoph's eyes dart across the room to Lotario's ungainly crash on the couch. "No. Lotario comes from the Vatican. Personally appointed by the Holy Father. He was trained as an exorcist in his seminary days and spent a decade in solitude at a monastery, training for this life. We—the knights—partner with the Vatican, with their specially trained priests. We hunt together in secret."

"Then who is the other knight? You're always alone. Everyone thinks you're practically a demon yourself. What they say about you." Cristoph's face scrunched up, anger and determination warring in his expression. "Who else is working with you? Why don't they defend you?"

Alain tried to speak, but the words wouldn't come. He squeezed his eyes shut as his arms wrapped around Cristoph's chest. He cleared his throat, but even then, when he spoke, his words caught in his throat, ripped apart by twelve-year-old grief. "He doesn't exist anymore. He's gone."

Silence. Alain felt the weight of Cristoph's burning curiosity hanging heavy in the air.

"I lost him," Alain breathed. He buried his face in Cristoph's neck. "I lost him, and I swore I'd never lose anyone ever again. Which is why I never wanted you to know all this. I never wanted to put you at risk."

"Hey." Cristoph pulled free, turning in Alain's arms until they were eyeball to eyeball. "I'm okay. I survived that incubus. We survived together." He frowned. "You know, I'm not totally worthless. I am a soldier. I've managed this far in life, haven't I?"

Alain looked away.

"And I'm glad I know what the fuck is going on," Cristoph pressed on, ducking to find Alain's gaze again. "Do you have any idea how pissed off I was knowing you were lying to me? Wondering what I'd done to make you hate me so much?"

"I don't hate you. Cristoph, God, I don't hate you."

"I really hope not." Silence stretched long. "I was running away," Cristoph finally said. "I couldn't take it anymore. The lies. The bullshit."

"Don't go." Both hands covered Cristoph's as Alain laced their fingers together. "Don't go," he repeated. "I can't keep you safe if you leave."

Cristoph frowned. "I've been taking care of myself for a long time."

"You don't know what's out there. What can happen—"

"Actually, I do, a little bit at least." Cristoph interrupted. "I do know what's out there. I just didn't want to accept it was real. But, I saw... something. Darkness. Evil. Something I couldn't explain at the time." He shook his head and sat back on his heels, pulling his hands free. Alain chased his grasp, tangling their fingers together again. "Before I applied to the Guard, I was assigned to the army disaster relief team. We were in West Africa during the Ebola outbreak. We did what we could, you know? We were in all four of the countries, collecting bodies every day. A never-ending stream of death. There was blood... everywhere. Jesus, it flowed like rivers." He closed his eyes.

Alain had seen the headlines, but it had been a distant news event to him at the time, something staticky in the background behind wraiths and hungry ghosts and revenants.

"There was this witch, the local shaman said. Who collected the blood, even though it was infected. She used it in her black magic spells. We had to go and get her." He shrugged, one shoulder rising and falling. "And... get rid of her." He inhaled, long and slow. "A shaman did it. There was this ceremony. A lot of drumming. Black smoke everywhere. And they—" He swallowed hard. "She died in the fire."

"That sounds like more than simple witchcraft," Alain breathed. There wasn't much difference between the spells Lotario cast and what witches cast, to be honest. But what Cristoph had described? His blood turned to ice in his veins.

"The shaman said it was evil that lived inside of her. That it had found a hole into our world because of the disease. Because of all of the death. The others in my unit, they thought he was crazy. They wouldn't help him with the witch. But..." Cristoph met Alain's gaze. "He was the one who said I should come here, to the Vatican, and try to find answers. Find the truth." Another shrug. "So that's why I came." A tiny, lopsided grin curled up one corner of his lips. "You asked once why I was here. I came to get away from what I saw. To try to understand it all. I guess, in a way, I have."

"Cristoph..." Alain shook his head, leaning in until their foreheads touched, warm skin nestling against warm skin. There were a lot of empty spaces in Cristoph's story, holes that Alain could read into. "I'm sorry. You came here to get away from the darkness. Not get pulled into it." His fingers stroked down Cristoph's cheeks, thumbs gliding over the high arches of his cheekbones. Cristoph's eyes fluttered closed, and he leaned into Alain's touch as his lips parted. A tiny exhale burned the air between them.

"While this is all very touching," Lotario drawled, "we really do have business to get to. A killer vampire to stop and a spy ring to break."

Alain flew back from Cristoph. He and Cristoph twisted, staring wide-eyed at Lotario. He'd sat up on the couch and was rubbing one hand over his face

"How long have you been awake?" Alain pushed himself to his feet, dusting off his pants.

"Long enough." Lotario eyeballed Alain before dropping his gaze to Cristoph.

Cristoph stared between the two men. Alain wouldn't meet his gaze.

"I can help," Cristoph said, standing. "I can help you both."

"Cristoph, no—" Alain said, at the same moment Lotario spoke. "Sounds like a great idea!"

Alain leveled a flat glare Lotario's way.

Lotario grinned back, all yellowed teeth and gums. "I'll lend you a shirt, Alain. Yours is fucked."

ALAIN BUTTONED UP THE BLACK SHIRT LOTARIO LOANED HIM, carefully skirting the burns on his chest while watching Lotario explain the banishment circle to Cristoph. The two men were kneeling down, Lotario pointing out sigils and signs and explaining the magical weights, the calculations he'd performed to balance the energies just right.

"Where did the demon go?" Cristoph traced a chalk sigil with his finger.

"Destroyed. I built this circle to trap and exterminate demonic energies. The power generated," Lotario gestured to both circles, "was enough to obliterate its energies."

Cristoph looked at Alain silently.

"Did you get the flash drive from Angelo, Lotario?" Alain shook off Cristoph's stare as he tucked in his borrowed shirt.

"Yeah, before he left. I don't have a computer though. Let's get back to your office at the garrison."

Alain nodded, and they filed out of Lotario's apartment one by one, Alain carefully avoiding Cristoph's gaze. Lotario steered Cristoph ahead, agreeing they could swing by the bar from the night before to pick up the duffel he'd left there when the incubus had pushed him out the back with a promise of a quickie. Alain closed his eyes against the sound of Cristoph's voice, hesitating on the stairs, but he started up again when Lotario barked up at him. He followed down to the street and slid into the backseat of the Bug, not meeting Cristoph's gaze in the rearview mirror.

Lotario called him out when they stopped at Moondust, after

Cristoph hopped out to check on his duffel.

"Alain—"

"Don't, Lotario. Just don't."

"You're *still* pushing him away? After all this?"

"Why are you encouraging him?" Alain snapped. "You know I won't let anything happen. You know how much it would kill me if someone I—" He looked away. "If someone I cared about was hurt. *Again.*"

"Your fear is paralyzing you. Are you really ready to throw this away? When you know how he feels about you?"

"And how does he feel about me?" Alain glared at Lotario through the rearview mirror.

"Enough that an incubus dressed as you in order to seduce him. His deepest desire." Lotario puffed on his cigarette, angrily blowing the smoke out the window.

Alain looked away.

"And don't think I didn't notice the incubus flicker to him once you were close enough to be caught in its thrall. That is *not* what I thought would happen if you were ever trapped with an incubus, but it just proves—"

Alain's eyes slid closed. His stomach tried to turn inside out. "Lotario?"

"Yeah?" Lotario flicked ash over the window, onto the street.

"Shut the fuck up."

Lotario chuckled, and then the passenger door creaked open as Cristoph folded himself back inside the Bug, carrying his lost duffel. He grinned over his shoulder at Alain, his eyes seeming to search for some sign or signal. All Alain could manage in return was a weak smile.

He stared out the window as they puttered back to the Vatican. When they arrived, news trucks blocked St. Anne's Gate, and there were ten extra Swiss Guards on duty at the entrance to the Vatican, harried and frantic and trying to direct Vatican traffic in and keep news vans, reporters, and oglers out.

Alain leaned over Lotario's shoulder at the gate, sticking his head almost out the window, and waved the nearest guard over.

It was Zeigler. Go figure. Alain schooled his expression to neutrality and ignored the harsh inhale from Cristoph, the whispered curse directed Zeigler's way.

"Halberdier," Alain addressed him as Zeigler approached.

Zeigler's eyes went wide as he took in the battered Bug, Lotario chain smoking, and Cristoph, looking exhausted with deep dark circles beneath his eyes.

"Sergeant." Zeigler straightened. He looked down his long nose at Alain.

"What's going on, Halberdier? What happened?"

"You haven't heard?" Zeigler's eyes flashed back to the street and a crowd of reporters trying to heckle a comment out of a group of nuns walking into the Vatican.

"What happened?"

"The secretary of state has died," Zeigler said. "Cardinal Carlo Nuzzi. The Vatican claims it was from natural causes and he died in his sleep, but someone leaked a photo of blood on the walls in the Apostolic Palace—"

"Drive! Now!" Alain pounded the back of Lotario's seat.

Lotario slammed the Bug into gear and floored the accelerator, gunning the choking engine and launching into the Vatican. They screamed through the Swiss Guard courtyard, slipped around the barracks, and drove up the hill toward the Vatican Bank. Lotario swerved, parking the car outside the back steps to the Apostolic Palace.

Alain dove out of the car, clambering out at the same time as Lotario. Cristoph followed, jogging behind as they took the entrance steps three at a time, bypassing the shocked Swiss Guards on post and running through the halls before anyone tried to stop them.

The Royal Staircase loomed ahead, and they jumped the gleaming steps two and three at a time, passing marble statues of angels staring downward, hands outstretched as if to smite the wicked. Archangels stretched skyward, blowing their trumpets in exultant glory, robes fluttering wildly in still stone. Nymphs frolicked, their sightless eyes still trying to flirt, with breasts and smooth thighs spilling from falling robes.

A long corridor led them to the turnoff to Cardinal Nuzzi's apartments. Along one wall, a gigantic fresco loomed, a pitched naval battle warring forever on tumultuous seas. Death, a sightless skeleton robed in swirling black, watched over the battle. Death's empty eyes seemed to follow their every step.

When they arrived at Cardinal Nuzzi's apartments, Commandant Best stood with Cardinal Santino Acossio, the Vatican undersecretary of state. They turned to the trio.

"Alain," Best said, his voice weary. "Halberdier Hasse. Father Nicosia."

Panting, Alain propped his hands on his hips and tried to look somewhat dignified. Lotario sagged beside him, doubled over with his hands on his knees. Cristoph stood to the side, trying not to fidget.

Cardinal Acossio watched with a single raised eyebrow and a slowly curling lip.

"We just heard," Alain breathed. "We were waylaid. There was a... situation in Rome last night. We've just returned."

Best nodded. "What have you heard?"

"The secretary of state. Cardinal Nuzzi." Alain shook his head. "He's dead."

Commandant Best turned to Cardinal Acossio. "Thank you, Cardinal Secretary. I will brief His Holiness and yourself as soon as I am through with my men."

The new cardinal secretary of the Vatican nodded once, turned on his heel, and left.

Best waited until Acossio had walked away. He turned to Alain, stepping close to the trio. "We've put out that Cardinal Nuzzi died of natural causes in his sleep. But a picture has leaked out."

"We heard. A blood stain?"

"A bloody geyser. It's terrible." Best shook his head. "Nuzzi was murdered."

"How?"

Best held his stare. "A vampire killed him."

CARDINAL NUZZI'S BODY WAS MANGLED ALMOST BEYOND recognition. Alain stood at the doorway to the cardinal's apartment, his shoes just out of reach of the pool of blood. Commandant Best stayed with him, questioning Alain on the state of their investigation, and what they knew—or didn't know—so far. Best didn't say as much, but the tightness in his eyes, the pale blanch of his face, the thin spread to his lips, made Alain's palms itch.

Alain's gaze lingered on Cristoph, crouched next to Lotario beside Nuzzi's bloodied head and neck. Cristoph looked so out of place in his faded jeans and his white T-shirt, dirty from the floor of Lotario's apartment and the exorcism. He didn't belong here. He'd wanted to send Cristoph away. Cristoph had lingered too long. He was supposed to head back to his dorm and rest. Recover his strength. The lingering drain of the banishment spell hung heavy on Alain's bones, and he knew it had to drag on Cristoph, too.

He chewed on the inside of his lip as Lotario pointed out the defining features of a vampire murder to Cristoph, gesturing to Nuzzi's body.

Nuzzi lay on his back on his French provincial coffee table, arms flung wide, as if his death were a parody of a crucifixion. The body was misshapen, broken in so many places. His spine was cracked in half, and the lower body twisted one hundred and eighty degrees from his upper body. Bruises dotted the old man's frail skin, deep purple and black eddies. Slashes and tears tore through his chest and his abdomen. His guts had spilled out, tumbling on either side of the table and pooling on the blood-soaked floor.

His throat had been slashed with talons and fangs. Shredded to ribbons, white bone protruding through the mess of muscles and fat and bloody skin. His face was practically ripped off, destroyed, beaten and torn almost beyond recognition. Parts of his skull shone the carnage where patches of his hair and skin had been ripped from his head.

Lotario's gruff voice pointed it all out to Cristoph. He asked questions, too, questions Alain remembered from twelve years ago. "Tell me what you taste in the air. What do you smell?"

Cristoph closed his eyes. His nostrils flared.

Alain's teeth scraped together.

"Blood. Copper. And... fog. Something wet. Like dirt."

"That's the grave dirt. Vampires keep grave dirt with them in their nests and when they're moving in the world."

"Also..." Cristoph frowned. "It's like lightning. The air after a storm. And something else." He shook his head. "Makes me think of snakes."

"Good." Lotario squeezed Cristoph's shoulder. "You're smelling ozone. Clings to vamps. Makes you feel like lightning is arcing in the back of your throat when you're close to one. And I get the snake smell, too. Sometimes you might think you're smelling sand, of dust."

Cristoph managed a smile for Lotario, even over the murderous tableau spread before them. He glanced over his shoulder, toward Alain, his eyebrows raised.

Alain looked away.

Best spoke, drawing his attention back. "Alain, I have to report to His Holiness in ten minutes. He's quite upset, as you might be able to guess. What can I tell him?"

Only days ago, it had just been a freak ghoul scavenging in the city. Then a vampire murdering a prostitute. But she was a prostitute who had been sleeping with the cardinal secretary of state and spying on him for a nest of vampires.

Vampires who wielded Demon Fire.

But now was a lone, possibly crazed vampire running through

the city as well, stirring up the etheric and the supernatural. A lone, possibly crazed vampire who had killed the girl.

And now, Cardinal Nuzzi was dead, too.

Why? How did it all add up? Why kill the girl? Why kill Cardinal Nuzzi? Why kill the spy and the target?

Why had an incubus appeared in the *Campo*? Why had Cristoph, of all people, been targeted?

Alain dragged his palm down his face. "Commandant..." He swallowed. "I don't know what's going on."

He repeated what he'd told Best before, about the nest of vampires under Rome, then added in Lotario's find of the abandoned solitary vampire's nest. The research they'd found, the signs that pointed to a crazed lone vampire wreaking havoc on the city. Angelo's call and the discovery that Madelena had seduced Cardinal Nuzzi and had spied on him.

"For who?" Best frowned. "Who was she working for?"

She was one of ours. "The vampire nest. The alpha knew her. Claimed her."

Best paled, and his lips drew tight, a thin line pressed against his teeth. "And now Cardinal Nuzzi is dead." He exhaled softly. "The pact is surely forfeit now. But why? What information did she steal? What have the vampires learned?"

"We just got the flash drive this morning. We still need to search through it. We spoke to the cardinal yesterday evening. He said he only had his laptop at her apartment three days ago. That would have been the only chance she had to rip the files."

"And she died..."

"Yesterday. That's not a large window to get the information to the vampires." Alain thought back to the vampire's bone cathedral, their nest beneath Rome. He shook his head. "They weren't gloating, though, when they captured me. They were shocked we were there. In fact, they were asking me questions, trying to get information out of me."

"What kind of information?"

"They didn't know what I was, for one. Or who. They thought

I was a priest. They wanted to know about the hunters in Rome."
He picked at his dark suit jacket, rumpled and covered in salt
grime and dust. "Guess the outfit works for something."

Best pursed his lips. "Could that be connected to what the girl
was stealing?"

"It's possible. But a full rip of the cardinal secretary of state's
laptop would have given anyone mountains of data on the Vatican,
on all sorts of secret dealings. Vampires have known of hunters for
centuries. We're nothing new. And that nest should definitely
know us."

"But you said it was a new alpha."

Alain nodded.

A heavy sigh as Best shook his head. "I don't like any of this.
It's not adding up right. If they did get the information they
needed from her in a single day, the nest could have been the ones
to kill her. She'd be useless to them. But then why leave the drive
in her possession? It's sloppy. I certainly don't think they have
laptops down there in their nest, but still. Leaving evidence behind
is careless. And vampires are anything but careless and sloppy."

"They weren't the ones to kill her. The alpha didn't know she
was dead."

"Suppose the nest didn't get the information she stole, then.
Someone killed her before she could pass it on, and made it look
like the nest was responsible."

"The lone vampire's blood was there. We think he killed her."
Alain frowned. "Which means he's working against the nest.
Against the alpha, and against their own spy. Why?"

"And now, Cardinal Nuzzi is dead as well." Best sighed. "There
are too many unknowns. Find out what is on that drive, Alain. Find
out what the vampires are willing to rise and kill for." Best nodded
to Cardinal Nuzzi's corpse. "Find the cardinal's killer." His eyes
softened, just slightly. "I am also glad to see you are training
Halberdier Hasse."

"I'm not—"

"Keep him close," Best interrupted. "I don't like that the

vampires are asking such questions about the hunters. We've kept a cloak of secrecy over our identities for hundreds of years. We all need to be careful now." He nodded toward Cristoph. "Everyone."

Alain gritted his teeth. "Yes, Commandant. I'll brief you on what we find from the drive."

Best nodded, clapped Alain on the shoulder, and headed out, slipping from the cardinal's apartment and shutting the door behind him.

Alain turned back to Lotario and Cristoph. For getting off on the wrong foot, the two seemed to be getting along as thick as thieves, now. Cristoph had taken to soaking up Lotario's gruff teachings and pearls of bloody wisdom. Despite himself, a smile curled the corners of Alain's lips, watching Cristoph crouched next to Lotario.

"What else do you see? Look at the whole scene." Lotario waved his hand over Nuzzi's corpse and the cardinal's sitting room. "What stands out?"

Cristoph peered around the bloody apartment. "The door wasn't forced. The vampire didn't come in that way."

Lotario smirked. His chin jutted toward the window and the lightly twitching curtain.

Cristoph sidestepped Nuzzi's corpse and the shattered glass and scattered silver, stepping between blood stains across the apartment to the windows overlooking the tiny San Damaso courtyard that sat in middle of the Apostolic and the Medieval Palaces.

"Window's busted," he said, pulling back the curtain.

Lotario nodded. "What else?"

Cristoph's eyes slitted as he took in the apartment, sweeping left and right slowly.

Alain's eyes burned, and he was suddenly standing in a similar room, over a corpse sliced to ribbons by another vampire, watching his fellow knight learn the ins and outs of a supernatural murder, twelve years ago. He forced himself to keep his eyes open, to not blink away the moment, to hold on to it for another second.

No. *It's the past. It's all in the past. And it won't happen again. I swear to God, the bastard, that it won't happen again.*

"The vampire crossed the room unnoticed. He got around the sofa. Then there was a struggle." Cristoph pointed to the toppled stained-glass lamp and the overturned silver serving tray bracketing the end of the couch. "Nuzzi was sitting. Drinking." A crystal goblet lay on the floor, dark wine mixing with the spilled blood. "He jumped up. The vampire attacked. Shoved him backward onto the table." Cristoph moved as he spoke, walking through the scene. "He was alive for a while. While all of this—" His hand swept over the disfigured corpse. "—was happening."

Lotario stood, his knees cracking. He tossed a wry look Alain's way. "Not bad. Not bad at all."

Alain nodded. He smiled thinly when Cristoph met his gaze. "No, not bad at all."

The warm look Cristoph gave Alain almost melted his bones. His breath shorted, and he coughed as he leaned against the doorway.

"Is it always this violent?" Cristoph looked between Lotario and Alain.

"Pretty much." Lotario wiped his hands and shoved them in his pockets with a sigh.

"But not this personal." Alain moved closer to the corpse, peering down at the cardinal's bashed-in face. His arms stayed crossed over his chest. There, at the edges of the cardinal's eyes, running down his temples. Salt tracks. Tears.

Silence. Lotario watched him carefully. "What makes you say that?"

"His face. Who beats someone's face in, especially after the killing bite to the neck? There's not a lot of bleeding around the face. These disfigurations were done after his neck was torn." Alain met Cristoph's gaze. "What do you think that means?"

"The vampire knew the cardinal. And he hated his guts," Cristoph said.

Alain nodded. "Death wasn't enough. He wanted to erase him."

Chapter Sixteen

LOTARIO TRIED TO CAST A LOCATING CHARM USING NUZZI'S spilled blood, the same blood-to-blood locating spell they had used on Madelena's corpse. They searched carefully for the dark vampire blood, a near-black sludge that pooled differently than human blood.

A drop had fallen next to the silver tea set. A smear of deep burgundy swept over the curved back of a spoon. Perhaps a careless brush, a burn against the vampire's skin? Lotario had Cristoph hold the spoon while he rolled the tip of the crystal through the vampire's blood and Alain set the map up on the cardinal's couch.

After explaining the locating charm behind the spell, Lotario handed the crystal to Cristoph and gestured him to the map. Alain gritted his teeth but stayed still as Cristoph held out the bloody pendulum. This wasn't right, training Cristoph. Not now. Not when so much was unknown and so much danger lurked in the shadows.

Not ever, if he was honest with himself. He never wanted to train Cristoph. He wanted Cristoph to be normal, safe, and far away from all of this.

He wanted Cristoph to be by his side as he kept him safe. Protected.

The contradictory thoughts made him want to puke. Cristoph wasn't a child, wasn't a feeble thing that needed to be protected. He was six feet of military muscle, and he'd stood up to Alain and his bullshit. And when he had every right to run away, forget Alain and all of his dark madness, he'd chosen to stay. He'd chosen to stay to learn how to hold a crystal pendulum covered in vampire blood, suspended over a map of Rome, and feel the first tendrils of the etheric work through him.

They all waited for the charm to spark, for the blood to call out to its owner, blood to blood, and swing across the map before shivering and dripping down, betraying the vampire's location.

Nothing happened.

"What the fuck?" Lotario scowled.

"Let me see that." Alain held out his hand. Cristoph gently passed the pendulum over. Lifting it to his nose, Alain inhaled, taking in a whiff of the blood-soaked tip. He turned his head away. Rot and putrescence, the hallmarks of vampire blood. And underneath, the betraying tang of pungent roots. "Monkshood." He wrapped the pendant back up in its silk cloth, still soaked in blood. "The vampire must have taken it before the murder."

Cristoph frowned.

"Son of a bitch." Lotario shook his head. "Fucker knew we'd try to track it."

Alain nodded.

"Monkshood messes with the magic?" Cristoph's eyes bounced from Alain to Lotario. "We can't find the vampire that did this?"

"Monkshood provides invisibility from tracking spells." Standing, Alain pocketed the crystal. "We can't track him this way."

"What now?" Cristoph's eyes lingered on Alain.

Alain struggled not to shake off the feel of his gaze. "We've got to check that flash drive. We need to know what was worth killing both Madelena and Nuzzi."

SANTINO SMILED TO HIMSELF AS THE ELEVATOR CREAKED AND climbed upward to the pope's apartments in the Apostolic Palace. Cardinal secretary of state. Just what he wanted. A whisper of wind shook his cassock. He turned, glancing to the side.

He wasn't alone any longer. A black shadow, the smoky shape of a man, roiled next to him. Asmodeus's face, the pure white Venetian mask, stared at him, frozen lips turned up in a fake smile.

"You killed Cardinal Nuzzi?"

"Not I." The smoke shivered. "One of ours, though. I trust you are pleased."

Santino smiled sidelong, eyeing Asmodeus's smoke.

"Our deal remains, Santino. You are in position. We require the information we have now bought and paid for. Find out what we need to know."

"What is so important about this hunter you seek? Why are you searching for him?"

"That is not your concern." Asmodeus's smoke trembled. The temperature in the elevator plunged.

A creak and a thud, and the elevator neared the top landing.

"I'll find him, as I said I would. But—" Santino faced the demon. "—I want to be rewarded when I do."

For a moment, Asmodeus stayed still, his shadows no longer twitching, no longer trembling. The elevator dinged, a heavy, brass bell chiming, announcing their arrival to the pope's guards and secretaries.

A rush of black wind swept through the elevator, swirling around Santino and knocking him sideways. The pressure rose, the shadow squeezing him tight, a coiled cobra ready to devour him. Roaring, like a train barreling through a mountain tunnel, filled his ears. He tried to scream, to fight the shadow off.

It vanished, the smoke and pressure disappearing with a crack as the elevator doors slid open.

Santino leaned against the side of the elevator, panting. Ice dusted the brass handle he grasped.

"Cardinal? Can I help you?" Captain Ewe of the Swiss Guard, standing outside the elevator with one of the Swiss Guard sergeants, extended his hand for Santino. "Is everything all right, sir?"

Santino's heart raced, a tympanic beat that thundered against his ribs. *I am watching you*, hissed in his ear. *And I will get what I want.*

LOTARIO LEFT ANGELO A VOICEMAIL AS HE FINISHED HIS cigarette outside Alain's office. "Angelo, I've got an idea. Pull up all the files you've got on any unexplained deaths. Any hint of a possibility of an etheric or supernatural murder. If there's a solitary vampire running loose in the city, then he's probably been killing for longer than we've known. If we can find a body he's drained, I can track the son of a bitch down." Lotario stamped out his cigarette and hung up.

Alain couldn't look at Cristoph as they headed for his office. Inside, Cristoph poked through his shelves, flipping through his tomes and spell books, his runes and relics and his collection of weapons. The loose pile of gendarmerie crime stats and pickpocket reports he normally kept everything hidden under had been tossed aside, Cristoph no longer caring about Alain's privacy, it seemed.

"I can help," Cristoph insisted when Alain turned his way, before Alain had opened his mouth.

"No. Not right now. This is too dangerous. It's too much. Maybe after this is all over—"

"Let the kid stay!" Lotario snapped. "He's doing good, Alain!"

"Stay out of this, Lotario!"

"I can take care of myself! I can help!" Cristoph glared at Lotario. "And don't call me 'kid'!"

Lotario smirked, laughing to himself.

"Help with what? You're not trained." Alain tried to turn away.

"Then train me. Teach me. I *can* help you." Cristoph pushed the scroll he'd been studying back on the messy shelf and crowded Alain, standing so close their chests brushed against each other. "I want to be here. I want to do this. I know I can help you."

Alain turned away from Cristoph's hot stare. "No."

"This is *why* I am here. This is why I came to the Vatican. God works in mysterious ways, doesn't he? This is meant to be, it has to be. You know that. Why won't you let me help?"

"You don't understand the risks! These are *vampires*. I can't let anyone else—"

"*Alain*—"

"I know a little bit about what I'm talking about, Cristoph! The last man who worked with me is *gone!*" His voice rose until he was shouting, bellowing in Cristoph's face.

"Alain..." Lotario tried to interrupt, a warning in his voice.

"Shut up!" Alain sent a scathing glare Lotario's way. Lotario shut his mouth, for once.

"I'm not him! I won't make the same mistakes he did!" Cristoph's gaze burned into Alain's. "Let me stay. Let me help."

"Damn it, Cristoph. They weren't *his* mistakes. They were all *mine*." Alain paced away, tipping his head back as a pulse pounded at the base of his skull. "I got him killed."

Silence filled the cramped office. Lotario looked down, scuffing his boots, and then cleared his throat. Smoker's phlegm curdled as he coughed. "I'll leave you two to sort it out. I've got bodies to examine." He slipped out, kicking the *Malleus Maleficarum* away from the door and closing it behind him.

"Cristoph—"

"No, *stop*, Alain. Don't do this. Don't shut me out again. Not after everything." He shook his head. "You need help. We both know you can't do this all yourself. I want to stay, with you. Let me do something, anything, to help you. Please."

"Helping me would be putting you on a plane and sending you to the Caribbean. Getting you far, far away from here."

"Only if you come with me."

His dream flashed in his mind again, Cristoph, naked, gloriously naked, and happy, stretched out alongside Alain in a bed overlooking a beach. Alain reached for Cristoph's hand, his shaking fingers barely brushing over the back of Cristoph's. "Promise me one thing."

"What?"

"If I tell you to go, you will. You'll run, and you'll stay safe."

Cristoph frowned. "Only if you're safe, too."

Stepping back, Alain cleared his throat. He pulled out the flash drive and sank into his chair in front of his computer. "We have to see what's on here."

Cristoph perched on the edge of the desk and watched as Alain plugged the drive into his dusty computer tower.

"Is everything in your office ancient?" Cristoph muttered into Alain's ear.

"Hush." Alain almost grinned. "Our budget isn't large. Petrol prices have risen over the years. Most of our funds go to getting around Rome."

The flash drive popped up a new window on Alain's monitor, listing the directory of files ripped from the secretary of state's laptop.

"I feel like I'm reading God's email."

Alain tossed Cristoph a dry look. He popped his knuckles and hovered his fingers over the keyboard. A moment later, he sorted the drive by folder and file date last opened.

"Personnel Files?" Cristoph read the most recent file over Alain's shoulder. Confusion hung in his voice.

Dread sank in Alain's stomach. *No. God, you bastard. No.*

He clicked into the folder. A substring of the Vatican departments the cardinal secretary of state oversaw opened. His eyes scanned the folders, searching.

Pontifical Swiss Guard. His breath stuttered.

The file had been opened two days ago. By Madelena. The spy. His eyes scanned the rest of the drive. Nothing else had been opened on that day. No other folders. No other files.

Holding his breath, Alain clicked into the Swiss Guard personnel file. One hundred and twenty folders popped up, last names followed by first names.

Alain frowned. One hundred and twenty? He scanned the list, searching for his name.

It wasn't there.

But Commandant Best's was, right up top. Recently opened. *Best, Gaëtan (Commandant).*

"Shit," he breathed. Clicking into Best's file felt like he was reading his father's diary. He didn't have a right to his information, to Best's service record. He didn't want to know what Best was like when he was a younger man, before he was the stalwart, strident knight who had recruited Alain and—

He shut down his thoughts.

It was all there. The date Best joined the Swiss Guard. His training scores. Alain raised his eyebrow as Cristoph chuckled. Their commandant had barely scraped by. Two years as a halberdier, two years as a corporal. And then, in his fifth year, a reassignment. *Best, Gaëtan. Promoted to sergeant and reassigned to Special Projects.*

"He was the knight before you, right?" Cristoph murmured. His breath tickled through Alain's hair next to his ear. "He recruited you?"

Alain shivered. "Yes," he croaked. Coughing, he tried to cover his slip. "And he was recruited by *his* commandant, Alois Sonnenberg. And Sonnenberg was knighted before him."

Cristoph squinted at Alain. "You gonna be commandant one day?"

Laughter erupted from him. "Christ, no," he snorted. "I'm—"

The door ripped open.

Whatever Alain was going to say died as Luca loomed in the doorway. Storm clouds darkened Luca's eyes and a harsh frown furrowed his brow. "Sergeant," he bit out. He nodded to Cristoph, slightly less hostile. "Halberdier."

Alain fought for breath. He stood, but his hands clenched his keyboard, white-knuckling around the plastic. "Luca. What do you want?"

Luca's eyes lingered on Cristoph, perched on Alain's desk so close he was almost touching Alain's leg. "I came to check on Halberdier Hasse," Luca said. His eyes dragged from Cristoph to Alain, his gaze searing right through to Alain's soul. "His injury seems to be doing better."

Cristoph opened his mouth.

Alain spoke first. "He's still healing," he said quickly. "I still have duties for him while he recovers." He held Luca's stare. "You assigned him to me, and I have duties for him to do. He's not ready for guard shifts yet. He needs more time."

Cristoph's jaw snapped shut.

Luca's eyes darted his way. "Halberdier. How are you?"

Slipping from the edge of the desk, Cristoph sagged sideways, making a show of limping on his formerly injured foot and falling to the chair beside the desk. "Still hurts, sir." He grimaced and rubbed his ankle. "I'm very grateful for the time you've given me to recover."

Alain rolled his eyes at Cristoph's terrible show of acting. Luca's eyebrows shot high. A pinched look of hilarious disbelief scrawled across his face.

"Anything else you need, Luca?" He stared Luca down, daring him to pick another one of their fights. *Not now, Luca. Not now.*

Luca's gaze held his, his eyes deep pools of chestnut brown so dark they looked black. "Not at the moment," Luca finally said, smooth voice purring over his words. "I'll be back," he promised. As he turned away, he paused, his gaze sliding to Cristoph. "Feel better," he barked.

Silence strained the office until the door slid closed once more.

"The fuck is his problem?" Cristoph exhaled, glaring up at Alain. "Has he never, ever been laid?"

The very last thing he wanted was to discuss Luca, or to have Luca involved in their case in any way. "We need to call the commandant. Someone—something—is searching for him."

"Because he was a knight? A hunter?"

Alain nodded. He punched in Best's cell phone number on his desk phone as Cristoph went back to perusing his shelves, his books. Something was out there searching for the hunters, the knights. Vampires had made Madelena a spy, had made her seduce Cardinal Nuzzi and steal his files. She had been guided to seek out the Pontifical Swiss Guard's personnel files and search for guards assigned to Special Projects.

A chill curled around his heart. Something out there was getting close. The incubus. It must have targeted Cristoph. The questions it asked, trying to find out information on Alain, and on the hunters. Too coincidental to be an accident.

Vampires and demons, both trying to find them. Vampires with Demon Fire. Demons tracking down information on hunters. A vampire spy searching computer files. The same goal. The same purpose.

Vampires and demons, unbelievably, working together. Something that had never happened before.

"You're getting your wish." Alain's throat clenched and his heart shouted, screaming for him to put Cristoph on the next flight out of Rome, to send him far away. "You're staying with me for now."

Cristoph's eyebrows shot up.

"We're—the knights— are being targeted. I think you were targeted by that incubus because of me. Someone, somehow, knew we were connected." His fingers clenched on the phone's handset. He didn't want to elaborate on that connection. "I'm not going to let anything happen to you."

The commandant's gruff voice breaking over the line cut off Cristoph's response. In the background, Alain heard the low tones of the Holy Father asking Best who was calling.

Chapter Seventeen

THEY STAYED IN ALAIN'S OFFICE FOR THE REST OF THE DAY. Alain showed Cristoph how to draw a demon's trap and a protective circle and had him practice on the cinderblock walls until he made a passable warding sigil.

He gave Cristoph the French treatise on Demon Fire and took the old Germanic poem for himself to study. They drank espressos and read the manuscripts, scribbling notes down and reading passages to each other when they stumbled. In the end, the poem revealed nothing new for Alain. He already knew demons and vampires didn't get along, that there was no history of any alliance between them, ever.

So what was happening now?

Cristoph's French treatise didn't have any new information either. Demon Fire, the monks found, could only be wielded by demons. When the monks tried for themselves, they ended up burning down first their monastery and then their village before a monk finally self-immolated and flung himself into the village well, poisoning the town's water supply.

"Well, we know how to put it out at least." Cristoph rubbed his eyes.

Alain shot him a dark look.

They were no closer to understanding why the vampires had Demon Fire, why the vampires were searching for the hunters, or why an incubus had targeted Cristoph.

"It's not that they were looking for what we do." Alain tried to puzzle through it with Cristoph again. "The dark creatures and the demons have always known about hunters. But why ask about a *single* hunter? What do they want with the commandant?"

"How many hunters are there? You said there were only one or two knights at a time nowadays." Cristoph leaned forward, bracing his forearms on his knees.

"There are only a few knights at a time now here in the Vatican. But we're not the only hunters in the world. The original Knights Templar sent out missionaries." He grinned. "Turned out, we were late to the party. Most everyone else already had hunters. Our missionaries became emissaries, and we learned from everyone we could. Prayers and scrying from India and China. More about possession from Africa. And, in the new world, we learned about shapeshifting."

He caught how Cristoph's eyes darkened when he spoke of Africa.

"There are hundreds of hunters in the world, across every culture. We share information. Work together when we can. Your shaman in Africa that sent you here? He was a hunter." Alain stood, stretching. The day had grown long. "What was Lotario's last update?"

Cristoph swiped on his phone screen. Alain's cell phone was still gone, but Cristoph had Lotario's number from two nights ago. A string of text messages between Lotario and Cristoph had kept them connected while Lotario went to work with Angelo, digging through records of bodies and unclaimed corpses.

"His last message, and I quote, was 'fuck this shit.'" Cristoph grinned. "He was heading for the potter's cemetery to dig up some bodies. Then back to the station. Angelo was going to bring him more corpses."

"The commandant sent an email, too. He's up in his apartment, tucked in tight."

"Do we stand guard for the commandant?" Cristoph looked ready to stand guard all night if Alain ordered it.

Chuckling, Alain shook his head. "The commandant is a knight, remember? He's got demon traps in the walls of his apartment and salt lines on his doors and windows. We all do. Wards high and low."

"Does he have armor and a sword, too?" Cristoph winked.

"We used to have a holy sword in the old days." Alain leaned back, crossing his feet as he sighed. Exhaustion weighed on him, and the light banter was a perfect escape for the moment. There wasn't anything they could do, not with so few answers and no leads. Lotario would find them a new lead, a location to scout, a vampire to track. He had to believe that, or he'd go crazy with nothing to do, nowhere to turn, with no answers and only ever-deepening mysteries.

But he could sit here and protect Cristoph. Keep him safe. Maybe even train him, just a tiny bit.

"The Knights Templar had a sword in the Order. I mean, every knight had a sword, but the Order had a special one. Almost six feet long, the stories said. It was a holy blade, possessed with some kind of power."

"Sweet. What do you have now?"

"Iron and silver blades. Stakes. Guns. Shotguns and pistols. Bullets tipped with everything that can kill the darkness. Herbs, holy water, saint's blood..." He ticked off the weapons on his fingers, counting aloud. "The blood you smeared me in? That was saint's blood mixed with the ash of a crucifix and the fang of a vampire. An antidote to vampire wounds. Not a bite. But wounds."

"Where do you get saint's blood?"

Alain took a deep breath. If Cristoph wanted to know... "We drain the popes' bodies after they die."

"Holy *shit*..." Cristoph's eyes bugged out as his mouth formed a perfect O.

"Oh. And we use overproof vodka." He tried to change the subject, quickly moving to safer territory.

"Vodka?"

"Lotario kills revenants and ghosts with vodka. One hundred and ninety proof. It's a local rotgut he gets from somewhere. He soaks the revenants and lights them on fire."

A part of Alain warmed as the sound of Cristoph's laughter slipped through his heart and soul. It was dangerous, so dangerous, to let Cristoph get this close. To let him smile and laugh and look at Alain in that way. Standing, Alain broke the moment that had stretched long, shared grins and soft gazes darting over each other's faces. "You hungry?"

"Starved." Cristoph rubbed his taut belly as he stood, stretching. His shirt rode up, revealing a thin strip of tanned skin above his sagging jeans stretched tight over defined hipbones.

He looked away, but his mouth felt drier than the Sahara. His palms itched, wanting to reach for Cristoph's hips, slide his hands under his shirt, feel the warmth of his skin.

No. No, you closed that door. No. Your dreams have to end. There's no future there. No future except in blood. You vowed. Remember? Remember your vow.

Alain led Cristoph to the canteen where they grabbed takeout containers of manicotti, salad, and garlic bread. They ignored all the blatant stares as they moved through the buffet line. Cristoph served as Alain held the containers open, and they chuckled as the manicotti slipped and slid all over the spatula before Cristoph managed to get it in the containers.

When Cristoph held up a piece of garlic bread for Alain to try, offering to feed him from his fingers, Alain's heart nearly burst. The canteen went silent, no longer pretending not to stare.

What was Cristoph *doing*? He knew Alain was ostracized. He knew he'd be on the outs for this.

He didn't seem to care. After Alain carefully chewed off the end—staying far away from Cristoph's fingers—Cristoph gobbled down the rest, stuffing his cheeks, his smile wide.

They headed out, Cristoph waving a two-fingered salute to the silent room as they left and headed up to Alain's apartment.

"You know you'll just get more grief for that." Alain stood on the opposite side of the elevator, keeping his distance from Cristoph. "Your friends already despise me."

"They aren't my friends. And I don't care what they think." Cristoph's gaze pierced his. "I want them to know I chose *you*. That you're not alone. I know where my loyalties are."

What could he say to that? No one stood with Alain. No one had, not in twelve years. It was too much, and he looked away, looked down, tried to escape from the heat burning out of Cristoph's gaze.

He led Cristoph to his apartment silently. They stood in Alain's kitchen and ate, sidestepping the scattered skulls and spilled tarot cards and the jars filled with blood. Alain pointed out everything, naming the animal or creature the blood had come from, how the blood was used in a spell, or what weapons to dip in which against which creatures.

Cristoph asked about each of the weapons hanging on the wall. There were silver blades and blades dipped in holy water, blades coated with lamb's blood and goat's blood. Shotguns with salt shells. A broadsword, but not, Alain said with a smile, *the* broadsword from the Order.

When they finished, Alain tossed their empty trays and then poured a shot of vodka for them both into chipped plastic cups. Cristoph *clinked* his glass and downed his shot.

Silence descended over the pair.

"Can I ask you a question?" Cristoph twirled his cup on the counter, slow spins, and didn't look up at Alain.

"Sure." Alain stuffed his hands in his pants pocket and hitched his shoulders. "I've answered everything else you've asked today. Even though I broke every rule of the Order to do so."

Cristoph licked his lips. He didn't look up. "It's about the incubus."

Alain stilled.

"I asked Lotario what incubi do—"

"When?" Alain frowned. He didn't remember that.

"Over text." Cristoph sent him a wry grin but looked back down to the chipped countertop. His finger picked at a crack. "I mean, you know I saw you. That the incubus became you." He looked up, straight into Alain's gaze. "For me."

Heat flashed through Alain, followed by ice. His jaw clenched. He couldn't do this. He couldn't take this, Cristoph confronting him about the truth of the incubus. The meaning he tried to ignore, tried to run from. He turned away, hands clenching the warped edge of his kitchen sink. A bare bulb above was the only light in the kitchen, burning down on Alain like a spotlight. He was being stripped raw beneath it. Like the light was flaying him open.

"Cristoph..."

"I haven't asked my question."

Alain's hands white-knuckled the counter. His heart pounded, crashing like the bass of St. Peter's bells.

"I know what you saw, too, Alain. I was pretty out of it. But I *did* see my face on the incubus. It was wearing *my* face when it pulled you in for a kiss." Cristoph's chin lifted. "And Lotario confirmed it."

Damn that man. Damn Lotario. Damn him to the blackness beyond the Veil.

Silence fell.

"I still haven't heard a question," Alain choked out.

Cristoph chewed on his lip. Shuffled one foot. "'Your deepest desire,' Lotario said. The incubus shows you what you want most."

The faucet dripped. In the courtyard below, a braying laugh burst out, one guard messing with another.

"Is it true?"

Finally, Cristoph's question. The one question Alain never wanted to hear, never wanted to answer. He didn't want to confront this, didn't want to answer for his feelings, for the way his heart had run away from his ironclad control. Because no matter what, no matter how he felt, no matter how Cristoph felt, and no matter how warm and wonderful and agonizingly beautiful it felt to have Cristoph look at him the way he did, just like in his dreams, *nothing* could happen.

Nothing could ever happen between them.

He coughed. Hitched his shoulders as he gripped the counter. "It doesn't matter if it is," he grunted. "Nothing can happen, Cristoph."

"What?" Cristoph's voice was soft, a shocked breath escaping his lips.

Alain shook his head. "I'm flattered, Cristoph, I am. You don't know what it means to me, that you would—"

"Alain—"

Alain whirled, facing Cristoph as he braced himself back on the sink. "I *can't*, Cristoph!" he hissed. "*I* can't!"

Cristoph froze, halfway around the kitchen counter. His eyes went wide as his lips parted. "Is this—" Cristoph shook his head once. "Is this about the guy you lost? The other knight? You and he— You were lovers, weren't you?"

Alain's eyes slid closed. His arms shook as he fought to remain standing. He was going to die. His heart couldn't take this, not this constant longing mixed with despair. The counter was going to crack beneath his grasp.

Letting go, he collapsed forward, falling to his knees on the worn linoleum of his kitchen. He tried to breathe, tried to drag in a ragged breath, but couldn't. "He's more than gone," he whispered. His body trembled, shivers that coiled up his spine. "He doesn't exist. Not anymore."

Cristoph kneeled in front of him, hands grabbing his shoulders as his big eyes stared into Alain's. "Jesus, Alain. He doesn't exist anymore? What the hell does that mean?"

He pitched forward, burying his face in Cristoph's neck. There were no sobs, no tears. Not after twelve years. "I can't survive that again. I can't let there be any risk of that happening to you."

Cristoph's scent burrowed into his nose, warm and bright. "I can't take that kind of loss again."

Cristoph tried to smile. It stabbed Alain in the center of his heart. "You don't want to start anything because you're afraid you'll lose me?"

Desperately, Alain tried to fight his body's reaction to Cristoph, to his warmth and his strength and his damned determination. "It's the only way to be sure." His eyes blinked past Cristoph's neck, studying his weapons hanging on the wall. Mental calculations flew through his mind, which classes of weapons worked best against each type of supernatural creature or etheric entity. Anything to keep his mind off Cristoph and his touch. Alain fought not to sigh into his arms. He stiffened. Tried to pull away.

Cristoph let him go. He sat back. "So, I want you, and you want me, but..."

Nodding, Alain grimaced. "But."

Cristoph pulled himself up. He held out his hand for Alain. Alain clambered up, unsteady. Cristoph held him until he was balanced.

"Alain..." Cristoph's dark eyes found his, burning with desire. Hunger. And sadness. "What do you really want?"

Time seemed to stop as Alain stared into Cristoph's eyes. He struggled not to scream or rage at God and the universe, or to seize Cristoph with both hands.

He wanted to fall to his knees and beg for forgiveness.

He wanted to grab Cristoph, haul him close, bury his fingers in Cristoph's hair, kiss him senseless.

Alain closed his eyes and stroked his hands down Cristoph's arms. His fingers found Cristoph's, tangled them together. He leaned close, pressing their foreheads together, nuzzling his skin. A sigh slipped past Cristoph's lips.

There was no end to this hurt, no bottom to his desire. Unrestrained, unbridled yearning burst from him, laced with a bitterly resigned anguish. Why did it have to be this way? Why couldn't he reach forward, close the single breath separating their lips? Why did he hold himself back?

One bloody night twelve years ago answered him in his memories. Alain shuddered. His hands rose, gripping Cristoph's shirt, tangling in the white cotton. Cristoph's breath hitched, a quiet gasp. Alain reached for the back of Cristoph's head, stroking his neck. Silken blond strands slipped through his fingers.

Alain's soul was screaming. His heart burned, thrashing and pleading and begging for what was right in front of him. For another chance.

"What do I want..." Alain breathed. His lips brushed against Cristoph's as he spoke, an almost-kiss that maddened his blood. They were too close. Shaking, he tried again as his fingers stroked through the hair on the back of Cristoph's neck. "I haven't let myself want. Not in twelve years. I thought I couldn't want anything anymore."

Cristoph blinked, but his burning gaze stayed locked to Alain's.

Alain licked his lips. Cristoph's eyes darted down, watching, and a soft moan escaped him.

"I want *you*," Alain whispered. "God, I want *you*." His voice shook, trembled. Nearly fractured apart as he tried to speak again. "I want you so *badly*. I want to kiss you. Have you. I want to make you mine." His voice dropped, nearly growling. "I want—"

"Tell me," Cristoph begged. "Tell me, Alain."

Alain shoved Cristoph hard, driving him backward. Cristoph's eyes went wide as he hit the kitchen wall, but Alain followed instantly, cupping his face. His thumbs rose, sweeping across Cristoph's cheeks. Noses brushed, sliding together.

He was flying apart. He'd leaped off a cliff, and he didn't know if there was anything there at the bottom. His teeth clenched, and a bitten-off curse caught in the back of his throat.

A tortured moan burst from his lips as one fist flew, punching the kitchen wall next to Cristoph's head hard enough to dent the plaster.

Cristoph didn't blink. "Tell me what you want."

"I want—" There was no going back, not after this. All of his fears blazed. All of his longing surged. "I want to *love* you," he growled, his voice dropping an octave. "And I want you to love me."

Cristoph's smile could ignite the sun. Could resurrect a god. Alain almost closed his eyes against the sheer brilliance. His soul reached, desperate, for Cristoph.

"Then do." Cristoph exhaled, nuzzling the side of Alain's face as Alain's bruised fingers scratched furrows in the hideous paisley wallpaper. "Love me. I'm yours, Alain."

That was the end of his control. He had nothing left, not after that. Nothing left to cling to, no power in the universe he could beg or pray to, no sign or sigil he could cast that could ward off his passion. Every defense, every bitten-off prayer, every silent plea, every moment he'd chained himself deep within his haunted soul, fled. Nothing stood against the force of his desire.

Twelve years, and he broke for a man who stood up to him, who called him an equal, and who stared into the darkness and asked for more, side by side with him.

Moaning, Alain brought their lips together, capturing Cristoph's mouth in a soul-deep kiss that tasted like sin and heaven all wrapped up in one.

Cristoph snaked his arms around Alain's head, his hands burying into Alain's dark, wild hair. One leg rose, slipping around Alain's thigh. Alain ground his hips into Cristoph's. His lips slid down Cristoph's chin, down his neck, teeth scraping over his skin and his Adam's apple. He laved at his pulse, at the pounding of Cristoph's blood, warm beneath his skin. Dropping his hands, he slid them down Cristoph's body, skimming broad shoulders, his firm back, landing on Cristoph's taut ass. Cristoph jerked.

Hefting him up, Alain lifted Cristoph into his arms, his hands sliding down to grasp his thighs. Cristoph's legs wrapped around Alain's waist, ankles locking behind him as he cupped Alain's face and dove in for another kiss. A growl slipped from Alain before he kissed Cristoph back, hard. Tongues dueling, Alain's mind spun as he carried Cristoph toward his bedroom for the second time.

Each step felt more unreal than the last. Each kiss was a damnation, a slide deeper into the place he'd vowed never to go again. Danger loomed ahead after this moment, dark and bloody, but he couldn't care. Not now.

His legs hit the edge of his bed, and he tossed Cristoph down before climbing on top. Their lips parted for a breath and then came together again. Alain mouthed down Cristoph's neck as his hands slipped up his shirt. A quick tug and the shirt was gone.

Cristoph's fingers shook as he tried to undo Alain's buttons. They kept slipping from his fingers.

"Rip it off," Alain grunted against Cristoph's lips. "It's not mine."

Buttons flew. Cristoph yanked Lotario's black shirt down Alain's arms. A brief struggle, arms tugging free from the remains of the shirt, and then Alain wrapped Cristoph up in his arms, laid him down on his bed. He started kissing a trail down Cristoph's chest. Between his pecs. Down to his belly button.

He popped the button on Cristoph's fly.

Cristoph's hands fisted in the sheets, his head thrown back, and he swallowed back a muffled scream as Alain tugged his jeans down and closed his lips around Cristoph.

"I want to hear it." He stared up at Cristoph from between his legs. "Don't hold back. Let me hear you."

Cristoph tasted amazing. Alain sucked screams out of him, long, wailing moans, curses, and pleas to God. He writhed under Alain's tongue, spasming against the bed. He chanted Alain's name and grabbed his hair. His toes curled in the sheets next to Alain's head.

Alain popped off, his lips wet. He dragged his nails down Cristoph's chest, over his nipples, skirting his belly button. "Not yet."

"Fuck," Cristoph gasped. His body hitched, curling almost in half.

He pressed a wet kiss to Cristoph's thigh and stood, quickly stripping. He was back on Cristoph in a moment. "If I look in your pants," he breathed into Cristoph's ear, "will I find a condom in your pocket?" Cristoph had been heading out of town, running away. Running from Alain, and he'd been in a bar. He'd bet his knighthood on Cristoph's plans.

Shuddering, Cristoph nodded, barely able to speak.

He slid back and grabbed the jeans. There, in the front pocket, was a single lubed condom. He tossed it on the bed.

"I've got to open you up."

Bleary eyes blinked, searching for Alain. One hand rose, reaching out. Alain wrapped his fingers around Cristoph's and pressed a kiss to his knuckles. Then he moved, his hands grabbing Cristoph's thighs and pushing his legs back, spreading them wide, leaving him open and exposed and bent in half.

Alain's hands landed on either side of Cristoph's round ass. Spreading him open, his tongue snaked down in between his ass cheeks and dragged over his hole, switching between hot licks and gentle sucks and deep sweeps before sliding deep into Cristoph's ass.

Cristoph went rigid, then flew apart, shaking beneath Alain's lips and his hands, so much that Alain had to hold him tight, arms wrapped around his hips, Cristoph's ass lifted off the bed. Cristoph sobbed his name, ripped the sheets from the corners of the bed, fistfuls of white cotton in his shaking hands.

Alain sat back and grabbed one of his pillows. He slid it under Cristoph's hips.

The condom wrapper tearing mixed with the sound of Cristoph's gasps, his heaving pants. "Alain," Cristoph breathed. "Alain, *fuck*." He threw his head back as he grabbed the edge of the mattress above him.

Alain gripped Cristoph's knees and spread him wide before leaning close for a kiss. His cock pushed against Cristoph's body at his saliva-slick hole.

"Do it," Cristoph whispered. "Fucking do it. I want you so bad!—"

Closing the breath that separate their lips, Alain captured Cristoph's mouth, his tongue parting Cristoph's lips.

The kiss broke as he slid inside, gasping at the sudden rush of sensation. He pressed his forehead to Cristoph's cheek and squeezed his eyes shut. His body was a live wire, burning from the inside, shocks of lightning zinging through his soul, and every muscle spasmed with too much feeling. "You're so fucking perfect," he breathed into Cristoph's hair, blond strands sticking to his lips. Slow, gentle thrusts had him sinking all the way into Cristoph. Cristoph's hands scratched down his back, nails digging into his skin.

Alain rocked into Cristoph—long, slow, deep—until his blood burned and his spine melted. Cristoph kept up a steady litany of begging, cries to God mixed with Alain's name slipping out in desperate whimpers.

His voice pushed Alain, faster, harder, deeper, until Cristoph was sliding up the mattress on every thrust, the sheets ruined, sweat-soaked and pulled free. Until Cristoph was screaming, begging for more and shouting his name, pleading to God, and urging him on. Cristoph grabbed Alain's cheek and the headboard behind him as he struggled to draw in ragged breaths between each rough thrust.

Alain's fingers dug deep into Cristoph's skin, leaving purple bruises on his hips. He couldn't stop. Couldn't make himself stop. Not ever. He was flying, racing toward the edge of a cliff, and his soul screamed, bared before Cristoph, every nerve in his body singing with rapture, all together, all at once.

It was so much better than every dream, every single dream. The reality of Cristoph in his bed was indescribable compared to the frenzy of his dreams, the pale imitations of Cristoph whipped up by his subconscious. Nothing could ever compare to him, to the reality of his existence.

Cristoph's body clenched, a roar bursting from his throat as his release exploded. Alain cursed, squeezed his eyes shut, and buried himself in Cristoph as his body crested, as he leaped from the peak of his soul, from the base of his heart, from the length of his yearning. He shouted Cristoph's name and swore to a God he didn't believe in, begged Cristoph for forgiveness as he whispered he loved him.

He didn't mean to admit that.

For a moment, he couldn't breathe, his heart racing like it was a single beat away from exploding. Alain squeezed his eyes shut as he gasped, his first inhale after his soul had erupted. Finally, he opened his eyes and looked down.

Dazed eyes stared up at him. Cristoph stroked down Alain's cheeks, over his chest. He pulled Alain down, kissing him like Alain's lips held the secret to life. His ass clenched, and Alain groaned, trying to thrust once more.

"Holy shit," Cristoph breathed. "Jesus fucking Christ." His eyes were still wide, still seemingly trying to gather his bearings, trying to see straight.

Alain grinned. His lips pressed against the side of Cristoph's mouth, against his chin. "Such language in the Vatican."

"What we just did..." Cristoph closed his eyes, and one hand dragged up Alain's sweaty, scratched back. "That was not Vatican approved."

He grinned again, ducking down and sucking at the skin behind Cristoph's ear. Cristoph moaned and curled into Alain, still trying to catch his breath.

Alain held Cristoph as he tucked his face against Alain's neck and his nose pressed against his skin, breathing him in. As one hand rose, holding onto Alain's hip, and his long legs pinned him down. As his eyes fluttered closed, and his breathing evened out, and sleep claimed Cristoph's soul.

Alain stayed awake, his fingers stroking up and down Cristoph's arm, his back. His eyes stayed fixed to the ceiling while his thoughts tumbled.

What have I done?

His soul was on fire, basking in the warmth of Cristoph, in the passion, in the release. His heart was screaming, begging for more and begging to run. To bury himself in Cristoph's arms and never let go. To fling himself from the bed and never return.

Aching fear seeped in around the edges of his searing bliss, quietly muting the wild passion he'd given himself over to.

What have I done?

Chapter Eighteen

CRISTOPH'S PHONE RINGING AT THREE IN THE MORNING SENT them scrambling, twisting half off the bed and searching for his discarded jeans in the ruins of the scattered sheets, clothes, and pillows.

Alain found Cristoph's jeans and pulled out the phone right before it rolled over to voicemail. "Hello?" He winced, hating how breathless he sounded.

Lotario, damn that man, noticed. "*The fuck is wrong with you?*"

"Nothing."

"*Why didn't you answer my texts?*"

Alain hesitated. "We were busy."

Silence. The sound of a deep drag on a cigarette and the soft rustle of ash burning away floated over the line. "*Busy, huh?*" There was a wide, ugly grin in Lotario's voice.

"Shut up, Lotario. Just shut up."

Lotario chuckled.

Cristoph had scrambled across the bed, leaning precariously off the edge as he'd searched for his phone. He halfheartedly rolled back, but stayed sprawled on his stomach, his bare ass exposed right in front of Alain. He pillowed his head on his arms, looking back over his shoulder, smiling.

Alain slapped his bare ass and then grabbed it, kneading a muscular cheek.

"*What was that?*" Lotario, sounding far too cheery and full of brightness for three in the morning, perked up over the line at the slap.

"Nothing. Why are you calling?"

"*Yeah, about that.*" Another drag of the cigarette. "*So I went through Angelo's records. There have been thirteen suspicious deaths in the past month, all buried in the potter's field. No next of kin, no one to press charges. The vics were all vagrants and indigents. No one anybody would miss.*"

Alain shifted, sitting cross-legged on his mattress, a clump of sweaty bedsheet tangled between his legs. He fumbled with the phone, finally finding the speaker button, and held it between him and Cristoph.

"How did the thirteen die?" Cristoph sat up as Alain spoke, one knee tucked up close to his chest. Alain's eyes were drawn down, between his legs.

"*They each appeared different. Some had their throats slit. Others were stabbed. Some looked like suicides. Slashed wrists. One had his leg torn off.*"

Alain frowned.

"*Do you know how hard it is to dig up thirteen graves? I mean, do you have any idea?*"

"You're showing off for Cristoph, Lotario. It's the potter's field. And it's only been a month. You only had to dig up one. Two tops.

A snort and an indignant guffaw rolled together, masking a deep chuckle. "*Yeah, yeah. Actually, none. The bodies were in the open trench, just wrapped up and taped in body bags. But—*" Another suck on the cigarette. "*—jumping into the trench is gross. And the stench. Fuck, the smell.*"

Cristoph's jaw dropped, his eyes wide. Alain laughed. "Okay, Lotario, you win. Cristoph looks like he's ready to puke. And yeah, I'll buy you a drink."

"You'll buy me ten."

"Fine." Alain rubbed his foot against Cristoph's thigh. "What did you find?"

"From what I could tell from the bodies that weren't already too far decomposed, they had been drained of blood."

"Vampires?" Cristoph spoke as he scooted forward, his eyes darting between Alain and the phone, a question in his eyes. Alain held the phone up for Cristoph and nodded.

"Vamps." Lotario sighed, the wet phlegm of his smoker's throat catching. Static filled the phone line. *"I found fang marks hidden on all their bodies. The other wounds, the things that supposedly killed them? They were all done after the vamps sucked them dry."*

"Our solitary vampire has been hunting around Rome for a month?" Alain rolled his shoulders. His back twinged. He looked away. It had been a long time since he'd fucked anyone, even longer since he'd been so vigorous.

"That's what I thought. Angelo got me blood samples from the vics' death records. The polizia didn't perform any autopsies, but they did pull what tiny bit of blood they could from the corpses for DNA evidence, in case someone reports them missing one day. 'Course, since the vics were drained, it was just bloody backwash from the vamps in their system, but that helps us. Guess what happened when I dropped each of the vics' vampy bloody backwash into the sample we got from Madelena's apartment? The one that traced back to the solitary nest, not the alpha?" Lotario paused. *"The blood burned."*

Cristoph reared back, frowning. Alain grabbed his ankle, one thumb stroking down the arch of his foot. "Vampires can't drink each other's blood. They can't merge blood with another vampire. If they try, their blood burns inside of them. It's a nasty death." He managed a tight grin. "Also a good way to kill them, if you can get your hands on vampire blood."

"Then it's not the solitary vampire who killed everyone."

"Nope." The flick of a lighter sounded. Another cigarette being lit. *"So get this. I said, what the fuck, and I dropped the bloody backwash*

into the first sample we took from Madelena, the one that took us to the main nest. And..."

Alain's stomach sank. Dread filled his chest. His head pounded, a deep ache at the base of his skull. "Don't tell me it flashed."

"Faint, but it was there. Every time."

Another frown from Cristoph. "When spilled vampire blood touches its owner—or, well, touches the vampire it bled from, the blood will flash. Like a spark."

"It happened with every one of the vics."

His mind reeled. Their theory that the solitary vampire was responsible for so many deaths was cast down, refuted. "The main nest killed thirteen people?" It was too much, too many deaths for any nest in so short a time.

"That's not all I found." Another inhale of smoke, and Alain finally got it. Lotario was nervous. He wasn't just sucking down cigarettes for his endless fix. A shaking exhale, and then Lotario spoke. *"The vics had sulfur on them. Every one."*

Cristoph's eyes snapped to Alain's. "Demons," Cristoph said.

Alain nodded. "Traces of demons on vampire kills." He shook his head and rubbed his temples. "They have to be working together."

"Demons and vamps, working together, killing a bunch of vagrants. And we still don't know what the solitary vamp is up to or who is hunting you lot." Lotario coughed, and the sound of a boot snuffing out a cigarette crackled across the phone. *"I've got a bit more to do here before I head back. Alain, you still got the blood from Nuzzi's corpse? With the monkshood in it?"*

He'd dumped the bloody pendulum in with the rest of his tools in his shoulder bag and left that locked in his office. "Yeah, it's here."

"I'll bring back the blood samples from both nests. We can't track the vamp who killed Nuzzi, but at least we can figure out which nest killed him. Maybe it wasn't the solitary vamp."

"Then he just killed the girl?" Alain shook his head. He stared at Cristoph. "Why would a vampire kill a spy against the Vatican?

Especially if she was working for the nest. Isn't that turning against his own kind?"

"*Maybe he really hates the demons. Hates whatever alliance they've got going on.*"

"Maybe. Lotario, call us when you're here. We'll meet you."

"*Yeah.*" Lotario scoffed. "*Don't let me interrupt anything.*"

"You're not." Alain clicked off the phone and tossed it to the side. His eyes burned as he took Cristoph in, naked on his bed, sitting there with his chin resting on his knee and a soft smile on his face.

"See something you like?" Cristoph spread his legs.

Oh yes, he did. Alain nodded.

"Come and get it."

HOURS LATER, THEY WERE BACK IN THE KITCHEN, CRISTOPH leaning against the counter in his boxers and a borrowed white T-shirt from Alain that stretched deliciously tight across his shoulders. Alain rummaged in his pathetically empty fridge. "I've got... some expired yogurt and half a bottle of orange juice?" He pulled back, holding out the food in either hand. "No idea if the yogurt is still good."

"It's yogurt. It's already spoiled milk."

Shrugging, Alain kicked the fridge door closed and brought the food to the counter, grabbing two spoons and an almost-empty bottle of honey on his way. He squirted the honey straight into the yogurt container and passed a spoon to Cristoph. He unscrewed the orange juice carton and set it between them.

"No glasses?" Cristoph's eyes twinkled.

"Both of my cups are dirty." He licked honeyed yogurt off the spoon. Cristoph's taste still lingered on his tongue, mixing with the sweetness. He almost moaned.

In no time at all, they scraped the bottom of the yogurt tub. *I'll have to get more food. I bet he eats a lot, what with that body.* Alain shook his head. *God, what am I doing?*

"What's it like being knighted?" Cristoph fiddled with the spoon, his eyes boring into Alain's.

"It was one of the best days of my life," he said softly. The memories cascaded back, soft and sweet, like a classic film reel playing highlights in black and white. "The Holy Father knights you. There's a small ceremony. When I was knighted, it was me, Best, Lotario, and—" He swallowed. Smiled to cover his slip, the name he'd almost spoken. Cristoph let it go. "We were kneeling. Best stood in front of us. He prayed, and then pressed his hands to our foreheads." He squinted. "I don't know if I can describe what happened next. I've never felt anything like it."

Cristoph tilted his head.

"You know how priests and clergy are ordained? By apostolic succession? An unbroken line of clergy who have transferred their prayers and their blessings forward, from the apostles to today?" Cristoph nodded. "It's the same with the knights. From the first ones who found the Well of Souls to now. Each knight has been blessed and prayed over by the knight before him, and he transfers this... blessing down to the next knight. That blessing, the power of it, has been carried down through the line since it was picked up in the Well of Souls by the first knights."

"Cool." Cristoph grinned. "You got some kind of magical super powers?"

"Well, *I* didn't get it. My partner got the blessing. He was supposed to be the superior knight."

"But didn't he—"

"I ripped it out of him." He stared into Cristoph's gaze. "I ripped it out of him the night he—" The memories shifted, no longer warm and happy. Instead, they were bloody, full of screaming. Terror.

He grabbed one of the blades off his kitchen wall. It wasn't long, about the length of his forearm. Thin, but not skinny like a rapier. He spun the blade around, hilt facing Cristoph.

The tension coiling through Cristoph's shoulders turned to curiosity. "What's this?"

"The blade I was knighted with. After the blessing, the Holy Father prayed over us, and then Best chanted the invocations. He touched our heads with our new blades, and then it was done." He dragged one finger down the top of the blade, staying away from the edge. "This blade has an iron core coated with silver. Feel how heavy."

Carefully, Cristoph wrapped his fingers around the hilt and lifted it from Alain's hands.

He looked good. He looked so damn good holding the blade. Holding Alain's knighted sword. Alain fought to clear his throat. "You've trained with the weapons in the armory?" The Swiss Guard had pikes and halberds, swords and daggers, and an arsenal of modern pistols and assault rifles.

Cristoph nodded.

"Good. Keep it. Learn how to use it."

"What?" Stricken, Cristoph stared at Alain like he'd lost his mind. "I can't, Alain. It's yours."

"I have another one," he said quietly. "I have my old partner's. And I want you to have this one. Mine. Maybe it's early to give it to you. But one day, you can hold it as your own."

Silence. "After you knight me? After you give me your knightly superpowers?"

What am I doing? This isn't right. Still, he chuckled, trying to break the moment as he looked away. "Well, I think I already gave you something tonight."

Cristoph barked out a laugh, but he kept holding the blade, gently testing the weight and the tang. He stepped back, gave it a few careful swings for practice, and then set it down gently on the counter.

"You said the knights before you were all commandants. Why won't you rise to that rank? Seems like it's tradition."

Alain shook his head. "No, I'm not the type. I wasn't supposed to be the superior knight, remember? I was just along for the ride.

I was supposed to be the muscle. My partner was the brains." Looking away, Alain bit his tongue, fighting back a swell of memories. "Luca is more the type, you know. To be a righteous knight of the Templar Order. Second-in-command, about to inherit the guard."

"I'm glad it's you and not him." Cristoph's hand snaked across the counter, his fingers resting over Alain's. "I can't imagine he'd handle learning about this stuff very well. He'd probably have a meltdown, completely lose his marbles."

The moment stretched long, Alain losing himself in the warmth of Cristoph's gaze. He couldn't tear himself from Cristoph. *I'm in too deep. I care too much about him. This is only going to end in tragedy.*

"Cristoph—"

His front door splintering open, broken down from outside, tore them apart in a flash. Cristoph grabbed the blade Alain had given him as Alain ripped down a shotgun mounted behind them. He pumped once and braced against the kitchen wall, next to the narrow doorway leading to the rest of the apartment. Cristoph stood opposite, holding the blade and keeping his eyes fixed on Alain.

"*Alain!*" A deep voice roared from the doorway. "Alain, I know you're in here!"

His breath *whooshed* from him, exhaling in a massive gasp. He dropped the shotgun, letting it clatter behind him on the floor as he motioned for Cristoph to lower his blade.

The noise from the dropped shotgun drew the intruder to them. Footsteps thundered toward the kitchen. Alain spun out into the hall, stopping the man before he saw Alain's kitchen, his armory. Cristoph followed on his heels.

Luca came up short, glowering at Cristoph before turning a murderous scowl to Alain.

"What the fuck do you want, Luca? It's—" He checked through the kitchen door to the coffee maker. The clock said five in the morning. "It's way too fucking early for this."

"I'm *so* sorry to disturb your morning, Alain," Luca growled. "You should have thought of that last night. When *I* was trying to sleep."

He frowned. Then it hit him. His bedroom wall was also Luca's bedroom wall.

They hadn't been quiet last night. Not at all. Not with him urging Cristoph to scream his name, to wail to God and the Vatican what Alain was doing to him. And then there was the bed frame, the hard, rhythmic pounding against the wall, for hours. His face flushed, burning.

"Prick," Luca snarled. He snarled at Cristoph. "If you're well enough to fuck, you're well enough to get back to your duties. You'll stand at your post until I tell you you're free, Halberdier."

"No, I still have my duties with Alain."

Luca's gaze burned and his lips pulled back, baring his gritted teeth. "Sergeant Autenburg—"

"Cristoph, it's all right. You should go back to your post." Alain tried to stem Luca's fury, tried to stave off the eruption brewing before his eyes.

"But—" Hurt flashed through Cristoph, followed by a pang of accusation. "But we have our *own* duties. Things we need to do."

Luca snorted loudly. He rolled his eyes.

Alain ignored him. "And when you're through with your shifts, you'll be back." A thin smile stretched over his lips. "It's better for you to be at your post right now. Safer. Don't draw attention to yourself."

Luca's eyes narrowed to slits. He stared at Alain. Wariness poured from him, but he shook his head and strode away, leaving them behind.

Cristoph waited until he was gone. "Don't push me away again."

Alain grabbed Cristoph's hand, bringing it to his lips. "I couldn't even if I wanted to." He kissed his fingers, the center of Cristoph's palm. "I'll see you later. I promise." Cristoph smiled, then turned. He heaved a sigh.

Like a guilty man going to his execution, Cristoph trudged for Luca. Luca waited, glowering. "Are you ready, Halberdier?"

"I need to get dressed—"

"You will. Into your own uniform. In your own dorm."

Cristoph's face twisted. He marched in front of Luca to Alain's broken door in just his boxers and Alain's borrowed undershirt. He'd walk the whole way back to his dorm like that with Luca on his heels, and with what had happened yesterday in the canteen, *everyone* would know. God, *everyone* would know what had happened.

Alain scrubbed a hand over his eyes. Too much, too much was happening too fast. He couldn't wrap his head around it, couldn't wrap his heart around it.

He felt a heavy gaze on him. He looked up.

Luca, half shrouded in the darkness of the hallway, stared at him. His face was cast in shadow, and only the reflected light from the Apostolic Palace made his eyes gleam, a stare that made the hairs on the back of Alain's neck stand on end. His blood turned to ice. He tasted electricity, felt the slide of snakeskin over a dry desert, sand and grave dirt choking the back of his throat.

"Luca," he breathed.

Luca stormed off. His deep voice echoed down the barracks hallway, dogging after Cristoph as he marched him to his dorm.

ALAIN MET LOTARIO IN HIS OFFICE, CLUTCHING HIS THIRD CUP of espresso, in no mood for Lotario's jokes.

"Where's your lover boy?"

"Shut up."

"Ooo, touchy. Was it not all you wanted it to be? Did he not put out?" Lotario's eyebrows wagged. "Or did you not?"

"I don't want to hear it."

Lotario spread his arms wide. "Your first attempt at being an actual living male in twelve years and you expect me to *not* make a big deal out of it?"

"I expect you to be a decent human being but that's clearly asking too much."

Lotario snorted. He pulled one of the rickety metal chairs out with his foot and twirled it around, sitting backward and hanging his arms over the backrest. "Welcome back to the world of sin, Alain. It's missed you."

Alain stayed silent. He sucked his top lip behind his bottom teeth as he paged through his email. All quiet on the internet, at least. Thank God for small favors.

"Where *is* lover boy?"

He fixed Lotario with a dark glare. "He's on post." He hesitated. "Luca barged in this morning and dragged him back on duty. We were... loud."

Lotario fought back his wild grin. One hand rose, covering his mouth. He coughed, looking anywhere but at Alain. "So that's why you're in such a wonderful mood."

"Did you bring the samples?" Ignoring Lotario, Alain slid the crystal pendulum with the vampire blood from Nuzzi's murder across the desk. The vampire blood had dried black on the crystal.

Lotario pulled out two vials of blood, hastily marked with tape and black marker. "*Nest*" read the first label. "*Solitary*" read the second. "Which one first?"

Alain grabbed the vial for the solitary vampire. He scraped some of the dried blood off the crystal, letting the small flecks rest on a cleared spot on his desk. Unstopping the vial, he tilted it, pouring a single drop onto the flecks.

Flame sparked as both parts of blood were consumed in fire.

Their gazes met and held. Lotario frowned and pulled out a cigarette as Alain scraped a new pile of dried blood onto the desk. Silently, Lotario passed over the second vial, the one labeled "*Nest*."

A single drop fell. The blood flashed, the dried flecks slipping into the droplet, becoming one. A black sphere of blood sat quivering on Alain's desk.

Lotario smashed it with his lit cigarette, rolling the embers into the blood drop. Smoke rose as the blood sizzled. Lotario left his smashed cigarette in the mess on Alain's desk. "The nest killed Cardinal Nuzzi."

"The nest had Madelena *spy* on Nuzzi."

"They might have been coming after what they didn't get from her. Trying to finish the job?"

Alain swallowed. "Did they?"

Lotario shrugged and let his head hang down over the back of the chair. He spread his hands wide. "What now, Alain? Where do we go from here?"

He didn't want to do this. More than anything else, he didn't want to do this. But they had to, especially now. With all signs pointing to the nest, with more unknowns than knowns, they had to track down the only leads they had. "We have to scout the nest."

Lotario sighed, hanging his head. "Are you sure that's a good idea? They've just snacked on thirteen bodies. They're super powered now. Hitting them in the nest sounds like a really fucking bad idea, actually."

"Not a strike. You're right, we can't take them. But we need to figure out what is going on. We need to talk to the alpha. The pact still stands, at least in writing. We should demand answers. Figure out what kind of alliance the demons and vampires have."

"How are we going to get in there? We didn't do so well the last time."

"I can backtrack the route I took through the river, follow the Tiber back underground. We can come up through the water. It will mask our scent."

"Should we wait for Cristoph?" Lotario sighed as Alain shot him a frigid glare. "All I'm saying is that more bodies would be helpful. We could use the backup."

"No. No *way*."

"Alain—"

"I will *never* bring him anywhere near the vampires, Lotario!"

Twelve years, and nothing seemed to have changed. Facing vampires, again. And his lover in the mix, again. "I will *never* put him at risk. *Never*."

Lotario pursed his lips, but nodded. He slapped his knees. "All right. All right, fine. Let's go. Let's go scout the damn nest. Try and talk to the alpha."

Chapter Nineteen

ASMODEUS SHIVERED INTO BEING. THE SMOKE AND SHADOWS OF his incorporeal form was all he could push across the shuttered Veil. For ten thousand years, the Veil had stood, separating Earth—and humans—from everything else.

From their home. From the garden, the land they all had been born in.

It was an endless torment, a ceaseless torture, carving out the humans from the rest of creation. The erection of the Veil had shattered their lands, sent their home into endless waves of darkness and warfare. So much had changed when the Veil descended.

So many had been lost that day.

So many never found.

But nine hundred years ago, there had been a moment, a slice in time, when the Veil had torn. The Veil tore at the ruins where the last battle occurred, Elohim's fight against Lucifer.

It was after that battle that the darkness had fallen, the Veil had risen, and their worlds had been torn apart, seemingly forever. A tear in the Veil at the site of those ancient ruins, the scorched and destroyed lands of the ancient battle, wasn't what anyone had been expecting.

But they could all feel the Veil tear apart, and more, they could feel his longing, his desperate, aching longing. For the first time in millennia, they all could hear him again, his voice raging in their minds, calling out for salvation and for justice, just as he had so long ago.

Nine hundred years ago, the Veil had parted, and, coming from the humans' world—from Earth—Lucifer's voice was heard again, a clarion shout singing through their lands.

They tried to come for him, tried to find where his *noumenon*— thought banished, thought destroyed and unmade for millennia —had gone.

The Veil closed before they could reach him.

Before it closed, they saw men in white tunics with blazing red crosses, dressed in shining plate armor, and they heard the men call each other Templar.

They had a purpose, after that. Find Lucifer. Find his *noumenon*. Rescue their leader.

Time didn't matter. They had eternity.

The search spanned centuries, crossed continents. The Templars—knights of Elohim's church—grew in power and then were nearly destroyed. They went to the shadows and seemed to vanish.

But they returned. Whispers spread amongst the creatures of darkness, filtering through the Veil. Hunters, the whispers said. The knights are hunters.

It took time, but they tracked the knights to Rome.

To do more, they would need to work on Earth. They'd need to cross the Veil. But nothing could, nothing but shadow and smoke, the barest hint of their powers. Only dark creatures lived in the human world, on the human side of the Veil.

An alliance, then. A meeting of purposes in the darkness. Dark desires fanning each other.

Even though vampires were the darkest scourge of creation, twisted and corrupted, they had their uses.

Asmodeus turned, his shadowed form moving silently in the vampires' bone cathedral. Green mist snaked over the walls, lit the skulls hanging on the walls. He recognized some of his fallen brothers. "Alpha Lycidas," he called. "I am here."

Lycidas emerged from the darkness, scowling. The evanescent gleam that slithered over his pupils caught enough light to give his glare an eerie glow. Asmodeus's smoke curled inward, nearly curdled, and if he'd had his body, his bones would have puckered.

"The cardinal is dead," Lycidas growled. His fangs were out, flashing in the dim light. "He didn't give up the information, even though I took my time with his death."

A pity. But not insurmountable. "You weren't able to strum the information from your whore, and you weren't able to take the information from a dying old man?"

Lycidas flew at him, fangs flashing, talons extended. He stopped short of Asmodeus's shadow, holding back his strike. "Speak carefully of Madelena," Lycidas's nose twitched. Disgust crawled over his face. "She was mine, and I loved her."

"She may have been your lover, and she may have let you feed on her, but she was useless to us in the end. And it was your carelessness that allowed the ghoul to follow you to her. Linhart followed the ghoul. You lost your little whore. A whore who bled out your secret, your blood in her veins, and led those priests to your nest." Asmodeus clucked. "You couldn't even pull information from the hunter you *accidentally* managed to capture here. And, you killed Nuzzi before he gave you any information. Your jealous blood rage against him obstructed your mission."

Lycidas's low snarl echoed through the bone cathedral. Growls rose in the darkness. "You didn't have to send *my* lover to seduce the cardinal." More braying, harsh grunts in the darkness, and talons slashing against stone, sparking.

"You would truly set your nest on me, Lycidas? Despite our

alliance?" Asmodeus grinned, sly. "Will vampires turn against us in the end?"

"You stink." Lycidas stalked away, slinking into the darkness. "You stink like damnation."

"Pretty words from creatures who smell like grave rot and death."

Lycidas stayed in the dark, silent.

Asmodeus felt a tug on his *noumenon*. Yes, he had to get going. Temeluchus, on the other side of the Veil, was getting restless. "Alpha Lycidas, you have failed at every turn. Even for a vampire, you're a disappointment. Every low expectation I had for your kind, you failed to meet." He turned, circling, able to spot Lycidas in the shadows despite the vampire's attempts to retreat to his darkness.

The vampires thought they owned the darkness.

No. Demons gave birth to the darkness.

"Everything we did for you. Your nest was strengthened by us. We fed you all those humans, all those possessed souls led into your arms, and in exchange for what?" His head tilted. His white mask was perpetually grinning, but if he could, he'd have smiled wider, practically beaming.

"We can still get the information," Lycidas barked. "We can still find out who the hunter is."

"Oh, I think now you're more useful for something else." Asmodeus pulled inward, drawing his strength together. A low chant started in the back of his mind. "You didn't think you were our only pawns, did you? Unfortunately for you, in the end, the others were simply so much more *useful*."

Silence, for a moment, and then the nest exploded. Snarls, the roars of furious vampires, fangs snapping and talons scratching against bone and stone. He saw them coming, racing for him in the darkness.

He spoke his chant aloud, his voice rising. His power curled, swirling within him. He blasted his spell and his shadowed form—

suddenly burning, suddenly flaming—turned to burgundy Demon Fire and arched through the nest.

Snarling vampires threw up their arms, trying to shield their eyes. They shrieked, falling to the ground, wrapped head to toe in freezing Demon Fire.

Lycidas howled, his voice like shattering glass and metal splintering apart. "What are you doing?"

Asmodeus, a whiff of shade, barely anything at all with his shadowed form turned to flame and stretched around the vampires, chuckled. "Turning on you, Lycidas. You vampires, you're despicable. The worst of creation." His flames leaped higher, his presence, his spell one and the same. "You know, you weren't even created by Elohim. You're an abomination."

"Damn you," Lycidas growled. "Damn you, Asmodeus."

Asmodeus's voice fell flat. "We are already damned."

His spell roared. The vampires shrieked, wailing and howling as their bones broke and their skin fractured and the blood within them—stolen blood, thirteen corpses worth—flowed free, bathing the bones of their cathedral, pooling on the ground. The taste of copper filled the air, the tang strong and sweet.

Lycidas lived, barely. He struggled against the flaming bonds as Asmodeus moved to him, circling the alpha. "I needed you for something beyond your search for the hunter, Lycidas. I needed you, and your nest, for this blood. To gather it here so that I could spill it as one."

Madness flared from Lycidas's eyes. "Burn, demon. Burn in the depths."

"No more depths for us." He pushed Lycidas down, the fires pulling him until he was flat on his back, lying in the pool of spilled blood from his nest. It rose around him, over his ears, his cheeks. Poured down his throat. Lycidas thrashed as smoke rose from his mouth, as his body started to burn from the inside. "We're bringing Lucifer back. Today."

Lycidas bellowed, his fangs snapping as he burned from the inside out.

Asmodeus's Demon Fire bonds cracked.

Lycidas's screams died with a wet snap.

———

SILENCE, THICK LIKE DEATH, HOVERED IN THE AIR AS ALAIN AND Lotario crept toward the vampires' bone cathedral.

They took the long way, snaking along the banks of the Tiber that broke off into a tributary underground. When they crept into the darkness, Alain passed over a set of night vision goggles he'd pilfered from the Swiss Guard armory.

Deep underground they pushed, communicating with silent gestures.

Alain motioned for Lotario to follow him carefully toward a pebble shore in the black depths.

He froze, the Tiber lapping at his shins as he crept up the vampires' rocky beach.

Something dripped from the bone walls, from the skulls and their guttered dark flames. Something wet.

He waited, listening. There were no sounds. No movement. Nothing at all in the darkness.

Alain folded up his NVGs and fished out his flashlight. Lotario held his own with his wrists crossed under the grip of his pistol, covering Alain. Alain hefted the knight's blade he carried. Lotario had raised both eyebrows when he brought it, but Alain hadn't said a word. This one wasn't his own. He'd left his as a gift for Cristoph back at his apartment.

No, the blade he held wasn't his.

He held it before him as he crept up the softly sloping pebble shore. The glow of their flashlights landed on the blood-drenched nest.

Blood was *everywhere*. The entire space was coated in it— running down the bone walls, lying in a lake in the center of the nest. Bodies lay in the shadows, unmoving. He stopped short at the sheer amount of gore. His throat closed against the smell of it, copper and iron on the back of his tongue, the taste of rot and grave dirt. But no ozone, no electricity arcing down his throat.

The vampires were dead.

Slaughtered would be a better word.

Lotario whistled. He coughed, choking on the death in the air. The beam of his flashlight moved to the center of the cavern and froze. "Alain."

A vampire, or what was left of him, lay in the center of the lake of blood. A ragged slice ripped down the center of his chest. His ribs flared out, peeled back at odd angles.

They moved closer, flashlights trained on the vampire's corpse.

"Jesus Christ, it's the alpha." Alain coughed and turned his nose away, trying to escape the stench. Death and putrefaction, and a sharper, deeper scent. Burning.

The alpha's eyes were open, staring at nothing. His fangs were out, lips pulled back, his face frozen in a last, desperate scream.

Blood swirled against their boots, almost up to their ankles.

Alain peered into the hollow, open cavity of the alpha's chest. Darkness stared back at him, a hole that ran straight through the corpse and opened into an endless void.

"What the hell?" Lotario squatted next to the body.

A shiver crawled up Alain's spine, slow taps like fingernails plucking his bones. "I know what this is," he breathed. "I've seen it before. In the secrets of the Order." There was a danger in the air, a stain, a brand of evil. Something that screamed in his mind, tore at his soul, shredded him apart. *Run! Run!*

A slithering voice, deep within, urged him to stay. To reach into the alpha's corpse, to fall headfirst into the black void cut through the vampire's lifeless body.

"It's a spell." He closed his eyes. The slippery voice buried under his soul was getting louder. "A portal through the Veil. It's the same kind of portal the first knights found in the Well of Souls."

Lotario was silent, save for the wet inhale of his ragged breaths. "Who could do this?"

Inhaling, Alain's nostrils flared. That burn, that acrid stench, slotted into his brain. "Demons."

Lotario's lips pressed together, thinning to a hard line.

"Can't you smell it? The burning? The sulfur?"

"I can't smell shit over all this blood." He peered at Alain, shining his flashlight into Alain's face. "You sure? You sure it's demons?"

Jump. Jump down. Cross the Veil, Alain. It was a whisper tugging on his soul, deep enough to rattle his bones.

"I'm sure of it." He pulled himself away from the alpha's corpse. "What else could destroy a nest of vampires and leave them soaked in gore?"

"I thought they were working together."

Panic bloomed, so suddenly, so fiercely, he stumbled, nearly fell into the lake of blood. "This is it, Lotario. Whatever they're planning, it's happening now. The demons, they must have double crossed the vamps. For this! This is a portal, like before. Like what the knights found. It's an opening, it's *the* opening. The Veil, it's—" Groaning, Alain dropped down, squatting as his mind screamed and the whisper inside him chuckled, dry leaves and old nails scraping across chalkboard.

He had to get back. He had to get to Cristoph. Why wasn't he right next to Cristoph, right now? Why had he thought, why had he *believed*, Cristoph would be safe away from his side?

"What's happening? What the fuck is going on with you?"

"I don't know! I don't fucking know!" He grasped his hair, almost pulling out strands as he groaned. His head throbbed, as if his skull was splitting in two. "We have to get back. Something's happening, Lotario. Something terrible. I can feel it."

Commandant Best made the sign of the cross over his chest and kissed his rosary before tucking the wooden crucifix back under his shirt. His gaze rolled up, eyes fixing to the painting he'd insisted on hanging in his office. A portrait of the Knights Templar, two knights bedecked in white tunics, emblazoned with red crosses, kneeling with their swords dug into the earth. Eyes turned up, the knights' faces held a look of rapture as they prayed, listening to God's word.

Where was divine guidance when he asked? Where was his rapture, his answered prayer?

He closed his eyes, his eyelashes brushing over his weathered cheeks. The years had grown long, perhaps too long, and it was getting time to consider stepping down and letting Luca take over the reins.

And yet, Luca...

Sighing, Best rubbed the beads of his rosary again.

His cell phone ringing jarred him out of his pensive thoughts. He didn't recognize the number. Still, he swiped to answer. "Commandant Best speaking."

"*Commandant!*"

It was Alain, but not Alain as he'd ever sounded. This Alain was panicked. Petrified.

"Alain? What is wrong? What's happened?"

"*We found a portal, Commandant. Through the Veil. Just like the legends say. A bloody gate and a black hole to the abyss. We found one down in the vampires' nest. It's the demons, Commandant, they're—*"

"Alain, slow down. What are you saying?" As Alain spoke, Best slowly rose from his desk chair. The blood drained from his face. "I have to warn the Holy Father. His Holiness will want to pray."

"*Be careful, Gaëtan!*" Alain's panicked voice was almost drowned out by the wail of a car horn. "*The girl searched you out, and the vamps killed Cardinal Nuzzi. They might have the same information she did. If the vampires knew about you, then the demons must too! They could be coming for you.*"

"I will be cautious, Alain. You must do so as well."

"*No, my file wasn't there. The only way they'll find me is if they get to you.*"

"I will be cautious. But I must inform His Holiness."

"We're on our way back. I'll find you when we get there. I need help, Commandant." Alain exhaled, a long, sorrow-filled sigh. *"I'm sorry, Gaëtan. I'm sorry I failed. I let this happen—"*

"Alain, there hasn't been a true demonic rising in centuries. And the last vampire rising, *you* stopped. You've been dealing with revenants and wraiths and hungry ghosts for over a decade, and you've been great."

"Commandant—"

"Speak no more of this, Alain. We'll talk when you get here. We will fight this rising. Together."

He heard Alain's swallow over the phone line. *"Yes, Commandant. I'll... I'll see you soon."*

Closing his eyes, Best sent a prayer to the heavens as he hung up. *Lord, deliver us now, as we place our faith and our future into your hands.* He pulled open the bottom drawer of his desk and took out a long box from the filing cabinet. The narrow, navy box had a simple clasp. He slipped the brass clip back and tilted the lid.

A silver-coated blade nestled against black velvet, laid in place twelve years ago, the last time he'd ever touched it. He hefted the blade, the grip still fitting his hand like it had for the decade he had been the knight on guard against the darkness.

Beneath the black velvet, a leather scabbard rested, fitted for his suit. The Swiss Guard wore rapiers and swords on their belts every day, for ceremony and for purpose, and it had been easy to carry this blade back then, hidden in plain sight, a holy weapon amid a sea of ordinary.

Alain had never carried his blade, not since that night twelve years prior.

Sliding the blade into the scabbard, Best slipped it into his suit jacket's inner pocket. He left his office and strode through the garrison. Luca was scowling at his computer monitor. Captain Ewe joked with one of the sergeants, tossing back his head and laughing out loud. Halberdiers milled, on their way to or from a posting, and tipped their heads in a salute as he passed by.

The walk to the Apostolic Palace was a short one. He smiled at the young halberdier guarding the elevator for the Holy Father's private apartment.

As the elevator doors opened, the heavy brass bell ringing, another man joined him, sliding to his side. "May I ride up with you, Commandant?" Cardinal Santino Acossio, the new secretary of state, smiled.

"Of course, Cardinal." Best gestured to the opening doors. "Please, after you."

"No, I insist. As a warrior for God, please do me the honor." Cardinal Acossio held out his hand.

Tipping his head, Best stepped in the elevator and pressed the button for the Holy Father's floor. The doors started to close.

"Such a trying time," Cardinal Acossio said, clucking his tongue. "Cardinal Nuzzi's death. So violent."

"We're working on finding the murderer, Cardinal. We will keep you safe. You and the Holy Father."

The brass doors slotted together. The elevator began to rise.

"But Commandant," Cardinal Acossio said, turning to face him.

Black smoke appeared in a vortex. Swirling, the smoke formed into the shape of a man, cracking and thundering. As quick as it appeared, the smoke vanished, revealing a being cut from darkness, long limbs stretched to grotesque proportions, lean muscles pushing out from midnight skin, and an angular jaw narrowed to a tip beneath a pointed skull. The creature grinned, all sharp teeth and fangs.

It was a demon in full form, summoned bodily through a portal ripped through the Veil.

Best reached for his blade.

Cardinal Acossio smirked. "Who will keep you safe?"

Acossio stepped back. The demon struck before Best could draw his blade, pinning him against the elevator. Smoke poured from its skin, sliding over Best's body, up his arms, around his throat, and into his mouth, open in a silent scream.

Best's eyes rolled back in his skull, shifting to black as the demon possessed his soul.

It had taken hours to crawl their way to the vampires' nest deep under Rome, but they didn't have that kind of time heading back.

Filthy, soaking wet, and drenched in spilled vampire blood, Alain and Lotario burst from Lotario's Bug half a mile from the Vatican and ran for St. Anne's Gate. A roadblock had stopped all traffic heading into the Eternal City. Two Swiss Guards waved people away, directing them to turn back.

"What happened?" Alain grabbed one of the guards, nearly running over the man. He was a corporal, three years in, but not someone Alain knew well. "What's happening?"

Eyes wide, the guard stared askance at Alain. His gaze tracked the blood and gore, the rot and the putrescence clinging to Alain's suit. He tried to jerk away, but Alain held him fast.

"Tell me!" Alain roared, shaking the young guard.

"Alain—" Lotario tried.

"It's the Commandant!" Petrified eyes darted between Alain and Lotario. He jerked again but wasn't able to break Alain's hold. "It's the Commandant." His voice wavered, warbled. "He's dead."

No. God, you bastard. No, damn you! Alain gripped the guard's arms until the younger man winced. "How?" he breathed as Lotario cursed.

The guard shook his head. "They found him in His Holiness's elevator. His—" His voice cracked. The guard looked down.

Alain shook him again. "Tell me everything!"

"He was decapitated!" the guard snapped. "He had some kind of blade with him, and it sliced his head off. But he was alone! How—"

Pushing away, Alain doubled over, his hands on his knees, trying to fight back the wave of nausea. Gaëtan was dead. His one anchor in the world, his friend, and he was gone. Ripped from his life.

Ripped from his life by *demons,* working with vampires.

If the demons had gotten to Best, then they knew everything Best knew. Which meant—

Whirling, Alain grabbed the guard again. "Where is Major Bader?"

The guard tried to pull free from Alain's ironclad grasp. "He's in the garrison. He's trying to keep a lid on this, but you're acting like a lunatic, Sergeant." The guard finally twisted free and stepped back, one hand on his service weapon at his hip. "Get a hold of yourself. You're making a scene."

Fuck him. Alain took off, ignoring the guard's demands to stop. He ran, Lotario beside him, and tore straight for the garrison offices.

A blur of color appeared, striped red, yellow, and blue. His soul wept as he recognized Cristoph, and he reached over and grabbed his uniform, hauling him close.

"I just heard." Cristoph ripped his beret off. "The major put me on post at the Door of Death for nine hours. I left."

He couldn't be mad about Cristoph ditching his post, not now. "Stay close to me."

They slowed as they reached the garrison, Lotario hacking through a wet cough as he doubled over while Alain ripped open the door. Cristoph's hand landed on his back as they crowded through, and even through his suit, the touch burned.

Chaos had descended on the Swiss Guard inside the garrison. Phones rang off the hook. Stricken halberdiers rushed to and fro as Captain Ewe barked orders in German into a radio in one hand and shouted into a phone in Italian in the other. Chaplain Weimers sat at a desk, staring at his folded hands, his eyes vacant and lost.

Luca stood in the center of it all, listening to his own radio and furiously scratching something down on a notepad.

"*Luca!*" Alain bellowed.

Luca's gaze rose and met Alain's.

Light and fury exploded through the garrison.

An eruption bloomed, bursting apart the brick wall of the

office. Shrapnel flew, shards of red brick sliced through the air. Molten heat washed the world in orange flames. Desks and computers blew apart, rocketing across the office, cords whiptailing behind the machines. Glass shattered, raining a stinging, razor-sharp grit. Shouts cut off mid-scream as the ceiling groaned and buckled, collapsing. Smoke and haze choked the air, lodging in Alain's throat and obscuring everything from sight.

Alain coughed as he peered through the wreckage, knocked to his belly and trying to see something, anything. Shattered glass sliced his palms. Brick dust hung on his tongue, mixing with acrid black smoke. His eyes watered, stinging. He twisted and found Cristoph's soot-covered face. A gash bled from his temple to his chin, but his eyes were clear, and he reached for Alain, squeezing his shoulder. "I'm all right," Cristoph shouted over the roar of devastation and the chaos of destruction. "You?"

He nodded as the fire sprinklers jetted on, red lights spinning as the two-note siren wailed.

A being made of darkness, of midnight skin and angular features, stepped through the blown hole in the garrison's brick wall.

Demon! Alain's soul shouted. *A demon from beyond the Veil! It crossed over!*

Next to the demon, a second being entered, also made of darkness, but covered head to toe in curling flames writhing over his skin.

Temeluchus, deep whispers breathed beneath Alain's soul. *My old friend. So good to see you again.*

Dread filled Alain, spreading to all the corners of his being. He scrambled up, slipping as he came to his knees. "*Luca!*" he shouted. "Luca, Goddammit, where are you?"

"Here." A voice he didn't know spoke. Alain turned—

Luca dangled by his throat, held aloft by the midnight demon. His fingers clawed at the demon's grasp, scratching at its wrists as he struggled for breath. The second demon tumbled flames from its fingers, curls of fire snaking toward Luca.

"No!" Alain charged forward. In his hand, he gripped the blade he'd taken that morning.

Both demons turned, heads snapping to Alain.

"Alain, *stop*—" Luca wheezed.

A shriek, like metal shredding against metal, like glass shearing in two, burst through the garrison. Light streaked over everyone as they grabbed at their ears and buried their faces in the debris-strewn floor. Screaming shattered the air, a lingering wail that curdled blood in veins.

And then, it was over.

***

CRISTOPH LEAPED TO HIS FEET, KICKING AWAY CEILING TILES and crumbled brick as water rained down on him from the sprinklers. He ran toward the center of the office, vaulting over splintered furniture, destroyed computers, and shattered glass. His torn uniform snagged on bits of wood and shorn metal.

He whirled, searching for Alain. "*Alain*! Alain, where the fuck are you?"

Alain was gone.

But he had been there, just a moment ago. What—

Something gleamed on the floor, a glint of silver. He reached for it.

Another hand grabbed it first.

Cristoph looked up. Luca's confused gaze met his. Luca rubbed his throat as he plucked Alain's blade from the debris, staring down at the sword with an expression Cristoph couldn't read.

He didn't have time for this. Those things, those creatures —*demons*—must have taken Alain. He didn't have time to fight with Luca. Not when Alain's life was in danger. Not when he had to find him, had to save him, and he had no idea how to begin.

"Lotar—" He spoke before he turned, shouting for the asshole priest who had become, inexplicably, his mentor. Maybe was starting to become a friend.

But Lotario wasn't there. He was *gone*. Vanished, like Alain.

"My God!" A new voice broke through the devastation as the gendarmerie captain arrived, the camerlengo in tow. "Major Bader? Major, are you in here? Are you all right? We've brought medical aid!" the elderly camerlengo cried. The wail of sirens and the deep horn of ambulances and fire engines echoed, the Vatican fire brigade on scene.

"We're here!" Luca hefted himself to his feet and tried to hide a wince that Cristoph caught. His hand closed around the blade, drawing it behind his back. "My people need medical attention! Please hurry!"

Firefighters and medics rushed in, darting through the destruction and the smoke. Captain Ewe already had a few of the guards up, guiding them free of the destruction as they held bleeding limbs and broken bones.

The camerlengo picked his way to Luca's side, mouth agape at the rampant destruction. "Major—" he started, crossing himself. "Commandant," he corrected. "His Holiness requires your presence. Immediately."

Chapter Twenty

CRISTOPH, BEDRAGGLED IN HIS FILTHY, DAMP UNIFORM, JOGGED alongside Luca, refusing to leave his side as they followed the camerlengo up to the Holy Father's private apartments.

Across the Vatican, sirens wailed, ambulances, fire engines, and gendarmerie vehicles all trying to render aid and set up a protective perimeter, keeping onlookers and bystanders away from the destruction of the Swiss Guard garrison. The carabinieri were setting a perimeter outside the Vatican, helping to push back the crowd of gawking civilians, and in St. Peter's Square, a line of halberdiers began to slowly push out the tourists and pilgrims praying outside the Basilica. The Vatican was closing ranks.

Luca never said a word, not to Cristoph, and not to the camerlengo. He still held Alain's sword, but he'd shifted the hilt, holding it like a dagger against his forearm.

I need to get that back. What would Alain say if he knew that fucking *Luca* had his blade? His eyes darted over the major. God, how was he supposed to do any of this? They needed to fight back, strike the demons that had attacked them. Find Alain and Lotario. But how was he supposed to do that if Luca stood in his way?

They skipped the cordoned-off elevator inside the Apostolic

Palace. Yellow gendarmerie crime scene tape blocked off the private elevator. Inside, Commandant Best's headless body still lay on the floor, covered with a sheet. There hadn't been time yet to take him to the clinic, to the small morgue in the back.

They were led to the stairs, Cristoph taking them two at a time while Luca helped the older camerlengo up. Impatient, Cristoph fidgeted at the top landing. The urge to run, to act, to do something, anything, nearly made him scream. He clenched his hands and tried to breathe.

The camerlengo guided them down the Holy Father's private hallway. Marble floors gleamed and the smell of beeswax hung in the air. One wall facing out over the courtyard was solid glass, a perfectly unobstructed view of the Vatican and Rome beyond. On the opposite wall, vivid frescoes and maps of antiquity stared them down. Seas and the continents of the Old World, the corners marked with mythical beasts and monsters that warned travelers of the perils of exploration off the edges of the map. The frescoes had been painted onto the Vatican's walls by the Renaissance masters themselves, and even hundreds of years old, the colors were still striking and brilliant. The weight of history lingered, mixing with the scent of candles and incense.

Cristoph spared a glance for the paintings and kept on, staying at Luca's side all the way to the gold door at the end of the hall. A silent, pale Swiss Guard stood his post outside the golden door, his jaw clenched so tight the tendons in his neck bulged. The sound of his teeth scraping together echoed down the hall.

Luca rested his hand on the guard's shoulder and leaned in, speaking softly in his ear. The guard's eyes slid closed. A single tear rolled down his cheek. He nodded once.

The camerlengo reached for the door handle. His gaze darted over Luca—his dark eyes raging, a tumult of confusion and fury, his uniform burned, a bruise blooming around his throat in the shape of a perfect handprint—and then Cristoph—his torn uniform dirty and wet, and probably looking like a dog about to bolt at any moment. "His Holiness is waiting for you inside."

Cristoph heard Luca's inhale, a rush of air hissing through his bruised throat.

The door opened. Cristoph stepped in, shoulder to shoulder with Luca.

In the center of the Holy Father's sitting room, praying with his face turned to the heavens, was His Holiness, Pope Clemente. Elected by conclave only the year before, he was younger than his predecessors, in his late sixties, and even though he was Italian, the world welcomed him as a breath of fresh air, a reformer of the church for the modern age.

Luca strode forward as Cristoph froze, stuck suddenly in place. Luca dropped to one knee before Clemente, genuflecting and bowing his head. He grasped the Holy Father's hand and pressed a lingering kiss to the papal ring. "Holy Father," Cristoph heard Luca whisper. "Holy Father... we need your guidance."

Clemente caressed Luca's cheek. Soot from Luca stained his pale fingers and dusted onto the front of his white cassock. "Commandant," he said carefully. "My heart is with you this terrible hour. Rise, my son."

Cringing at his new title, Luca rose stiffly, staring at the carpet. "Holy Father," he began, his voice gruff and grinding over his words, "I'm..." He skipped his new title. "Luca Bader. And this is —" Luca's gaze met Cristoph's. He tried to speak, but no words came out. He shook his head. "This is Halberdier Cristoph Hasse."

"I know who you are, Luca Bader." Clemente smiled, his eyes crinkling at the edges. "You, though." Crossing the sitting room, Clemente stopped before Cristoph. "You, I don't know."

God, what should he do? Should he drop to his knee, genuflect and kiss the ring like a proper Catholic? *Was* he even a proper Catholic anymore? After Africa, he hadn't known what he was, and he'd run for the Vatican on a whim. Going through the motions with the Swiss Guard was one thing, but face-to-face with the Holy Father was entirely another. What did he believe?

And what did any of his beliefs mean cast against the new reality he'd been thrust into, where vampires and demons and dark creatures existed? There was evil in the world, he'd always known that, but he had thought it had just been human evil. Evil from men's hearts.

What did it mean that evil, pure evil, existed in the universe? What did that mean for God?

Clemente's smile widened as Cristoph faltered, struck dumb with indecision. Jesus, the fucking pope was waiting on him to decide what to do and he was standing there like a moron.

Warmth radiated from Clemente, a gentle wave of peace and acceptance that lapped at the edges of Cristoph's soul. He seemed to shine, to glow just faintly, as if there was something under his skin that couldn't quite be contained. Alain seemed like that sometimes, when he smiled. When they were together. And, just like with Alain, Cristoph wanted to step forward, bury himself in Clemente's robes and wrap his soul up in that feeling. His breath hitched.

"Cristoph Hasse. I do not know you yet." Clemente's eyes were soft. "Tell me, my son. What do you need?"

It all came tumbling out, words crowding in his throat and fighting for freedom. "God— *Shit*, Holy Father, I don't even know where to begin—" He shook his head. Behind the Holy Father, Luca's dark eyes fixed on Cristoph.

I report to the pope.

"I work with Alain Autenburg," Cristoph blurted out. "He's training me. Him and Father Lotario Nicosia. I've been helping with their hunt. This, right now, what's happening. It's *vampires*. A vampire killed a woman who was spying on Cardinal Nuzzi, and then more vampires killed Cardinal Nuzzi. The woman was trying to find out information on the hunters in Rome. On the *knights*. Someone, something, was trying to track them all down, I think. She had Commandant Best's file. I think they're trying to kill all of the knights. All of the hunters. And then there was the attack on the garrison just now, and they *took* Alain. And Lotario."

Clemente's quiet exhale shook the crystals dangling from the gilded chandelier.

Cristoph chanced a glance at Luca. His dark eyes had narrowed to slits, disbelief scrawling across his twisted features.

"Oh, my son," Clemente breathed. He grasped Cristoph's hand, squeezing. "What took them? And how?"

He fumbled for words, starting and stopping as he shook his head. "It wasn't vampires." He shuddered, a wracked inhale shaking his chest. Dark creatures, one flaming, the other with gleaming, mad eyes. "I don't know," he whispered. "God, I don't know. I'm sorry."

"We'll find them." Clemente's hand squeezed again. "We will. We have to." Clemente turned back to Luca. He straightened his spine, squared his shoulders. "There are things you need to know now that you are the commandant."

"What is all of this, Holy Father?" Luca's voice trembled. His chin jutted toward Cristoph. "What does he mean?"

Cristoph looked down.

"You're the first commandant who hasn't also spent time in service as a knight of the Secret Order of the Resurrected Knights Templar. I am very sorry that you have to learn this way, my son." Clemente spoke as he crossed the room toward Luca. A quiet exhale, and then he was explaining everything as he took Luca's hand in his own, raising the curtain of secrecy on the existence of demons, of vampires and ghosts and wraiths and revenants, of ghouls and shape shifters and witches and zombies, of nightmares that were real and walked the Earth.

Luca paled, and his breath came fast and weak, but he held his ground, staring at Clemente.

"Our world is divided from the rest of creation by the Veil. It separates the world of the supernatural from our existence. The realms of the holy and the damned. Sometimes a demon's essence can sneak across the Veil. Minor demons, like incubi and succubae, can filter through. But the major demons can only cross through a portal."

"A portal?" Luca's gruff voice broke on the question.

"A bloody gate made of suffering and sorrow and horror. The

Knights Templar found a portal when they found the Well of Souls, and they were the first to discover the Veil and cross over to the other side. What they found... Well, they've never revealed in full to any outsider. But they closed the portal and sealed the Veil, and their Order was founded on the vow of those knights to protect our world from the other side. Their true mission was kept from the world, and even after they fell, they lived on, continuing in secret, passing on the mysteries of the knights and the Order every generation. The Swiss Guard is the current incarnation of the Knights Templar, though the true number of knights has dwindled through the centuries." Clemente sighed. "Alain Autenburg is the current knight, given his knighthood from *his* predecessor, Commandant Best, and *my* predecessor."

Luca looked away, blinking fast as his jaw clenched.

"And this young man," Clemente gestured to Cristoph, "is Alain Autenburg's recruit. We'll take our lead from his knowledge. Tell me, my son, how long have you been in training?"

Cristoph swallowed. Luca's dark gaze fixed to him, melting his spine. "A day," he managed to stutter.

Clemente blinked.

"And a night," he added quickly.

"Oh my Lord." Pacing, Clemente moved across the living room, his white cassock shuffling softly across the carpet. His hand rose, covering his mouth as he stared out the bay window overlooking the back dome of St. Peter's Basilica. "We must find out what happened," he finally said. "And where our knight has been taken. And why."

Glass shattered next to Clemente as the window burst inward. Clemente fell back, stumbling and throwing his hands up, trying to shield himself from the shards of wood and window flying through the air. Luca roared and leaped for Clemente, trying to reach the pontiff and shield him with his body. He raised the blade in his hand, twirling and brandishing it toward the creature who'd swooped inside. Cristoph crashed to the ground, staring at the hulking creature that had broken through the Holy Father's top-floor window.

Luca dropped to one knee in front of Clemente and pointed Alain's blade at the invader. "Halt!" he bellowed. "Don't dare take one more step!"

Dark eyes opened. Yellowed irises sat deep in a harsh, lean face, sallow skin stretched over angular bone. Sigils and runes were carved and scarred in a line reaching from his temple to the long cut of his pointed jaw. Angled ears stretched along his skull, and bits of bone and gold rings jingled along his earlobe. His lips pulled back, revealing a full set of fangs, hooked and razor sharp, curving over his teeth.

"Vampire," Cristoph breathed. He scrambled to his feet. "Vampire!" he shouted. Running, he crossed the Holy Father's sitting room in four strides and launched himself at the vampire before he could strike Luca or Clemente.

The vampire hissed and backhanded him, swatting him to the carpet. He tumbled in midair and crashed to the floor.

Luca swallowed and jabbed the point of Alain's sword toward the vampire. He stayed down, shielding Clemente as the Holy Father clutched his shoulder and crossed himself.

Groaning, Cristoph dragged himself to his feet, swaying. His hands came up, loose fists in front of his face.

A dry laugh bubbled out of the vampire. "I am not here to *fight* you," he hissed. His voice sounded like the deep embers of a roaring forest fire, like a bellows filling and a thunderclap, all rolled into one. "I am here to *help* you."

Eyes squinting, Cristoph stared at the vampire. Luca didn't move, but his eyes darted to Cristoph, then back to the vampire. He didn't drop his blade.

It clicked for Cristoph a moment later. "Jesus Christ," he mumbled, dropping his fists. Clemente glared sidelong at him. "You're the lone vampire. You turned against the nest." He shook his head. "You killed the girl. The spy."

The vampire nodded.

"You're *helping* us?" Cristoph watched Luca slowly rise and help Clemente to his feet. "Why? Why turn against your nest?"

The vampire snarled like a lion under challenge, fangs bared. Cristoph's blood iced over, but he stood firm.

"The alpha made an infernal deal," the vampire growled. "He believed those blackened spirits would truly ally with him. He was a fool, and he has paid the price for his foolishness."

"He's dead?"

"The entire nest is. The demons, Asmodeus and Temeluchus, slaughtered them to cast open the portal." The vampire turned to Clemente. "You described it thusly. A portal made of blood and sorrow. Two demons crossed through one cast at dawn's light. It's closed now, but they *will* open another one."

Clemente stepped around Luca's protective cover. Luca protested, but Clemente silenced him with a touch to his shoulder. He squared his shoulders as he faced the vampire. "What is your purpose here?"

"I know what it is they plan. I know where they have taken your knight and kin." He nodded to Cristoph. "We must stop them before they slay your knight and release the *noumenon*."

"The what?" Cristoph spoke before Clemente could.

"The secrets you spoke of," the vampire rumbled, turning back to Clemente. "What has passed through the centuries from knight to knight is not just a simple blessing. There's a power there, holy, sacred, and *profane*. Power that gives the knight the ability to combat the darkness, but is tainted with the shadows of its own form. For darkness calls to darkness and knows it as its own kind."

Alain's gentle words—had it only been that morning?—and his smiling recollections, his story of his knighting and the blessing from Commandant Best, the passing on of the knightly superpowers as he'd teasingly called the indescribable power Alain had mentioned, came back to him. Alain had said it felt warm and beautiful.

That he'd ripped the blessing from his lover and had taken it as his own.

Whatever it was, Alain had it deep inside him, and the demons wanted it. "What the hell is it? What is inside of Alain?"

"Lucifer's *noumenon*, the closest thing demonic forces and angelic beings have to a soul. The true essence of their identity, regardless of their physical body. That which is them, wholly and purely." The vampire's yellow eyes fixed to Cristoph's.

Silence stole the air from the Holy Father's apartment, full and complete. Wind twitched against the curtains, silk shifting on silk, and a shard of glass tumbled from its shattered fracture, tinkling to the carpet. Cristoph could feel his heart pounding, and he thought he could hear Luca's raging heartbeat, too.

"Lucifer?" Cristoph breathed. "*The* Lucifer? The Devil? Evil incarnate?"

"The fallen prince of Elohim," the vampire corrected. "Leader of the rebellion. Murderer. Destroyer of the universe."

"How do you know all of this?" Clemente stepped forward, his shoes crunching on broken glass. He stood tall before the grotesque vampire, staring into his gaze.

"I have been a vampire for hundreds of years now," he rumbled. "I have heard tales from the darkness and whispers across the Veil. Stories and legends of old, from millennia far before me. And..." He dropped to one knee before Clemente and bowed his head. "I was once a knight, though never a chosen knight to carry the *noumenon*. I fell defending my Holy Father's life and was turned on May 6, 1527."

Cristoph and Luca started, sharing a long look. Swiss Guard history came droning back, Luca's voice lecturing the recruits about their unbroken history and their heraldry. Their greatest sacrifice, long ago.

"May 6, 1527, is the date of the Stand of Swiss Guard, when one hundred and forty-seven guards gave their life to protect the Holy Father's flight from the Vatican when invaders sacked Rome. The commander, Kaspar Röist, died in the battle, passing leadership to Hercules Göldi who led the Holy Father to safety in the fortress of Castel Sant'Angelo."

"My name is Linhart Claus." The vampire looked into

Clemente's eyes. "I was one of the original Swiss Guard to journey to the Vatican. I died defending my captain, Kaspar, and his second, Hercules, as Kaspar passed on the *noumenon* to Hercules. I died watching Hercules rush the Holy Father away. I bled out on the steps of St. Peter's."

Cristoph couldn't breathe. He couldn't think. Couldn't react in any way. His gaze darted back to Luca. Luca wasn't any better, pale and staring at the vampire with broken eyes and a dropped jaw.

"How did you turn, my son?" Clemente cupped Linhart's cheek as gently as he had Luca's.

Linhart exhaled, a breathy whimper, and turned his face into Clemente's palm. "Dark creatures always find their way into war, into battle, and into despair. Into sickness and tragedy." He licked his pale, cracked lips. "A vampire crawled over me. It's the last thing I saw, before—"

Clemente's thumb stroking across the harsh line of Linhart's jutting cheekbone, down the sigils on his cheek. Linhart closed his eyes, a rapturous expression crossing his face.

"You can help us, my son?" Clemente said softly. "You can guide us to our people? And help us stop these demons?"

Linhart swallowed, and Cristoph watched him gather himself together and rise. "Yes, I can take you to them. I tracked their teleport across Rome. I can help you rescue my knight brother." He turned to Cristoph, a tiny smile stretched across his lips. "I can see how much you care for him in your soul. We will find him. I swear it."

He shouldn't have taken comfort in the vow of a vampire, but he clung to anything he could, anything in this crazed world that promised he'd see Alain again. He nodded. "What do we do? Where do we go?"

"We need weapons. The knights' weapons. Where is their armory?"

That, at least, he could answer. "Alain's kitchen. I can get what we need. Silver, iron, salt?"

"Bring everything." Linhart turned to Luca. "Retrieve the

halberds and pikes from the Swiss Guard armory. They have silver cores. We can use those weapons as well."

Luca nodded. His fingers tightened on Alain's blade.

Linhart noticed. "And keep that blade close. It's a knight's blade. You seem to know how to hold it and the blade is comfortable in your grasp."

Cristoph frowned. He wanted to take Alain's blade back. He didn't want Luca to keep it.

"We also need transportation." Linhart scowled between Luca and Cristoph. "I cannot carry both of you across Rome—"

"I am coming with you." Clemente spoke slowly, but there was the weight of authority in his voice, the heaviness of a man who wasn't argued with. Ever.

"Holy Father..." Luca tried. "You *can't*. This is too dangerous, Your Holiness."

Clemente arched his eyebrows at Luca. "My son, this is a battle against the darkness. Where else am I supposed to be?"

Cristoph shrugged when Luca tossed a harried glance his way. What could they say to that? Luca shook his head and closed his eyes, but the fight had gone out of him.

"Lotario has a car. He keeps it parked by the barracks."

"That rusted-out yellow monstrosity?" Luca snorted. "It runs on faith alone."

"That is all we need." Clemente smiled at Luca, and Luca's sneer fell instantly. "Cristoph, go get what you need. Luca, you and I will get the car. Linhart, meet us there. I trust you know how to stay hidden?"

Linhart nodded. "One more thing, Holy Father. Do not, for any reason, trust anyone in the Vatican. This place is full of darkness. Evil has corrupted men's hearts. There is no trust here. Not anymore. Stick close to only those you know."

"Wise words." Clemente crossed himself. "Go. We'll meet back up in the courtyard in five minutes."

Chapter Twenty-One

CRISTOPH BURST THROUGH ALAIN'S BROKEN FRONT DOOR, knocking it out of place from where Alain had propped it after Luca had kicked it in. He bounced off the wall, skittered down the hallway, and slid into the kitchen.

He grabbed everything he could. Knives, daggers, swords, shotguns, pistols. He kicked open the chest with the toe of his boot and grabbed all the bags of herbs he could find, shoving them into his pockets and down his shirt when he ran out of space. He didn't know exactly what he was grabbing, but hell if he was leaving anything behind.

Whirling, he started to leave.

And stopped.

On the kitchen counter, right where they had shared breakfast, was the blade Alain had given to him, resting gently in a navy box atop a sea of black velvet.

The blade Luca has. It must be from the other knight.

A slip of paper was tucked under the box.

Cristoph,

This blade belongs to you now.

Dizziness stole through Cristoph, followed by the sinking

weight of dread. He really had given it up, given to him wholly and completely.

As if he knew he wasn't going to get the chance to give it to him in the future. As if he knew he wasn't coming back.

He grabbed the blade and took off.

No matter what, he was bringing Alain back. No matter what.

THE GENDARMERIE WAS TOWING LOTARIO'S RUSTED-OUT BUG when Luca arrived at the Swiss Guard courtyard next to St. Anne's Gate.

Twirling red lights and the warning claxon of the tow truck blared. Lotario's Bug was being loaded onto a flatbed outside the blasted-out garrison. Gendarmerie officers and members of the Vatican fire brigade were still picking through the smoldering wreckage, working with headlamps and flashlights instead of floodlights to keep away the gawkers and news helicopters.

Luca pressed Clemente against a column alongside the barracks, hiding him from sight. The Holy Father had traded his cassock for a pair of soft track pants and a sweatshirt, and instead of his zucchetto, a Juventus football beanie sat low on his head, pulled down over his eyebrows.

Luca stormed across the courtyard. An exchange of harsh words, and then one hundred Euros from Luca's wallet, and the rusted Bug was dropped in place, the tow truck departing.

Captain Ewe appeared, his filthy face stained with dirt and blood, haggard and weary from the day's tragedies. "Commandant Bader," he said. "We've secured the garrison and removed all the wounded. We've set up a triage facility in the canteen, and the most critically injured have been taken to hospital. No fatalities, thank the Lord, but there are some badly wounded halberdiers. Broken bones and such. The halberdiers who are still able to stand guard have been placed around the Vatican, and we have an extra squad clearing St. Peter's Square. I've enacted emergency protocol for the night." He waited, watching Luca. "Commandant? What are your orders?"

Luca shook his head. He couldn't think straight, and a haze had settled through him. Disparate urges tore him apart. He should return to his men, to the Swiss Guard, and stay with them through the night. Be the leader they deserved, that they needed. Especially now.

But His Holy Father and Cristoph were about to battle dark and evil forces and try to save Alain, all with the help of a vampire, a vampire that was one of their own from centuries past.

He didn't know what was real anymore. Maybe he was really unconscious, laid up in hospital, and this was all some farcical fantasy.

He could only hope.

"Captain, excellent work. Continue through the night. I have to attend to duties with His Holiness."

"The Holy Father? Shall I pull a squadron of guards for you?"

"No! No, what you've done here is remarkable." He couldn't put any more men in danger, not after so many had been hurt already. Not when none of them had been trained for any of this, and even Cristoph, Alain's recruit, had only just barely begun his own training. Whatever that meant. "Carry on, Captain."

Captain Ewe jogged off. Luca waited until he was alone, achingly alone, before heading back to Lotario's Bug.

Clemente had already climbed into the driver's seat. Luca passed the Bug by and headed for the armory, grabbing pikes and halberds by the armful. He eyed the silver breastplates and then grabbed two, hauling the heavy armor back to the Bug.

When he got there, he shoved the pikes and halberds in as far as they would go, silver tips down and buried in Lotario's trash heap of cigarette packs and fast food wrappers. He shimmied into one of the breastplates, hurriedly tying the leather straps beneath his arms, and then clambered into the back of the Bug.

From the front, Clemente and Linhart turned as one, the Holy Father smiling at Luca as Linhart appraised his armor with the critical eye of a Swiss Guard captain inspecting a junior soldier. With a start, Luca realized that he was wearing armor that Linhart would have worn, wearing armor, in fact, that one of the survivors of that battle Linhart had given his life in had worn.

His eyes darted between the Holy Father and the vampire. "Jesus fucking Christ," he muttered.

"Language, my son." Clemente's eyes narrowed, and he shared a quick look with Linhart, who had pulled back his lips and bared his fangs at Luca's curse.

What happened to the world? What happened to my sanity? Luca's eyes slipped closed.

He found the hilt of the blade he'd tucked into his belt, fingers squeezing around it. Out of everything that had happened in the past hour, the blade in his hand felt the most real. It felt right to hold it close. He hadn't known what he was doing when he brandished the blade at Linhart, but he'd moved as if he did, the sword slashing through the air like an extension of his arm. Like an extension of him.

His eyes slitted open, staring at the back of Linhart's dark, messy head. Matted hair twisted into locks gave the vampire a crazed, dangerous air. Linhart made his bones scream and his skin crawl, made him feel like he was about to jump out of his body. He wanted to run, to get as far away from the vampire as he could, and take His Holiness with him.

But another part of him, something deeper, wanted to slide close to Linhart. Wanted to bare his throat and sink to his knees, offer himself up. Dark words, hoarse and indistinct, echoed deep in his mind, a low chant that he couldn't make out.

Finally, Cristoph arrived, dropping a heaping pile of weapons into Luca's lap before clambering into the Bug. "Let's go!" he said, slapping at the back of Clemente's seat.

"Do you have the keys?" Clemente, seemingly ever calm, even crammed in a car with a vampire and more weapons than were legal to possess in Italy, smiled faintly over his shoulder.

Luca groaned. He slammed his head back against the seat.

"Uhh—" Cristoph bit his lip A flush crawled up his neck. "I can — Here, let me—" He crawled forward, sliding between the two front seats and laying his body across Clemente's lap.

Luca watched him pull out a blade identical to the one he'd grabbed after Alain had vanished and slice into the wiring beneath the Bug's steering column.

Silence resounded as Cristoph hot-wired the car in front of the Holy Father and a vampire. The engine sputtered to life, choking as it turned over.

"Excellent," Clemente said with a smile. He turned to Linhart. "Where to?"

"The *Santa Maria del Priorato* church, in the *Piazza dei Cavalieri di Malta*. It was an old Knights Templar castle in Rome before they were disbanded. The demons want to channel the power from the knights' history there."

Clemente shifted into gear. They slid past the Swiss Guards at St. Anne's Gate, their flashlights shining briefly over their faces before waving the car through.

CRISTOPH TUGGED HIS CELL PHONE OUT AND DIALED THE number for the Italian *polizia* after he tied on the breastplate Luca tossed on his lap.

"I need to speak to Angelo, please. He's an officer working on special assignment with the Vatican. It's urgent." He tapped his foot against the floorboards, through Lotario's trash, as he waited for the operator on the other end of the line.

"*I'm sorry, sir,*" she said, heavy Italian accenting her words. "*There is no officer who works in the polizia on special assignment with the Vatican.*"

"No, I *know* he exists. I *know* he works there. I *know* he's on some kind of special ultra-top-secret assignment to the Vatican." His voice rose. "I know he's there. Put him on the line! Connect me to him!"

"*I'm sorry, sir. I can't help you.*"

"Dammit, connect me to him! I need his help!"

The operator disconnected the line, leaving Cristoph in silence. "Dammit..."

Luca watched him, the streetlights illuminating his face for a half second at a time. "We're on our own," Luca breathed.

Cristoph nodded. He watched out the front window as Clemente drove across Rome. They passed the Coliseum, and the Bug belched and stuttered, the engine knocking out black smoke as Clemente shifted gears. The *Ponte Sublicio* took them across the Tiber, toward a park and a bus station and a stand of restaurants. Italians walked in the street, laughing in the warm summer evening, ignorant of the rusted-out Bug and their mission.

Clemente turned up the Lungotevere and then turned again, winding up Aventine Hill toward the *Piazza dei Cavalieri di Malta*, the courtyard of the monastery and church dedicated to the Knights of Malta after the fall of the Knights Templar. It had been the Templar's home in the heart of Rome, once, on a hill across the river from the Vatican.

Darkness enveloped Rome, night falling across the bustling city. A black moon hung low in the sky. Linhart seemed to fade into shadow in the front of the Bug. Everyone stayed silent as the car lurched and rattled up the hill.

Ahead, the tower of the monastery gleamed. Clemente rocked the Bug to a stop in the center of the piazza. Night, at least, took the tourists away.

The monastery and church were secured behind a steel-reinforced wooden gate. It was the only entrance in an unbroken fence, taller than two men, that encircled the grounds.

Cristoph opened his mouth, about to offer to boost Luca up over the fence, when Luca pulled out one of Alain's shotguns.

"Stand back," he growled.

Luca blasted the center of the gate, blowing away the lock. Wood splintered, and one side of the gate slipped open, hinges creaking.

Linhart had curled around Clemente, shielding him as Luca fired. Cristoph watched Linhart quickly check over Clemente before they rushed the gate.

"We don't know what's in there," Cristoph said, striding to the front of the group. He held Alain's blade in one hand and a pistol loaded with silver- and iron-tipped bullets in the other. Luca walked beside him, shotgun and blade in his hands. Linhart held two halberds and guarded Clemente.

"We just need to get out alive with Alain and Lotario." Cristoph met Luca's gaze. He raised his blade. Luca crossed his blade with his own, a sidelong salute.

"I will distract the demons," Linhart growled. "You both retrieve our brethren."

"Your Holiness," Luca pleaded. "You can stay outside. You can stay safe."

"I will be with you, my children. I will fight the way I know how. With prayer."

The monastery and church were supposed to be dark, shuttered for the night. There wasn't supposed to be anyone within. But the windows were illuminated with a shimmering light, wreathing the church. As they neared, the air grew colder and their breath misted before their faces.

Alain, I'm coming. Just hold on. Hold on. We're here. I'm here.

ALAIN CAME BACK TO CONSCIOUSNESS SLOWLY, HIS VISION fading in and out. Shapes and shadows moved around him, flickering in and out of darkness. Smoke tickled his nose, and the wet, warm taste of blood coated his tongue and the back of his throat.

He tried to move.

He couldn't.

Awareness returned in a flash. Charging forward after seeing a demon holding Luca. The clap of a demon's teleportation. They'd grabbed him, clinging to his soul as he was hurtled through space.

Where was he? What had happened? Where was Cristoph? Hopefully far away, someplace safe, someplace protected. Lotario would see to that. He'd make sure Cristoph stayed safe.

A muffled groan to his right had him trying to turn his head. Pain fractured his mind, his sight, but he fought against bindings holding his arms and legs down, and something lashed tight across his forehead, pinning his head in place.

As the haze in his vision cleared, the interior of a church came into view. Scattered pews, tossed aside, were tumbled against one wall. Stained-glass murals rose around the nave. Bronze chandeliers hung above, filled with candles half melted. He was in the apse, secured to the altar and surrounded by a ring of burgundy Demon Fire, the ice-cold flames licking at his sides.

Moaning echoed again, and he searched for the sound. He finally spotted Lotario outside the ring of flame, bound at his feet and his hands and tied to a stake, a broken beam of wood from a shattered pew embedded in the marble floor of the church.

On his face, a sigil of silence had been carved into his skin. It stretched from his forehead to his chin, crossing over both eyes and his lips. Blood wept from the ragged edges of the sigil.

"Lotario?" He coughed. Something wet and coppery trickled from the corner of his lip. He swiped his tongue around his mouth but couldn't feel a cut. "Lotario?"

Slowly, Lotario's eyes swiveled to him, bleary and dim. Lotario tried to open his mouth, tried to speak. The sigil shattered his voice, broke his words into nothing. His eyes slid shut again.

Alain struggled, scraping the back of his skull over the rough stone of the altar. Shadows, movements outside the Demon Fire, caught his gaze. A low chant was building, voices speaking out of sync but all saying the same thing. He wanted to shut his ears against the noise, against the sound of fire crackling and hyenas braying, a dark howling that grated over his bones. The words made him want to run, to flee, to leave his body behind and escape everything.

But beneath his soul, a whispering voice called out to that same crackling darkness. *Soon*, it breathed. *So soon.*

CRISTOPH'S BREATH CAME HARD AND FAST, BUT HE KEPT HIS EYES locked on Luca's, watching his silent countdown as they bracketed the entrance to the church. Inside, burgundy flames circled the front altar, and they spotted a man tied to a stake, slumped and unconscious.

Two beings chanted, one of darkness and one of flame, as they moved in the shadows. It seemed like a hundred voices burst from their throats.

Luca's fingers counted down to *three*.

Cristoph inhaled. Held his breath.

Two.

He exhaled.

One.

They moved together, sliding around the door frame and clearing the corners of the church quickly before sliding shoulder to shoulder and striding up the central aisle. Luca held his shotgun and his blade at eye level. Cristoph held his in a cross-wristed grip as he aimed his pistol at the demons behind the altar.

Linhart slid above in the rafters. Clemente walked well behind him and Luca, quietly praying.

"*Demons!*" Cristoph bellowed. "We're here to stop your evil shit!"

He felt Luca's groan through their pressed shoulders.

The man tied to the altar thrashed. He twisted, trying to look their way. Cristoph's throat clenched. "Alain?"

"Cristoph!" Alain shouted. "Jesus Christ, why are you here? You shouldn't be here! God, get away!" Alain's eyes darted to Luca. He roared, "*No!*"

"I'm not leaving you, Alain." Cristoph set his jaw and stalked forward, walking in step with Luca. They slowed in the center of the church, watching for the dark forms of the demons.

The demons had vanished.

"Get the fuck out of here!" Alain hissed. "*Now!*"

Flames burst through the stained glass above the altar, barreling for Cristoph and Luca. They ducked and rolled as the fireball consumed the front half of the church, skipping the altar, and roared down through the main aisle.

"Alain!" Cristoph howled.

The demon covered in writhing flames strode out of the fireball. It was featureless, no eyes, no mouth, just an embodied flame in the shape of a man. A bone-screeching wail tore from it.

Luca fired his shotgun at the center of the demon's chest.

Staggering back, the demon's hands rose, and it seemed to stare down at the blast, at the rock salt embedded in its chest. It surged forward, shrieking, a twirling ball of flame building in its palm.

Cristoph had just enough time to cringe and curl into a ball, and to wish he'd actually managed to save Alain instead of dying in a demonic fireball. Luca threw himself around him, shielding Cristoph's face with his shoulders as they waited for the blast.

A lion's roar bellowed from above. Linhart leaped from the rafters as twin halberds flew toward the flame demon. The vampire snarled as he landed in front of Cristoph and Luca and slashed at the flame demon with his talons. Where he slashed, black smoke tumbled free from the demon's form, followed by purple light blazing through the cuts.

The demon backed away, one hand covering the tears in its abdomen. Linhart roared, stalking the demon across the church.

Cristoph spared a panicked glance to Luca before they scrambled to their feet.

CLEMENTE KNELT NEXT TO LOTARIO, CRADLING HIS FACE IN HIS

aged hands. "Father," he called, gently shaking the priest. "Father, open your eyes."

Lotario's eyes fluttered open. His gaze was unfocused, wandering through the church before falling on Clemente. His eyes went wide, and he struggled against the bonds holding him to the stake.

"Shhh," Clemente hushed him with a gentle smile. "I'm here to rescue you. I will not leave one of my flock behind, Father." He pulled out a blade he'd hidden, taken from his private apartments in the Vatican, and started cutting Lotario free.

"Holy Father. You care so much for your flock."

Behind Clemente, a lilting voice mocked his rescue. A familiar voice, one he knew from the Vatican. He turned and came face-to-face with Cardinal Santino Acossio.

"Santino, I was warned you were ambitious. But I underestimated your desires. I didn't know they included murder and damnation."

"Your crown and keys will be mine, Father," Acossio purred. He lunged, teeth bared in a feral scream as he raised a heavy crucifix in his hand, swinging for Clemente's head.

The blade slipped through the last of the bonds holding Lotario. Twisting, Clemente spun and brought the blade in front of him and shoved it straight up, straight through Acossio's chest, through his lungs and up into his heart. The jeweled hilt of the blade pressed against Acossio's cassock-covered chest.

Slowly, the green jewel faded, losing its color. A hollow tube embedded within the blade emptied the poison hidden in the hollowed-out gem.

"The *misericorde* was the favored weapon of popes through the middle ages," Clemente whispered as Acossio coughed around the blood rising within him from the wound. "It was the Borgias who added a poison vial. A fitting legacy for them."

The last of the poison emptied into Acossio's heart. Clemente pushed him back, letting his body fall to the stone floor of the church. Boils erupted on his skin, across his face and over his arms and legs where his cassock had flown up. Blood sizzled from the boils, and he writhed, trying to scream through the gurgling in his throat.

Lotario had managed to untie the bindings around his ankles, and he toppled forward, weak. Clemente turned away from Acossio as the cardinal breathed his last rattling gasp and wrapped his arms around Lotario.

Lotario, again, tried to speak. A strangled moan was all that came out.

"Don't speak, my son. You've been silenced. It will take time to undo this curse. You'll only hurt yourself more if you try to talk." Clemente wrapped one of Lotario's long arms around his shoulders and headed down the center aisle.

Lotario fought him, trying to turn back to the altar, and to Alain.

"Those flames are too high. I need to get you to safety first, my son. But we *will* rescue him."

Sagging, Lotario's head fell against Clemente's shoulder. Clemente all but carried him down the church's aisle as he prayed for Lotario's soul.

THE BURGUNDY FLAMES ROARED, CLIMBING HIGHER AROUND THE altar. Alain had lost sight of Cristoph and Luca. He thrashed, struggling against the bonds, screaming with every pull.

Darkness appeared next to him, the angular shape of the midnight demon rising beside the altar. It grinned.

Blood dripped from the demon's skin, soaking him from head to toe and splattering on Alain. A drop landed on his lips.

"It's almost time," the demon breathed. "Almost time for you to come home."

"Fuck you." Alain spat, blood and spittle flying from his mouth and striking the demon's face.

The demon laughed. It disappeared, vanishing outside the

circle of ice-cold flames. Alain's frantic eyes tried to track the demon's movements, as much as he could while restrained. It reappeared, dragging Cardinal Acossio's body through into the circle and dumping him at the head of the altar.

"We were going to use that priest's body," the demon said, its voice layered with smoke and darkness. "Your fellow hunter. He was going to be the portal. But the cardinal works just as well." The demon plunged his hands into the cardinal's chest. It tugged, ripping Acossio in two, a vertical slit that rent the cardinal from neck to waist. He kneeled and whispered an invocation over the mangled body.

A shrill scream tore from the corpse, but not from its mouth. From the center of the destroyed chest, a wail built as a swirling wind kicked up, a sudden tornado rising from the corpse's chest.

Acossio's corpse sucked inward and then blasted out, bits of bone and blood flying. The chest gaped open, revealing a void, a portal carved of blood and sorrow that punched through the Veil.

The stench of sulfur and death hung heavy in the air.

A thrum rushed through Alain.

So soon. So soon.

LINHART HAD CHASED THE FLAMING DEMON AROUND THE church, throwing pews aside when the demon sent flaming debris toward him and breaking apart the heavy blocks of stone the demon ripped from the walls and flung his way. Cristoph and Luca followed behind, using him as cover as they shot at the demon.

Leaping, Linhart captured the flame demon against the broken stained-glass windows. He dug his talons into its fiery flanks. The demon screeched and sent a pillar of flame into the side of his face. Linhart refused to let go. "Now! Strike him now!"

Cristoph and Luca charged, Luca firing his shotgun at the hand burning the side of Linhart's face. The demon's hand exploded into scattered purple light. Cristoph swung Alain's blade into the demon's chest where its heart would have been had it been a man. Purple light flashed, exploding from the demon's body. It jerked, thrashing under Linhart's hold, struggling for freedom. Cristoph backed away as Linhart released the demon. Linhart panted, moving with shaking steps.

The demon shuddered and fell to its knees, purple light flaring through each of the tears and cuts Linhart had inflicted and the gaping wound over its chest. It writhed on the stone floor of the church.

Bellowing, Luca swung his blade, slashing through the demon's neck and severing its head from its body.

A blinding burst of light exploded from its body. They fell back, shielding their eyes as the demon's body crumpled and collapsed, flames consuming its shrieking form. Purple light swallowed it whole, shrinking the demon down to a pinprick that winked out of existence.

All at once, the wailing stopped. Cristoph only heard Linhart's exhausted, wet gasps and Luca's trembling exhales.

Screaming from the front of the church made Cristoph whirl. Demon Fire roared around the altar, so high it licked the rafters. Alain shrieked within the flames.

"*Alain!*"

Cristoph raced to the front of the church, but the wall of fire kept him back, pinning him away from Alain. Alain's screams grew. "*Alain!*" he bellowed. Luca hovered at his side, his gaze darting over the burgundy flames. Ice coated the stone floors. "I can't get through!"

Luca paled as another shriek from Alain tore through the church. He looked like he was about to tear the church apart with his bare hands, rip stone from stone. His fingers tightened on the hilt of his blade. "We need—"

Linhart leaped over Cristoph and Luca, barreling through the flames.

ALAIN TRIED TO WIGGLE AWAY FROM THE DEMON AND ITS bloodied, taloned hands, but there was no escape. He was trapped, tied down.

"It's time." The demon smiled down at Alain. Its hand rose, blood from Acossio's corpse still warm on its midnight skin.

The hand dropped, talons slicing into Alain's chest. Alain screamed, his back arching as the demon tore its way through his skin and muscle and ripped apart his chest, slowly.

Until his heart lay exposed.

Frigid air shivered over his torn body. He felt his lungs shiver, heard the frantic liquid pull of his blood pumping within him.

One long, taloned finger stroked down the outside of his heart.

Alain threw back his head and shrieked.

His thoughts turned to Cristoph, somewhere on the other side of the flames. *Stay safe, Cristoph. God, stay safe. I wish I could be there to keep you safe for the rest of your life.*

His breath hitched, caught in his chest as the demon's talon sliced down the center of his heart. *I know my sins, Cristoph. And I don't regret them. I thought that I could hold my life together by my strength alone, but I didn't know I needed my rock. You became my rock, Cristoph. My Peter, even for just these short moments. I'll love you forever for that. For giving me these last days.*

Agony lanced through him, tears building in his eyes, pouring down his face as his throat tore, his shrieks shredding his vocal chords. *Goddammit, I wanted so much, Cristoph. I wanted a life with you. I wanted a future with you, a future away from this. I wanted the chance, at least, to be the one to make you happy.*

Blood poured out of his sliced heart, pooling in the demon's cupped palm. Alain watched the demon step back, cradling his heart's blood, and breathe an invocation over his cupped palms. His vision began to fade, blacking out around the edges. His lungs seized, no longer dragging in breath. He struggled for air, trying to watch the demon walking away with his heart's blood. With his life.

The last thing he saw was the demon igniting his blood, a burst of blue flame rising from its hands before it flung his heart's blood down the gaping hole in Santino Acossio's corpse.

IT WOULD ALL COME DOWN TO THIS MOMENT.

Asmodeus released the knight's blood through the portal, sending it across the Veil. Lucifer's *noumenon* burned inside spilt blood.

On the other side, their allies committed to resurrecting their leader and fallen prince rallied, cries of joy and salvation rising through the ether.

They would have the spell in place, the mix of bones and dust and water ready to swirl together when the *noumenon* returned.

Lucifer's body, remade. His *noumenon*, rejoined.

Asmodeus stepped back. And waited.

LINHART LEAPED THROUGH THE FLAMES, SHARDS OF ICE slamming through his body, slicing him from every angle. He collapsed, coughing black blood on the stone floor.

He struggled to stand. He wasn't going to survive this.

Linhart's gaze landed on the altar and the destroyed body lying there, unmoving.

Brother...

He recognized Alain. Sigils were drawn on his arms in blood, binding seals holding him down. Runes lined the altar, carved and burned into the marble floor.

They should have worked together. He should have reached out sooner to the knights.

Swirling wisps of Alain's soul clung to his body, refusing to depart the world just yet.

At the head of the altar, the dark demon—Asmodeus—stood over a second corpse, staring into a dark hole.

The corpse at Asmodeus's feet jerked. It twisted, writhing over the tear in the Veil it was joined with. Blood spread over the stone, and the crack of snapping bones echoed in the circle of flames. The corpse's ribs flared, arching outward. A wail pierced the church, inhuman, primal.

The corpse bowed, jerked, and bowed again, trembling.

A hand appeared, blood-soaked, using the corpse as an anchor to crawl up out of the void in the corpse's chest.

Linhart froze.

Another hand appeared, then arms. A bowed head. Shoulders.

It was a man, or at least, it appeared to be a man. Lithe and strong, pale skin gleaming. Long, bloody hair, dripping with bits of bone and gore.

The man looked up. Burning eyes stared through Linhart.

"Lucifer..." Beside the corpse, Asmodeus dropped to its knees, his arms outstretched, and helped Lucifer crawl out of the bloody portal. Lucifer stumbled, falling sideways into the demon. He wrapped his arms around the demon's midnight shoulders.

One shaking hand rose, pointing to Linhart.

Asmodeus snarled and bared its fangs. Linhart roared and raised his talons. He didn't have enough strength left in him for this, but he had enough, at least, to die fighting.

Hissing sounded from behind him. The ever-present crackle of the Demon Fire faded, replaced with the whistle of steam, of water dousing flame. A break ripped through the Demon Fire as Clemente appeared, dousing the flames with bottles of water stolen from a tourist shack and wrapped with a length of rosary.

Homemade holy water, blessed by the Holy Father himself.

Linhart roared and lunged for Asmodeus. It snarled, flung a bitten-off curse at Linhart and wrapped Lucifer tight in its arms. There was a flash, a burst of blinding white light, and the whole church shuddered, every stone quaking.

When the flash faded, Asmodeus and Lucifer were gone.

On the floor, Acossio's corpse shuddered, bowing up again.

"More are crossing through!" Linhart bellowed. "Destroy it!"

Luca raced to his side. "How?" He paled, watching Acossio's mangled corpse writhe on the stone floor.

"Do something!" Linhart shouted.

Luca thrust his blade into the corpse, over and over, stabbing it everywhere. He kicked, trying to shove the mangled body as it began to collapse in on itself, into the void. He kicked harder, shoving the corpse until the raging wind died and the roar from the void faded.

Linhart watched the body as Luca gasped, doubling over with his hands on his knees.

He was the only one who saw the corpse shift.

"*No!*" He shoved Luca back, taking the brunt of the portal's blowback as he threw himself down on the corpse and the void. A wave of gore exploded beneath him, warm and fresh and run through with the stench of rot and death and burning sulfur. He stayed down, taking the blast to the center of his chest.

He felt the portal collapse, fall away from him into the void. He almost fell with it, tumbling into the darkness.

Somewhere, there was screaming. Shattered stone. The ground shook beneath him.

And then, there was silence.

Linhart laid his head down, half on the corpse and half on the blood-drenched stone. He should have been excited about this much blood, should have reveled in it. Should lick the floors and roll in it.

But he couldn't.

Exhaustion clung to him. The weariness of death.

Hands grabbed him. Spun him around. Luca's face appeared, worry staining his eyes and darkening his expression.

Somewhere beyond Luca, a man wailed, bellowing his sorrow at the top of his lungs. A blade clattered to the ground.

Brother. Brother, don't go. Not yet.

Chapter Twenty-Two

CRISTOPH COULDN'T SPEAK WHEN HE SAW WHAT HAD BEEN DONE to Alain. He couldn't do anything except scream out his soul to the shaking rafters of the crumbling church.

Clemente closed his eyes and crossed himself. He whispered prayers over Alain's breathless body. Tear tracks spilled from the corners of Alain's still eyes, salt lines drying on his skin.

Alain's blade clattered to the floor as Cristoph buried his face against Alain's stomach, his hands fisting in the remains of Alain's cut-away shirt. His tears soaked the fabric beneath his face. It wasn't supposed to end this way.

Luca's shout broke through the rumble of the church. "We have to leave, *now*! This place is coming down!" He appeared at Clemente's side, blood-spattered and sweat-stained, his normally perfect hair standing on end, soot marring one side of his face.

The Holy Father finished his prayers over Alain's body before he let Luca bustle him away from the collapsing apse.

Stone crackled above Cristoph's head. One of the bronze chandeliers swayed and fell, crashing behind Luca and Clemente's footsteps. A rafter collapsed, the wooden beam splintering as it hit the ground.

"You must go."

Cristoph gripped Alain's shirt tighter and turned toward the weary voice.

Linhart.

"I don't want to leave him." A caught sob warbled his voice, but Cristoph set his jaw and held his ground.

"He's not gone. Not yet." Linhart's gazed at Alain's body, at a space just above his shredded heart. "His soul clings to his body, even now. For you, I suspect."

Cristoph grasped Alain's shirt, his ruined body. "I love him," he whispered. He couldn't have had the realization at a worse time.

Linhart nodded. His breaths were weak and wet, and he leaned heavily on the altar. One hand rose, holding Cristoph's dropped blade.

He sliced from his wrist to his elbow, opening his veins and letting the last of his vampiric blood flow into his palms.

"I can give him another life." Linhart held his cupped palm, full of vampire blood, over Alain's lips.

Cristoph's breath faltered. Alain, back from the dead. Alain, at his side again. Alain, *alive.*

No, not alive. A vampire. Undead. Would Alain even want to be reborn as a vampire? Would he even want to live as a dark creature?

Could he live without Alain?

Tears blurred his vision. "*Please...*" he breathed.

Linhart let his blood pour from his palms, coating Alain's lips. He poured more into the ruins of Alain's heart, into the sliced and torn muscle.

For a moment, nothing happened.

Alain heaved, a shuddering, rattling gasp rocking his body. His eyes flew open, and he stared up at Linhart, wild terror in his gaze. His hand rose, grabbing Linhart's wrist. "*No!*"

"You have the choice, brother. You *can* choose your fate. You do not have to be a slave to darkness." Linhart struggled against Alain's hold. Dark blood oozed between Alain's fingers, dripping down their joined arms. "You can stay in your life. You do not have to leave, Alain. Stay." Linhart's eyes darted toward Cristoph. "Stay with the one you love."

Alain's gasps shortened, growing weaker. His eyes flicked to Cristoph. Fresh tears flowed from the corners of his eyes, running down his face.

"Cristoph—"

"*Please.*" Tears poured from Cristoph's eyes, ugly hot tears. "Stay."

Alain's breath faltered again.

Cristoph screamed through gritted teeth. "*Alain!*"

Eyes closed, Alain grabbed Linhart's hand and dragged it to his lips, sucking down the vampire's blood. He moaned as the blood flowed into his mouth, some escaping past his lips and dribbling down his chin.

The tears at his eyes shifted, changing to tears of blood cascading down the sides of his face.

Linhart smiled as Alain drank, and he lay his head down on the edge of the altar. His eyes slipped closed.

The church shuddered again, stone behind the apse tumbling free. Cristoph threw himself over Alain, covering him as Alain sucked the last of Linhart's vampire blood from his body.

"We have to go." Cristoph grabbed him, wrapping his arms under and around Alain and hefted him into his arms. The demon locks shattered. Alain sagged into him, rolling his blood-covered face against Cristoph's chest.

Staggering, Cristoph stepped around Linhart's body. Linhart fell back, and before his corpse could hit the floor, his body—unmade through his act—dissipated into dust and ash, sweeping around Cristoph's ankles.

He ran down the center of the church as the walls came down around them. Glass shattered, wood splintered, and stone crumbled to dust, a cloud of destruction billowing behind him as he carried Alain out of the desecrated and destroyed church.

Cristoph collapsed to his knees and fell over Alain, pitching his forehead to the ground.

Clemente ran to their side. He wrapped Alain with a gaudy "I heart Rome" jacket lifted from the cart of souvenirs for sale left in the corner of the piazza. Luca squatted by the Bug, one hand on Lotario's shoulder. Lotario was still out of it, his head lolling against the side of his car.

Alain's bloody hand rose. He cupped Cristoph's face.

Cristoph looked down, into Alain's yellow eyes.

"For you," Alain whispered. Blood burbled on his lips. "For you."

Two Months Later

CRISTOPH WOKE FACE DOWN, HIS FACE PRESSED TO ONE OF THE last of Alain's dirty shirts. His arms slid beneath his pillow, and his feet poked off the end of the bed.

Off the end of Alain's bed.

When they'd returned to the Vatican—a bedraggled band of wounded holy warriors, a pope, and a barely alive vampire— Cristoph had *ideas* of what would happen next. He'd care for Alain, watch over him as he healed. Or recovered. Or whatever it was called when vampires were newly turned. Whatever it was, he thought he'd be by Alain's side through it all. He thought they'd be together.

Of course, that wasn't what happened. Not at all.

The night they got back, Angelo had been anxiously waiting for them at the ruined Swiss Guard garrison. Cristoph had collapsed into his arms, exhausted and worn through and wrung out, and Angelo had taken him away, a heap of broken nerves and frayed spirit. He'd cleaned his cuts, bandaged his wounds. Listened to the whole story in silence.

Angelo had closed his eyes and bowed his head when Cristoph whispered what Alain had become.

The next morning, when he went searching for where the pope had taken Alain and Lotario, he was too late. They were gone. Clemente had whisked them away, taking them in a midnight helicopter ride off to Castel Gandolfo, the pope's private retreat.

His heart had cracked, then, the first bit.

He tried texting Lotario next, but a stunning silence met every one of his one hundred and seventeen texts.

He moved into Alain's apartment, bringing his single duffel up and setting his things alongside Alain's. His T-shirts hung next to Alain's button-downs in the wardrobe. His jeans went beside Alain's black suits. His toothbrush lay next to Alain's in the tiny bathroom.

Did vampires need to brush their teeth?

Would Alain ever return?

He spent the first month in Alain's office, reading through texts and journals and books, trying to learn everything he could. He cleaned and repaired and then organized Alain's office, filing loose papers and alphabetizing the books. Magical artifacts went on one shelf. Weapons on another. Tools on a third. He wanted it to look perfect when Alain returned.

Scattered on the floor, blown there by the blast through the garrison, were notes from a murder investigation Alain had filed away as unsolved. A dead end. A young priest, a clerk in the Vatican archives, drowned in the Tiber by melusine. An apparent suicide, but the unusual circumstances suggested supernatural murder.

A note in Alain's scrawled, looping handwriting caught his eye. *Victim was researching early Swiss Guard history at the Vatican.*

He closed his eyes. At the end, it was easy to look back and see the connections. The demons had infiltrated deep in their quest to find the knights. To find Alain.

He went back to the Vatican archives and pulled up the young priest's work. It was a slog, poking through ancient mementos and rotten remnants of journals, of sketches and half-bitten-off thoughts sketched on scraps of paper, the writer not intending for their words to last an eternity.

A torn and yellowed note written by Linhart made him pause. It was a bawdy tavern song, rewritten to sing of the Swiss Guard, and, if Cristoph squinted, he could see a double meaning. A song for the knights in hiding.

He found what the clerk had been researching: burial records for the first of the Swiss Guard. The first captain, the man who led the knights back to Rome, Captain Kaspar von Silenen, was buried in the Teutonic Cemetery in the Vatican, back when it had been an empty hill and a grove of quiet trees. A place of solace for eternity.

He'd been buried with two swords. A charcoal sketch yellowed with age showed both. His knight's blade, identical to Alain's—to Cristoph's—and a larger, longer broadsword, almost as long as the captain was tall.

The artist had gone to great pains to show the gleam of the broadsword, little lines of light and shadow falling from the rubbed charcoal, even hundreds of years later.

Cristoph headed to the Teutonic Cemetery, an oasis of overgrown trees walled in on all sides, sitting in the ominous shadows of St. Peter's Basilica. Red snubs of candles burned on Commandant Best's headstone, the drops of wax bleeding down the front like blood, heading for the fresh dirt of his burial. He picked his way past Commandant Best's fresh grave and wound his way toward the earliest tombs and the forgotten graves.

In the corner of the cemetery, the weeds thickened, the brambles grew waist high, and branches from cypress and orange trees seemed to block out all life, keep away all trespassers. Rotten fruit lay spoiled on the ground, and freshly fallen oranges waited to wither, nestled between fallen leaves and dead earth. No one, it seemed, came to the earliest graves and tombs.

He sighed when he found Captain von Silenen's grave.

No one came to the earliest graves except for demons and grave robbers.

Captain von Silenen's grave had been dug out, his bones open to the sky in the loose black dirt.

His hands were empty. The Templar Sword was gone.

He reburied Captain von Silenen as best he could and watched the sun set while sitting beside his grave, one hand on the mound of dirt covering him.

His life felt different, somehow. Larger, longer, now that he was connected to these men. Now that he shared their history and their lineage. He was one of them, part of something larger than himself, and after a lifetime of being disconnected, always on the outside, always at right angles to the world, he'd finally found a place to belong.

A place of the dead.

There would be no more running. Not from this.

Days rolled on, the heat of high summer descending over Rome.

No one bothered him. No one spoke to him. He was a ghost, as ignored as Alain had ever been. He caught the sidelong glares and silences that followed his every move.

Luca, especially, avoided him.

LUCA KNEW IT WOULD COME, THE SUMMONS TO CASTEL Gandolfo.

He just didn't want to go.

He'd sent over half the guard to the Holy Father's summer residence under Captain—now Major—Ewe's leadership. He'd stayed behind in the nearly empty Vatican. He and Cristoph haunted the halls of the barracks and the rebuilt garrison offices.

He stayed far, far away from Cristoph.

Memories ghosted after him, like wisps of vapor and incense, or whispers muttered just out of reach. He woke every night drenched in sweat, clutching his sheets, nightmares of blood and flame tearing through his soul.

And different dreams. Thoughts he couldn't file away, shadows of memories he couldn't place. Like the way he knew how to wield the blade. Suspicion grew within him like a cancer, scratching at his soul.

When the summons came, he dutifully climbed into the Vatican car and sat in silence for the forty-five-minute drive across Rome. The city faded, turning to countryside and the villa-dotted landscape outside Castel Gandolfo. Fields of golden grasses and olive trees snaked across the countryside. A cloudless blue sky, unending and serene.

A perfect image of a perfect day.

It wasn't a day for sorrow, but Luca felt the pull on his soul, the certainty that he wouldn't survive this summons, not as he was now.

He was left alone at the front of the mansion, and it was up to him to climb the steps and enter. The heavy door closing behind him echoed throughout the spacious hall. He closed his eyes against hollow echo in his heart.

A note left on a tray by the door told him to head to an unused guest room in a corner of the summer residence the Swiss Guard hadn't monitored in decades. As he walked through the empty, dust-filled hallways, he knew it was a place his men still didn't venture.

He hesitated outside the door, trying to breathe. He didn't want to face this. Didn't want to face what was on the other side of the door. Sweat soaked through his suit, covered his neck. He gripped the strap of his messenger bag tight, his short nails biting into the leather.

Luca slipped inside.

Wet copper, the tang of iron, and a warm heat lay heavy on his tongue. He smelled damp earth, like a fresh grave. The beginnings of rot. Of something just past gone, a body needing to be buried. Mist seemed to cling to his skin. Lightning crackled behind his molars.

The room was dark, kept so by heavy drapes drawn over the

window. A crack of light burned through the curtains, streaking a sunbeam across the floor.

Alain stood at the curtains, peering through the slip of light. A single ray curled across his sallow cheek.

Luca stared at the lines of Alain's body, the lean form he'd served next to for twelve years. He tried to spot the differences, the changes that had already altered his existence. Linhart had been so far from human it hadn't even been fathomable to call him once a man, but Alain was Alain, a man Luca had spent almost half his life beside.

"I can hear your heart beat." Alain spoke first, his voice barely a whisper, but deep enough to shake his bones. "I can taste your fear."

"I'm not afraid of you. Not of what you've become."

"Then you're an idiot."

Luca snorted. So easy to fall back to insults, to twelve years of hatred and malice. And yet... "How are you? Really?"

"Really?" The curtain twitched back. Darkness closed around the room. "I'm a vampire. I'm a monster."

Silence. "You're still here, though. You're alive."

"I'm not alive."

"You're *here*, Alain."

"I'm a monster. I'm everything I despise. Everything I hate most in the world. Everything I swore I would destroy." The gleam of Alain's yellow eyes burned into Luca. "I should be hunted and killed. I would kill myself, but the best part is... I can't."

"Don't say things like that."

"I can't even go suck down another vampire's blood. It just so happens that there are no more vampires in Rome. The demons destroyed them all. I'm *alone*, Luca. Utterly alone. Do you know what happens to vampires who are alone?"

Silence.

"And!" Alain chuckled, the sound dark, like broken church bells. "I get to continue on, existing for who knows how long, knowing I carried the Devil's soul inside of me. I let him back into the world!" Alain's fist slammed into the wall. The whole room shook. Plaster fell from the ceiling.

"Linhart called it a *noumenon*. He said the demons don't have souls."

Alain fixed Luca with a dark glare, more heavy and dangerous than when he was alive.

Luca's spine shivered. "Why did you call me here?"

It was Alain's turn for silence. He collapsed into a chair by the window, his long legs snaking before him. His hair was a mess, all wild angles and standing on end. He grabbed a crystal tumbler and swirled it around, a heavy burgundy liquid coating the cut lines of the glass, falling in slow drags.

Luca's stomach curled.

"The Holy Father has been kind enough to feed me." Alain saluted Luca and then knocked back the glass with a single swallow. "He believes that saint's blood will have some kind of effect on me. Will keep me—" Alain shrugged and dropped the tumbler onto the table. "—somewhat human."

"It could work."

"No, it *can't* work. It can't work because there is only one way to stop a vampire from turning, and I'm beyond that point. I've already fed."

Alain's rage called to Luca's, as it always did. He could feel his hackles rising, his temper simmering. His eyes rolled. "And what is that? What secret, special knowledge do you know that no one else does?"

"I know because I've done it before!" Alain leaped to his feet, bellowing, and the force of his voice nearly blew out Luca's eardrums. "I've stopped a vampire from turning! I gave everything to stop it!"

"Then why couldn't you stop yourself?"

Alain turned away. "You shouldn't have come. It was a mistake to call you."

"I'm here now. You didn't want me here for this. To argue. What do you really want?"

Alain's hands gripped the chair. Wood splintered in his grip. The crack stilled Luca's steps.

"Why were you there?" Alain finally asked. "Why did you come with Cristoph to rescue us?"

Why indeed. Even he didn't have an answer for that. Something between *What else could I do?* and *The blade in my hand told me to go.* "It felt right."

"Do you still have the blade?"

Reaching into his messenger bag, Luca pulled out a thin navy box, a box he'd found in Commandant Best's destroyed office. Alain's blade had fit inside. He kept it there, when he wasn't pulling it out to cradle it, or gripping the hilt to try to feel something—anything—again. He didn't want to let the blade go, and he couldn't say why. He held out the box and closed his eyes. "We buried Commandant Best with his blade. The ceremony was private. He's in the Teutonic Cemetery in the Vatican."

"You held it well." Alain didn't move, didn't reach for the box. "Like you knew how."

Sighing, Luca dropped his arm. "Alain... What is this about?"

"Do you remember nothing?"

Flashes played through his mind, moments in time he couldn't file, memories he couldn't identify. Scenes from another man's life flying through his mind and vanishing before he could stop to examine each one.

Laughing with Alain, drinking cheap wine on the roof of the barracks, watching the sun set on the Vatican. Best's watching them both in training. Shaking Lotario's hand and squatting beside him as he learned the hallmarks of a vampire kill. Laughing with Lotario over beers, catching Alain's gaze as what felt like the whole world spread before him, happiness rooted in the center of his soul.

Kneeling before Best and feeling a warmth suffuse his being, down to the marrow of his bones.

Walking into a darkened warehouse, the smell of salt air and dead fish and corpse rot in the air. Hearing a snarl and a roar.

Fangs sliding into the back of his neck.

Burning. Fire sliding through his body as his blood was sucked out and the vampire's poured in, changing him.

Turning him.

Luca doubled over. Heaving, he puked rancid vomit, brandy from the night before rising and emptying on the Oriental rug. He closed his eyes. Covered his mouth with his palm. "What is this?" he breathed. His voice shook. "What are you showing me?"

"I'm not showing you anything, Luca. Your memory block is fracturing. I was afraid it had when you could wield that blade so well. When you knew how to kill a demon."

Slashing the throat. Beheading the flame demon. Luca swallowed back the bile rising in him. He stood. "Memory block?"

Alain's yellow eyes fell closed, all the coiled tension in his body leaking away. He moved soundlessly across the room, standing too close. Luca held his ground, staring into Alain's vampire eyes.

"I can smell your fear," Alain whispered.

"It's not fear of you." Luca swallowed. "What am I going to see?" His words splintered apart when they left his lips.

"Lotario and I blocked your memories twelve years ago." Alain stroked one hand down the side of his face, his thumb dragging over his bottom lip. "We were knights together, Luca." Alain's fingers were cold, almost freezing. "Christ, we were so young. We had forever and happiness in our hands. But one night we were on a hunt. I was leading, as part of our training. We were tracking a rogue group of vampires that had wandered into Rome. They had murdered so many. The city thought there was a crazed serial killer on the loose. We knew the truth." He took a shaking breath.

"The Roman vampire nest asked for our help to destroy these new vampires. They said the new group was going to slaughter them and take over Rome. That they were far beyond anything we'd ever seen, depraved in their violence and wickedness. That they wanted to step out of the darkness. Destroy humanity. The Roman nest couldn't fight back alone. Not without bringing all of Rome down. We made a deal. You negotiated it with the old alpha of the nest. They gave us the information to kill them.

"We tracked the invading nest to the docks. We studied them. We built our plan, thought it was perfect. And then we went in to slay the leader and torch the nest." Alain exhaled. "But... I walked us into a trap. They were waiting for us. They'd been playing us while we scouted them."

"Alain—"

"They jumped you. Bit you. Tortured you. You started to turn."

Flashes of memory played in Luca's mind. He shook his head, trying to make sense of the swirling images. "I don't remember any of this."

"We got you back to the Vatican." Alain swallowed. "We asked the Roman nest for help. They told us there is one way to stop a vampire from turning. And we did that to you."

Luca waited as Alain's eyes moved down his body. "We opened up your veins and bled you out. Emptied your body until your heart stopped. Once you were bled dry... we put half the blood from another human back into you."

Dizziness stole through him. "How— *Who*—" His thoughts bumped into each other, clamoring to be spoken next. "Who could you take that much blood from? That would kill a man!"

Alain's eyes closed. "Me," he breathed. "I gave my blood to you. And yes, I nearly died. And I didn't care. That's our faith, isn't it? We are made to sacrifice for our brother. For those we love. Greater love has no one than this, than to lay down one's life for one's friends."

Silence.

"But you still were drawn to the vampires, Luca. Even after you woke, you still wanted to go back to the nest. You were desperate to join them. Something had changed inside of you. All you wanted anymore was the vampires."

Turning away, Alain's teeth clenched, his lips bared, and Luca saw the curve of his fangs. "Even after the nest was burnt. Even after they were destroyed. You still were deranged. You were mad. Crazed. You tried to attack us. Said you wanted to kill us. Said you wanted to drink the city's blood. They did something to you. God, they destroyed you—"

"So you took my memories?"

"It was the *last* thing we wanted." When Alain looked back, pure sorrow bled from his soul, tragedy and grief raining from his yellow eyes. "It was the last thing *I* wanted. I didn't want to lose you. I lo—" He clamped his lips closed. "But I had to save your life, Luca. I would have given anything to save you."

Alain inhaled carefully. "It was a spell. I cast it. I wove all of your memories together, everything about hunting, about being a knight. Of the vampires. Every memory of us. I took them all and I buried them deep in your mind, deep in your soul. They're hidden away with a word lock, Luca, words I knew I could *never* say to you again after that moment." One bloody tear pushed free from the corner of Alain's eye, starting a slow trek down his pale cheek.

"What words?"

"When I say them, you'll remember everything. Are you ready for that?" Alain barely breathed his words, his voice so soft Luca strained to hear him.

Was he? Alain spoke of a Luca he didn't know. Part of his life wasn't his own. What would he find, if he opened this door? Sleepless nights and dark nightmares made of memories and images he couldn't place flickered through his thoughts.

He nodded, short jerks of his head up and down. Alain smiled, thin and weak like it pained him. He stood before Luca, and both hands cradled his face too tenderly. He bit his lip, the tips of his fangs piercing his red skin. One thumb brushed over Luca's lips. Alain breathed out, the warm air caressing him. "Luca," he started. His voice shook. "I *love* you."

It all came crashing back.

A flood of recollection, of understanding.

His life as a knight, as a hunter. Himself, happy.

In *love* with Alain.

Their life together, meeting in the Guard. Like lightning, they'd been drawn together from the first moment they'd met. Inseparable, they'd turned from best friends to lovers quickly. They'd been the talk of the Guard, the gossip of the Vatican.

Afternoons and midnights and sunrises and sunsets in the gardens, on the rooftops of the barracks, in each other's beds. Making love, dreaming of the future. Fantasies of their future as knights, as leaders of the Swiss Guard. All the good they would do together. Endless nights wrapped in each other's arms, kiss bruises and sweat all over their bodies.

Father Lotario's gruff voice, his hand squeezing Luca's shoulder, his warm smile filling the empty spaces Luca's family had left. For the first time in years, he'd felt what it was like to have a father again.

They'd been happy, deliriously, joyously *happy*.

The hunt against the vampires. The pain of the bite. Of the turn.

Desperation, a seemingly endless need to get back to the nest. To complete the turn, to join them and become one with the darkness. He'd wanted damnation, wanted to rend his soul to darkness and eternity. He wanted to bathe in blood, and he'd wanted to start with Alain's.

Alain's pleas, his endless prayers to God to save Luca's soul, to save his life.

The last memory he had was of Alain kissing his lips and laying him down on their bed, tears running down his cheeks as he promised that he would save him, no matter what.

Luca tore away from Alain. He stumbled and collapsed, falling to his hands and knees. "You stole my life!" Alain was silent. The bloody tear shivered before it fell from his jaw to the carpet. "You took everything! You tore us apart!"

"The Luca I was in love with ceased to exist that day. You died. Everything that you were, everything that *we* were, it all died. I lost you."

He glared over his shoulder, his vision blurred by a burst of rage. "How could you do this to me? To us?"

"I would have done anything to save your life, and this was the only way to do it." Yellow eyes met his. Another bloody tear slipped from the corner of Alain's eye. "And I was the one who had to live with it. You didn't remember a single thing about me. You didn't remember anything. When you met me again, instead of love, you hated me. This choice has always been my cross to bear."

Luca fell to his ass, landing in a sprawl. "I remember now," he breathed. "Being with you. Like it was yesterday."

"I can take it all away. Do you want me to lock the memories away again? You can go back to the way it was. You don't have to remember anything."

Did he want to forget? Did he want to bury the memory of Alain's love again, the feel of his skin, the taste of his kiss? Forget their dreams, the happiness they'd had? The wild nights, the laughter, and the *hope*, God, the hope that had burned through them, had made them feel so alive.

His bones ached as he pushed to his feet. His body was old, older than he'd been when he'd fallen in love with Alain. Memories were out of sequence, his mind living in the past as his older body tried to catch up.

Three steps took him to Alain, took him to yellow eyes and bloody tears. Alain held his ground, waiting for Luca's rage, his wrath, ready to take whatever Luca was going to throw at him like he had taken everything else for the past twelve years, silent and sentinel.

"Is there—" Luca's voice cracked. "Can we—" He shook his head. Squeezed his eyes shut. "Is there any way that—" His throat clenched. He gave up speaking.

He grabbed Alain behind the neck and pulled him close.

Memories flared as his lips closed over Alain's. Every kiss they'd ever shared burned through him, thousands of memories sparking in his mind. Alain's lips were warm, slightly chapped like they always had been. He sighed into the kiss, drawing closer to the love of his life.

The tip of a fang sliced his lip, cutting him. His blood welled, spilling onto Alain's tongue.

Alain flew back, shoving him away.

He stared at Alain, motionless.

Alain shook his head. "We *can't.*"

"I don't care about what you are." He wiped his torn lip on the back of his hand, smearing his blood over his skin. Everything in him begged to rush to Alain, to fall into his arms and to never, ever let go. "I don't care, Alain. I love you." His voice shook. "Please."

"Luca..."

"I don't *care* what you are. I don't."

"Luca, twelve years is a long time."

Luca's heart stuttered. His breath shorted, his lungs collapsing.

Twelve years of raging at Alain, of them rubbing each other the wrong way. Of shouting matches that shook the walls, of punching out his window when he just wanted to throttle Alain. Of a scratch under his skin, something he couldn't reach.

He thought it had been hatred.

"It's been a long time," Alain breathed.

"It feels like yesterday to me." His vision blurred. He tried to blink through it. Hot tears spilled down his cheeks.

"It's been a long time," Alain repeated, "for *me.*"

Cristoph. Stubborn, independent Cristoph, insisting on being exactly who he was. He'd stood up to Luca, he'd stood up to Alain, and, despite everything against him, he'd become a knight. He'd become Alain's *lover.* He'd done the hard work of getting through Alain's defenses, his isolation. He'd been there for Alain through the rising. And he was still waiting for Alain, living in his apartment.

Of course he was the man Alain would fall for, would *love.*

"And you've moved on." He managed to say it without his voice shattering to pieces. "You love someone else."

Alain looked down.

Fast blinks pushed more tears down his cheeks. He sniffed. Tried to swallow his heart. Tried to stop it from breaking. "You—

You should reach out to him. He's worried about you." Luca nodded, trying to tell himself he was doing the right thing. He was, he was. They loved each other. "Cristoph, he's... He's a good man. I know I was hard on him—" He gritted his teeth, groaning, trying to get through the next moment. "He loves you so damn much."

A quiet exhale was the only reaction. Luca sniffed again, angry snot and his wet swallows the only sounds in the room.

"I can't be with him like this," Alain whispered. "I'm dangerous. I'm a monster." His face twisted. "Why would he even want me now?"

Luca smiled, and it was agonizing, but he did it anyway. "Alain, he loves you. He wants you any way he can have you. And, I know you. I know you would never hurt the ones you love." Another gulp, like trying to swallow shards of glass. "For what it's worth... I wouldn't turn you away for anything. Definitely not for this. He won't either."

Yellow eyes lifted. Met his gaze. "I am sorry, Luca."

He stared at his blood, smeared on Alain's lips. "I'll survive. It's what I do, right?"

THE DAYS CONTINUED UNINTERRUPTED, UNCHANGING, UNTIL Cristoph was summoned to Luca's office.

The Vatican was still empty, the Holy Father and most of the guard winding down the summer at Castel Gandolfo. He padded down the empty garrison offices to the commandant's office and leaned against the doorframe.

"Hey."

Luca sent him a quick, unreadable look, too many emotions buried with each other. He looked away. "Good afternoon, Mr. Hasse."

"You called?" Actually, it had been an email, a one-sentence request.

Luca nodded. His gaze stayed locked on his desk, and he

seemed to fidget, straightening the edges of his notepad, lining his pens in perfect rows. One hand dragged a folder across his immaculate desktop, almost as if he was holding it down.

"I've heard from His Holiness," Luca began, clearing his throat. "The ranks of the knights need to be filled again."

The words sank heavy in the afternoon heat, settling like grave dirt. "The rank of *one* has to be refilled?" Cristoph didn't want to hear it confirmed, hear that Alain wasn't returning. *He gave you his sword. He knew. He knew he wasn't coming back.*

"Yes. We need a replacement." Finally, Luca looked up. He couldn't hold Cristoph's gaze. He looked instead past him, over his shoulder. Cristoph spied a cut on his lip, a scab that hadn't healed. "You've been studying Ala—Sergeant Autenburg's work?"

He couldn't speak. Couldn't form the words. *It was always going to end this way*. He looked away. "Where is Lotario?"

"I was told he's recuperating at the monastery where he trained." Cristoph watched Luca bite the inside of his lip. "You're the man for this, Cristoph. We need you."

He closed his eyes. Exhaled. And nodded.

Luca cleared his throat and flipped open the file folder. "Effective immediately, Mr. Hasse, you are promoted to the rank of corporal and you are assigned to the Special Projects division. You will continue to study the material of the Secret Order of the Resurrected Knights Templar and take up the duties of said knights, including defense and protection of the territories of Rome and the Vatican from all dark, etheric, and supernatural creatures and events." Luca bit his lip, worrying the scab with his teeth. He blinked when he met Cristoph's gaze. "Do you accept?"

What else could he do? There was too much out there, and running now felt like a sin against Alain's memory. He couldn't do that to the man or to his memory, run from what they had built together. One day and one night was all he got, but everything between them had created this future. His path. Walking the path of the knights.

Confronting the darkness. Avenging Alain.

And one day, finding Lucifer.

A lull had settled over Rome since the battle in the church. No risings, no ghosts, no revenants. No vampires, now that the Roman nest was dead. And no demons, despite Lucifer rising from the Veil, corporeal and alive once again.

The quiet wouldn't last. He needed to be ready.

"I accept," he said, his voice soft.

Nodding, Luca stood, and raised his right hand, extending his thumb, index and middle finger and spreading them wide. It was supposed to symbolize the Holy Trinity.

Cristoph straightened and raised his right hand, mirroring Luca. It was tradition.

Luca spoke first, half of the oath spoken over the Guardsmen, an oath they were to listen to and swear their lives to if they held the words in their soul. "I swear I will faithfully, loyally and honorably serve His Holiness, Holy Father Clemente and his legitimate successors, and dedicate myself to them with all my strength, sacrificing my life to defend them. I assume this same commitment with regard to the Sacred College of Cardinals whenever the See is vacant. I promise to the Commandant and my other superiors respect, fidelity, and obedience."

Cristoph answered, the words of his part of the oath rolling off his tongue with ease, so unlike the first time he uttered them. "I, Cristoph Hasse, swear diligently and faithfully to abide by all that has just been sworn to me."

Luca finished with the refrain. "This I swear. May—" Luca stuttered, his voice catching. "God and our Holy Patrons assist me."

"This I swear." Cristoph held Luca's gaze and lowered his hand, ending the oath early. He couldn't speak about God and faith, not yet. Maybe not ever. He couldn't swear to something he didn't understand and couldn't know. What it all meant—God, the devil, and evil in the world. The questions were too big.

Luca sat, not saying a word about the omission.

"Congratulations, Corporal." A short nod. "I am sure you have lots of work to do."

And just like that, he was dismissed. Promoted, casually knighted, and dismissed. It was nothing like Alain's memories, nothing like the best day of his life.

Cristoph slipped out of Luca's office and headed back for Alain's—now his—office.

DAYS ROLLED ON, THE LATE SUMMER HEAT BLEEDING ALL OVER the city and suffocating Rome. Nighttime shimmered with heat waves cast from the ground, stars from distant times occasionally twinkling overhead. The city lights were more prevalent than starlight. Cristoph watched from Alain's window, counting neon glows and repeating wishes he'd wished a hundred times already.

Luca skirted his existence, leaving the canteen when he entered, turning away in the garrison offices if Cristoph neared. The guards who had remained at the Vatican left him alone, and his isolation grew, surrounding him in an impenetrable bubble.

And then, one evening, the door to Alain's apartment was ajar when he returned.

He pulled out his pistol, silver-tipped bullets locked and loaded, from the shoulder holster he wore beneath his black suit jacket. A priest's suit was so much easier to wear than the Swiss Guard uniform, and he had traded in the striped ensemble for the black suit a month prior. It got rumpled, though, when he was researching in the archives or practicing his runes and seals with salt and chalk.

He slipped into the apartment, clearing the corners in the front hallway and sliding along the wall. A quick check of the kitchen revealed no one and nothing stolen. He backed out and braced against the wall at the arched entrance to the study.

A shadow stood in front of the windows, gazing over the Vatican.

Cristoph leveled his weapon at the shadow's back. "Freeze, evil bitch," he barked. "You're trapped." A demon's trap lay under the rug, carved there by Alain and reinforced with silver inlay and salt by Cristoph.

A warm chuckle broke through the apartment. "'Freeze, evil bitch'?" Yellow eyes glanced over one dark shoulder. "You have to get better lines, Cristoph."

The pistol dropped with a clatter, hitting the floor hard. His jaw fell open, lips parting. "Alain?"

Alain turned around completely, facing Cristoph. He looked like he always had, save for the yellow eyes and the tightening of his skin, the hollows of his cheeks and the sharper cut of his jawline.

The taste of blood and fog hit the back of Cristoph's throat, copper and damp earth, and a hint of rot. "Alain... Are you back? Are you—" He swallowed. He didn't want to say it. Didn't want to ask if Alain had escaped, if he was on lockdown because he had gone evil, or if he had just been gone for so long because he wanted to be gone. Wanted to be away from Cristoph.

A soft inhale curled the air between them. "I'm back," Alain whispered. Fangs curving over each of his teeth flashed as he spoke. "If..." He swallowed. "If you'll have me."

Striding forward, Cristoph buried one hand in Alain's wild, messy hair, the other wrapping around his hip. He tugged him forward and captured Alain's lips in a searing, bruising kiss. Alain refused to part his lips, despite Cristoph's probing, and he settled for nibbling on Alain's lower lip. "I'll never let you go," Cristoph breathed. "I've missed you so much."

Alain grabbed Cristoph's arms. The strength in his grip shocked Cristoph. He felt bruises form beneath Alain's hold. He watched Alain, trying to gauge his reaction.

His eyes were closed, the yellow gleam covered. His breaths came fast and harsh. "Your soul," Alain finally whispered. "It's so bright. So beautiful."

Cristoph quirked a tiny smile, the corner of his lip curling upwards. "'Cause I'm happy you're back."

Alain's yellow eyes slitted open. His fangs shone, sharp and deadly as he spoke. "You're sure?" His voice trembled. "You're *sure* you want me? Like this?"

"I want you always. Every way. Every day. Forever."

Alain's eyes slid away. "I don't even know if I want me like this, Cristoph. I don't know if I can live like this—"

"Hey." Cristoph grabbed his face, dragging Alain's gaze back to him. "We can get through this. Together."

Slowly, Alain nodded, though his face fell and his expression cracked, slow tears of blood leaking from the corners of his eyes. "Shit!" Alain tried to turn away, tried to curl out of Cristoph's hold. Cristoph fought him, and even though Alain was strong enough to break free, he fell against Cristoph instead of fleeing, burying his face in Cristoph's neck. They sank down, falling to the floor on their knees, wrapped together.

Cristoph stroked Alain's back, whispering soft noises and sweet nothings in his ear. "We *will* get through this, Alain," he breathed. "I swear it. I swear on my life. I will *not* lose you."

Alain gripped him tighter and pressed his lips to Cristoph's neck, right over his pulse, over the pounding blood flowing through his veins. "For *you*."

Afterword

The Poor Fellow-Soldiers of Christ and of the Temple of Solomon, also known as The Order of the Knights Templar, were one of the most prominent Christian military orders in the Middle Ages. In 1119, the Templar formed in Jerusalem in secrecy, and their power grew sharply over the next two hundred years before their swift and dramatic downfall.

The Order was fanatically secret about itself from the beginning. Rumors of occult and mystical practices followed the Order for two centuries while they amassed incredible power. The Order held hundreds of castles and large tracts of land, owned and managed their own powerful naval fleet for both military and commercial endeavors, and created the Western world's first form of banking. They were said to hold more wealth and financial power than many of the kingdoms of Europe combined. The knights answered only to the pope and were exempt from following the laws of the nations they resided in. They could freely cross borders and paid no taxes.

Templar knights, dressed in white mantles with a distinctive red Templar cross emblazoned on the front, were considered the greatest skilled and most courageous knights in the Crusades. In 1177, 500 knights defeated 26,000 soldiers from Saladin's army in the Holy Land.

In 1307, King Phillip IV of France, in deep debt, convinced Pope Clement V to issue an arrest warrant for the Knights Templar, which commanded all Christian monarchs to arrest the knights and seize their assets immediately. King Phillip and other western European leaders arrested almost 15,000 Templar knights on Friday October 13th, 1307. They were imprisoned and tortured, and many knights confessed to heretical, mystical acts, denying God, and sodomy.

More Templar knights escaped, disappearing into history. The Templar naval fleet set sail from their base at La Rochelle before the arrest and was never seen again.

In 1312, Pope Clement V disbanded the Order permanently through the Papal bull *Vox in excelso*.

In 1314, the Grand Master of the Knights Templar was burned at the stake in Paris, France. His last words were a curse upon Pope Clement and King Phillip IV. Both men died that year.

At the same time, small groups of people living in the Swiss Alps began to unite in opposition against the power of the Holy Roman Empire, the powerful, yet distant, rulers who claimed to rule over the Swiss lands. This became known as the Swiss Confederacy. Swiss legends and folktales tell of white-mantled knights with blazing red crosses on their chests riding into the mountains and training the Confederacy as well as joining their ranks. After the Confederacy defeated the Holy Roman Empire and gained their autonomy, the Swiss, in a matter of one hundred years, became the most powerful army in all of Europe with the best-trained knights and soldiers. Their military prowess remained unchallenged for over two centuries.

In 1506, one hundred and fifty Swiss soldiers marched to Rome, the first contingent of the Pontifical Swiss Guard, the new army of the Vatican.

The author wishes to give special thanks to Charlotte and Justene for their help with this novel.

Vatican City Map

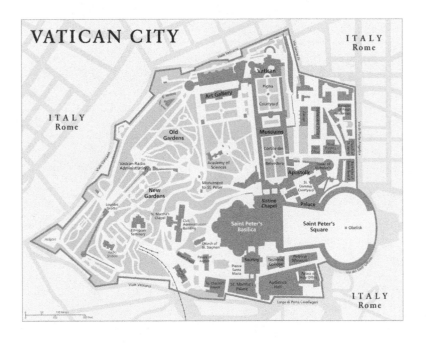

About the Author

Tal Bauer is an award-winning and best-selling author of gay romantic thrillers, bringing together a career in law enforcement and international humanitarian aid to create dynamic characters, intriguing plots, and exotic locations. He is happily married and lives with his husband and their Basset Hound in Texas. Tal is a member of the Romance Writers of America.

Drop Tal a line at tal@talbauerwrites.com. He can't respond to every email, but he does read every single one.

Check out Tal's website: www.talbauerwrites.com or follow Tal on social media.

facebook.com/talbauerauthor

twitter.com/talbauerwrites

amazon.com/author/talbauer

Also by Tal Bauer

Hush

Whisper

The Executive Office Series

Enemies of the State

Interlude

Enemy of My Enemy

Enemy Within

Made in the USA
Monee, IL
25 April 2023